Critics are head-over-heels for bestselling author Susan Mallery's

Married for a Month

"*Temptation Island* meets *Oprah* in [this] contemporary romp. . . . [T]his sweet story will delight as it provides food for thought."

—*Publishers Weekly*

"Compatibility, passion, and love are all on the line in this wonderful book. . . ."

—*Romantic Times*

Sweet Success

"The humor, warmth, and rich characterizations make this a must read."

—*Romantic Times*

"[A] sweet tale from beginning to end. . . . A delightful read."

—*Rendezvous*

"[An] exceptional book . . . filled with warmhearted laughter and wonderful relationships. . . . Delightful."

—*The Belles and Beaux of Romance*

"*Sweet Success* is a wonderfully fast-paced delight! . . . You can never go wrong with Ms. Mallery's fascinating storytelling!"

—*Romance Reviews Today*

"Witty dialogue, plenty of romantic tension, and delicious characters."

—*Publishers Weekly*

"A warm, reassuring romance."

—*Old Book Barn Gazette*

"*Sweet Success* is a treat. . . . The characters seem to jump off the page."

—*Romance Journal*

Also by Susan Mallery

Sweet Success
Married for a Month

And the *Marcelli Sisters* trilogy

The Sparkling One
The Sassy One
The Seductive One

SUSAN MALLERY

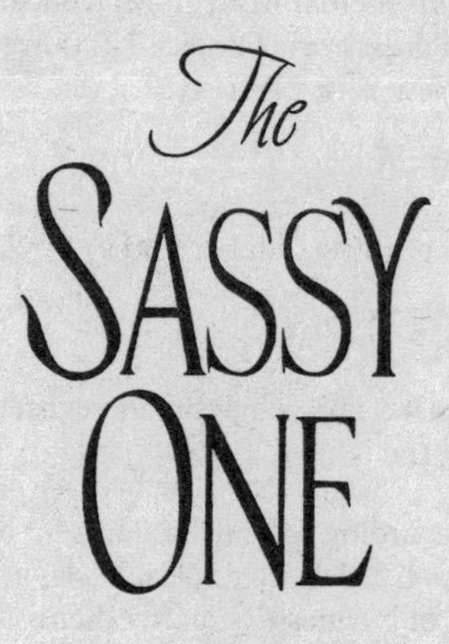

POCKET STAR BOOKS
New York London Toronto Sydney Singapore

This book is a work of fiction. Names, characters, places and incidents are products of the author's imagination or are used fictitiously. Any resemblance to actual events or locales or persons, living or dead, is entirely coincidental.

An *Original* Publication of POCKET BOOKS

A Pocket Star Book published by
POCKET BOOKS, a division of Simon & Schuster, Inc.
1230 Avenue of the Americas, New York, NY 10020

ISBN: 0-7434-4395-0

First Pocket Books printing October 2003

10 9 8 7 6 5 4 3 2 1

Designed by Melissa Isriprashad

Front cover illustration by Frank Accornero

Printed in the U.S.A.

To Amy Pierpont, my editor, for ever so gently asking,
"What would happen if he didn't know about the kid?"
and to Irene Goodman, my agent,
who loved the trilogy idea from the very beginning.

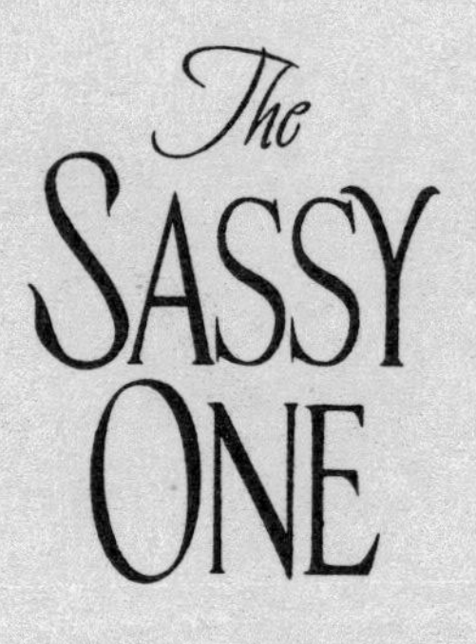
The
SASSY
ONE

1

Francesca Marcelli had only been pregnant for twenty minutes and already her back hurt.

"Talk about realistic," she muttered, adjusting the straps that held her fake eight-months-pregnant belly in place. The size was daunting enough—she couldn't see her feet or find a comfortable sitting position—but the weight was the real killer. Someone with a twisted sense of humor had decided to simulate what felt like the pressure of a baby elephant. The small of her back screamed out in protest, while unexpected pressure on her bladder made her want to duck into the nearest ladies' room.

"All for a good cause," she reminded herself.

Francesca shifted to ease the throbbing in her back and leaned against the heavy cart she'd maneuvered into the service elevator of the six-story bank building. When the doors opened, she shoved her overloaded cart into the main hallway. Stacks of boxes wobbled precariously and threatened to tumble onto the carpeted floor.

It was just after five on a Friday afternoon. All around her dozens of businesspeople headed for the main elevators to start their weekend. Francesca pushed up her glasses and paused to smooth down the front of the ugliest maternity dress she'd been able to find. The oversize collar dwarfed her shoulders and made her head look too small. The pinks and roses of the busy floral print sucked all the color from her pale olive skin. She'd brushed powder into her hair to lighten it to a mousy brown. The little makeup she'd put on had been applied to make her look tired, drawn, and unattractive.

She glanced at her watch, then squared her shoulders as she prepared to begin work.

"Show time," she said softly, not that anyone was listening.

Three men from the insurance office at the end of the hall walked past her without even giving her a nod. Francesca continued to push her pile of packages slowly against the flow of foot traffic. Two women in suits gave her a quick, sympathetic smile. A man and a woman, both carrying expensive-looking briefcases, followed. The woman looked, the man didn't.

Another corridor branched to the left. Francesca shifted her cart to make the turn. Several boxes went tumbling. A single man walked by without breaking his stride. A college-age girl stopped long enough to help Francesca pick up the boxes, then hurried toward the elevator with a call to "Wait for me!"

Five minutes later Francesca reached her destination—an office she'd scouted out the previous week, chosen because the company had recently shut down. There she was, pregnant, lost, overloaded with more than a dozen boxes to be delivered, and no one to accept them. Had she been any sort of an actress, she might have been able to force out a tear or two.

The rules stipulated she was not allowed to directly ask

for help. It had to be offered. She would wait for the required thirty minutes, mentally tallying who ignored her, who smiled, and who, if anyone, stopped to actually offer assistance.

This was a high-powered crowd with expensive tastes and busy lives. She didn't hold out much hope for rescue. In her experience—

"You look lost."

Francesca whirled around to see a tall man standing beside her cart. A tall, *good-looking* man in a dark blue power suit.

"Hi," she said before preparing to launch into her canned speech about needing to deliver packages to a non-existent firm. Except she couldn't remember anything she was supposed to say.

The man waited patiently. He had dark blond hair and sort of tawny-colored eyes. There was an intensity to his expression that reminded her of predators watching prey. A shiver rippled through her as she thought of gazelles being brought down for the kill. Unfortunately in her current condition she was more water buffalo than gazelle.

He looked confident, important, and powerful. Not the sort of person who should be stopping to help an unattractive pregnant woman in trouble. Men like him sent assistants to take care of life's unpleasant details.

"Do you speak English?" he asked, enunciating each word clearly.

"What? Oh. Of course." She sucked in a breath, not sure what could be wrong with her. She would blame her sudden mental hiccup on food poisoning, only she hadn't eaten anything that day. "I'm, ah—" Francesca cleared her throat. Brain function returned and she launched into her spiel.

"Hi. I'm Francesca. I'm supposed to be delivering these packages here—" She motioned to the closed and locked office door. "But there seems to be a problem."

The man glanced first at the boxes, all carefully addressed to the defunct company, then to the door where a hand-lettered sign said that Malcolm and White Data Tech was no more.

"Bringing these here was the last thing my boss told me to do before he left town," she went on. "If I don't get them delivered, he's going to kill me."

In an effort to look terrified, Francesca thought about how little she had in her checking account and how that pesky electric bill was going to come due soon. Eventually she would reap the rewards of her postgraduate education, but until she could actually slap the letters Ph.D. after her name, she seemed destined to a life of poverty.

"You'll have to risk his fury," the man said calmly. "These boxes aren't going anywhere today. That company closed the door about ten days ago. From what I've heard, the main players skipped town with the last few dollars left, leaving several employees with lots of angry customers and no paychecks. What's your name again?"

"Francesca Marcelli."

He smiled at her. A genuine, happy-to-meet-you smile that made the corners of his eyes crinkle and caused her palms to suddenly start to sweat. This was the most fun she'd had in days.

Her rescuer introduced himself as Sam Reese.

"Let's get you out of this hallway, and we'll figure out what we're going to do next."

We? They were a *we?*

Sam took charge of the cart, wheeling it down the hallway with an ease that made her envious. Of course, he didn't have to worry about a pregnant belly getting in the way of his actions. She trailed after him, wondering what the next step would be. How far was Sam willing to take things? In situations like this—a nonemergency—people generally stopped at the point of inconvenience.

"Just through there," he said, pointing to a set of double glass doors.

Before Francesca could read the name of the company, one of the doors opened and a huge man stepped into the hallway. She involuntarily came to a stop to stare.

The man had to be at least six feet seven. He was built like a mountain with a massive neck and shoulders broad enough to support a couple of trailer homes. Dark-skinned, with penetrating eyes and a firm, unsmiling mouth, he looked both dangerous and more than a little scary.

"Sam," the man said, glancing between her rescuer and herself. "Is there a problem?"

"I think there might be." Sam looked back at her. "Ms. Marcelli was trying to make a delivery to Malcolm and White."

"They split last week."

"As I explained to Ms. Marcelli." He motioned to the cart. "Take this inside, Jason. Store it in one of the conference rooms." He turned his attention back to her. "If your employer's expecting payment for a delivery, that isn't going to happen. At least not right now. Come on inside and we'll get this situation straightened out."

Francesca found herself being ushered into a plush office with a gray and burgundy waiting area. An attractive woman in her early forties manned the front desk. She spoke over a headset as they walked by, pausing only to nod at Sam.

"I can search out Malcolm and White," Sam said as they moved down a long corridor decorated with elegant prints and the occasional slim table pushed up against a wall. "I've been looking for an excuse to track them down."

He sounded fierce as he spoke, as if he had a personal beef with the missing businessmen. Francesca trailed after him, torn between wondering why Sam Reese would care if a company in his building closed and trying to figure out what she'd gotten herself into. They passed several large conference rooms, what looked like classrooms, and a few offices containing large desks, computers, and file cabinets. All generic stuff that didn't hint at the kind of business done here.

At the end of the hall they made a left, then a quick right before stopping in front of an open foyer containing a large desk and computer setup manned by a well-dressed young man wearing a sport coat.

"Jack, this is Ms. Marcelli."

The young man, probably around twenty-five and built like a football player, rose to his feet. "Nice to meet you, ma'am."

Francesca walked to the desk to shake hands. As she did so, her purse slipped down her arm and plopped onto the ground before she could catch it.

"Oops," she said, bending down to pick it up.

As she straightened, all the blood rushed from her head, causing the room to spin and her body to sway. For a split second she thought she was going down.

Less than a heartbeat later a strong arm encircled her, holding her in place. "Ms. Marcelli? Are you all right? Is it the baby?"

Baby? What . . . oh, *the baby.*

Francesca shook her head slightly. Her sense of equilibrium returned enough for her to realize she was standing amazingly close to Sam. Close enough to see the surprisingly dark lashes framing his eyes. Speaking of which—she stared more intently—seen from such a close range, his eyes were the most unusual color. Light brown, shot with gold. Otherworldly eyes. Cat eyes.

Cat eyes on a powerful man. She felt both the heat of him and the strength. Somehow she'd always assumed that executives in expensive suits were sort of wimpy under all that designer wool. She had been seriously wrong.

"Ms. Marcelli?"

Tension filled his voice. She shook her head again and tried to shrug free of his hold. When he didn't release her, she gave him a quick smile.

"I'm fine."

"You nearly fainted."

"I know. I haven't eaten today. I do that sometimes. Work distracts me. Then I get low blood sugar."

"That can't be good for the child."

As there was no child, his concern made her feel a little guilty.

"I'm fine," she repeated. "Really."

He slowly removed his arm from around her waist. "Jack, bring Ms. Marcelli some herb tea. There's a selection in the coffee room. Nothing with caffeine. Also, check to see if there are any sandwiches left from the lunch meeting."

Francesca thought about protesting again, but before she could figure out what to say without blowing her cover, she found herself being ushered into an office the size of Utah.

Floor-to-ceiling windows offered a view of Santa Barbara and mountains from one wall and Santa Barbara and a hint of ocean from the other. Tasteful paintings decorated the remaining walls. Two large leather sofas formed a conversational area in a corner. Between them and the desk was enough room to hold a kickboxing class.

Sam settled her on the sofa, then sat next to her. Before she knew what was going on, he had her hand resting in his and his fingers on the inside of her wrist.

"Your pulse is rapid. Would you like me to call your doctor?"

She generally went to student health services whenever she needed a checkup. Somehow she didn't think her friendly chitchat with the nurse practitioner qualified as having a doctor of her own.

Although she *would* have to admit that having her hand cradled by a handsome man held a certain thrill. He was warm, solid, and plenty sexy. Had she looked slightly more appealing than something gacked up by a stray cat, she might have tried smiling, flirting, and witty conversation. Not that she could think of anything witty right at the moment.

"No doctor calling," she insisted, reluctantly drawing her hand free of his. "There's nothing wrong with me. Although I have been taking up too much of your time."

She started to rise. Sam kept her in her seat with nothing more than a steady gaze.

"Have some tea," he said. "You'll feel better."

Both were an order.

Before she could protest, Jack appeared carrying a tray. There was a steaming mug of tea, along with a wrapped deli sandwich.

"We only have turkey left," the young man said apologetically as he set the tray on the glass coffee table.

The small amount of guilt she'd felt before doubled in size. "Look. You're being really nice—both of you. But there's no need to fuss."

The men ignored her. "Get on the computer," Sam told his assistant. "See if you can track down either Malcolm or White. You'll find a file in the usual place." He turned his considerable attention back to her. "You said your boss had left for the day. How do you get in touch with him? I want to let him know that the boxes can't be delivered. I'll also make arrangements for them to be returned to him." His fierce expression softened slightly. "He should never have left you to take care of them yourself."

"I didn't mind," she said weakly, feeling the floor beneath her crumbling into quicksand. In a matter of seconds she was going to sink so deep, no one would ever find her. "And you can't get in touch with him. He's, um, heading for the airport. To, ah, get on a plane."

She mentally winced. Lying had never come easily to her. Heading to the airport to get on a plane? Why else did people go to the airport?

Francesca sighed. Somehow this experiment had gotten out of hand. According to her research, Sam shouldn't have stopped to help her, and he should never have taken things this far. The man was messing with her data.

"What airline? What flight?" He pulled a small leather-covered notebook from his jacket pocket.

Francesca didn't know what to say. "You won't be able to track him down."

"Try me."

Uh-oh. She was in way over her head. She gave Jack a frantic "rescue me" look which he either didn't get or chose to ignore. Jason, the big and strong, poked his head in the office to inform them that he'd put the boxes in Conference Room 2. Jack disappeared with Jason, closing the door behind them. Leaving her very much alone with a man obviously capable of ruling the universe.

"So, Ms. Marcelli, your boss's flight? His name would help, as well."

"Please call me Francesca," she said and reached for the tea. Her stomach growled, but she refused to touch the sandwich. Not while she was here under false pretenses. "Can you really get in contact with someone on a plane?"

"If I have to. It would be easier to reach him before he left. Is he driving down to Los Angeles, or taking a corporate flight out of Santa Barbara."

Francesca thought of all the times she'd created situations to find out if strangers would take the trouble to stop and help her. She'd had nice old ladies offer her rides, friendly couples give her directions, even the odd schoolkid help her find a lost dog. But never had anyone taken things as far as Sam Reese.

She drew in a deep breath. "You've been great," she said. "Really terrific. I don't know how to thank you."

His tawny gaze settled on her face. She regretted her dull-colored hair and oversize glasses, not to mention the deliberately unflattering makeup. Successful, gorgeous men like him didn't much inhabit her grad-school world. Why couldn't she have put on her sexy biker-girl disguise today instead of ugly-pregnant-woman?

Sam waited patiently. As if he had all the time in the world. As if he was used to people being reluctant to give up information.

"If you don't want me to track down your boss, that's your decision," he said. "At least eat something. For the baby, if not for yourself."

She really wished he would stop mentioning the pregnancy. Okay, so in all the years she'd been doing this sort of thing, she'd never once been put in a position of coming clean, but hey, this wasn't her fault. She was being overwhelmed by guilt. Well, guilt and a more-than-mild attraction to a handsome guy.

"I'm not pregnant," she said.

His gaze never left her face. One point for his side. She pulled off her glasses and tossed them on the table. It was a small gesture of vanity, but under the circumstance—wearing the world's ugliest dress, sensible shoes, and an unflattering hairstyle—it was the best she could do.

"I'm a grad student studying social psychology. I observe how people react under different circumstances. In my work I'm trying to see if social standing, appearance, or gender influence behavior."

Sam tucked his notepad back into his jacket pocket. One eyebrow rose slightly. "Will busy people eager to get home on a Friday afternoon stop and help a pregnant woman?"

"Exactly."

His eyes narrowed as he studied her face. She wanted to say something stupid, like she cleaned up real well, but held back.

"What's in the boxes?"

She cleared her throat. "Mixed paper recycling."

"You deliberately chose to address them to a company that had recently closed?"

"Yes."

This time his gaze dropped to her protruding stomach. "And that?"

"A medical condition."

His eyes widened.

She laughed softly. "Just kidding. It's a device to simulate pregnancy. I borrowed it from a maternity store. Women use it to see how clothes will look as the baby gets bigger."

He picked up the glasses and glanced through the lenses. "Clear."

He smiled. A slow, sexy smile that made her long to trade in her black sensible shoes for a pair of red strappy sandals.

"I'm not an easy man to fool, Francesca," he told her. "In fact, I can't think of the last time someone did. You're impressive. The fainting was a nice touch."

She shrugged. "Actually that part was real. I haven't eaten all day and that messes with my blood sugar."

He motioned to her protruding belly. "You spend your day like this in the name of scientific research?"

"I don't always dress up with a pregnancy belly. Sometimes I go out in a wheelchair, or tattoos and black leather."

He leaned back against the sofa. "That would stop traffic."

She smiled. "That depends on where I am." She reached for the tea. "There have been dozens of studies done about the effect of appearance on behavior. Do you know that more people will stop to help an attractive person than an unattractive one?"

"Men are visual creatures."

"But it's not just men. Women do it, too. I'm studying—" She stopped and put down her tea. "Sorry. I get on a roll. My studies fascinate me."

"I can see why. Who are you going to be tomorrow? If your costume involves black leather, feel free to stop by."

She laughed. "Actually I'm supposed to be done with

the research phase. My project for the summer is to write my dissertation. But the thought of spending all that time at the computer makes my skin crawl, so I've been putting it off."

"What do you want me to do with the boxes?"

"Oh. I can take them with me. I need to return the cart, too. I borrowed it from the building maintenance guy."

"So he gets full points for helping out the pregnant lady?"

"Absolutely."

"What about me?"

Sam had a great voice, Francesca thought as a shiver rippled through her. Deep, rich, seductive.

"You get bonus points," she told him.

"Good to know." He angled toward her. "How about I let you keep the points and in return you join me for dinner tonight?"

Under normal circumstances Francesca never would have accepted the invitation. She didn't know Sam Reese from a rock. Yes, he was plenty appealing, but in the scheme of things, did that really matter?

"Dumb question," she murmured as she maneuvered her truck through the early evening Santa Barbara traffic. It was early June, with the tourist season in full swing. Sidewalks were crowded, restaurants full, and traffic moved at a crawl down State Street.

"Appeal matters."

So did those cat eyes, the tempting smile, and easy conversation. But the real reason she'd said yes was she needed to have sex. After all, a promise was a promise.

Francesca grinned as she thought of Sam's reaction if

she'd told him that particular truth. Would he have bolted for safety or started unbuttoning his shirt? She liked to think it would be the latter, but she'd taken a good look at herself when she'd gone home to change and her out-loud shriek hadn't been from pleasure. Nope, the man would have run for his life.

One shower with three shampoos to get the powder out of her hair, a quick change of clothes, and a light dusting of makeup later, she was ready to if not dazzle, then at least intrigue. She figured with as bad as she'd looked before, anything would be an improvement.

So she was off to dazzle Sam Reese and see what she could do about keeping her promise . . . the one she'd made to have sex with the next attractive, single man to cross her path.

2

Francesca knew she wasn't in Kansas anymore when the restaurant's valet parking cost more than a recent lunch at McDonald's. She smiled brightly as the well-dressed, blond surfer valet looked disgustedly at her ten-year-old truck, then took the keys with a shake of his head. She could only imagine what the guy would have done if she'd still been pregnant and, well, ugly. No doubt he would have shown her to the back of the restaurant.

Francesca dismissed him from her mind and instead focused on the beauty of the evening. The sun hovered at the horizon, casting a golden glow over the courtyard entrance to the restaurant. She was about to have dinner with a very nice man who, if he played his cards right, would help her fulfill the commitment she'd made to her sisters.

Two months ago, after too much wine and way too many cookies, she'd promised Katie and Brenna she would do the wild thing with the first normal single man she met, thus ending a self-imposed three-year celibacy. Her willingness to do something so completely out of character had a whole lot more to do with the lack of romance and fun in her life than it did with the dare itself. Not that she wanted a commitment. Been there, done that. But a sexy man and warm summer night . . . that was another matter.

In the past sixty-three days she hadn't come across one appropriate candidate, which said something about the state of her social life . . . or lack thereof.

Then Sam had appeared. He'd rescued her, made her pulse quicken, *and* asked her to dinner. She didn't need her tea leaves read to recognize a sign when she saw one, she thought with a smile. As this one had been in all capital letters and italics, she couldn't have missed it.

"What's so funny?"

The smooth red-wine-and-chocolate voice came from behind her, causing her to jump. She turned and saw Sam standing next to a gleaming silver car. She couldn't quite see the type of sedan, but she didn't doubt that it was expensive.

"How do you do that?" she asked. "This is the second time you've been able to sneak up on me."

His tawny gaze settled on her face . . . which gave her a distinctly *unsettled* feeling. He stood about six two or three. She was five nine and had put on two-inch heels, but still had to tilt her head slightly to study his face.

"I sneak by profession," he said. "You look terrific."

She glanced down at the black dress she'd pulled on. She'd bought it on impulse from a guy selling them out of the back of a truck on campus. With the designer label cut out and not a tag in sight, she'd had a feeling the merchandise hadn't been exactly legal. But the price had been amazing and the dress made her feel elegant and sophisticated. Two things she knew she would need tonight.

She held out her arms, sucked in her stomach and turned slowly. "The miracles of modern medicine."

"Did you have a boy or a girl?" he asked.

"It was more of a beanbag mound. Undetermined gender."

As she came to stop in front of him, she flipped back her long hair, a gesture she'd perfected at age fourteen and hadn't had reason to use in years.

This was fun. Maybe she'd been too hasty in settling in to her years of celibacy. There was something to be said for appreciation in a man's eyes.

Sam took her hand and placed it in the crook of his arm.

"Shall we?" he asked, motioning to the open courtyard of the restaurant.

"Why not?"

Why not? Well, for one thing, there was a growing knot of nerves in the pit of her stomach. Sam was smooth. The men of her acquaintance didn't dress like *GQ* and act like James Bond. The guys in grad school were more jeans and Taco Bell.

Oh, well. She'd said she was going to get back in the swim of things and had decided throwing herself in the deep end was the quickest way. If her plan backfired, she would dog-paddle to the side and drag her wet butt out of the pool.

The visual metaphor made her smile.

As they walked into the restaurant, Francesca curled her fingers and felt the softness of Sam's wool jacket and the hint of powerful muscle just beneath the fabric. Very masculine. Very not her life. Very something she might want to experiment with.

They reached the podium, where the hostess smiled at Sam. "Good evening, Mr. Reese. Your table is ready."

"A man with his own table," Francesca murmured.

"Wow. If you come here often enough, do you get other pieces of furniture?"

"Sure. Last year they gave me a chair and a sideboard."

She smiled. "I'm impressed you know what a sideboard is."

"I'm an impressive guy."

Sam placed his fingers over hers and squeezed slightly. The soft pressure, not to mention the heat of his touch, nearly made her stumble.

"So you're confident," she said as they were shown to a table tucked into an alcove. Several tall, potted plants gave the space a sense of privacy.

Sam released her hand and moved to hold out a chair. As she sat down, she tried to remember the last time anyone had done that for her, and came up with the answer.

Never.

He moved around the table and settled across from her. The hostess put menus on the table and left.

"Always."

"What if you're not sure? Do you fake it?"

He leaned toward her. "I never have to fake it."

"One could think all that bravado was covering up for something."

"Then one would be wrong."

She laughed. "Fair enough. Although I can see I'm going to have to be on my toes with you. I'm glad I have a background in psychology."

"It's not going to help."

"You say that because you're not the trained professional."

"Sure I am."

The waiter appeared with a wine list. Sam waited until the server left, then held up the list. "Do you have an interest?"

Francesca considered the question. "Not as much as my sister, but I'll look."

Sam watched Francesca slowly turn pages. Her long dark hair rippled with her every movement and caught the light. The rich brown color was a contrast to the mousy brown it had been earlier.

She'd discarded her glasses, the pregnancy belly, and the unflattering dress. In their place she wore a black dress that hugged slender curves and long, sexy legs. Her skin was clear, a pale olive color that appeared luminescent. Hazel eyes—more green than gold or blue—widened as she read an entry. She had the kind of mouth that got a man in trouble, and he found himself wanting to be first in line for whatever she might be offering.

On the way over he'd told himself he was an idiot for asking her to dinner. He'd first offered to help because she'd been in trouble and that's what he did.

Then he'd looked closer and he'd seen . . . possibilities.

She closed the wine menu and passed it to him.

"You see anything you like?" he asked.

"I'm going to let you pick."

"Is it a test?" he asked.

"Maybe." She turned her attention to her menu. "What's good here?"

"Everything."

"Do you already know what you want?"

He waited until she'd glanced up before answering. "I know exactly what I want."

The words got the reaction he'd been hoping for. Her eyes widened and her take-me-I'm-yours mouth curved.

"One point for your side," she murmured.

"Are we keeping score?"

"I think I have to."

"What's the prize for winning?"

"What do you want it to be?" As soon as she said the words, she held up a hand. "Pretend I didn't say that."

He chuckled. "Getting in over your head?"

"A little. I'm not going to ask if you are. I can already guess the answer."

"Fair enough. What do you want for dinner?"

"I'm not sure."

"Are you a vegetarian?"

She frowned. "No. Why would you think that?"

"Psychology major. It's a touchy-feely fringe science. Attracts a lot of vegetarians."

She delighted him by laughing. "As long as you haven't allowed yourself to be swayed by ill-informed stereotypes."

"Not my style."

"I'm not about to ask what your style is."

"I'd be happy to tell you."

"I'll bet. So what are you ordering?" she asked.

"Steak."

"That's a little clichéd."

"I can't help myself."

The waiter appeared and discussed the evening's specials. Francesca chose a baked chicken dish, while he had his usual. He ordered a bottle of Wild Sea Vineyards Cabernet.

"Interesting choice," Francesca said. "The wine I mean."

"They're local. Central California."

"I know." She tilted her head, her hazel eyes bright with emotions he couldn't read. "So, Sam Reese, why did you invite me to dinner?"

"Easy question. You fooled me. That doesn't happen very often. I was impressed."

"By my disguise?"

"Sure. I should have been able to see through it and I didn't. When you fainted, I was terrified we were going to be delivering a baby right there in the hallway."

"It would have been a shame to spoil such nice carpeting." She smiled. "I was pretty unattractive. I'm surprised you didn't run in the opposite direction."

Their waiter returned and showed Sam the bottle of wine. When Sam nodded, the young man opened it, then poured a small amount into Sam's glass. He took a sip.

"Very nice."

Francesca waited until the waiter had left before tasting her wine.

"Do you like it?" he asked.

"As you said, it's very nice."

There was something in her voice. Something he couldn't place. Amusement? Annoyance? Both?

"Why did *you* accept my invitation to dinner?" he asked.

"Because I wanted to."

Good answer, he thought as his gaze settled on her lush mouth.

"Tell me what you do," she said. "I saw a very nice office with lots of room, but no clues."

"I run Security International. We're based here in Santa Barbara, although we operate all over the world."

"What kind of security?"

"Personal. We provide bodyguards on a temporary or full-time basis. We have a security consulting division, and we will train other people's bodyguards."

She looked startled. "Like the movie?"

He knew which one she meant. "My people get fired for sleeping with a client."

"That seems harsh."

"They're paid to stay alert, not get lucky."

"Any famous clients?"

"Yes."

She waited expectantly, then laughed. "You're not going to give me any names."

"Not even a hint."

"That really big guy back at the office. Jason. He's one of your bodyguards?"

Sam nodded.

"He wouldn't exactly blend in."

"Sometimes that's not what the client wants."

"Everybody armed?"

"Sure."

"Even you?"

He gave her a slow smile. "Especially me."

She picked up her wine. "Even now?"

"Want to see?"

Francesca was willing to bet Sam hadn't spent more than fifteen minutes without a woman circling in his orbit. Her specifications had been clear—she would throw herself at the first eligible, attractive guy she ran into. She'd thought the situation might be nerve-racking and awkward; she hadn't considered she would be a bush-league rookie playing with the pros.

"I'm not sure you want to flash the staff," she said. "This is an upscale restaurant, and they frown on that sort of thing."

She sipped her wine, which actually wasn't bad. Not that she would be telling her sister.

"Afraid?" he asked. "The safety's on."

As if they were talking about the gun. "I'm cautious and sensible. Not afraid." She put the glass down. "How long have you been in the security business?"

"All my life. My grandfather founded the company."

She knew all about family concerns. "Any siblings to share the responsibility?"

"No." He shrugged. "My father died when I was a kid. My mom passed away a few years ago, though we were never close. Now there's just my grandfather and myself."

The waiter appeared and set their salads in front of them. Francesca stared at the artful arrangement of baby greens, apple slices, blue cheese, and walnuts. Her mind whirled with possibilities.

Married? No. That wasn't an option. Her luck couldn't be that bad. There was no way the first guy she'd been attracted to in the past three years could be—

"You're not married, are you?" she blurted.

Sam paused in the act of bringing his fork to his mouth. He set the utensil down.

She braced herself for a joke or teasing, or something snide. Instead his expression turned serious. "I wouldn't have asked you to dinner if I were married or involved."

Relief blended with the flavor of the cheese. "Okay."

"And you? Any current or former Mr. Marcellis floating around?"

"No. Actually, Marcelli is my maiden name. But I was married several years ago. He passed away."

"I'm sorry," Sam said. "You must have married young."

"At eighteen. Right on time, according to my rather twisted family's expectations." She speared a slice of apple. "I come from an Irish-Italian family. Very large, very traditional. We're supposed to marry young and procreate with abandon."

"Kids?"

She bit back a smile. "Not that I know about."

He chuckled. "I had an ill-fated marriage. I was all of

twenty-two, off in Europe, out of college, and on my own. We didn't make it to our first anniversary." He shrugged. "We were both too young. No kids, which is good. Divorce is tough on them."

"I agree."

He picked up his wine. "Enough serious conversation. Do you plan to seduce me later?"

If Francesca had been drinking, she would have spit. All promises and plans made in the presence of her sisters aside, this was a first date. She might want to throw herself in the deep end, but not in the first hour.

She was reasonably certain Sam was teasing, but just in case there was a grain of truth to the question, she decided on the most sensible, mature course of action.

She ignored it.

"Has your company always been based in Santa Barbara?" she asked.

Sam chuckled. "Chicken."

"Cluck cluck. Now graciously accept the change in subject, please."

"Okay. My grandfather had a branch office in Los Angeles for a while, but the base of operations has always been here."

They talked about the changes in the city in the past ten years, how celebrities both wanted and thwarted a bodyguard's ability to protect, and the various experiments she'd set up to help her with her research.

Sam had nearly finished his steak when he glanced at her nearly full glass.

"Don't you like your wine?"

She touched the stem. "It's fine."

"Francesca. What aren't you telling me?"

"I'm not a big fan of Wild Sea Vineyards."

"Why?"

"It's a long story."

"Do you have any other plans for tonight?"

Plans? With him? Now that he mentioned it—

She deliberately broke off in mid-thought. "Not really."

"I can't think of anywhere else I'd rather be," he said. "So tell me a story."

"All right." At least this was a safe topic. No double entendres, not even a hint of sexual tension.

"In 1923 two friends, Antonio Marcelli and Salvatore Giovanni, came to America from Italy. They were both second sons with no hope of inheriting their families' businesses. They vowed to show their respective families that they would be big successes. They settled in Central California and carefully tended the treasures they had brought with them." She paused and smiled. "Grapevines."

Sam leaned back in his chair. She was one surprise after the other. "Francesca Marcelli? As in Marcelli Wines?"

"That's me."

He motioned to the bottle on the table. "The Giovanni family, I presume."

"Uh-huh. The virgin soil, the windswept hills, the temperate climate were all perfect for growing grapes. Antonio and Salvatore bought land next to each other. They shared labor, celebrated victories, and together toasted their first harvest. In time they returned to Italy to marry, then came back to California and settled down to have happy lives. Wild Sea Vineyard and Marcelli Wines were born. Antonio and Salvatore each had one son and two daughters."

She paused to take a drink of water. He leaned forward. "You grew up listening to that story."

"I've heard it a thousand times."

"Your voice changes when you talk about the family

history." More than her voice. Her eyes stared past him to focus on a long-ago place.

"My grandmother talks about the old days. I guess I'm repeating what she says."

She drew in a breath and continued. "Events in Europe in the late 1930s worried the friends. With the German occupation of France and threats to Italy during the Second World War, there was great concern for the state of the vineyards. Would generations of healthy stock be destroyed? Antonio and Salvatore went to Europe, where friends offered cuttings. They traveled, collecting more and more cuttings from the most famous vineyards in France and Italy. Then they returned home to graft their legacy to their strongest vines. Whatever happened in Europe, the traditions would continue in America."

"I've noticed a more European flavor to Wild Sea wines," he said, "but I wouldn't say the same about Marcelli wines."

"I know." She shrugged. "No one knows exactly what happened or why. At first both sets of cuttings did well, but over time those planted on Marcelli lands began to die. Antonio accused Salvatore of cursing his lands or poisoning his grapes. The two men had a falling out, as did the families. Friendships ended, engagements were broken. To this day, Marcelli Wines and Wild Sea Vineyards are mortal enemies."

He liked the story, but then he found that he liked everything Francesca had to say.

"Any spilt blood?" he asked.

"Not our style," she said with a smile. "We're more the heated conversation types. Actually my grandfather, Antonio's son, is the one most interested in carrying on the feud. My parents have never been that enthusiastic about old fights, and my sisters and I don't really have the invested emotions."

"Who runs Wild Sea now?"

"Salvatore's great-grandson, Nicholas." She rested her fingertips on the bottle. "They flourished with their new European cuttings. While we're a successful enterprise, they are an international conglomerate."

"You study psychology, not wine. Why?"

"Grandpa Lorenzo says the vines must be a passion. They never were for me. My sister, Brenna, has them in her blood."

Their waiter took away the plates. Francesca shook off an offer of dessert. Sam handed him a credit card.

"Thank you for dinner," she said when they were alone again. "I've enjoyed this evening."

"Me, too." Sam smiled. "I'd like to see you again."

Heat sparked to life inside her midsection. "Me, too."

"Tomorrow night? Unless you already have plans."

She supposed she *should* play hard to get. That's what Mia, her baby sister, was always saying. Francesca had never been very good at following directions.

"Tomorrow is fine."

Sam pulled a business card from his jacket pocket and wrote on the back. "My home number," he said when he passed it to her. He drew out another card. "Yours?"

As she told him the number, he wrote it down. When he was finished, she glanced at his business card. She scanned the information, then visually stumbled when she read the title under the name.

President and CEO.

"You run the company," she said, trying not to panic. Of course he did. Why would that change anything?

"For a few years now."

She raised her gaze to his face. "How old are you?"

"Thirty-four."

The waiter interrupted them when he handed Sam his credit card and a receipt to sign.

When Sam had finished, he glanced at her. "Have I converted you to Wild Sea wines?"

She chuckled. "Unlikely. I'm not sure I've had Wild Sea Cab before. It was actually pretty good. Not that I'll tell my grandfather."

"He would probably want to cut you out of his will."

"That or throw me out of the family."

Sam tucked the receipt into his jacket pocket, rose, and moved behind her. As she stood, he pulled the chair away, then settled a hand on the small of her back.

She felt the heat of his palm and fingers all the way through to her skin, and found herself fighting the instinctive urge to step closer.

Surfer valet met them by the courtyard. He gave Sam a quick salute and pointed down the street. Francesca followed the direction and saw her truck parked behind a gleaming silver sedan. Sam held out his free hand, and the valet dropped two set of keys into them.

"He's not going to get the cars?" she asked, confused by the circumstances.

Sam handed her the truck's keys and slipped the others into his jacket pocket.

"I arranged for our cars to be brought around and parked down there."

"Why?"

"It's more private. It's not as if I want an audience when I kiss you good night."

3

Francesca told herself that a man with a plan was a good thing. She should applaud Sam's sensible nature. Instead she suddenly felt awkward, nervous, clumsy, and just a little tingly. The odd combination of apprehension and anticipation did not sit well on her baked chicken entrée.

The hand resting on the small of her back propelled her up the street. Sam drew her off the sidewalk, between her truck and his car. She had to admit it was private. And quiet. Very quiet. Voices from the restaurant seemed distant. Somewhere a radio played. The night was warm and clear. Everything was in place and pretty darned perfect—except for her sudden need to throw up.

What had seemed sensible, even funny, when she'd talked with her sisters about having sex with a stranger now seemed insane. What had she been thinking? If she threw herself into the deep end, she was going to end up wet, cold, and quite possible caught up in a riptide. Not that pools had riptides, but still. There were—

Sam took her face in his hands, then bent low and kissed her. Just like that. She was stuck holding her purse and her keys, which meant she had nothing for *her* hands to do but sort of twist there on the ends of her arms. Real attractive. If she was the least bit—

Long dormant nerves came back to life with a loud *yippee*. She went from intellectual awareness of what he was doing to actually feeling it in a nanosecond. Sam was kissing her. His warm firm mouth brushed against hers, moving slowly, discovering, touching. She could feel heat, from him and within herself. His long fingers stroked her cheeks, then he dropped his hands to her shoulders. She felt both limp and energized. Nothing could have compelled her to move. She wanted the kiss to go on forever.

He tilted his head and pressed a little harder. Tingling sensations shot through her, making her heart pound harder. For the first time in years she remembered that her breasts were exquisitely sensitive. Her skin tightened everywhere, anticipating the touch of his hands. Hunger filled her and she realized she'd been starving for this kind of intimacy for what felt like three lifetimes.

He stroked her lower lip with his tongue. A shiver rippled through her as delight overtook whatever common sense she might have once possessed. She raised one hand—the one holding the keys—and wrapped her arm around the back of his neck. He was just tall enough that she had to go on tiptoes. Sam responded by pulling her close so that they touched . . . everywhere.

Hard to her soft. She'd heard the words a thousand times, read them in books, but never before had they made so much sense. Every part of him was hard, solid, and unyielding. Her curves molded around him. She felt soft and feminine. She felt safe. When he licked her lower lip again, she parted to admit him.

At the first brush of his tongue against hers, she felt as

if she could fly. At the second, fire consumed her, heating without burning, exciting her to the point of confusion. She couldn't remember sensations like this. Not when she'd been kissed in the past. She must have been doing something wrong before—or something right this time.

She wanted more. She wanted all of it. She wanted him to kiss her until she couldn't think, couldn't breathe, couldn't do anything but feel and want and need.

She tried to move closer. When that wasn't possible, she started to kiss him back. Which was when he moved away, forcing her to pull her arm from around his neck.

"Street," Sam said, stepping back a little.

Francesca stared at him. "Street?"

His gold-brown eyes seemed darker than they had before, and brighter. His lips were damp, making him look even more sexy and powerful. Desire swamped her.

One corner of his mouth turned up. "We're standing on the street."

Okay. And that mattered *how*?

Then reality sank in. The street. She glanced around and realized there were several houses nearby and cars. People out walking their dogs, patrons from the restaurant.

She swallowed. "You're right. I guess—"

She stopped talking because she didn't know what to say. A confession that she'd been overcome by passion would only be embarrassing. If not for him, then for her.

"Are you all right?" he asked.

All right? She was perfect. She was so good, she could have started singing opera.

She went for a cool, confident, I-do-this-sort-of-thing-all-the-time smile. "Absolutely."

She turned toward her truck and headed for the driver's

door. Whatever sophistication she might have faked crumbled when she completely missed the door lock and nearly put the key through the side of her truck.

She felt herself blush. "Oops," she muttered.

"Francesca?"

She glanced over her shoulder and saw him standing behind her.

"I'll call you tomorrow afternoon and set up a time for tomorrow night. Will you be in?"

In? She would probably be curled up on the sofa, reliving the best kiss since Kelly McGillis and Tom Cruise did the tongue thing in *Top Gun*. "Sure. I have to work on my dissertation."

"I'll talk to you then."

She nodded and climbed into the truck. Sam stepped close.

"Thank you for tonight," he said and carefully closed her door.

She wanted to respond in kind, or say something clever. But her mind was still reeling from the kiss. So she settled on a wave, then she started her engine and pulled out onto the road.

As she drove through the intersection, she began humming a peppy tune from Toscanini.

Francesca didn't sleep much that night, and woke with the sun the following morning, so it took half of a second pot of coffee to get her brain functioning.

Once she was able to think in complete sentences, she cleared her tiny kitchen table of a stack of textbooks, grabbed a sheet of notebook paper and sat down to make a list.

There were the usual chores of laundry, grocery shopping—always a challenge with her budget—and vacuuming. Then there was the outline for her dissertation that had been due ten days ago and was yet to be started. Finally there was the thrill of doing her best *not* to think about Sam, their previous date, their future date, and the impending phone call.

She felt giddy. She felt wonderfully alive and in tune with the cosmos. She felt more than a little stirring low in her belly. Her heretofore silent female bits were currently line dancing in anticipation of rousing activity.

"You don't actually know he's going to want to have sex," she told herself sternly as she poured a fourth cup of coffee. "One kiss does not a physical relationship make."

True. But it had been an amazing kiss. One that deserved, if not its own national holiday, then at least a stamp.

The way Sam had pulled her close and taken charge. The feel of his mouth on hers. The taste of him, the heat that they'd—

A knock on the door interrupted her musings. Reluctantly Francesca banished her R-rated thoughts and crossed to the door. When she pulled it open, she found Mia, her baby sister, standing on the threshold.

"I came to say good-bye," Mia said as she stepped into the small apartment. "Do you have coffee? Something for breakfast? I'm starved."

Francesca laughed. "Anything else in your list of demands? How about money? You want a loan?"

Mia hugged her. "No way. You're broke."

On that cheerful note she led the way into the kitchen.

Francesca followed, then leaned against the door frame as Mia poured coffee and added a large splash of milk. She took a sip, then set the mug on the counter and opened the freezer door.

"Did Brenna leave any doughnuts in here?" she asked as she rummaged through a couple of frozen entrées, ravioli sent over by Grandma Tessa, and an emergency pint of Ben & Jerry's.

"I don't think so," Francesca said, then shook her head as Mia held up a foil-wrapped container.

"Don't you check for stuff like this?" she asked. "Brenna lived with you for almost a month after she and Jeff split up. Didn't it occur to you that she would have put doughnuts in the freezer?"

"Honestly, no."

"For someone with a degree in psychology, you sure don't know your twin."

Francesca laughed. "I thought she'd take the doughnuts with her."

"Uh-huh."

Mia finished unwrapping the Krispy Kremes and slid them onto a paper towel. Then she set them in the microwave and punched in fifteen seconds.

The old machine whirred and shook slightly as it hummed to life. Mia frowned.

"Is this safe? Are we going to get radiation burns from this?"

"I don't think microwaves use radiation."

As if not willing to risk any potential danger, Mia took a step back. Francesca grinned.

When the timer beeped, Mia pulled out the paper towel and carried it to the table. "Come on," she said. "I'll share."

"I should hope so. If Brenna left the food in the house, then it's legally mine."

Mia grabbed her coffee and pulled out a chair. Despite the relatively early hour on a Saturday, she looked alert and rested. Her big eyes were bright and clear. Her dark hair had been freshly streaked with blond highlights, and for once she wasn't wearing enough makeup to make a Vegas showgirl proud.

Francesca settled across from her and took one of the steaming doughnuts.

"Where's your face?" she asked.

Mia wrinkled her nose. "Mom begged me not to look slutty this summer while I'm in D.C. That was her exact word. Do I look slutty to you?"

Francesca studied the pretty features, the round cheeks and grinning mouth. "Not now."

Mia balled up a napkin and threw it at her. "Katie's always getting on me about my makeup, too. I think it's because you're all so old. You're just jealous."

"I'm sure that's it."

Mia finished her doughnut and reached for another. "My plane leaves early tomorrow. The folks are driving me into L.A. this afternoon, and I'm spending the night at an airport hotel. In-room movies and room service. Wanna come? It's on them. And don't say you don't mooch. This is different."

Francesca was more concerned with her date that night than sponging off her parents. "I know it's different."

Mia rolled her eyes. "You're so stubborn. You know Mom and Dad would love to help you out financially. Why don't you let them? I'm in college and they help me. Should I feel guilty?"

It was a familiar argument. "Of course not. Mia, you're eighteen, you're brilliant, and of course the folks want to pay for your school."

"So you're old. That doesn't mean they wouldn't help."

"I'm going to ignore the 'old' part," Francesca told her. "I was married. I've been on my own. It was my choice to go to college after Todd died, and it's important for me to pay my own way. I want to be independent—it's one of the reasons I took back my maiden name."

"You'd think that old poophead would have at least left you a few bucks," Mia grumbled.

"You'd think," Francesca agreed. "But he didn't and I'm doing fine."

Mia eyed the small dark kitchen. "If you say so."

"I do. Now let's talk about you. Are you excited to go to Washington?"

Mia shimmied in her chair. "D.C. is going to be so great. I still wish I was taking my language class in Japan, but this is nearly as good. I figure when I'm not studying, I'll hang out by the Capitol and meet some cute congressional aides." She sipped her coffee. "I mean, I *am* recovering from a broken heart."

Francesca shook her head. Mia might have recently broken up with her fiancé, but there weren't any broken hearts in sight.

"You seem to have moved from 'recovering' to 'recovered,' " Francesca said.

"I guess. Which means it's really good I didn't marry David, huh? So what are you doing today?"

"The usual. Errands." She motioned to the list she'd started.

Mia picked it up.

Exactly two seconds later Francesca realized her mistake. Mia got it about five seconds after that. Her baby sister's mouth dropped open, she snorted, then gave a strangled gasp-laugh.

"Check your diaphragm? Somehow I know we're not talking about breathing devices."

Francesca refused to be embarrassed. She reached across the table to take back her list.

Mia held it out of reach. "Uh-uh. No way. First you talk. Then I return personal possessions."

"Fine. It's no big deal." She picked up a doughnut and took a bite.

Mia stared at her. "Five words doesn't count as talking. I want details. Start at the beginning and speak slowly."

Francesca figured there was no point in putting off the inevitable. Mia had the same stubborn trait as all the Marcelli sisters. "When I was married to Todd, I had a bad reaction to being on the Pill, so I started using a diaphragm. In the years since, I've had occasion to dust it off once or twice, and I was curious if it was still around."

Mia dropped the list and slapped her hands on the table. "You are such a liar."

Francesca nodded. "I know. I was practicing to see if I was any better at it. What do you think?"

"You stink. Now spill your guts, woman."

"After Brenna moved back home, she, Katie, and I were talking one afternoon. Actually we were drinking wine and eating too many cookies, but that's a different story."

Mia pouted. "Dammit, why do I always miss the fun stuff? You guys are always hanging out and not including me. I hate that. It's because you and Brenna are twins and Katie's only a year older. I'm the leftover kid."

"I'm sorry, Mia. It wasn't on purpose. And for the record, we all love you to pieces. You're not the leftover kid."

"Okay. Maybe. But that doesn't make it any less annoying. So tell me what happened."

Francesca drank more coffee. "We were talking about boys we'd liked in high school but hadn't slept with. We talked about Jeff and Todd and Zach. They got on me about not dating."

"Or having sex," Mia added.

"That, too. Basically I agreed to sleep with the next normal, available guy I ran into."

Mia's eyes widened. "So you're just going to cruise the neighborhood?"

"No. I met someone yesterday. I was working and—"

Mia groaned and leaned forward until her head was resting on the table. "Please. Not the tattooed biker chick. Tell me you weren't her."

"I wasn't. I was pregnant."

Mia straightened, then gagged. "That's gross. He asked out a pregnant lady? What's wrong with him?"

"From what I can tell, nothing. He helped me out. We went back to his office, where he guilted me into telling him the truth."

"How did he do that?"

Francesca shrugged. "He was really nice."

"Wow. Nice. That must have been painful. Tell me he's at least good-looking."

"He is. *Really* good-looking." She reached for her purse and dug out his business card, then passed it to Mia.

Her sister took it and read. "President and CEO? Okay, I take back the gross comment." She set the card on the table. "If you're just now hunting for birth control, I'm guessing you didn't do it last night."

Francesca was shocked. "I do not have sex on the first date."

Mia looked unimpressed. "You don't actually know that. It would take you dating to find out."

"Good point. Okay. No, we didn't do it. We kissed."

"And?"

"It was a religious experience."

Mia chuckled. "Way to go, Sis." She tilted her head. "Let me guess. He's the reason you can't join me in Los Angeles for a night of in-room movies and room service?"

"Exactly. We have a date."

"I'm proud of you." Mia rose and stretched. "So let's find that diaphragm of yours. I want to see what it looks like and you need to practice. It sounds to me like someone might be getting lucky."

Francesca followed her into the bedroom. "I thought guys got lucky and girls put out."

"Whatever." Mia flopped down on the bed. "So start looking."

Francesca walked to her dresser but didn't pull out any drawers. She'd added the diaphragm to her to-do list on impulse. She wasn't actually expecting to get naked with Sam, was she? She'd been a virgin when she married Todd, and after his death she'd never been all that sexually active. There was an assortment of reasons, most of which could be the subject of their own psych term paper.

Yes, she'd promised her sisters, and yes, keeping that promise was the only way she was going to enter the mainstreaming dating world, but still. Sex with a stranger? She reminded herself that simple sex beat a complicated relationship any day.

Mia groaned. "I can hear you talking yourself out of it from here. Francesca, come on. It'll be fun."

"You don't actually know that."

"Yeah, I do." Mia flipped onto her stomach. "Trust me. Life with sex is pretty thrilling."

"I can't believe my eighteen-year-old sister is offering me advice on this."

"I can't believe my twenty-seven-year-old sister needs it. Now, start looking."

Francesca didn't have to look. She knew exactly where the device in question was parked. She opened the top drawer and moved a pile of socks. The slim blue case sat in the corner.

When she pulled it out of the drawer, Mia sat up. "How does this thing work?"

"It provides a barrier against invading sperm," Francesca told her. "You put a gel on first, then fold the diaphragm in half and insert it."

Mia looked doubtful.

Francesca opened the case and took out the birth-control device. Mia peered at it.

"Are you sure you can't go on the Pill?" she asked.

"I don't know. Like I said, I had a bad reaction last time. The problem is, even if I could, I have to wait until I can get to a doctor for a prescription."

"Yeah, and then you have to wait for your period to start. Bummer." She poked at the diaphragm. "I guess this could work, but I gotta tell you that putting it in will really break the mood."

Francesca hadn't thought that part through. "Good point. I guess I can put it in before I leave, although that seems so sleazy. Like I'm expecting something to happen."

So many issues to work through, she thought as she walked into the small bathroom and took the diaphragm from its case. She turned on the water and rinsed it.

Mia followed. "Aren't you?"

Francesca laughed. "Not so I want to admit." She liked Sam. They'd had a good time the previous evening. And the kiss, well, she'd already spent plenty of time reliving that. Was she ready to take things to the next level? Did she—

"That can't be good," Mia said.

Francesca glanced down at the diaphragm. She'd filled it with water, and now the liquid dripped out the bottom. Panic swept through her.

"No," she muttered. "It can't have a leak."

"How old is that thing?"

"I got it the first year I was married."

Mia shook her head. "I don't think they're supposed to last nine years, kiddo."

Francesca dumped out the water and held the diaphragm up to the light. Sure enough, there were three tiny holes. "Just perfect. I finally decide to do the wild thing, and this is what happens."

"It's no big deal," her sister told her. "The guy's supposed to wear a hat, anyway. Just make sure he does. Or make him wear two."

Francesca tossed the birth control into the sink, then sank onto the edge of the tub. "This is so unfair."

Mia crouched next to her. "It's no big deal. Really. Condoms are perfectly safe. Or if you're really worried, then don't have sex with him. That solves the problem, too. On Monday head over to the health clinic on campus and talk to someone there. Maybe you can try something slightly more modern in the birth-control department."

Francesca brightened. "Good point. I don't have to do it with Sam. I can just say no."

"Not yet," Grandpa Lorenzo said as they walked through the rows of Cabernet Sauvignon. Not yet, meaning they hadn't started to ripen.

Brenna Marcelli barely saw the clusters of pea-size green grapes. Instead a gently sloping track of land filled her mind. One that sat in the way of a cool ocean breeze, tucked between hills that blocked out early-morning and late-afternoon sunlight. A place shrouded by morning fog. Perfect conditions for the high quality Pinot Noir growing there. Perfect and possibly up for sale.

She'd already driven by twice, but she hadn't had the nerve to stop. Not when she knew that seeing the land would cause her to dream of four perfect acres that she would never own. She didn't have the money herself and knew the futility of trying to talk her grandfather into purchasing the acreage.

Probably just as well, she thought grimly. Why buy more when there were rumors that her grandfather was going to sell Marcelli Wines? Persistent rumors that didn't go away.

"When does the bottling start?" he asked, crouching in front of a cluster of young grapes that had yet to begin ripening. The Cabs always came in last.

"Middle of the week," she said. "That's when we've booked the crew."

"Are you ready?"

Brenna thought about the intense process of bottling wine. The various machines were linked together by conveyor belts that wound around like a noisy snake doing the rumba. Bottles clinked and jerked along the line, being blown clean, filled, corked, labeled in a mechanical dance that made her long for the time and manpower to lovingly fill each bottle by hand.

She hated bottling—knew how the wine could be bruised or aerated or traumatized by the rapid and brutal journey from quiet barrels to jostling bottles. A thousand and one things could go wrong with the equipment. She would check in a few times a day but otherwise planned to avoid the process.

"The Chardonnay is ready," she said. "We'll get it all done in time."

The bright sun made her pull her baseball cap over her forehead and squint to see, the vineyard stretching out for what felt like miles in every direction. The smell of earth mingled with the fragrance of grapes. The scent wasn't rich as it would be at harvest, when simply walking through the vineyard could be intoxicating. But it held promise of a good crop and a great wine.

This was her home, she thought contentedly. This land, these vines all existed within the confines of the only world she had ever loved. It had taken coming back to discover that.

She knew now she should never have left. That taking what had seemed to be the safe choice had been a mistake she'd paid for over and over again during the past nine years. Now it appeared she would be paying the ultimate price when her grandfather sold the winery. *If* he sold the winery.

Brenna couldn't get confirmation of the rumors, but there were so many of them, she couldn't help believing them true.

"People are talking," she began slowly. "About the winery. I've heard them say you're considering selling."

Her grandfather picked up a handful of dirt and let it run through his fingers. He rubbed a few leaves, then straightened and glanced up at the sun.

"A good day," he said. "A good season."

She didn't say anything. Her heart seemed to have

frozen solid in her chest. Despite the heat of the afternoon, every part of her was cold.

Finally he turned to look at her. "You asked me before. I told you. I'm not selling."

She studied his weathered face. He was a stern man who ruled his family with outdated laws and discipline, but he didn't lie.

Relief poured through her, hot and welcome. Her heart began to beat again. She sucked in a breath, then another. As long as she had the winery, she had a reason for living. It didn't matter that her personal life was in the toilet and that she was twenty-seven and had just moved back home. The grapes were everything. They—

"Not yet," he said. "Maybe soon."

Brenna stared at him. "No," she breathed. Sell? Marcelli Wines? Her chest ached as if someone had stabbed her. "You can't. This land has been in the family for over seventy years. Why would you turn all we've worked for over to a stranger?"

"I'm an old man."

"I'm not. I'm here and working hard."

His dark eyes narrowed. "For now. But then what?"

They'd had this conversation before. The unfairness of it burned like a brand. All her life she'd been told her duty was to get married as soon as she turned eighteen. Which she had done. That relationship had taken her away from the vineyard she loved.

She turned and walked away. Her body ached, but that pain was nothing when compared with the emptiness of her soul.

Her grandfather blamed her for leaving. After all those years of telling her to get married, he now punished her for listening to him. Worse, Brenna almost couldn't argue his point. She couldn't figure out why she'd given up the vineyards to marry her ass of an ex-husband who was knee-deep in preparations for his wedding to wife number two.

Her eyes burned, but she didn't cry. Not over Jeff. Not anymore. She'd moved past hate, regret, and revenge. Now she simply wanted that chapter of her life over. Let him get married again. Let him get married a dozen more times. As long as she had the grapes . . .

She crested a rise and turned to look back at the land. She'd been born and bred to work the vines, and she had walked away from them all. If only—

The bright sunlight made her squint. In the distance, on neighboring Giovanni lands, she saw movement. Was it Nic? She was too far away to tell.

If only what? If only she'd listened to her heart instead of taking the easy way out and marrying Jeff? Things would not have turned out much better with her grandfather. There were no *if onlys*. There was now and the fact that she'd finally found everything she wanted only to lose it again if her grandfather sold.

She'd learned her lesson. Unfortunately the education had come too late. What did it matter now if she never again trusted her heart and soul to a man? Without Marcelli Wines she was nothing.

4

Francesca hadn't spent much time in Montecito, an upscale neighborhood just east of Santa Barbara. She glanced at the directions she'd scribbled down, then back at the street signs and wondered what she was going to do if she got lost. No doubt the local police would want to impound her truck for being the wrong type of vehicle, the wrong age, and definitely the wrong price. In this neighborhood even the maids drove Volvos.

Francesca chuckled as she recalled her terror when Sam called and suggested a barbecue at his place, or what he'd referred to as Montecito's best grill kitchen. Her first thought had been she couldn't—she had faulty birth control. Her second had been wild temptation, followed by bone-numbing fear. Obviously she needed to get out more. Pitifully, she'd accepted his invitation when he'd mentioned a live-in housekeeper who would act as chaperon.

Less than five minutes later she found the right street and the right house. Make that the right gate. Both sides of the narrow street were lined with tall fences and gates. Some stood open, but others were firmly closed. Francesca pulled in front of Sam's, then opened her truck window to press the button on the control panel.

After a couple of seconds a familiar voice said, "Hello, Francesca. Glad you could make it."

Sam's words made her heart flutter like hummingbird wings. She felt giddy and nervous, but excited. "Hi, Sam."

"Come on in."

The large double wrought-iron gates swung open, allowing her to drive onto the property. A few hundred yards later, after rounding a bend, she stopped in front of an old two-story house built in the 1920s. The mock Tudor facade blended perfectly with the formal gardens stretching out on either side.

So the security business paid well, she thought as she opened the door and stepped onto the cobblestone driveway. Despite Sam's elegant offices and his title as CEO, she'd never considered their economic differences. If she compared family fortunes, she would probably be in the ballpark, but personally she didn't have a penny. Marcelli Wines belonged solely to her grandfather.

She glanced down at the simple sundress she'd worn. She'd taken the time to curl her long hair and put on a little makeup, but other than that, there wasn't much she could do to dazzle anyone. Funny how she found herself wanting to dazzle Sam.

She crossed to the front door, which opened before she could knock.

"Hi," she said before she got a good look at him. Which was well timed, because *after* she looked, she wasn't up for much in the way of conversation.

She'd been picturing him in a suit, not that she'd wasted her *entire* day dreaming about him.

He wore a red polo shirt tucked into worn jeans and no

shoes. Somehow the sight of his bare feet shocked her—as if she'd stumbled into his bedroom and accidentally seen him naked. They were just feet, she told herself. *Big* feet.

She held in a smile as she thought of what her sister, Brenna, would say about her observation on the feet front.

"Thanks for coming," he said, smiling at her.

She found herself getting lost in those tawny-colored eyes she'd admired last night. His dark blond hair was tousled, as if he'd been running his hands through it. What was it about a slightly rumpled man that women found appealing? Why did he seem more dangerous now than he had before?

"Thanks for the invitation." She glanced around the foyer. "So this is the great grill place, huh?"

"Actually the grilling magic happens on my back patio. There's going to be a write-up in *Food and Spirits* next month."

"You're going to be busy. I'm glad I could get in before the rush."

"I'd make room for you."

"You mean in time I could get my own table?"

"Maybe a chair, if you're good."

This is the place where a sophisticated, *experienced* woman would purr something about always being good. The words hovered on Francesca lips, but she held them back. Throwing herself into the deep end was one thing, but promising an Olympic performance instead of the ungainly flailing that was likely to follow seemed like a mistake.

"I'll give you the nickel tour," he said. "You can meet Elena, so you'll know I wasn't lying about her, then I'll take you out to the patio and impress you."

His low voice seemed to brush across her skin like warm

velvet. She found herself wanting to move closer, to stretch until all the kinks were out, then rub against him. Maybe she could purr without words.

He took a step, then paused. "Take your shoes off if you want."

Francesca hesitated a second, then slipped out of her sandals and dropped her bag next to them. Somehow the thought of both of them barefoot was more than a little scandalous, but she was playing with the big guys now.

She followed Sam across the hardwood floor of the entryway, past a large living room. She caught a glimpse of a library, a home office, and a dining room.

"Big place," she said. "I can see why you have live-in help."

Sam smiled at her. "I didn't used to. Somebody came in and cleaned. My grandfather lives a couple of miles from here. He's getting up in years and needs more help than he used to. Not that he'll admit it. I wanted to get him someone, but he's stubborn and wouldn't agree. So I complained about wanting to hire a full-time person and not having enough work. He pretended to believe me. Elena spends most of her time with him, but she has a suite of rooms here. It's a game my grandfather and I play, but it works."

They crossed by the kitchen and entered a small hallway at the back of the house. Sam knocked on a closed door.

"Elena? Francesca is here."

A small, redheaded woman in her early fifties opened the door. She was casually dressed in sweats and a T-shirt.

"Elena, this is Francesca. Francesca, Elena runs the house. My grandfather and I would be lost without her."

"Nice to meet you," Francesca said.

"You, too." She grinned at her employer. "Okay. I agree. This one was worth the wait."

Sam sighed. "You weren't supposed to say anything to get me in trouble."

Elena's smile broadened. "Me? What did I say? Did I mention a word about a man living alone for too long with only an old woman for company? No. Not a word. Did I say it was time he found himself a good woman? Not even close. I mind my own business. That's what I'm paid to do. I keep my mouth shut."

"Speaking of shutting," Sam said, interrupting her. "I'm closing your door now. You sure you don't want me to cook you a steak?"

"Yes. Red meat will kill you."

"Without it, life isn't worth living."

"You need to eat more vegetables."

"Good night, Elena," he said and drew the door closed.

"Good night," she called. "Have fun."

Sam shook his head, then led the way back to the kitchen. "She makes me crazy."

"You adore her."

"I do. She's great with Gabriel. He can be a real curmudgeon, but she doesn't mind. As you may have noticed, she gives as good as she gets. He thinks she's great, although he'd rather eat worms than admit it."

Francesca glanced around at the spacious rooms they passed on their way through the house. "Do you rent out rooms?"

"I could. If the security business ever tanks, I'll think about it." He led the way into the kitchen.

She had a brief impression of bleached cabinets and tiled counters. French doors led to an open deck with the ocean in the distance. But she was more distracted by

Sam's words than the view. Very nice, she thought. Too nice. If Sam was so all that, why wasn't he married with six kids?

"What are you thinking?" he asked as he took a step toward her.

"Nothing much. I'm in observation mode."

"Exploring your environment?" he asked as he moved a little closer.

"Sure." And him. Flawed or not, she wouldn't mind exploring him.

"You look beautiful," he said.

"You're not so bad yourself."

He grinned. "You like my 'executive at home' look?"

"It doesn't stink."

He chuckled, then stepped in front of her and rested his hands on her waist. She had a half second of warning before he bent low and kissed her.

The light brush of his mouth made her sway toward him. Body parts slowly stirred to life. She rested her fingers on his shoulders, feeling the strength and heat of him.

Her insides warmed, then melted. Legs quivered. She sighed and leaned into him. This was going to be good.

And it was. He ran his hands up and down her back, then swept his tongue across her lower lip. She never thought of protesting, or even worrying that they were standing in a kitchen. There were counters and tables and lots of possibilities, not that she could think of even one when she parted her lips slightly and brushed her tongue against his.

Erotic excitement sizzled. Every inch of skin quivered as they pressed together. He smelled good—male, clean, sexy. He tasted even better. They danced and stroked and explored. He dropped his hands to her rear and squeezed.

She instinctively arched against him, which brought her belly in contact with his erection. The proof of his arousal both delighted and terrified her.

He broke the kiss and stared at her. Fire danced in his gold-brown eyes.

"So you're the kind of girl my grandfather always warned me about. The ones who get guys like me in trouble."

His hands were still on her waist. She liked the weight of them there. She lightly squeezed his shoulders. "How on earth would I get you in trouble?"

"I can think of a thousand ways."

She could only think of a couple, but she wasn't prepared to share lists.

She studied his face, enjoying the way he watched her. As if he liked what he saw. They weren't moving, weren't touching, except for where their hands rested. The moment shouldn't have been special or intimate, yet it was both.

The aching inside of her grew. It moved low in her belly, then flared out to her thighs. Her body felt heavy. She felt thick, swollen, and wet. All this and they'd only kissed.

She didn't want to know. Well, okay—maybe she did.

"What are you thinking?" he asked.

"Nothing I'm going to tell you."

He laughed. "That sounds promising. Come on. We'll open a bottle of wine and go sit on the deck. While we stare at the ocean, you can tell me about your day."

He released her and crossed to the counter. As she watched him move, she realized she was completely out of her element. Sam obviously knew what he was doing. If she wasn't careful, she was going to find herself well and truly seduced.

She walked over to lean against the counter. The sight of the familiar label made her smile.

"I see I've converted you," she said, touching the Marcelli Wines bottle.

"It didn't take much convincing."

He pulled out the cork and poured them each a glass of Merlot, then led the way out onto the deck. The afternoon sun had warmed the redwood and the wicker chairs. When Francesca sat down, Sam pulled an ottoman over, positioning it between their chairs.

"To summer nights," he said, holding out his glass.

She touched hers to his, then took a sip. Summer nights. She couldn't remember one quite like this. There was still an hour or so to go until sunset. The view of the ocean stretched out in the distance, the vastness of the water offering endless possibilities. A handsome man who made her skin tingle and her heart flutter sat next to her. This was definitely a top-ten moment for the week.

"Tell me about your day," he said as he shifted and lifted his feet to the ottoman. Francesca had already stretched out her legs to rest her heels on the white wicker. Their bare toes, the proximity, the casual acceptance all made her feel as if they'd done this a thousand times before. It was disconcerting. It was very nice.

"My sister, Mia, came to see me," she said. "She's leaving for Washington, D.C., in the morning. Mia is eighteen, a junior at UCLA, and brilliant. She's majoring in political science and is probably going to take over the world some day. As if all that isn't enough, she's amazing with languages. This summer she's taking a six-week language course. She'll be studying Japanese."

Sam glanced at her. "Is she your only sister?"

Francesca thought about her family. "How scared do you want to be?"

"I already know about your family history. Is it more intimidating than that?"

"You'll have to tell me." She sipped her wine. "My fraternal grandparents, my maternal grandmother, and my parents all live in a hacienda up by the vineyard. I have a sister, Katie, who is older by a year and a fraternal twin, Brenna. Mia is the baby—she's nine years younger than me."

Sam looked impressed. "I won't complain about Gabriel anymore."

"You'd better not. Grandma Tessa, my father's mother, is pure Italian. For her, everything in life can be healed with more pasta. Mary-Margaret O'Shea is my mother's mother. We call her Grammy M. She's Irish, tiny, but strong-willed. We're Italian-Irish and Catholic. The family is loud, volatile, and rosaries appear at the drop of a hat."

He smiled. "You love them. I can hear it in your voice."

"I do. I can't imagine what it would be like to grow up with a small family."

"There are pluses and minuses." He set his wine on the table between their chairs. "I'm going to delight you with my culinary abilities."

"Really?"

"Sure. I already have potatoes baking in the oven. Elena made a salad earlier, and I'm going to grill steaks."

She laughed. "I'm so impressed I can barely breathe. Will you actually take the potatoes out of the oven yourself?"

"Absolutely. Although if it makes you feel better, you can help."

"It's almost too much. I'm going to bet that next you'll be telling me you can pour milk on cereal and make toast."

"How'd you guess?" He rose. "Come on. You can watch and marvel."

She set down her wine and stood. "So much for you hiring Elena for your grandfather. You sound like you need a keeper, too."

"No way. I can order take-out as well as any other guy."

"I guess I shouldn't make fun of you. I'm not much of a cook, either. Although I can boil up frozen ravioli like nobody's business."

"That's something," he said, and took her hand in his.

Francesca allowed him to lead her inside. She felt good. Better than good, she was tingling. Being around Sam made her physically aware in a way that was new and exciting. She liked how they teased and laughed. So far there hadn't been any awkward pauses or stumbling conversations, and this dating stuff was looking pretty good.

He walked into the family room, where he released her and moved over to a stack of complicated-looking electronic equipment.

"Any musical preferences?" he asked.

"Not really."

While he flipped through several CDs, she walked around the room. A large, overstuffed sofa faced a widescreen television with massive speakers on either side. To the left was the electronic tower Sam held court over; to the right was a set of French doors leading to the patio.

Francesca moved to her right, where open shelves displayed everything from books to pictures. There were several of Sam with an older man she guessed was his grandfather, a few shots of foreign locations, and none of his parents. No other women, either, which she supposed was a good thing.

Magazines lay on a coffee table. *Time, Fortune, Car and Driver*. Talk about a guy. She smiled.

As she completed her circuit, soft strains of music filled the room.

Sam touched her shoulder, causing her to turn toward him. He moved close, putting both his hands on her waist.

"Dance with me," he said.

Awkwardness filled her. "Here? In the family room?"

"Would you be more comfortable in the kitchen?"

"No. I just—"

He didn't wait for an explanation. She had the feeling he didn't wait for much. Instead he began moving her to the slow beat, pulling her closer with each step until they were pressed against each other. She gave into the rhythm and raised her arms so she could link her hands behind his head.

She found herself caught up in his steady gaze, in the feel of his body against hers. There were defining moments in life, she thought hazily. And magic ones. This dance, this night, this *man* fell into the latter category. If she was interested in reacquainting herself with a journey exploring life's possibilities, he seemed like the perfect guide.

He leaned down and brushed his mouth against hers. This time she immediately recognized the aching for what it was. Desire.

She gave herself up to the sensation and the kiss. His tongue stroked her lower lip before slipping inside her mouth. She welcomed him, surging against him. The edges of the world blurred, then faded as she lost herself in the passion of the moment.

He kissed her deeply, thoroughly, slowly. Over and over his tongue stroked against hers, circling, teasing, until she only wanted to surrender. Their bodies continued to move to the rhythm of the music, a steady erotic beat that matched the thundering of her heart.

Hunger filled her, pulsing, driving, and demanding. Hunger, but not for the promised steak and salad. Instead she starved for this man. Her sisters had teased her about it being too long, but she hadn't really believed them. Not until this moment, when she felt empty and malnourished. She wanted to be touched all over and to touch in return. She wanted to feel slick heat and surging surrender. She wanted to give herself up to the moment, to the man, and then spend the next forty-eight hours in a sensual fog.

Between her legs, flesh swelled and wept in anticipation. Her panties grew damp. Her breasts ached as her nipples tightened. Her skin was suddenly too small, her clothes too confining. She ached . . . all over.

The kissing wasn't enough, she thought, fighting frantic need. She pressed harder against Sam, desperate to rub against him, to feel friction and contact and pleasure. Her brain began to shut down as instinct took over. The hunger grew and burned. Unfamiliar, powerful, it should have frightened her. Maybe with another man it would have, but not with Sam.

He pulled away and stared at her. Passion tightened his features. His breathing was as fast and hard as her own.

"Hell of a kiss," he murmured, his voice thick and low.

She stared at him without speaking.

He swore. "Francesca, do you have any idea what your eyes are telling me? If you don't mean them to say yes, you'd better speak up right now."

She waited for good sense to take over. Nothing happened.

"I guess I don't have anything to say," she whispered.

He rubbed his thumb across her mouth. "You're pure fantasy material, you know that?"

Her? A fantasy? That worked. She reached up and kissed him.

Sam responded with a deep groan that shook her down to her toes. He cupped her face and kissed her deeply. Sometime in all this they'd stopped dancing. She didn't mind. Nothing really mattered except the fire inside of her and the man in front of her.

He dropped his hands to her shoulders, then slid them down to her hands. Even as he kissed her cheeks, her jaw, her chin, he was pulling her out of the room. They made it to the hallway, where they clung to each other for a second before racing up the tall, wide flight of stairs.

On the second floor Francesca saw little more than hardwood floors, windows, and doors before Sam was pulling her along the hallway. At the end he entered through double doors, and pushed them shut behind her. Then he was drawing her close and touching her . . . everywhere.

He stroked her back, her rear, her hips, then slipped around to settle his hands on her waist. At the same time he kissed her. His tongue brushed against hers with a passionate tenderness that made her catch her breath.

She touched him in return. The width of his shoulders. Hard muscles contrasted with the softness of his shirt. She traced the breadth of his chest, then circled to his back. His hands climbed toward her breasts, hers dipped to his rear. They reached their destinations at the same time, and as her fingers dug into high, tight flesh, he brushed against her hard, sensitive nipples.

They both gasped.

The ache inside of her intensified. She couldn't remember the last time she'd been touched there. How many years had it been since she'd felt the pressure of a firm caress on tight, hungry skin?

He cupped her curves, then broke the kiss to bend down. Through the layers of her dress and bra, she felt the heat of his breath. He bit down gently and she nearly screamed.

He reached for the buttons running down the front of her dress. At the same time she tugged his shirt out of the waistband of his jeans. She vaguely recalled that in the past she'd been somewhat shy and restrained in bed. And she probably would be again. Just not now. Not with the need pounding inside of her like a drum. She ached. Between her legs, the dampness surged until she was wet and slick and ready. She wanted his hands on her—her breasts, between her legs. She wanted his mouth everywhere. She trembled, she shook, she needed.

He finished with the buttons and pushed the dress off her shoulders. She straightened her arms and let it fall to the floor, leaving her wearing bikini panties and a bra.

Sam's gaze swept over her, and he sucked in a breath. "Stunning," he said.

"My turn." She tugged on his polo shirt. "Take this off."

He grinned. "Yes, ma'am."

He went one better. After tugging off his shirt, he unfastened his belt, then his jeans and pushed them to the floor.

She took in the well-toned muscles, the blond hair dusting his chest, the narrow waist, and his erection straining against his briefs. Big feet was right, she thought, mesmerized by the length and thickness of him.

Then she couldn't think, because he was touching her. He explored her shoulders, her rib cage, then her back, where he easily unfastened her bra. When the bit of lace had fallen away, he cupped her breasts in his hands and kissed her.

The combination was electric. Warm fingers teased her breasts, while his mouth worked its magic on hers. She moaned, she squirmed, she nearly came in her panties.

She touched him back, wanting to get closer. She ached to wrap her legs around him and have him plunge inside of her. She wanted to beg, to scream, to demand. When he began moving them toward the bed, she nearly moaned in relief.

Once they arrived, Sam pulled open a nightstand drawer and set a condom on the surface. The sight of something that practical should have brought Francesca to her senses, but she was too far gone. She glanced at it, had a moment of gratitude, then slipped off her panties and climbed on the bed.

He was right there with her. They surged together, naked, hungry, needing. Even as he bent down to kiss and lick her sensitive breasts, he slipped a hand between her legs.

At the first brush of his fingers, she pulsed against him. She felt ravenous and wanted to swallow him whole. Need made her pulse her hips impatiently.

"More," she whispered, clinging to him. "Touch me—ah."

He'd found the spot. That single place of pleasure. He pressed his fingers against it, rubbing firmly, gently, perfectly. She dropped her head to the pillow and sucked in a breath.

It was too good. It had been too long, and damn if Sam hadn't figured out exactly what made her shake.

He circled that tight spot, shifted until he could caress her with his thumb, then slipped a finger inside.

It was too much. Her body contracted, convulsed, and she was gone. Just like that. Her orgasm swept through her, making her shudder and pant and moan. She lost herself in the pleasure.

So much better than she remembered, she thought

hazily as wave after wave of warm, liquid release filled her. Way too good for mortal man.

When the contractions slowed, she opened one eye, then the other. Sam looked both pleased and stunned. She couldn't help grinning.

"It's been a long time," she admitted.

He continued to gently stroke her. "And here I thought you were going to tell me that I'm really good."

"That, too."

She studied his eyes, his mouth, the way the blond hair fell over his forehead. She might have had her appetizer, but she was still hungry for the main course.

She reached between them and took his impressive arousal in her hand. With one slow stroke she had him groaning.

"I thought maybe we'd take this guy for a test-drive," she said. "What do you think?"

"You're my kind of woman."

He grabbed the condom and quickly put it on.

Francesca felt her body stretching as he filled her. It took every ounce of self-control not to lose herself in the first thrust. When he was in all the way, he shifted so he was staring down at her. His eyes dilated.

"Don't hold back on my account," he said, his voice low and husky. "You're so damn wet and hot, I'm about to lose it."

She placed her hands on his back and stroked him. "How do you feel about screaming? I never have before, but I have a feeling I might have to this time."

"I consider it the highest praise possible."

"Oh, good."

With that, he began to move. She closed her eyes and lost herself in the pleasure of him filling her over and over again. Within a few strokes, tension built to unbearable and she couldn't hold on any longer.

"Oh, Sam," she breathed, then lost herself in the pleasure. She surged against him, dropped her hands to his rear and pulling him in deeper and deeper.

Thick, powerful contractions rippled through her. She gasped, she writhed, she surrendered. She might have even screamed.

And still her orgasm went on. It crested at the moment he shuddered and stilled. His body tensed, then he collapsed against her.

Francesca lay there, under his body, and slowly opened her eyes. She felt good. Better than good. She felt capable of performing miracles. The lovemaking had been great. Amazing. Sinus-clearing. She wanted to do it again. She wanted—

Reality chose that moment to crash her party. One second she was basking in afterglow so bright she could tan by it, and the next she was hardly able to breathe. Panic swept through her, making her squirm slightly.

Sam raised himself on his arms and smiled sheepishly. "Sorry. I didn't mean to squash you."

"It wasn't that," she said, trying not to push him away and bolt for freedom. Unfortunately, she wasn't able to school her expression as well as she would like.

He frowned. "What's wrong?"

"Nothing." She swallowed, then knew she had to come clean. "Everything. I just . . ." She sucked in a breath. "There's absolutely no way I want to get married."

5

Sam's dick chose that moment to shrink to the size of a peanut. Sam pushed up into a kneeling position, pulled out of her, and slid to the edge of the bed. When he'd tossed the condom, he turned back to Francesca.

She lay on her back, her mouth swollen, her skin flushed. She was gorgeous. Sexy as hell. And quite possibly crazy. Damn.

He knew better than to make love this soon. He'd given that up nearly a decade before. He preferred to get to know a woman before getting into her pants, and with good reason.

Francesca bit her lower lip. "That came out wrong. I mean I know you didn't propose or anything."

"Okay." That was a step in the right direction.

He stood and grabbed her panties, bra, and dress, then tossed them to her. He collected his jeans and pulled them on, not looking at her until she slipped into her dress and started on the buttons.

When she'd secured the front of her dress, she sank back on the mattress. "This was really great," she told him, motioning vaguely to the bed, then to him. "I haven't been with anyone in a while and . . ." She stopped and sighed. "So my sisters made me promise . . ." She stopped again.

He was still wary enough not to approach the bed. "You said you didn't want to get married."

She brightened. "That's right. I don't." She smiled. "What I mean by that is I'm not looking to get involved." She shook her head. "I'm not really into the whole romance-marriage thing. I was married once, and I didn't like it. After Todd died, I tried dating some, but guys always want to take things to the next level. Does that sound too horrible?"

"No." Some of his wariness eased. "You think because I slept with you I'll want to marry you?"

She covered her face with her hands. "That sounds so horrible." She dropped her hands to her sides and looked at him. "It's just that I gave up on the whole male-female thing because it was such a pain. I'm guilted enough by my family. They want my sisters and me to settle down and have dozens of babies. I live with the guilt because I can't seem to let it go, but it's not enough to make me do what they want. I have my school and a great career just a couple of years away. Until recently, that's been enough. It's just I sort of miss, well, um . . ." She cleared her throat and shifted on the bed.

He got it immediately. "Sex," he said with a grin.

"That would be it, yes."

His wariness faded completely, and he mentally apologized for thinking she was crazy.

"You don't want to get involved with me," he said.

"You're very nice," she told him. "A really great guy."

He chuckled and moved closer to the bed. "Be honest."

"Okay, I don't want hearts, flowers, or forever."

"Uh-huh." He sat next to her and took her hand. "But you wouldn't mind a little slap and tickle."

Her eyes widened. "I don't think I'd like any slapping."

"Spanking?"

"Only if I get to do it to you."

He grinned. "No way. I'm the dominant male around here."

She angled toward him. "I'm sorry I blurted out the marriage thing. The sex was so good and then I panicked."

"Me, too. I thought you'd gone postal."

She chuckled. "No. I was overwhelmed by my physical response is all."

He touched her face. Beautiful, responsive, and not interested in forever. And honest. The one quality he valued above all others.

"I'm into serial monogamy myself," he said as he cupped her cheek. "No plans to get married."

"Really?"

"Sure. I didn't like my experience, either."

She drew in a breath. "Okay. At the risk of moving too fast, would you be open to a monogamous sexual relationship with no emotional ties?"

He didn't have to think twice. Not when the woman in question was as appealing as this one. "Absolutely."

Francesca thought her experience with Sam had peaked with her orgasms, but maybe she'd been a little hasty in her judgment. Was it possible to have everything she wanted and nothing she didn't?

"We'll see each other when we want," he said. "Good conversation, lots of laughs, and plenty of time in bed. When one or both of us want to end it, we will. No expectations. No hard feelings. Deal?"

She felt wicked. She felt excited. God was probably

going to punish her, and if the Grands ever found out, they'd have her hide. But it would be worth it.

"Deal."

When Francesca arrived at the hacienda for brunch the following morning, she had a bad feeling that everyone was going to guess something was going on with her. She felt radiant, her skin was glowing, and she just couldn't seem to stop grinning.

Not that it was all her fault. After striking their deal, she and Sam had spent the entire night making love. They'd crept downstairs about midnight to grab something to eat and then had retreated to the quiet, sensual darkness of his bedroom.

The only way she'd been able to drag herself from his presence was the realization that if she didn't show up for her weekly brunch with her family, the Grands would set the FBI on her trail. And she couldn't very well bring Sam with her. The sight of her in the company of an eligible man would fill the house with the sound of wedding bells. Something neither of them wanted.

Francesca climbed out of her truck and headed for the back door of the big Spanish-style house. It was early June, which meant every form of plant life was lush, green, and growing. Tall trees provided shade over the rear of the house. The vegetable garden by the garage soaked up the bright sunshine. In the distance acres and acres of vines rustled and danced in the light breeze.

The flowers on the grapevines had dried up, while the small pea-sized grapes had appeared. From what she had seen on her drive up to the hacienda, they were going to have a banner year. But there was still a lot of time left until harvest, and Brenna would be happy to tell her all the things that could go wrong between now and then.

The back door burst open. "Francesca!"

She glanced up and smiled as Grandma Tessa held out her arms. "Come, child. We have missed you."

Francesca ran toward the house and up the three steps, then hugged her grandmother close. "How are you? Feeling all right?"

"I'm old, eh? Things don't work as well as they used to, but I'm here. That's enough." She released her granddaughter, reached up, and pinched her cheek. "Still a pretty girl. But you're not so young anymore. You need to be married, Francesca. You need *bambinos*. It is time."

Normally she found the family pressure a little exasperating, but today nothing could puncture her good mood. "Before I'm too old, right?"

"Single women over thirty," her grandmother said knowingly. "I read. Easier for you to be taken by aliens than find a man. You only have three years, Francesca. Don't waste them."

Francesca laughed. Her cheek stung from Grandma Tessa's enthusiasm, but the pain was as familiar as the entreaty that she marry and produce offspring. Over the past three years the hints had become much less subtle. Fresh off the success of her older sister's engagement, the family had increased the pressure.

If she mentioned Sam, they would get off her back about finding a man. Of course, they would also want to meet him and find out if a wedding date had been set. Knowledge of her "no commitment" agreement with him would send both grandmothers scuttling for their rosaries and force her parents to have a long talk with her. Better to play along.

"Talk to her," Grandma Tessa said as they entered the open and airy kitchen.

Grammy M—Mary-Margaret O'Shea to the rest of the world and Francesca's maternal grandmother—glanced up from the dough she'd rolled out on the granite counter.

"Francesca! My darlin' girl." She wiped her hands on the apron she wore.

Francesca walked over for another hug—this one without a cheek pinch—and bent down to embrace the tiny woman.

"Grandma Tessa wants me to get married again," Francesca said with mock surprise. "What do you think?"

Grammy M shook her head, causing her white curls to bounce. "You're supposed to be respectin' your elders, young lady, not makin' fun of them. We want you to be happy."

"You want me pregnant." Francesca snatched a scone from a cooling rack.

"Married and pregnant," Grandma Tessa corrected.

Grammy M grinned, her blue eyes dancing with humor. "Oh, I don't know, Tessa. I'm thinkin' we could probably find it in our hearts to forgive Francesca if she found herself with a wee one in the oven."

Francesca chuckled, but didn't even try to get in the middle of *that* conversation. Instead she broke the still-steaming scone in half and took a small bite. The firm, golden-brown crust gave way to a soft, perfectly baked, orange-flavored center that made her mouth water even as it dissolved on her tongue.

"Amazing," she breathed. "Grammy M, we're going to have to try another scone lesson. I want to be able to do this at home."

Her maternal grandmother gazed at her fondly before

shaking her head and returned to the dough she'd rolled out.

"You're a lovely girl, but you don't have much success in the kitchen."

"I took that cake-decorating class a couple of years ago."

"Your father nearly choked to death on that piece he ate," Grandma Tessa reminded her.

Francesca knew they were right. She was a disaster when it came to cooking, although she continued to take classes. Mostly because despite a degree in psychology, she couldn't seem to talk herself out of the guilt she felt for not caving to family expectations about marriage and kids. So she substituted a quest for excellence in the domestic arts.

"The flowers on the cake were pretty."

"That they were," Grammy M agreed. "And you make a lovely radish rose."

Francesca took another bite of scone, then crossed to the cupboards above the dishwasher and grabbed a glass. "Is this your way of telling me my cooking has style but no substance? I was thinking of taking a class on Chinese cooking this summer."

"We're telling you that if you want to win a man's heart, come by and pick up some ravioli," Grandma Tessa said cheerfully. "I always have them in the freezer, along with a nice, thick meat sauce."

Winning a man's heart was *not* a place she wanted to go. "Did Mia's flight get off all right?" she asked to change the subject.

"You just missed her call to say she'd arrived in Washington," Grammy M said. "I know she'll enjoy her language course, but we'll all be missin' havin' her around."

"I'm sure she'll miss us, too," Francesca said, then

remembered Mia's plans to hang out with congressional aides. Somehow under those circumstances, she thought her very pretty little sister might be too busy to be homesick.

She reached for another scone, only to have her hand slapped by Grandma Tessa. "Brenna's out in the vineyards, so you'll have to set the table yourself. Wash your hands first."

Francesca laughed. "Yes, ma'am."

Her grandmother turned to stare at her. Dark eyebrows drew together as Grandma Tessa tried to look fierce.

"I love you both very much," Francesca said impulsively, hugging the Grands before moving into the hallway and the bathroom tucked under the stairs.

"Use the good china," Grandma Tessa called after her.

"You've been on your own a long time, dear," her mother said, gazing at her intently.

Colleen O'Shea Marcelli was a petite woman with attractive features, dark hair, and a fashionable dress sense. Even at a casual brunch she looked well put together enough to be in a photo shoot. Francesca had slipped on a sleeveless summer dress because Marcelli daughters weren't allowed to wear shorts or pants to dinners or any meal on Sunday. While her mother shopped at expensive boutiques that specialized in designer originals, Francesca favored the extra-reduced racks at outlet stores and the occasional castoffs from Brenna, the only one of her sisters to be within two inches of her height.

Across the large table Brenna and her grandfather talked about the coming harvest. The Grands chatted about which movie they would head out to see later, while her father, Marco Marcelli nodded at everything his wife said. Which meant her parents had planned their attack in advance.

"Five years," her mother said. "Francesca, your devotion to Todd's memory is a credit to your marriage, but you're still a young woman. Are you going to mourn him for the rest of your life?"

Francesca thought about pointing out that her grandmother had informed her she was reaching the age of no return, at least in the marriage market.

For the thousandth time she thought about coming clean and simply confessing that nothing about being married appealed to her. Her marriage to Todd had been a disaster. The on-the-surface successful banker hadn't been interested in an actual person for a wife. Instead he'd wanted only arm candy. His premature death in a car accident had led her to discover that their lavish lifestyle had been financed by credit, not income. She'd been left with plenty of debt, which had forced her to sell everything. In the end she'd walked away, not richer but wiser.

Brenna had married Jeff and had spent the next nine years of her life supporting him through medical school, internships, and residencies. She's given up her true love—the winery—to be a good wife. Her reward? Jeff dumped her for someone younger. Yes, their parents were happy, and Grandpa Lorenzo and Grandma Tessa had been married for generations, but that wasn't enough to convince her. As far as she was concerned, love was highly overrated and marriage wasn't in her future.

Not that her parents would understand. Which meant they had the "why don't you find a nice boy and settle down" conversation at least twice a month.

"I'm not mourning Todd," she said truthfully and

thought of making love with Sam the previous night. Mourning had been the last thing on her mind. Still, she wouldn't mind skipping the lecture.

She drew in a breath. "You're right. I do need to start going out."

Silence descended on the table. Everyone turned to stare at her, even Brenna, who raised her eyebrows and placed her hand on her chest in mock surprise. Francesca shot her a warning look.

Grandpa Lorenzo, still tall and powerful despite his seventy-plus years, pounded on the table. "About time you realized that, young lady. You're the prettiest of my granddaughters. When I think about all those years you've wasted going to college when you could have been getting married and having babies."

Francesca was used to the lecture, but even after all this time the words stung.

Brenna's eyes flashed with temper. She turned to her grandfather. "At some point you're going to have to realize we're in a new century, Grandpa. Women don't need men to make them feel whole anymore. We're fine on our own."

"If you'd spent a little more time paying attention to your husband, maybe he wouldn't have left you," the old man shot back.

"Lorenzo!" Grandma Tessa said, and looked sympathetically at Brenna. "We know you were a good girl. We should never have let you marry that ex-husband of yours. You need a nice Italian boy. My cousin, Marie, has a grandson who lives in Chicago."

Brenna shook her head. "No, Grandma. No relatives, or friends of relatives. I'm not even legally divorced yet. Give me a break on this, okay?"

Grandma Tessa didn't look ready to back down. Francesca

understood exactly what her sister was feeling. While she loved her family, they really knew how to get on her nerves. She decided to give them both a break.

"Have Katie and Zach set a wedding date yet?" she asked.

That got everyone's attention. Her mother reminded her about the family meeting later in the week to get the event planned. The Grands started arguing over the menu, and Grandpa Lorenzo threw out several possible wine suggestions.

Brenna picked up a bottle of Marcelli Wines Chardonnay and poured herself another glass. She held out the bottle.

"Make mine a double," Francesca murmured so only her sister could hear. When Brenna had filled her glass as well, they raised them to each other.

"To surviving our family," Brenna whispered. "May God save me from Cousin Marie's grandson."

"International oil brokers with families and death threats should not be allowed to travel for pleasure," Sam said wearily as he tossed a file folder onto his desk.

Jason reached forward and picked up the papers. "You're kidding."

"Not even close. He called yesterday."

Jason flipped through the pages, then put the folder back on Sam's desk. "Africa?"

"Safari. His daughter is something of an animal lover. This is part of her birthday present."

"Couldn't he just buy her a bike?"

Sam grinned. "That's not how the rich and powerful do things."

"Then get the kid a bike store. Africa?" The big man's dark eyes narrowed. "They're not going to stick to the tourist spots are they? Rich and powerful types like the unusual and out-of-the-way. Right?"

Sam nodded. "We're talking about camping in the wilderness, visiting native villages."

"I hate the outdoors," Jason muttered. "Why can't they vacation in Monaco? I could really get into Monaco."

"Guess you're going to have to go there on your own time."

Jason scowled. "So tell me why I volunteered for this job?"

"Because you love a challenge. Want to change your mind?"

Jason picked up the folder again. "Africa. We're talking ticks and leeches. I hate slimy things."

"That's the jungle. You're going to be on the savannah."

"Great. So I only have to worry about malaria."

"You might see a lion."

Jason's scowl deepened. "Hate cats, too."

Sam chuckled. "They're leaving in September. You have that long to put together the team. He's letting you pick them all. His regular protection is going on vacation."

"Bet they're not planning to hang out with ticks." Jason sighed. "At least I don't have to worry about some pantyass European bodyguards." He slammed the folder shut. "Hell, I've got to get shots, don't I?"

"There's a list in the back."

Before Jason could complain any more, a familiar uneven footfall sounded in the hallway. Step, clunk, slide. Step, clunk, slide.

"You didn't tell me the old man was here," Jason said.

"I didn't know. It's Sunday." His grandfather never came in on the weekend, although he still made regular appearances during the week.

"It's Sunday, for God's sake," Gabriel Reese announced from the entrance to Sam's office. "Why aren't you all in church?"

Jason rose to his feet and nodded at the older man. "Afternoon, sir."

"Jason. Is my grandson making you work on Sunday?"

"I volunteered."

"Good man. I'm the one who told Sam about you. Did he ever tell you that?"

Jason grinned. "Yes, sir."

Sam motioned to the second chair in front of his desk. "Have a seat, Gabriel. Do you want something to drink?"

"Whiskey, but don't bother telling me it's too early in the day. I'll wait until I get home." He braced his arms on his cane and slowly sank into the seat. "You've always been a good man in business, Samuel, but a real pain in the ass when it comes to my health."

"I don't want you dying on me."

"I don't plan to die *on* anyone," Gabriel snapped. "I'll be alone in my bed. That's how men *should* die."

Sam got up and crossed to the coffeepot on the small cart in the corner. He poured some in a mug, added generous amounts of sugar and cream, and carried it to his grandfather.

Gabriel took a sip, then eyed Jason, who had finally returned to his chair. "Heard you were going to Africa. Wish I were young enough to take your place."

"Me, too," Jason said glumly.

Sam grinned. "Jason's concerned about the wildlife. Snakes, leeches. That sort of thing."

Gabriel nodded solemnly. "Dry socks," he announced. "That's the key to a healthy safari. Oh, and plenty of bug spray."

"Well, hell. Bugs. I didn't think about them." Jason eyed Sam. "I want a trip to Monaco when this is over."

"We'll have to see what we can do."

Jason grunted, got to his feet, and said good-bye to both men. When he was gone, Sam leaned back in his chair.

"Elena's sister called this morning," Sam said. "She fell, broke her hip, and has to have surgery. Elena will have to go stay with her for a month or so."

Gabriel shrugged. "What do I care? She's *your* housekeeper."

Sam ignored that. "I can get someone in to clean with no problem," he told the older man. "Cooking is going to be more of an issue."

Gabriel scowled. "I've been taking care of myself for over sixty years, Sonny. I can manage until my toes curl up."

"I thought you might like to move in with me until she gets back."

"Not even on a bet."

Sam knew that the knee-jerk refusal didn't mean his grandfather had made up his mind. "We could go cruising for chicks together."

Gabriel's scowl faded as the corner of his mouth twitched. "I'm too old for chicks." His gaze narrowed. "But you're not. You work too hard."

"I learned that from you."

Gabriel gave a snort. "Good answer, but there's a difference. I had you to go home to. What do you have? Some mouthy housekeeper who doesn't know her place? Soon you won't even have her. You're thirty-four."

"I know."

The old man scowled. "You need a woman. When are you going to get married again?"

"When you do," he told his grandfather.

The old man chuckled. "There's still some life left in me, Samuel. I just might find someone who strikes my fancy. Then what will you say?"

"Enjoy."

Gabriel laughed, then pushed himself to his feet. "I'm going to head home. Don't you work too late."

Sam thought of Francesca's promise to be at his place no later than five. Anticipation made him grin. "I won't."

This time when Francesca arrived at Sam's place, the gate was wide open. One part nervous, three parts wild with excitement, she drove onto the property and parked in front of the impressive house.

When she'd turned off the engine, she reached for her oversize tote bag. Sam had asked her to spend the night, which meant dealing with logistics like a toothbrush and fresh undies for the morning. While she didn't want to show up with a suitcase and scare the man—she'd already done that once in the past twenty-four hours—she didn't want to be without her stuff.

"You should never have let your subscription to *Cosmo* lapse," she told herself as she stepped out of her truck. "They always cover this sort of dilemma."

She headed for the front door, which opened just before she knocked. Sam grinned.

"Hey, gorgeous."

"Hey, yourself."

They stared at each other. His hair was mused, his

expression amused. His mouth curved in what Texans would have described as a shit-eating grin. He was a man who knew he was about to get lucky.

She took in the Hawaiian-print shirt, worn jeans, and bare feet, and thought he looked good enough to be a poster boy for sin. She wasn't sure what he saw when he looked at her, but he liked it enough to pull her close and kiss her senseless.

"This time I really plan to feed you dinner," he said when he released her. He kissed her again. "But it might be late."

"Late works for me."

He drew her into the house and shut the door behind her. "How about some wine?"

"Sure. Get me drunk. So typical."

He chuckled, put his arm around her, and guided her to the kitchen.

"How was your day?" he asked as he opened a bottle of Marcelli Wines Merlot.

"Good. I drove up to see my family. We have a brunch every Sunday morning. It's something of a command performance unless you're out of town. They make me crazy, but I love them. What about you?"

He poured the wine. "I went to work. I don't usually on Sunday, but I felt restless." He raised his eyebrows. "Your fault, I believe."

"Me? What did I do?"

"For one thing there's that sound you make when you—"

"Okay, then," she said, cutting him off. She'd been doing her best *not* to think about the wild abandon she'd displayed in Sam's bed . . . and shower. She'd always thought of herself as sexually conservative and not very passionate. Apparently she'd been wrong.

She clutched her wineglass in both hands and mentioned something that had been bothering her. "I hope we didn't disturb Elena. That would be really embarrassing for me."

"Not to worry. Her room is downstairs at the opposite end of the house. There's no way she could have heard. But if it makes you feel any better, she's not going to be around for a while."

"What happened?"

"Her sister fell and broke her hip. Elena flew out this morning to stay with her for about a month." He shifted toward her. "So it's just us. No adult supervision to be had."

The closer Sam got, the more her heart raced, her breathing quickened, and before he even reached for her, she felt her muscles tensing in anticipation.

She put her wine on the counter and reached for him. "So we can be as bad as we want?"

"You got it. In fact, I've been having a very vivid fantasy that involves you, some champagne, and the kitchen counter."

She shivered with delight. "Count me—"

His mouth claimed hers. Francesca surrendered to his passionate kiss. Her mouth parted and she stroked his tongue with hers. Instantly her breasts swelled, her panties got damp, and her bones turned to al dente pasta.

The hunger returned. Despite the pleasure she'd experienced the night before *and* this morning, she wanted him again. Touching her. In her. It was as if she'd never experienced lovemaking before being with Sam. It was—

The ringing of the telephone cut through the quiet of the kitchen. Sam barely raised his head.

"The machine will get it," he murmured as he trailed

kisses along her jaw, then down her neck to her collarbone.

"What if it's one of your women?"

He chuckled. "I don't have any women right now. No, I take that back. I have you."

He returned his attention to her mouth. The phone continued to ring three more times. On the fourth she heard Sam's voice telling the caller to leave a name and number. There was a click, followed by a voice.

"Dammit, Sam, if you're out of town . . ." The woman speaking sighed heavily. "It's Tanya. *Again.* I've already called five times without leaving a message. Now I guess I don't have a choice. You need to call me right away. It's an emergency."

She kept on talking as she gave her number, but Francesca stopped listening. Sam had stiffened and pulled back.

"That's my ex-wife," he said. "Why the hell would she be calling?" He glanced at Francesca. "I haven't heard from her in years. Ten, maybe twelve."

She gave him a little push toward the phone. "She said it's an emergency. You should pick up."

Sam hesitated, not wanting to spoil the moment, then realized it was too late for that. He grabbed the phone. "Tanya, it's Sam. I'm here."

"About time," she said, sounding both frustrated and impatient. "It took me the better part of the morning to find your damn number and then you weren't there."

"It's nice to speak to you, too," he said sarcastically. "It's been a long time. How are you doing?"

She exhaled loudly. "Okay—good point. I'm being a bitch and you have no idea why."

Her nature, he thought grimly.

"The thing is . . ." she continued. "Oh, crap. I don't know how to tell you this. It's been too long. It's all your mother's fault. If she—"

"My mother?" Sam interrupted. His mother had died nearly eight years ago. "What does she have to do with anything?"

"Just her usual meddling. I had these plans, Sam. I worked damn hard, and no one is going to take it away from me now."

"Tanya, I have no idea what you're talking—"

The doorbell rang. Sam turned toward the front of the house and frowned. He'd closed the gate after Francesca had arrived. How had anyone gotten inside?

"What was that?" Tanya asked. "Oh God, was it the doorbell?"

"Yes. I'll be right back."

"Sam, wait." Tanya's voice dropped. "I'm going to hang up. In a few minutes you're going to want to call me back. I just left my number on your machine. I'll be here."

With that, the line went dead. Sam stared at the receiver for a second, then set it back on the base. The doorbell rang again.

He turned to Francesca. "I don't have any idea what's going on. Tanya didn't make sense, and I need to get the door."

She smiled. "I'm fine. Don't sweat it, Sam."

She looked calm, content, and too sexy for words. He grabbed her, quickly kissed her, then smiled.

"This won't take long," he promised. "Then I'm taking you upstairs and having my way with you."

"Promise?"

"You bet."

He released her and hurried to the front door. He pulled

it open, not sure who would be standing there. He didn't expect to see a girl with red curly hair, freckles, and big green eyes.

Sam glanced from her to the gate, which was still closed. "How'd you get in here?" he asked.

"I climbed." She shifted her large backpack. "Are you Sam Reese?"

"Yes. Who are you?"

The girl—he didn't know anything about kids, but he would guess she was in her early teens—squared her shoulders. "I'm Kelly Nash. Your daughter."

6

Sam *stared at the girl.* She stared back. Neither of them blinked.

He hadn't heard her correctly, he told himself. Or *daughter* had become one of those words that had multiple meanings. Like *bad* meaning "good."

"What?" he demanded.

Kelly pushed past him and entered the house. "Your daughter. You know. Your kid, your offspring." She dropped her backpack on the floor and glanced around. "Nice place. Didn't Tanya call you? It's not like she didn't know where I was going."

He closed the door. What the hell was going on?

"Tanya?"

Kelly turned back to him and rolled her eyes. "Tanya Nash. Your ex-wife. My mother. I bugged out this morning. I figured she'd get in touch with you and let you know what was going on."

"I've been out," he said, speaking slowly because he didn't know what to say. "She called right before you knocked on the door."

"Oh. Let me guess. She hung up and said you should

call her back. She's not real big on taking responsibility, you know. I'm starved. Is there anything to eat?"

"Sam?"

He saw Francesca enter the hallway. She smiled. "Are you all right?"

Kelly glanced at her, then back at him. "The new wife?"

He shook his head. This wasn't happening. Not really. His daughter? With Tanya? He hadn't seen his ex-wife in years. They'd been divorced. She'd never said anything about being pregnant, and she sure as hell wasn't the type to raise a kid on her own.

"How old are you?" he asked Kelly.

"Twelve." She sighed heavily. "Yeah, yeah, I know. Right when you divorced. Can I help it if you couldn't keep your pants on? Do you think this is what I wanted? But I didn't have a choice. Tanya's leaving the country, okay? And she's not taking me with her."

Francesca's eyes widened. "You're—"

"Sam's baby girl," Kelly said brightly. "I know. It's a special family moment. Look. I haven't had anything to eat since the plane. The tip for the limo ride up from the L.A. airport took all my cash, so I couldn't stop or anything. You got food in this place?"

Francesca looked as stunned as he felt. Kelly stared at them both, then shook her head. "Okay. While you two sort this out, I'm gonna go get something to eat. Feel free to talk amongst yourselves while I'm gone."

With that she sauntered down the hall and turned into the kitchen.

Sam watched her go. No way this was happening. It couldn't be. A child? A daughter?

Francesca walked toward him. "You look shocked."

"So do you." He ran his hand through his hair. "A kid.

She can't be mine. Tanya and I . . ." He looked at Francesca. "She wouldn't have agreed to the divorce if she'd known she was pregnant. She would have said something. Hell, she was always looking for an angle. All these years. Why wouldn't she have come after me for child support?"

"I have no idea."

"Of course you don't. Sorry." He swore under his breath. "This is crazy. I need to call Tanya back."

"I can't wait to hear the story."

He smiled grimly. "Seems like I'm going to have one to top the winery feud you told me about the other night."

He headed for the kitchen. Francesca stopped him.

"Don't call from there."

"Why not?"

"You're probably going to fight, and Kelly shouldn't hear that."

Sam stared at her. "What?"

She shrugged. "I'm twenty-seven and I *still* hate to hear my parents fight. Dorky, but true."

"Parents? I don't know that she's mine."

"She could be," Francesca told him.

"I need a drink," he muttered as he led the way into the kitchen.

He found Kelly spooning leftover enchiladas onto a plate. She glanced at him.

"These look good. Take-out?"

"My housekeeper made them."

Kelly nodded. "Live-in? Mom said you were loaded. I guess she was right, huh?"

He ignored her and crossed to the answering machine, where he played back the partial message from Tanya. He jotted down her number, then stalked out of the room.

Francesca was right. He would take the call in his study, where he could vent his rapidly growing frustration.

Francesca walked into the kitchen as Kelly put the plate into the microwave. The girl studied the control panel, then punched several minutes. The state-of-the-art machine barely hummed as it began to cook the food.

"So if you're not the wife, are you the girlfriend?" Kelly asked as she settled on a stool.

"Sam and I are friends."

"Oh. Friends. So you're having sex, but it's not serious, right?"

Francesca did her best not to react. Precocious didn't begin to describe Sam's daughter. Still, there was something about the air of bravado that was painfully familiar. Francesca remembered being out of step with the world, yet desperate to convince everyone she was fine. Maybe it was just a part of growing up, but that didn't make it any less painful.

Kelly leaned back and rested her elbows on the counter behind her. She was pretty. Slender with big eyes and a head full of beautiful red curls. Freckles dotted her nose and cheeks. She wore a cropped peach T-shirt and low-rise jeans. Both looked expensive.

"Friends are different from 'special friends,' " Kelly said. "Special friends means the woman wants to get married and the guy doesn't. He uses the word *special* to fake her out. Special for her, but not for him. Basically he's looking around for something better, but doesn't have the balls to leave without someone else to sleep with. Tanya says that most problems between men and women happen because the woman gives in too soon. Sexually, I mean."

"I see." Francesca leaned against the counter, mostly because her head was spinning and she didn't want to lose her balance. Sam was right. Kelly was forty on the inside.

She mentally replayed Kelly's comments. No doubt they'd been deliberately chosen to get a reaction. She settled on responding with something less controversial.

"You call your mother Tanya?"

"Oh, sure." Kelly brushed a loose curl off her forehead. "See, she lies about her age all the time. Half the guys she goes out with don't even know she has a kid. Just in case we're ever spotted together shopping or something, she wants me to call her Tanya. That way I can be her much older sister's kid. Guys think that's really sweet. Like she's all maternal or something." Kelly rolled her eyes. "Most guys are so stupid."

Okay. So this line of conversation wasn't any safer. "Where do you live?" she asked.

Kelly nodded. "New York. The Upper West Side. New York is pretty cool. I didn't want to leave, but Tanya wouldn't let me stay in the apartment on my own after she moved to Europe. I don't think Raoul even knows about me. So typical. I mean I have all my classes there. I can't believe how much I'm going to miss while I'm out here. Santa Barbara isn't exactly a big city."

Francesca was losing ground. "You go to school in the summer?"

The microwave beeped. Kelly slid off the stool and walked to the machine. "Ballet," she said impatiently. "I dance."

"Oh. That's nice."

Kelly pulled out her steaming plate and carried it back to the counter. "It's more than nice. I work hard. I plan to be a professional dancer. I did find this one school here on the Internet. The teacher used to be a principle dancer with several big companies. So that's okay. Sam will have to call her in the morning and get me an audition right away. I would have done it myself, but I only decided I was leaving yesterday."

Francesca wished this was a movie so she could push the Pause button. She needed a few minutes to catch up.

"Decided? Why?"

Kelly began opening drawers. She found the one with the flatware and pulled out a fork. "I finally found out my dad's name. Until a few months ago I thought he was dead. Tanya had always told me he was. Then I overheard her talking about me with one of her friends." Kelly looked at her. "A girlfriend. Anyway, she mentioned Sam, so I knew he was alive. I started bugging her to tell me who he was. Yesterday we had a really big fight and she blurted it out. Once I had his name, I waited until Tanya went out with Raoul, then I went through her stuff. I finally found his address in some old files."

This was the second time Kelly had mentioned Raoul, and as much as Francesca wanted to know who he was, she had a more pressing question.

"How did you manage to get here on your own?"

Kelly took a bite of the enchiladas and chewed. When she'd swallowed, she said, "Easy. I bought the ticket over the Internet. I have this credit card I can use to buy pretty much what I want. My grandmother's estate pays for all my expenses, so Tanya doesn't care. Anyway, I bought the ticket, arranged for the limo, and prepaid that. I forgot about the tip, though, which is a bummer. I guess Sam will give me more cash."

She considered the problem for a second, then continued. "Tanya spent the night with Raoul, so she wasn't home. I got a cab, went to the airport, and got on the plane."

"It couldn't have been that easy," Francesca said.

"Sure it was. I'm old enough to fly on my own. I just waited until the flight was boarding, then I went up to the gate person and announced myself. She started to freak, asking about my parents. I said my mom was parking the car. Have you been to JFK airport? Do you have any idea what a pain that is? She knew if she waited for someone to show up, they'd never get the plane out on time. Oh, and I lied about my age. I said I was fifteen. She believed me. So I got on board and here I am."

Kelly sounded calm and competent, but Francesca couldn't help thinking no twelve-year-old should have to fly across the country on her own to find a father she'd never met because her mother was moving to Europe.

"Is there anything to drink?" Kelly asked, eyeing the open bottle of Merlot.

Francesca crossed to the refrigerator. "How about some milk?"

Kelly rolled her eyes. "Fine. I need the calcium."

"What the hell are you talking about?" Sam demanded. He held the cordless phone to his ear and paced the length of his office.

"I don't know how your mother found out I was pregnant," Tanya said. "For all I know she paid off my doctor. That's not the point. What I'm saying is that two weeks after you and I agreed to get a divorce and I moved out, I found out I was expecting. I didn't know what to do."

Sam snorted. No way that was true. Tanya would have been calculating how much having his baby would earn her.

"Two days later your mother showed up on my

doorstep. She knew about the divorce and the pregnancy. She didn't want me going back to you or even telling you about the baby."

He leaned against his desk and rubbed his eyes with his free hand. "She knew I wouldn't have divorced you if I'd known you were pregnant."

"Right. At that point she was willing to do anything to get me out of your life. Even give up her own grandchild."

Sam didn't want to believe it, but he understood his mother. She'd spent her entire life manipulating people and events to suit her purpose, including him.

He knew his mother and he knew Tanya, which made the next question easy. "How much?"

"Does it matter?"

"Yeah, it does."

"Fine. Two hundred and fifty thousand up front, five thousand a month until she was eighteen or went to live with you, and payment of all her expenses. In return I was to move to New York and make sure you never found out about Kelly."

He was numb. "Why now?"

"Because I've worked my ass off for the past twelve years, Sam. I've married twice to men with money, and by God I earned every penny of my settlements. I'm finally financially secure, and I'm ready to live my life."

"And Kelly would get in the way?"

"I'm thirty-four. That's practically middle-aged. I can't have a twelve-year-old daughter." She hesitated. "I'm getting married and moving to Europe. Kelly can't come with me. I was going to put her into a boarding school, but when I told her, she freaked out. She wanted me to let her stay in the apartment. She's involved in ballet and that's all that matters to her. I suppose with the right staff . . .

but I couldn't risk it. All it would take is one emergency, and Raoul would find out about her."

Sam swore. "You're marrying a man who doesn't even know you have a daughter?"

"I never told him about her. I've been careful to keep them apart."

All he could do was wonder what he'd ever seen in Tanya. Then he remembered. He'd been twenty-two, fresh out of college, and abroad on his own. Tanya had been beautiful, charming, and the living, breathing embodiment of every fantasy he'd ever had.

"I've left a message with your mother's law firm telling them you now have custody of Kelly," Tanya said. "They'll take care of the paperwork. I've dealt with her for the past twelve years, Sam. Now it's your turn."

"This means you'll be giving up the money," he said cynically.

"I know. I can afford to. She's actually not that much trouble. Get her into a dance class and a private school, and you'll barely notice she's around."

Her callousness stunned him. "She's your daughter."

"Don't make me out to be such a bitch," Tanya said. "Kelly's done fine. She doesn't want for anything."

"How about parents?"

Tanya laughed. "Right. Because if I'd come back twelve years ago, you would have been so happy to find out we were having a child together. You hated me, Sam. You wanted me gone and you were willing to pay any price to get that. So here's the rest of the bill. I'm having her things packed up. They'll be there by the end of the week."

"That's it?" he asked.

"What else is there?"

"Don't you want to talk to Kelly?"

"No, and I doubt she wants to talk to me."

She hung up.

Sam slowly pushed the Off button on the phone and set it on the desk. As he did so, he glanced at his watch. It had been less than twenty minutes since Kelly had walked into his house. Twenty minutes during which his entire world had spun out of control.

Now what?

Sam walked into the kitchen to find Kelly finishing off her plate of enchiladas. Francesca stood by the sink, a glass of wine in her hand. He couldn't blame her for that, although he wanted something stronger than Merlot.

"I talked to your mother," he said.

Kelly carefully put down her fork, then wiped her mouth on a paper towel before turning toward him. Her wide green eyes didn't show any emotion.

He studied her face, looking for similarities. He thought he might see traces of Tanya, maybe in her high cheekbones and the shape of her mouth, but he wasn't sure. Nor did he see any resemblance to himself. Was his ex-wife lying?

He dismissed the question. Tanya might be out for the easy buck, but she wasn't stupid. Why would she try to pass someone else's kid off as his? All it would take was a DNA test to determine paternity. If he wasn't the father, he would hunt Tanya down and return Kelly. If Tanya was really running off with some guy who didn't know about Kelly, she wouldn't want to risk Sam showing up with her kid.

"Did she tell you about Raoul?" Kelly asked. "His father is some minor count or something. Euro-trash. But Tanya is totally into the title thing and Raoul's the heir. His dad is pretty old, but Raoul is only like twenty-five. They're going to live part-time in Paris and part-time at some big house Raoul has in the south of France."

"She only mentioned that she would be living abroad."

"And that you're stuck with me."

She spoke the words casually, as if they didn't matter. Sam tried to see past them. Wouldn't a twelve-year-old girl care that her mother had abandoned her? But Kelly met his gaze calmly, barely blinking, displaying no emotion.

"She said you're into ballet," he told her, avoiding the "stuck with" part of Kelly's statement.

"Apparently there's a prestigious teacher here in Santa Barbara," Francesca said. "Kelly did some research on the Internet."

Kelly nodded, her curls bouncing with the movement. "You're going to have to set up an audition. I brought workout clothes with me in my backpack, but that's all. So I guess I need to go shopping for some stuff. You can drop me off at a mall in the morning. Or can I take a cab? Do you have cabs out here?"

Sam held up his hands. "Hold on. One thing at a time. Your mother said she was sending your things. They'll be here at the end of the week."

Kelly rolled her eyes. "And between now and then what am I supposed to do? Tanya never said you were cheap."

"I'm not—"

He shook his head. He wasn't going to argue with her about shopping. There were more important issues. School. No. It was June. School was out for the summer. Shit. Which meant she was going to be around all the time. Could he leave a twelve-year-old alone while he went to work?

He thought of her ability to travel from New York to Santa Barbara. Leave her alone? It sounded more like he was going to have to lock her up.

"We have a lot of things to figure out," he said.

Kelly shrugged. "Whatever. I just want to get back to dance class right away. You'll call in the morning, right? I have the number in my backpack."

Dance class would keep her busy—probably a good thing. "Yeah, I'll call."

Kelly slid off the stool. "Good. I wrote down the names of my teachers and where I've been studying. Be sure to sound forceful when you call. Dance teachers respond to pressure from crabby parents. You might want to mention you're rich. They like that, too."

The longer she spoke, the more he could see his ex-wife in her. "Thanks for the advice," he said dryly.

"No problem."

She left the kitchen. Francesca crossed to the counter and picked up her dirty plate. "At least she's not a wallflower," she murmured as she carried the dish, fork, and glass to the sink.

"You say that like it's a good thing." He swore. "I can't believe Elena left this morning. Talk about timing."

Francesca's eyes widened. "I didn't even think of that. You can't leave her alone all day."

Kelly returned before Sam could ask Francesca why not. From what he could see, the kid could sure take care of herself.

He glanced at the backpack. "You don't have any more luggage than that?"

"Nope. I didn't want to bring a lot of clothes. I didn't know what would be in style out here. I mean, is it West Coast chic or just backwoods ugly?"

Sam didn't know how to answer the question, so he ignored it. Instead he led the way out of the kitchen and upstairs.

On the second floor he walked to the far end of the hall—at the opposite end of the house from his bedroom—and pushed open a door.

While there were five bedrooms upstairs, only three were furnished. He'd given Kelly the largest guestroom. The big, open space held a queen-size bed, a dresser, a desk, and an armoire with a television. The attached bathroom was as spacious as the bedroom.

Kelly dropped her backpack on the bed and prowled the room. Her stride was long and graceful. She held her head high. Years of dance training, he thought, then wondered if she was going to need some kind of workout room. Didn't dancers need hardwood floors and a wall of mirrors?

Kelly pushed open the closet and examined the space, then pulled on the armoire's doors. "Oh, good. A TV. Do you have cable or satellite?"

"Cable."

She tilted her head. "There isn't a DVD player. We'll need to take care of that this week. I'm sure Tanya will be sending my DVDs along with my other stuff. Once I'm settled and stuff, we need to redecorate this room." She wrinkled her nose. "Blue isn't my color."

Sam looked at the light blue walls and the multicolored quilt on the bed. Elena had taken care of fixing up the two guest rooms. His level of involvement had stopped at signing the check.

He was five seconds from overload, he thought and grabbed the door handle.

"Do you need anything else?"

Kelly shook her head. "I'll just watch TV, then go to bed

early. I'm still on East Coast time. Plus I got up early for my flight."

He hesitated, not sure what to say to her. Then he simply nodded, wished her good night, pulled the door shut, and stepped back into the hall.

He found Francesca still in the kitchen. When he walked into the room, they looked at each other.

"How are you doing?" she asked.

"I have no idea." He thought about their plans for the evening. No way that was happening now. "I'm sorry about all this messing up our evening," he told her. "You didn't sign up for anything like this. If you want to take off, I'll understand."

She smiled. "Thanks for giving me an out, but I don't mind sticking around. I have a feeling you're going to need someone to talk to."

Some of his tension eased. "You sure?"

"Absolutely. We're friends." She hesitated over the last word, then shook her head. "I'm glad to help. I might not have kids of my own, but I used to be one, just like you. We can brainstorm."

"Good idea. But first I need a drink."

She pointed to the bottle of wine. He shook his head.

"I want something a lot stronger than that."

Kelly listened at the door. When she couldn't hear anything, she slowly pulled it open. There was only a faint murmur of voices from downstairs.

Good, she told herself as she returned to the bed and opened her backpack. She was tired, just like she said. Being alone was better than hanging out with someone she didn't even know.

She pulled out her dance clothes and tucked them in a drawer. She'd brought a change of clothes, a bathing suit, a small bag of makeup and skin-care stuff, and a toothbrush. Tucked in an interior zipper compartment was the credit card she always used. If Sam didn't take her to the mall, she would order what she needed online. It wasn't as cool as actually trying stuff on, but she'd done it before. She checked that the card was still there.

Some kids had parents who took care of things like buying clothes and CDs and stuff. Tanya had never been into maintenance. Kelly couldn't remember her mother ever cooking for her, or laying out clothes. Whatever maid was around did that kind of stuff. At least she used to. Kelly had been handling that herself for years.

After she'd washed her face and brushed her teeth, she changed into cotton pjs and carried her backpack to the closet. But before stuffing it on the top shelf, she opened it one last time and pulled out a worn, tattered Pooh bear. The fur was rubbed off one side of the face. One arm hung at an awkward angle, and the cheerful yellow T-shirt the bear had been wearing had faded to a dingy gray.

Kelly studied the stuffed animal, then shoved the backpack in the closet and closed the door.

She would be fine, she told herself. Except she didn't believe it. After years of threatening, her mother had finally gotten rid of her. What if her dad didn't want her, either? If he threw her out, where was she going to go?

She didn't want to think about it, so she climbed into bed and pulled up the covers. After tucking Pooh under one arm, she tightly closed her eyes. But no matter how hard she squeezed her eyelids, she couldn't stop the tears from escaping and dripping down her cheeks.

7

Sam poured himself a scotch, then moved to the sofa where Francesca had already settled.

"This is crazy," he said, leaning his head against the back of the sofa and resting the glass on his flat belly. "Twelve-year-olds do *not* fly across the country on their own."

"This one did. Kelly explained the process." Francesca told him about the Internet purchases and the limo service.

"She's resourceful," he admitted. "Independent. Mouthy."

And used to being taken care of, Francesca thought, remembering the dishes Kelly had left on the counter. She was not a child who picked up after herself.

He took a sip of his drink. "She informed me that the room was acceptable, but she needed a DVD player, and when things were settled she wanted to talk about redecorating." He glanced at her. "Apparently blue isn't her color."

"She's not afraid to ask for what she wants."

"Somehow I'm not sure that's a good thing." He closed his eyes and sucked in a breath. "A daughter. After all this time."

Francesca knew *she* felt shell-shocked, and she was only an interested bystander. Sam must feel as if he'd been hit by a truck.

"Are you going to check paternity?" she asked.

He opened his eyes and looked at her. "DNA test? I thought about it. I guess I'll have to at some point. But while Tanya has no problem lying to get what she wants, she's not stupid. She knows I wouldn't keep a child who wasn't mine, and the last thing she wants right now is Kelly being returned to her. I don't know. Do you think she looks like me?"

"A little. Around her mouth. But she didn't get that hair from you."

"You're right." He stretched out his legs. "I don't know what to think about all of this. I had no idea. When Tanya left—hell, I don't remember much about that except wanting her gone. All these years I never guessed."

"Why would you? You had no clues. She's been living on the other side of the country. It's not as if you ran into her and Kelly."

"Good point." He took another drink. "I should be mad or something. I missed out on Kelly growing up. But I can't get angry."

She leaned toward him and lightly touched his arm. "Give yourself a break. Right now you don't feel anything, and that's not so bad. You'll start processing the information over time, and with that will come emotion."

He glanced at her and smiled. "That's your degree talking."

"Sure, but I have to use it every now and then or it gets dusty."

"Okay, Ms. Psychologist. What's my next move? Is it mentally healthy for me to run for the hills?"

"Probably not. As for what's next, you're going to have to play that by ear. You and Kelly need to get to know each other. That will take time."

"Time, huh? Want to give me a ballpark of how long it's going to take?"

"I haven't a clue."

"Me, either. About any of it." His smile faded. "The bitch took money."

It took Francesca a second to figure out who he meant. "Tanya?"

He nodded. "My mother paid her off to keep Kelly a secret. Two hundred and fifty thousand up front, five thousand a month, plus expenses."

Francesca felt her mouth drop open. She consciously pressed her lips together. "But why would she want to get rid of her own grandchild?"

"You'd have to know my mother to understand that." He took another drink. "Lily Reese liked to rule her kingdom, and she would use any means to keep her subjects in line. My father died when I was pretty young. I don't remember him much. When Lily was around, her word was law. When she was gone, which was most of the time, I lived with my paternal grandfather. Gabriel."

"The one you hired Elena for."

"Right. He was sane and normal. Two claims my mother couldn't make. God, they fought. He threatened to sue for custody more than once, but she got right back in his face. She was more than willing to take him on. She had money, power, and was fearless."

The tone of his voice told her he didn't mean the words as a compliment.

"By the time I was ten, I had already learned to mistrust everything she said. She lied because she liked to.

Because it worked. As I got older, I was sent away to prep school. I spent holidays with Gabriel. After college I escaped to Europe, where I met Tanya." He raised his glass. "A Miss California runner-up, well traveled, but not rich. She wanted money, I wanted . . ." He shrugged. "We met, I fell in love, or so I thought, and we got married two months later. My mother was furious."

"Didn't she like Tanya?"

"They loathed each other because they were so much alike. In one of those humorous twists of fate, I'd traveled all the way to France only to find the one woman exactly like my mother." He glanced at her. "You could write a paper about me."

She winced. "People fall for partners just like one of their parents all the time. If that parent is a good, loving person, the relationship works."

"If the new wife is lying and manipulative, it doesn't," he said. "It took me three months to figure out my mistake. By then my mother was already campaigning for the marriage to end. I was torn between my own happiness and doing what she wanted. Rebelling against that kept me in the marriage another six months. Then I ended it. All Tanya wanted was a big settlement. There were no broken hearts on either side."

He told the story easily, as if it no longer mattered. As it had been twelve years ago, Francesca didn't doubt Sam was long recovered. He'd moved on. Until Kelly had arrived, literally at his door, bringing the past back to life.

"So when she found out Tanya was pregnant, she paid her off to keep her away from you," she said.

He nodded. "If I'd known she was pregnant, I would have put the divorce on hold, at least until the baby was born." He frowned. "A baby. I still can't believe it."

"She's not a baby anymore."

"You have that right." He straightened. "So what do I do with her? Are you sure she's not old enough to be left alone while I'm at work?"

Francesca shook her head. "She's certainly capable of taking care of herself for a few hours, but I wouldn't leave her in the house by herself all day. She's into ballet. That gives you a place to start."

"That's right. She mentioned a school or a class. That will fill some time. Then what?"

"Then you get to know her."

"But what does she eat? How much? What about clothes? She wants a DVD player. Should I buy her one?"

She held up a hand. "You can't solve all the problems at once. Having a child dropped in your lap with no warning is going to offer some logistical challenges. Take them one at a time."

He grinned. "Logistical challenges? Is that the professional term for this?"

"Yes, and I hope you appreciate that I'm volunteering all this information for free. I'm a highly paid professional." She smiled. "Well, I *will* be in about eighteen months."

He shifted so he was facing her. After setting his glass on the coffee table, he stretched out his arm along the back of the sofa and touched her shoulder.

"You're being great. I appreciate it."

"I told you, I don't mind helping."

What she didn't tell him was the way he'd handled the entire situation had made her like him more. He wasn't just a pretty face and great in bed. He could have gone ballistic when Kelly showed up. Instead he'd remained relatively calm. Despite the shock he had to be feeling, he was planning things through, worrying about his daughter, and not blaming anyone.

He leaned forward and kissed her. His mouth was warm, firm, and tender, but not passionate. Francesca understood. Having an unexpected child show up had a way of changing the flow of a date.

"I don't have much going on over the next few days," she told him. "I should be working on the outline for my dissertation, but I'm practicing creative avoidance instead. Would you like me to come over tomorrow morning and help out with things?"

He hesitated. "You have no idea how much I want to say yes. But this isn't your problem."

"You're right. It's yours. So? Do you really want to do this all on your own?"

"No way. But we had that definition of great sex and no complications."

"I'll make an exception this one time." She looked into his eyes. "I mean it, Sam."

"Then I'll stop pushing back and say thank you." He glanced at his watch, then shook his head. "I can't make any arrangements tonight, so I guess I won't be going into work tomorrow." He touched her face. "If you wouldn't mind coming over, that would be great. At least then there will be two of us on the side of the grown-ups. You think that will make things even?"

Francesca thought about Kelly's precocious sophistication. "She'll probably still outthink us, but at least we can band together."

He chuckled. "You're terrific. Thanks for all of this."

His words made her feel warm inside. Sort of melty and squishy. Good thing she'd sworn off romantic entanglements years ago, or she could be in real danger here.

She rose. "I'm going to head home. We're both going to need our rest for tomorrow."

He stood. "When we face the terror of the preteen?"

"Exactly. Just remember. You're the adult."

"Oh, *I* know that. Kelly's the one we have to convince."

"You sure she's not dead?" Gabriel asked as he leaned back in the kitchen chair. "It's after nine. Maybe you should check on her."

Sam didn't think Kelly had passed away in the night. He doubted he'd been lucky enough that she'd run away. Of course, her leaving would be only a temporary reprieve. He would be forced to find her and drag her back. Not exactly how he wanted to start his day.

"I'll give her another half hour, then go check on her."

Gabriel shrugged. "She's your daughter."

Sam still hadn't made peace with that concept. A child. It didn't seem right. Not after all this time. And from what he'd seen of Kelly, she wasn't exactly the kid he would have chosen.

"What are you going to do with her?" his grandfather asked.

Sam glanced out the large window over the sink. "Hell if I know. Get her settled. She wants to take some ballet classes."

"What about carting her around? She can't drive. You're going to have to hire someone."

"I know." He'd already spent some time on the phone, but professional day care for preteens was sadly lacking. "The nannies all want to work with little kids and babies. I have a few people checking. They're supposed to get back to me."

His grandfather picked up his coffee mug. "Tanya's a bitch."

"Tell me about it."

After Francesca had left the previous evening, Sam had called his grandfather to tell him what had happened. Gabriel had been furious at the deception, but not surprised. He'd shown up bright and early to examine his great-granddaughter, but Kelly had yet to make an appearance.

"At least the kid isn't an idiot," Gabriel said. "It took brains for her to travel all this way herself. You should be proud."

"Uh-huh." Sam was trying not to say much until Gabriel had met Kelly. Maybe she would be better this morning. Maybe last night's demands and attitude had been more about being tired than anything else.

Unlikely, he thought grimly. Very unlikely.

"Whatever happens, I'm taking responsibility for her," he said.

"You make me sound like a dog you brought home," Kelly said as she breezed in the kitchen. "Do I get my own leash and water bowl, too?"

So much for a good night's sleep improving things, Sam told himself.

"Good morning," he said. "Gabriel, this is my daughter, Kelly. Kelly, this is your great-grandfather Gabriel."

The old man looked her over. Sam saw she'd pulled on the same low-rise jeans and yet another abbreviated T-shirt. This one was green, tight, and proclaimed "Girls Rule." She was barefoot. Her toes were painted, her skin pale.

Kelly tucked several curls behind her ears as she walked past them and headed for the refrigerator. "Whatever. So is there anything for breakfast?"

Sam's temper boiled, but before he could say anything, Gabriel pounded his cane on the tiled kitchen floor. Kelly jumped.

"What?" she demanded.

"You should lock this one up until she learns some manners," he said.

Kelly planted her hands on her hips. "We're not in that century anymore."

Gabriel's eyes narrowed. "You didn't say she was a smart-mouth, Sam. She got that from her mother."

Kelly rolled her eyes. "Are we done? Can I eat now?"

"I don't know," Gabriel said. "Can you?"

Kelly stared at him as if he'd started speaking Russian.

Sam sighed. "May I eat now," he told her. "*Can* is ability. *May* is permission."

"Oh. You're one of those." She turned back to the refrigerator and muttered something about "weird old men."

"You have a lot of freckles," Gabriel said.

"Gee, thanks," Kelly said. "Because until this moment I hadn't been sure. I kept scrubbing my face, but they wouldn't come off. Freckles. Who knew?"

Gabriel scowled. "Can we send her back?"

I wish, Sam thought. "We all need time to adjust."

Kelly shut the refrigerator. "I'd rather be back in New York. Tell you what, Grandpa. Just set me up in an apartment and I'll be fine. I'll go to school, then my ballet classes, and you won't even have to remember that you ever met me."

Gabriel grumbled something under his breath. Sam wondered if he was doing the math to figure out how much it would cost him.

"You're not going back to New York," Sam told her. "It's

been less than twenty-four hours. Why don't we back off for a few days."

Kelly scowled. "Tell *him* to back off." She walked to the pantry. "What did the ballet teacher say when you spoke with her?"

"I haven't."

Kelly turned on him. "What? I asked you to do one thing. Just one. Not twenty, not even five. And you couldn't do it. Why? Is this just to torture me or do you have a reason?"

"I've been busy."

"With things that are important to you. Not with things that are important to me."

Sam gripped his coffee mug so tightly, he thought he might snap it in two. His first instinct was to send Kelly to her room and ground her for life. Not that he knew what terms would be considered grounding. Locking her up sounded pretty damn good, though.

He thought about telling her she'd just lost her chance at ever attending a ballet class, but quickly reconsidered. Getting her out of the house for a few hours a day could be a blessing for both of them.

He sucked in a breath. "You know that DVD player you wanted?" he asked. "You can forget it until you learn to speak politely and respectfully."

She stared at him. "You are so kidding."

"Not even close, kid."

"Whatever. I'll buy it myself."

That's right. The credit card, compliments of his mother's estate. He would have to take care of that next.

"When are you calling the ballet teacher?" she asked through gritted teeth. "I want you to do it now."

"I will get to it when it's convenient for me. You can

hurry the process along by being civil or you can wait. Your choice."

She glared at him. "You're not the boss of me."

"That's where you're wrong. I absolutely am. I know you've been through hell, and I'm sorry about that. However, your circumstances don't give you the right to mouth off."

Kelly looked at him as if he were dog crap on her shoes. "If you're so worried about what I say, then you shouldn't swear in front of me. Or do the rules only apply to me? Don't you have to be civil, too?"

With that she turned on her heel and left the room.

Sam clutched his mug, not sure if he was going to drink the contents or throw it across the room.

"She's a handful," Gabriel said.

"Tell me about it."

"I guess locking her up would be against the law," Sam said.

Francesca wasn't completely sure he was kidding. "You know it would be. *And* it wouldn't solve any problems."

"Maybe it would. You could report me and the state would take her away."

"Is that what you want?"

He shook his head. "No. What I want is for this to be easier."

"It's only day one," she reminded him.

It was mid-afternoon. She'd arrived about an hour before to find Kelly eating lunch by herself and Sam holed up in his office. Neither of them seemed to be speaking to the other, and Kelly had barely acknowledged her.

She and Sam were out on the deck, enjoying the warm

afternoon, with a soft ocean breeze blowing over them. He was holding her hand, which made her want to talk about tangled sheets instead of his daughter. But that wasn't an option right now. Which was really too bad.

"It's been a long day," he told her, then explained what had happened that morning when Gabriel had been over to meet Kelly.

Francesca winced. "Okay, so we won't describe her as shy or timid. What did your grandfather say?"

"Nothing I can repeat in mixed company. He wasn't a fan of my ex-wife's, either, and to his mind, Kelly is too much like her."

"For what it's worth, I think you handled the situation really well. If she wants a DVD player, that gives you something to hold over her head." She glanced at him and smiled. "I mean that figuratively, not literally."

"I know. I'm not interested in hurting her. What I would like instead is to deal with a regular child instead of Teen-zilla."

"Does she have access to a computer?"

"Yes. In the other guest room."

"Then she could go buy the player herself. She's good at that."

He grinned. "Not anymore. I've canceled her credit card."

"How?"

"I contacted the law firm handling my mother's estate. Tanya had already told them that I had custody of Kelly. The lawyer I spoke with said I was entitled to the same monetary provisions Tanya had—Kelly's expenses covered plus five thousand a month." He shook his head. "I told them that wasn't necessary."

"She's going to be crabby when she finds out she can't shop at will."

He chuckled. "I know. I figured I'd let her find out for herself." His humor faded. "The lawyer told me something else. When Kelly was born, my mother had the paternity checked. The kid is mine."

Francesca was afraid to ask if that was good or bad. "At least you know."

"There wasn't a whole lot of doubt, but yeah, I know." He shrugged. "I got in touch with that ballet teacher, too. Angelina something. She's willing to see Kelly tomorrow. Apparently there's an audition process to get into this class. It must be a big deal. She has an appointment at eleven."

"Want me to take her?"

Sam looked at her. "You have your own life and it doesn't include Teen-zilla."

Francesca smiled. "Agreed, but I was serious when I said I would help. Hey, I spent the morning organizing my closet just to avoid working on my outline. Driving Kelly to her ballet audition would be a far better displacement activity. I could come here first thing and you could go to work."

He looked as hopeful as a drowning man spotting a rescue boat. "Yeah?"

"Absolutely."

"I'll be sure to return the favor." He brought her hand to his mouth and lightly kissed her knuckles.

The brush of his lips against her skin sent heat racing through her body, but before she could do something wild like throw herself at him and beg to be taken, he lowered his arm back to the table between their chairs.

Oh, well. Maybe next time.

"I have this theory about Kelly," she said. "I was thinking about her while cleaning out my closet. I think she's in a lot of emotional pain."

Sam looked at her. "From her mother dumping her on me?"

"It's more than that. The way Kelly talks about her life in New York, she was completely on her own. Even if you factor out a child's inclination to exaggerate, it's still pretty awful. You mentioned that Tanya was seeing someone she wanted to marry who never knew about Kelly. Combine those elements and you have a child who feels unloved and unwelcome. In her mind she could be thinking she's so horrible, she has to be kept a secret. Then her mother abandons her, and she meets a father she never knew about. Kelly has to be terrified, lonely, and really hurting."

He considered the information. "You think that's why she's being so difficult? She's lashing out like a wounded animal?"

"Exactly. With some time and positive attention, she'll be a completely different person."

"What if that person is worse?"

Francesca chuckled. "She won't be."

"You can't know that for sure." He rubbed his thumb across the back of her hand. "I went online, looking for some parenting books. There are a bunch on raising teens, and the descriptions scared the hell out of me. I want to back up and get her younger. Or when she's eighteen. Plus none of them had any practical information on things like what to feed her and how much sleep she needs."

Francesca did her best to ignore the tingling brought on by his light stroking and instead pay attention to the conversation. "She's not a llama. She doesn't have a special diet. Offer her healthy food and let her pick what she wants. As for sleep, by the end of summer you will know how much she needs so she's alert for school."

"Healthy food? I was going to order in Chinese tonight."

"That's fine once in a while. You don't have to dine on tofu every night."

"I'm not dining on tofu ever."

"Still a steak guy?"

He turned toward her. "I'm a man of simple tastes. I know what I like and I go after it."

She melted. Right there on the chair. Sam leaned forward and kissed her. Just as she parted her mouth, a door slammed in the house. Sam swore.

She considered the single word, then sighed. "Maybe next time."

8

"*And one, and two,* and three, and now!"

Kelly moved in time with the music. She swept her arms up in the air, then bent low at the waist, turning slightly. Her young face was the picture of concentration. Despite the plain black tights and leotards, with her hair pulled back and her skin bare of makeup, she reminded Francesca of a butterfly in a flower garden, flitting with grace and delight on a perfect summer day.

As she had learned in the past hour, the reality of ballet was far more about hard work than flitting, but the end result was just as beautiful. As the music swelled slightly, Kelly rose on her toes and began to turn slowly. Her little skirt swayed with the movement.

Francesca knew she should be working on organizing her paper, or reading the research book she'd brought with her, but she'd been unable to tear her attention away from Kelly's dance audition. What she knew about ballet and classical music wouldn't fill a thimble. She'd seen *The Nutcracker* a couple of times, but other than that her cultural education had been limited to the occasional trip to the opera.

Sitting at the edge of the practice room, she could see firsthand how difficult the moves were. The first half hour had been devoted to specific moves done at slow speed. But the lack of speed didn't make it easy. Parts of different dances had filled the second half hour. The instructor had called out the name of a ballet and some other instructions in French, then Kelly had performed.

Francesca watched her. The slender preteen moved with a grace that made Francesca envious. With her hair pulled back, she looked older than twelve. Her eyes seemed more green than they had the night before. She was already pretty—becoming beautiful was only a few years away. Sam was going to have plenty of trouble when the boys started to come calling.

The instructor—Miss Angelina—spoke in rapid French. Francesca had taken a couple of years of Spanish in high school and knew a smattering of Italian from her father's family. For all she knew, Miss Angelina was telling Kelly to get ready to rob a convenience store. But instead of reaching for weapons, Kelly curtsied.

Miss Angelina nodded and left the room. Kelly stared after her.

In that moment, longing tightened the girl's features. She looked alone, vulnerable, and very young.

Francesca stood. "What happened?" she asked.

Kelly shrugged. "I'm in. No biggie. You saw those other girls when we got here. Some of them are good, but the rest . . ." She shrugged and started toward the dressing room.

Francesca wanted to follow her and shake her. Being accepted into the dance class *was* a big deal. Why couldn't Kelly be excited? Why didn't she jump around like a normal kid? Or had life taught her not to show emotions because they could be used against her?

"I have Kelly's application papers here," the instructor said as she walked back into the studio. Her voice was lilting, and tinged with a French accent. "She will join my upper-intermediate class. If she works hard, she'll be with the advanced students within a year."

Angelina's eyes narrowed. "You are her mother?" She sounded doubtful.

"No. A friend of the family."

Angelina looked her over. Francesca fought against the sudden need to stand straighter and square her shoulders.

"She will need a practice room. Class is five days a week in the summer, but when school begins it is only three times a week." She shrugged delicately. "She will have to dance on her own the other days. Unless you hire a private tutor, she must attend academic classes, yes?"

A private tutor? So she could dance the rest of the time. This was so not her world. At least Sam's house had plenty of bedrooms. One could probably be converted to a practice room.

"I'll pass the message along to her father."

"My bill." The teacher handed her another sheet of paper. "This is for a month's worth of lessons."

Francesca glanced down at the total at the bottom and nearly fell over. She could easily live on that amount for two months.

"Anything else?" she asked, trying not to look shocked.

Angelina shook her head and smiled. "The rest is up to Kelly. Soon we will see if she has the backbone and the drive to devote herself to the ballet. She has much talent, but at this stage in her career, success will be about hard work. *Oui?*"

Kelly was only twelve. Francesca didn't think anyone

should be using the word *career* in reference to anything she did.

"Thank you so much for your time," Francesca told her.

Angelina nodded gracefully, then returned to her office. Seconds later Kelly emerged from the dressing room.

"That was something," Francesca said as she approached. "I'm amazed and impressed. I had no idea a class could be so much work."

"That wasn't a regular class. Miss Angelina wanted to see what I could do. Is that the application and stuff?" she asked, pointing at the folder.

"Yes. I'll give it to your father when we get back to the house. Speaking of which, do you want to head home or go out for lunch? It's only a little after noon."

Kelly gave a heavy sigh of the long-suffering. "Lunch would be okay."

Francesca wanted to tell her not to put herself out, but she held back. As she'd told Sam the previous evening, Kelly was acting up because she was scared. Somewhere under that prickly exterior was a charming young woman waiting to blossom. At least, that was the fantasy.

Thirty minutes later they were seated on a patio table in the shade. Kelly had left her hair up, but had pulled on jeans and a T-shirt over her ballet clothes. Francesca studied the menu and mentally winced at the prices. Twelve-fifty for a salad? If this was lunch, how much would dinner cost?

Not her problem, she reminded herself. That morning Sam had handed over cash, along with phone numbers and instructions to have fun. She'd been uncomfortable taking money from him, but as he'd pointed out, she was taking care of *his* daughter. That was favor enough without making her pay for anything.

She had agreed, mostly because she didn't have a choice. Places like this weren't in her budget.

The waitress arrived. They each ordered a Chinese chicken salad. Kelly asked for a cup of soup to start with while Francesca decided to content herself with the incredible French bread they'd brought.

When the two of them were alone, Francesca looked at Sam's daughter. The girl watched her carefully, as if not sure what was going to happen. Okay, so the situation was a little strange for both of them. Less than forty-eight hours ago neither had known the other existed. As the adult, Francesca knew it was up to her to make Kelly comfortable.

"You're an incredible dancer," she began, buttering a piece of bread. "How long have you been studying ballet?"

"Since I was six. I took a lot of different kinds of dance. Tap, modern, and ballet. Then a couple of years later I decided to focus on ballet."

Francesca tried to remember focusing on anything but having fun with her sisters when she'd been that age. "Does it hurt to go up on your toes?"

"A little. You get used to it. I've been dancing on pointe for over a year. It's no big deal."

Francesca doubted that. "It seems like a big deal to me, but then, I've never been very coordinated. If I tried any of those moves you were doing, I'd probably take someone's eye out."

Kelly started to smile, then pressed her lips together. "Did you ever dance?"

Francesca knew she wasn't talking about flailing about at school dances. "I was a cheerleader in high school. Does that count?"

Kelly rolled her eyes. "Not even close."

"I didn't think so. I can't even say I was really good at it. I was enthusiastic, but I didn't have a lot of talent. Some of the other girls had studied gymnastics, and they could do things with their bodies that astounded me. Of course, I never saw the point in being a human pretzel."

Kelly reached for the bread and took a slice. "Are you divorced?"

The change in topic startled Francesca, but at least they were having a normal conversation. "No. I was married before, but my husband died."

Kelly's eyes widened. "For real? Was he old?"

"No. He was twenty-eight. He was killed in a car accident."

Kelly stared at her. "I've never known anyone who died. Is it really spooky having to go to the funeral?"

"I don't remember much about it." Todd's death had been unexpected, and the days that followed had passed in a blur. "I moved back home for a few weeks, and that made a big difference. My whole family was around me. My sisters especially."

"You have sisters?" Kelly actually sounded interested.

"Three. Katie is a year older. Brenna is my twin, and Mia is nine years younger than me."

Kelly leaned forward. "You have a twin?"

She nodded. "We're fraternal, though, so we don't look that much alike."

"That is so cool."

"My grandparents really wanted my folks to have a boy, but I kind of like that it's only girls."

Kelly's expression turned wistful. "I would have liked a sister, but there was no way Tanya would ever get pregnant again. I was an accident." She picked up another slice of bread. "She used to say a mistake. She said that nothing was worth feeling sick and being fat. Plus I guess labor is really bad. You didn't have any kids, huh?"

Too much information, Francesca thought. "Todd and I wanted to wait a couple of years to start our family."

"And then he was gone. Bummer." Kelly eyed her. "Are you going to marry my dad?"

"No."

She started to say they were just friends, but then she remembered Kelly's definition of the word. While it described her relationship with Sam very well, she was uncomfortable with a twelve-year-old assuming she and Sam were having sex.

"He's rich," Kelly informed her. "Tanya always said that was the most important quality a man could have."

"Not to me."

Kelly snorted. "Oh, please. You drive an old truck and wear cheap clothes. Why wouldn't you want someone with plenty of cash?"

Francesca bristled, then reminded herself Kelly was pushing back to get a reaction. "I'm in graduate school. Being poor comes with the territory."

"That's like college, right?"

"Yes. I have a bachelor's degree. That took four years. Now I'm in a program for my master's and my Ph.D."

"What about your parents? Why aren't they paying for stuff?"

"Because I don't want them to. Going back to college was my decision. I want to pay my way."

Kelly looked genuinely shocked. "Why?"

"Because it gives me a sense of accomplishment. I want to be independent. This decision is about who I am as a person."

"You're stupid," Kelly muttered as her soup arrived. She picked up her spoon.

"Why do you dance?" Francesca asked, ignoring the "stupid" remark. "It's a lot of hard work. You sweat, you get sore. No one pays you. You might be able to have a career as a dancer, but what if you don't? You'll have put in years of hard work, and what will you have to show for it?"

"That's different."

"Actually, it's pretty much the same. We both have long-term goals that require a lot of us."

"Yeah, but I expect Sam or Tanya to pay for it."

"That may change as you get older."

"No way."

Kelly ate her soup. After a couple of minutes she said, "What are you studying?"

"Psychology."

"Oh, perfect. So you're going to tell my dad everything you think is wrong with me."

"Probably."

Kelly's green eyes narrowed. "I'm very smart."

"I know. You're also resourceful, independent, and self-motivated."

Kelly started to smile.

"Unfortunately, you have no sense of community, you don't seem to care about anyone but yourself, and you have no respect for authority or rules."

The smile faded.

Francesca shrugged. "It's okay, Kelly. We all have flaws."

The girl looked at her. "I don't care what you think."

"I'm sure that's true. So what do you want to do this afternoon? I was thinking we could go shopping and get you a few things to tide you over until your belongings arrive."

Kelly glanced at Francesca's sundress and shook her head. "No, thanks. I don't like bargain shopping."

Did the kid know how to lob the insults or what? Francesca sipped her iced tea. "No problem. I'd thought going to a movie after shopping would be fun, but if you're not interested, we'll just go back to the house."

Kelly dropped her spoon and glared, but didn't speak. Francesca could feel her outrage. Sam's daughter didn't like being maneuvered into a corner, but Francesca didn't know any other way to teach her lessons about courtesy. If Kelly wanted to blow everyone off, that was her business. But it was going to cost her things like movies and trips to the beach. With a little luck, and time, she would see the value of being more gracious.

Of course, Francesca could be wrong about all of this. Underneath the angry, hostile teen facade might be a really unpleasant kid. She hoped not, for Sam's sake. And for Kelly's.

"I come bearing Italian food," Brenna said as she stepped into Francesca's small apartment. "More important, I brought wine."

Francesca took the offered bottles and carried them into the kitchen. "Good. I need a drink. I was getting so desperate, I was about to go to the grocery store and buy a bottle of something." She looked at the chilled bottles of Marcelli Reserve Chardonnay. "This is much better."

Brenna set a large Styrofoam container on the counter and pulled off the top. She wore her short dark hair pulled back with a headband. A loose shirt hung to mid-thigh, nearly covering her cutoff jean shorts.

"School giving you trouble?"

"I would have to have actually *started* my dissertation for it to be a problem. Right now it's just nothing."

Brenna pulled out foil-wrapped plates. "Chicken Marsala, roasted potatoes with red and yellow peppers, and green beans with almonds à la Grammy M."

Francesca's stomach growled. "Thanks for calling and suggesting this. I could use some company."

"You could have come to the hacienda for dinner."

Francesca shook her head. "That's not the kind of company I need. Besides, you sounded like you were looking for an escape."

"I was." Brenna carried the serving dishes to the table, then dug around for a corkscrew.

Francesca grabbed plates, napkins, and flatware. When the table was set, she collected a wineglass for each of them, then pulled out a chair.

"Grandpa Lorenzo is making me crazy," Brenna said as she poured the wine. "I've heard several rumors about him selling the winery. A couple of our neighbors have talked to me about it. I'd already asked him once, and I thought we had things settled. But with all the talk, I had to ask him again."

"And?" Francesca asked as she slid a golden brown chicken breast onto her plate.

"And he says he's considering selling."

Francesca froze. She met her sister's troubled gaze. "That's not possible. Marcelli Wines is family."

"That's what I said." She scooped a spoonful of green beans onto her plate. "We're talking nearly seventy years of tradition. I just . . ." Brenna picked up her wineglass and took a long drink. "Damn him. He's saying he has to sell because he can't depend on me to stick around. For the first eighteen years of my life, all I heard was that I had to find a man, get married, and have babies. I married Jeff right on schedule. Like I was supposed to. And now our grandfather is complaining."

Francesca felt her twin's pain. "It's unfair. If you'd stayed, he would have complained about that, too."

"I know. The thing is, I'm back. I've learned my lesson about men. Since Jeff and I split up, I've buried myself in work. Within two days I realized I shouldn't have left. There's nothing I love more than the vineyards and making wine. That's all I want to do. If he sells . . ."

Brenna angrily cut off a piece of chicken and shoved it in her mouth.

"Have you talked to him about this?" Francesca asked, even though she already knew the answer.

Brenna shook her head. "Do you think it would help?"

"I don't know. If he understood how much you cared, it might make a difference."

"He's not going to listen. He only wants things his way."

Francesca knew that was true. Her grandfather ruled the family with an iron fist. Make that an iron fist from the nineteenth century. His outdated rules and ideas about family life meant anyone disagreeing with him could be tossed out at a moment's notice. The exiles were usually temporary, but still painful.

"I have so many ideas," Brenna told her. "There are these wonderful Pinot grapes coming up for sale. I desperately want to buy them, but he won't listen. Worse, the land could be going on the market. I'd kill for that."

Francesca might be floating just above the poverty level because of her studies, but Brenna's precarious financial situation was thanks to spending the past nine years supporting her soon-to-be ex-husband through his medical training. Once established as an up-and-coming cardiologist, Jeff had dumped his wife for a newer, younger model.

"What about the divorce settlement? Can't you use that money to buy the grapes?" she asked as she bit into a piece of the chicken and tried not to moan. As usual, the Grands had created something delicious, tender, and addictive.

Brenna shrugged. "It would help, but then what? I'd have grapes and no way to process them. Renting equipment and space. Jeez, Francesca, we're talking hundreds of thousands of dollars. I don't know."

She poked at the grilled potatoes on her plate. "Okay. I've been whining long enough. What's going on with you? I called last night and you were out. Give me good news. Tell me you've met a fabulous new guy and you were having hot monkey sex for hours and hours." She laughed. "On second thought, I might find that information a little depressing."

Francesca pushed a few green beans around her plate. "Funny you should say that," she told her sister.

Brenna's mouth dropped open. "No way."

"Way. Sort of."

Brenna laughed, then raised her glass. "Good for you, girlfriend. I can't believe you had sex. Are you sure? Were you all naked?"

"As there were only two of us in the room at the time, I'm pretty sure I can remember that part. Yes, we were naked."

Brenna hooted. "This is so cool. Okay, start at the beginning. How did you meet? Who is this guy, and what on earth made you give up your quest for nunhood?"

Francesca told her about her experiment, and Sam's rescue.

"I'm thrilled that you found someone willing to rescue

helpless pregnant women, but slightly put off by him asking you out while you looked like that."

Francesca sighed. "That's what Mia said when she was here on Saturday. I'd already told him I wasn't pregnant. He's in the security business and was impressed that I could pull one over on him."

"Fair enough. Now get to the sex part."

Francesca grinned. "It just happened. I was attracted to him, and he seemed to be attracted to me. Normally I avoid that sort of thing."

"Sure. Because it's so much more interesting to go out with guys you're *not* attracted to."

Francesca ignored her. "I remembered what we'd talked about a few months ago. When you and Katie made me promise to fall into bed with the next normal guy I met."

Brenna had been drinking. She nearly spit out her wine. "Francesca, we were kidding. If I remember correctly, we were drunk. Jeez, you can't take that kind of stuff seriously. Is that really why you slept with him?"

"Sort of. Maybe." Francesca remembered the night and her feeling of being so aroused, she was out of control. "I've spent the past few years avoiding relationships because I don't want to get married again. But talking with you and Katie made me wonder if maybe there was a compromise. The occasional casual relationship with a man, complete with perks, and no ring."

"I'm in favor of that," Brenna said. "Marriage is trouble. So is love." She cut off a piece of chicken. "Looking back on my sorry excuse for a marriage, I'm not sure I ever loved Jeff. He was the safe choice. At least, that's what he looked like then. Now I know he was nothing but a lying weasel dog."

"Todd didn't lie," Francesca said slowly, remembering

her late husband. "But he wanted arm candy instead of a partner. I hated that."

"I remember. Every time you expressed an opinion, he practically patted you on the head. As if you were as cute as a puppy performing a trick."

Not what she'd wanted for her life, Francesca thought. Not then and not now.

"So this Sam guy isn't like that?" Brenna asked.

"Not at all. Plus, he's no more interested in a commitment than I am. Especially now."

Brenna raised her eyebrows. "What happened?"

Francesca told her about Kelly's arrival. Brenna dropped her fork as her mouth fell open.

"A kid? He has a kid?"

"Teen-zilla, according to him. I don't think Kelly's all that bad, although she is a handful. Her mother ignored her, gave her everything she wanted just to shut her up, and never set down any rules. Kelly is more than independent, she's dictatorial."

"Sounds like a fun kid. Are you sure the sex is worth it? Didn't this unexpected arrival mess up your plans?"

"Sort of." Sam had been worried about that, too, Francesca thought. "Sometimes I really like her, but she makes everything a challenge. I feel bad for her. She needs to be loved."

Brenna's eyes narrowed. "I recognize that tone. It's the same one you used every time you wanted to drag home some stray dog or cat. You're too soft-hearted for your own good. Do *not* go falling for this guy and his kid. Do you really want to take on a ready-made family? Now? You're less than two years from finishing school."

"I know and I agree. I don't want to get married. I used to think I'd have children, but lately I'm not sure. If I don't want a husband, then I'm stuck doing it on my own. I don't know that I could stand the guilt of getting pregnant without being married. I mean, the whole family is Catholic and the Church really frowns on that."

"You'd send the Grands into a Hail-Mary frenzy. Grandpa Lorenzo would have your hide."

"He'd throw me out of the family."

"Some days I don't think that would be such a great loss."

Francesca shrugged. "It's not an issue. I have no plans to get pregnant, and I'm not falling for Sam."

"Or the kid," Brenna told her sternly. "Don't you even think about rescuing her. You hear me?"

"Yes, ma'am."

"All right." Brenna refilled both their glasses. "Now I want to hear all the details about the sex. I haven't even seen a naked man in months, and I'm going to have to live vicariously through you."

"I do *not* kiss and tell."

"Fine. Then make something up. I won't know the difference."

Kelly typed in the Internet address for one of her favorite clothing Web sites. "Cool," she murmured. "Free shipping."

After studying several camis and tops, she selected three of each, then moved on to skirts. A mock wrap with a slit caught her attention. Not that she went out all that much, but maybe Sam would take her to dinner or something.

"Not likely," she told herself. He was turning out to be a real pinhead. Francesca?

Another no, especially after what had happened that afternoon.

She guessed she knew that Francesca was only trying to be, like, nice with her offer to go shopping. Kelly had really *wanted* to say yes. A trip to the mall would have been fun. And a movie. The one on the plane had been totally dumb. But she'd reacted without thinking. Not just saying no, but being mean, too.

Kelly shook her head. It was all Tanya's fault. How many times had her mother asked her something like that? "Do you want to go shopping, Kelly?" Or if not shopping, then to the ballet or the theater. And *if* she said yes or acted interested, Tanya always gave her that smirky smile and shook her head.

"Well, I'm not taking you. Ask Mary." Or Rosa or Sarah, whoever was currently in charge of taking care of her.

Kelly had a feeling that Francesca wasn't like that. That she really would have taken her to the mall. But what if she'd just been playing, too?

Pushing the question to the back of her mind, Kelly completed her order. She changed the ship-to address on her account, so the clothes would come here instead of to the New York apartment, then clicked on "Place my order."

But instead of the cheerful notice telling her that her order had been placed, there was only a single line explaining that her credit card had been denied.

Kelly frowned. That didn't make sense.

She fished the credit card out of her backpack and checked the expiration date. It wasn't until 2006. So what . . . ?

Horror filled her. She remembered Sam yelling at her, telling her she wasn't getting her own DVD player and her claim that she would simply buy it herself. He'd looked mad when she'd said that. He couldn't have canceled her card, could he?

Three minutes later she hung up the phone and screamed. She flew out of her room and down the stairs.

"What did you do?" she screeched as she ran into the kitchen.

Her father stood at the stove, which was weird. Except for a couple of gay chefs her mother knew, she'd never seen a guy cook. Not that she cared right now.

Sam put down a spatula and faced her. "What's your problem?"

She curled her hands into fists. "You canceled my credit card."

"Yes, I did."

"You had no right. It's not yours. It's not in your name."

"You're twelve, Kelly. You don't need a credit card."

His eyes were a really weird color. Sort of brown, but gold, too. Right now they were dark and cold and he looked mean.

But she wasn't scared, she told herself. She was mad. "It was mine," she insisted. "How am I supposed to take care of myself if I can't buy stuff?"

"I'll buy what you need."

"No. You'll buy what you want me to have. You won't care about what I want." Without her credit card she was stuck.

He sighed. "We'll talk about the logistics of what and where the purchases will be after dinner. You're just in time to wash your hands and set the table."

"No! We'll talk about it now."

"I said later."

"I don't care what you said. I don't even have any clothes to wear."

"That's because you turned down Francesca's offer to take you shopping. Now you'll have to wash what you have and wait for the rest of your things to arrive."

Kelly's eyes burned. She turned away as betrayal cut through her. She couldn't believe Francesca had told Sam what had happened about the shopping. It wasn't fair.

Sam sighed. "Kelly, I'm not trying to make your life miserable, although it may seem that way to you. Things are going to be different here. You're not going to buy whatever you want, whenever it suits you. I will take care of you, but on my terms."

So she didn't matter at all. She squeezed her eyes shut.

"Your things will arrive on Friday. That's only three more days. If you don't know how to do laundry, I'll teach you."

She spun back to face him. "I don't *do* laundry. That's why you're supposed to have a maid."

"Ours is gone right now. Either you do it yourself or you wear dirty clothes. I don't care which. Now wash your hands and set the table."

He turned off the grill set in the center of the stove. Two chicken breasts lay there. They were pale and unappealing.

"I'm not eating that," she told him.

"It's healthy."

"It's disgusting looking. Did you cook them?"

His expression hardened. "Yes. And I made the salad."

She turned toward the table. There was a bowl of iceberg lettuce in the center. "That doesn't even count as a vegetable."

"It's healthy," he repeated.

"No, it's not. So you're not going to get me any clothes to wear, and now you're trying to starve me. You're really a lousy father."

He took a step toward her. "It's been forty-eight hours since you showed up, and I think I'm doing a hell of a job. If you've got a complaint, then put it in writing. Otherwise, wash your hands, set the table, and eat dinner."

She glared at him. "Go to hell," she said, speaking each word slowly, then walked out of the kitchen.

There was a moment of silence, then something slammed into a wall.

But Kelly didn't feel victorious. She didn't feel anything at all except empty, hungry, and very much alone.

9

"*I've decided to run away,*" Sam said after dinner. "Want to come?"

Francesca curled up against him on the family room sofa and closed her eyes. "Where would we go?"

"Somewhere hot. An uncharted island in the South Pacific. You'd have to spend the day naked."

She smiled. "There are parts of me I don't want sunburned."

He shifted so his mouth pressed against her ear. "We'd be making love all the time, so they'd be covered."

The low, sexy words made her stomach clench and her thighs relax. "What about food and water?"

"It would be there. We'd do take-out."

"On an uncharted island? How would they find us."

He wrapped both arms around her and drew her close. "Shh. You're spoiling the fantasy. There would be plenty of food and water. A big bed, champagne. Ready to sign up?"

She thought about the feeble start she'd made on her outline and Sam's child sulking upstairs. They were halfway through the first week, and things weren't looking any brighter.

"Sure. When do we leave?"

"You're my kind of woman."

He kissed her, pressing his mouth against hers as he pulled her close. She felt surrounded by sensual heat. Need sparked to life, making her part her lips.

As he swept his tongue inside, he groaned low in his throat. The sound of masculine need made her tremble. Wanting grew, as it had the first time they'd been together. It enveloped her until it was all she could think about. Until rational thought wasn't possible. She ached for him.

"Sam," she breathed as she rubbed her palm against his chest.

He swore, then kissed along her jaw and down her neck. Her breasts swelled and her nipples tightened.

As she arched against him, he slipped a hand under her T-shirt and cupped her left breast. She gasped as his thumb brushed across the sensitized peak, then shuddered as he continued to caress her.

Despite her need to get lost in the moment, she was aware that they weren't alone in the house.

"We can't," she whispered, even as she covered his hand with hers, urging him to keep touching her.

"I know. I'm just playing."

If this was play, she thought as he nibbled her neck and made her skin break out in goose bumps, what would it be like if he got serious?

But she already knew. She'd made love with Sam, experiencing the sureness of his touch, the ease with which he pleasured her. Her insides tightened as she recalled how he'd filled her, thrusting deeply until she'd lost herself. She wanted that now—his body covering hers, touching and teasing.

Think about something else, she told herself as need

turned frantic. Her breathing increased, as did her heart rate, and she couldn't find the strength to push him away when he slipped his hand from her breast to the waistband of her shorts.

Any halfhearted protest she might have made died away when he unfastened the waistband and drew down the zipper.

"Just for a second," she whispered, even as his fingers slid between curls and settled against swollen flesh.

He pressed his mouth to her ear. "You're wet," he whispered.

She sagged back against the sofa and closed her eyes. "I can't help it. You're touching me."

"I like touching you."

He rubbed against the one sensitive spot and she gasped. "What about Kelly?"

"We'll hear her if she comes downstairs." He bit her earlobe. "Just a couple of minutes. You don't have to like it."

"Yes, I do."

He circled around, then slipped a finger inside of her. At the same time he pressed in with his thumb. The unbelievable combination made her gasp. Her hips pulsed slightly as her body surged and tensed.

She was close in a heartbeat. A few more strokes, a little rubbing, and she would lose herself in the pleasure.

Awareness of her surroundings made her hesitate. She put her hand on his wrist. "We have to stop."

Sam looked at her, then nodded. "You're right. If things get going too much, we *won't* hear Kelly." He withdrew his hand.

Half relieved, half disappointed, Francesca fastened her shorts. She felt aroused, edgy, and in serious need of some satisfaction.

"Did you know I have an original Picasso?" he said.

She blinked at the change in topic. "No."

"It's in my office. Come have a look."

He stood and drew her to her feet, then led the way toward the front of the house. There was a small hallway just past the formal living room. The first door on the right led into a bookcase-lined study, complete with runway-sized desk and heavy drapes.

She barely had time to notice the small painting on the far wall when the door closed and Sam turned the lock.

"No condom," he said, pulling her close. "We'll have to be creative."

His mouth settled on hers. The relief was nearly as sweet as the need was sharp. Under the circumstances—no birth control, limited time, and strange surroundings—she probably should have told him to forget it. But she couldn't. Not when his hot, deep kisses made her rub herself against him. Her swollen center came in contact with his hard, thick erection and they both groaned.

"You first," he said, pushing her back until she settled against the desk. He was already fumbling with her shorts.

She helped, then pushed them off, along with her bikini briefs. Then his tongue was in her mouth and his fingers were between her legs, and nothing mattered but the way he made her feel.

It was too good, she thought, barely able to stay standing. She clung to him as she sucked on his tongue and parted her thighs even more. Fingers plunged in and out of her. His thumb rubbed and circled and teased. She was seconds away from losing herself when he broke the kiss and crouched down.

"I want to taste you," he told her.

She was hardly going to protest. With one quick push,

she sat on the edge of the desk. Sam knelt on the floor and drew her swollen flesh apart. He leaned close, then placed an open-mouthed kiss on the very heart of her.

The orgasm came from nowhere. One second she'd been anticipating the intimate act and the next she was caught up in a whirlwind of pleasure and release. She bit back a scream as she clutched at his head. He licked and sucked, forcing one orgasm into two, then three. She shuddered and gasped, finally stilling.

When she was done, he straightened and smiled at her. Francesca felt more than a little embarrassed.

"I, ah, should have taken longer."

He grinned. "You're going to make me think I have super powers."

"You do."

She slid off the desk and reached for the front of his jeans. "Your turn."

He covered her hands with his. "You don't have to do that."

Now it was her turn to grin. "I know."

They exchanged places, with him leaning against the desk and her standing in front. She unfastened his belt, then the button. When the zipper was released, she pushed jeans and briefs down his thighs. His erection sprang free.

He was already hard. She pressed her mouth to his neck as she took him in her hand. He tasted sweet and salty, and he felt like barely controled power encased in baby-soft velvet. The first stroke made her wish they'd brought a condom with them. The second stroke made them both moan.

"I'm going to beat your record," he whispered.

"Promise?" She rubbed her thumb against the tip of his penis.

He shuddered. "Oh, yeah."

Smiling, she knelt on the thick carpeting and took him in her mouth. He clutched the edge of the desk and muttered something about control. She held in a chuckle and began to move.

Francesca wasn't sure he beat her record, but he certainly matched it. In thirty seconds he was breathing hard, in forty-five he was swearing, and somewhere around a minute, he lost it completely.

"I like your enthusiasm," she murmured as they straightened their clothing. "It's inspiring."

He dropped a kiss on her forehead. "So are you. But now I'm starved. Is there any pasta left?"

"Are you kidding? I'm half Italian. There were three of us for dinner, so I brought enough for, oh, twenty."

Sam grinned, then crossed to the door. After unlocking it, he glanced into the hallway, then nodded.

Francesca could hear Kelly moving around upstairs as they made their way to the kitchen.

While she reheated ravioli and sauce, Sam poured them each a glass of wine.

"Did I thank you for bringing dinner?" he asked as he leaned against the counter.

"About four times."

"It was really good."

He'd already told her about his attempt to provide a "healthy" dinner the previous evening. She'd done her best not to laugh.

"The Grands know how to cook," she said. "Grandma Tessa does all the traditional Italian dishes, while Grammy M could bake her way into heaven."

She pulled steaming bowls out of the microwave and tried not to notice the delightfully squishy sensation that lingered after their quickie. She felt satiated, content, and just a little bit wicked.

"Do you cook?" he asked.

Francesca pulled out a chair at the kitchen table and sat. "No. I've taken tons of classes on every kind of cooking. I do fabulous garnishes, but I'm lousy at real food. Honestly, I don't even like cooking."

"So why do you take the classes?" he asked as he settled next to her and picked up a fork.

"Guilt," she said cheerfully. "I'm not interested in the traditional marriage role, and in my family that's about as blasphemous as not acknowledging the Pope. So I study cooking."

"You can rebel enough not to remarry, but not enough to tell them you don't like to cook?"

"I know it sounds crazy, but even being aware of what's happening doesn't take away the guilt. I'm Irish, Italian, and Catholic. Guilt is my birthright."

Sam chewed a mouthful of ravioli. It had been pretty good at dinner, but after what they'd just done in his office, it was delicious. As was Francesca. Her mouth was swollen, her skin flushed. She looked content and satisfied, which pleased him.

"I'm not trying to make trouble here," he said, "but shouldn't your professional training make a difference?"

"Psychologist, heal thyself?" she asked, then laughed. "You'd think it would, but then you'd be wrong. Besides, without guilt, I'd have too much mental free time."

"Good point." He grinned. "I never did show you my Picasso."

She looked at him, blushed slightly, then laughed. "Oh. Yes, well, we'll have to do that another time."

"Just say the word."

Not that he wanted to make a habit of five-minute sex. Not with her. Their night together had been too extraordinary. But with Kelly in the house, everything was different.

"I can tell by your change in facial expression that you've shifted to another mental topic," she said.

He nodded.

Francesca leaned toward him. "It's only been a few days."

"I know. We both have to adjust. It's going to take time." He pushed the bowl away. "I understand all that, but I'm ready to get on with fixing the problem."

"Have you defined what's wrong yet?"

Yeah, some kid he'd never known about had unexpectedly entered his life. Instead of being someone he could relate to—a boy, or quiet, or *normal*—Kelly was difficult, stubborn, and ill-mannered.

"We don't exactly get along," he said instead.

"That will come. First you have to get to know each other."

"Not easy when she spends all her time pissed off at me." He picked up his wine. "Was I wrong to cancel her credit card?"

"Of course not. I'm shocked her mother let her have one. The thing is you have one set of expectations and she has another. You're going to have to find some middle ground. And maybe next time warn her before you cancel her card."

"Good point. Too bad her idea of middle ground is for me to do everything she wants and stay out of her face." He took a sip of wine, then set the glass on the table. "She's going to be annoyed when she finds out I've hired a nanny."

"You found someone?"

He nodded. "The service wasn't thrilled to be providing car service and baby-sitting for a twelve-year-old, but for the right money, they'll do it. She starts Monday." He reached across the table and took her hand. "You've been great helping me out, but I can't take up all your time."

"I haven't minded. If nothing else, I'm learning about ballet." She hesitated. "I've been debating this for a while and I'd like to take Kelly to my folks' place after class. My older sister is getting married, and we have a 'girls only' planning meeting scheduled."

Sam squeezed her fingers and released them. "She's going to be in the way. I'll take the day off work and cart her around myself."

"You don't have to," she told him. "I don't mind taking Kelly to meet my family. I think they'll overwhelm her with attention, and that won't be such a bad thing."

"Are you sure?"

"Yes."

"Then why did you say you'd been debating it for a while?"

She wrinkled her nose. "My family. They're going to read too much into the situation and start planning a double wedding."

He could see why that would make her uncomfortable. "So don't take her. I can play hooky for the afternoon."

"It's not that simple. I understand a lot of what Kelly's feeling. Or I think I do. When I was growing up, there were a lot of times when I felt like an outsider. But the feeling didn't last long because I had my family to adore me."

He shifted uncomfortably. No way he adored Kelly. "It's not that I dislike her," he said.

"I know." She touched his arm. "I wasn't trying to

make you feel bad. My point is I think my family could be good for her."

He understood more than she was saying. Even though it meant setting herself up for unwelcome matchmaking, Francesca was willing to take Kelly home because it was the right thing for the girl.

"You're a hell of a woman."

She smiled. "Not really, but I'm glad *you* think so."

"Thank you. For everything."

"Don't thank me yet. I have no idea what my family might say to Kelly, so I'm warning you in advance."

"I have no idea what Kelly is going to say to them, so we're even."

"Good. Kelly is going to be cheek-pinched and hugged and fed until she's one big ball of good feelings."

"That will be a change."

Francesca's smile faded. "Sam, have you thought anymore about what I said? About Kelly acting out because she doesn't feel secure?"

"I've thought about it. You're probably right, but that doesn't make it any easier to deal with her."

"She needs to be loved."

"She's not very lovable."

"That doesn't change the need."

He knew she was right. Funny, he would have thought loving his own child would be immediate and overwhelming. As it was, he had trouble *liking* Kelly.

"So are you going to charge me billable hours?" he asked.

She grinned, leaned forward, and lowered her voice. "I was thinking more of taking it out in trade," she whispered.

• • •

Francesca whispered something Kelly couldn't hear, but it didn't matter. She was so mad, she was shaking. She *hated* her father. Hated him with all her heart.

The smell of food had lured her from her room a few minutes ago. She'd come downstairs and had heard Francesca and Sam in the kitchen. She'd just decided she would maybe join them when she'd heard Sam say she wasn't very lovable.

Spinning on the ball of her foot, she ran to the stairs and raced back to her room.

He was a horrible man. She should report him to the police or something for child abuse, and then they would lock him up and he'd have to spend the rest of his life in prison. That's what he deserved.

Kelly threw herself on her bed and pulled her Pooh bear close.

"Francesca's not so bad," she whispered into the scuffed fur. "But he's the worst."

She hated him and she would never, ever forgive him. No matter what.

Halfway to the hacienda the next day, Francesca still hadn't come up with an explanation for Kelly's presence. It was hardly as if the Grands wouldn't notice.

She glanced at Kelly, who had changed into shorts and a shirt after her morning ballet class. The preteen stared out the window without saying much. Francesca tried to figure out the best way to admit she had a problem. A big problem.

She cleared her throat. "Did I mention that my father's side of the family is Italian?" she asked.

Kelly turned to look at her. Not a flicker of interest showed on her face. "No."

"They are. My mother's family is Irish. Basically we're talking about grade-A European meddlers."

Kelly continued to watch her without speaking.

"Their idea of perfection is to see all four of their daughters happily married with five or six kids, which, to date, hasn't happened. But there is a ton of family pressure."

She waited to see if Kelly would say anything. Sam's daughter simply watched her.

"I'm going to tell them that your dad and I are friends," she continued. "The thing is, they're not going to believe me. So brace yourself for a lot of very unsubtle hints about weddings, marriage, engagements, not to mention questions about how many brothers and sisters you want. Okay?"

"Okay." Kelly shrugged and turned her attention back to the view out the window. "I understand. Parents can totally overreact."

Francesca had a feeling that comment was a slam on Sam, but she ignored it. "The other thing I need to warn you about is that my grandmothers love everyone. They're going to make a big fuss over you, which I know you'll think is totally uncool. So you need to be prepared."

Kelly's expression turned wary. "What do you mean, a big fuss?"

"Oh, they'll hug you and tell you you're pretty and try to get you to eat a lot of cookies and stuff. They're grandmothers." She smiled. "The usual boring stuff."

The wariness faded. "I can probably handle it."

"I'm sure you can. I just wanted to let you know it might be a real drag."

Francesca didn't want to back Kelly into a corner. If she was enthused about her family, then Kelly would have to take the opposite side and instantly hate them. The girl had a defense ready to go in every situation.

Instead, she had decided to make it all sound like an imposition. Kelly's natural reaction to be stubborn meant she might actually *want* to like the Grands. Francesca had a feeling that an afternoon at the Marcelli hacienda just might shrink the massive chip on Kelly's shoulder.

She saw the arched entrance to the Marcelli property. As she turned under the arch and onto the long paved road, Kelly swung around and gaped at her.

"You're Marcelli Wines?"

"Sort of. My grandfather owns the winery, not me, but this is where I grew up."

"Drinking wine?"

Francesca laughed. "Sometimes."

"Wow!"

Kelly turned in her seat, glancing first to the left, then to the right. Grapevines stretched out for acres. It was the first excitement she'd shown since arriving nearly a week before. Francesca was thrilled.

"So these will be wine soon?" Kelly asked.

"Sure. I think so." Francesca glanced out her side window. "I'm not the expert. If you have any specific questions, you should talk to my sister Brenna. She's the one who knows everything."

Kelly asked a few more questions, then fell silent when they rounded the corner and she saw the three-story Spanish-style hacienda. The pale yellow structure was topped with a tiled roof. Wrought-iron balconies decorated the front windows, and a porch circled the entire structure. Coordinating outbuildings lay in the distance.

Francesca pulled to the side by the multicar garage her

parents had built when their daughters had started driving their own cars.

Kelly turned to her. "Your family is rich. Why don't you have money?"

Francesca laughed. "My grandfather is rich. He's the one who owns the winery."

"But when he dies, doesn't this all go to the family?"

"That's a complicated question."

She stepped out of the car and slammed her door shut. Kelly followed suit. As they approached the rear door of the house, Francesca put a hand on Kelly's shoulder.

"Brace yourself."

Kelly stalled in mid-step. Francesca saw the hesitation in her eyes, but before she could head back to the relative safety of the truck, the backdoor opened and the Grands appeared.

"Francesca," Grandma Tessa called. "We thought maybe you were too busy to come to plan your own sister's wedding."

Grammy M smiled as she hurried behind her taller in-law. "Don't be scoldin' her, Tessa. She's here. And with a wee one."

Francesca wrapped her arm around Sam's daughter. "This is Kelly, the daughter of a friend. She's joining us for the afternoon. Kelly, these are my grandmothers. Grandma Tessa is married to Grandpa Lorenzo." She leaned close and lowered her voice. "They're the Italian side of the family."

Kelly nodded. "Nice to meet you, ma'am."

Ma'am? Francesca nearly fainted. Was Kelly being polite?

"And this is Grandma Mary-Margaret. When we were little, her name was a mouthful, so we call her Grammy M."

"Hi," Kelly said.

The Grands exchanged a look.

"A friend?" Grammy M asked. "Would this friend be a man?"

Francesca glanced at Kelly. "Here goes."

Kelly actually smiled. "Francesca dates my dad."

"You don't say," Grammy M murmured, her pale eyebrows rising toward her hairline. "Well, don't just stand there, Kelly. Come give us a hug."

The Grands descended. Francesca stepped out of the way as Kelly was hugged, kissed, and cheek-pinched. The latter caused her to wince in pain and rub the affected patch of skin. But her look of "rescue me" quickly changed to wonder when they were all hustled inside and she caught a glimpse of the food spread set out for the afternoon meeting.

Francesca was used to the array of cookies, cannolis, scones, cakes, and pastries that were her grandmothers' hobbies, but she doubted Kelly had seen anything like it outside of a bakery.

The girl had just been seated at the table with a plate and two hovering grandmothers when Brenna strolled in. She glanced from Kelly to Francesca.

"Is this who I think it is?" she asked as she leaned on the counter.

"Sam's daughter."

Brenna took off her baseball cap and brushed her short hair off her forehead. "Sam of the hot, naked sex?" she asked, her voice low enough to keep Kelly and the Grands from hearing.

Francesca refused to think about what had happened the previous night. Seeing her blush would only encourage Brenna. "I don't actually know any other men with children."

Brenna reached for one of the cookies and took a bite. "How long are you on baby-sitting detail?"

"Just today. He's hired someone from a service."

Brenna glanced at the Grands, then lowered her voice. "And the naked part?"

"Oh, that's still going great."

Brenna grinned. "Good for you!"

The backdoor opened and Katie breezed in. There were hugs all around, then Francesca introduced Kelly to Brenna and Katie. More hugging followed.

Katie gave Francesca a speculative glance as she looked at Kelly. Obviously there were going to be plenty of questions later.

Francesca watched Kelly closely to see if this was all too much for her, but the preteen seemed to be soaking up the attention.

"Am I the last one to arrive?" Francesca's mother asked as she hurried in from the hallway. "Your father and I have that sales trip in two days, and I'm still trying to get ready."

She kissed each of her daughters, then smiled at Kelly. "Hello. I'm responsible for these girls being here. But please don't hold it against me."

Kelly carefully wiped her hands on a napkin and stood. "Nice to meet you, Mrs. Marcelli."

Once again, the shock of the girl's excellent manners nearly made Francesca fall into a coma.

Francesca's mother smiled. "Call me Colleen." She turned back to everyone else. "Are we ready?"

There was a chorus of agreements. The six of them headed for the dining room. Francesca pulled Kelly aside.

"We're going to be talking about Katie's wedding. Planning it and discussing the dress she wants. You're welcome to join us, but if you think you'll be bored you can watch TV in the family room."

Kelly ducked her head. "I'd like to stay with everyone."

"Absolutely. But if you change your mind, it's okay."

Kelly nodded and followed her into the dining room.

In a matter of minutes they were working their way through wedding details like dates and how many for the guest list. Katie sat at one end of the table, with her mother next to her. Francesca sat next to her with Kelly beside her. The Grands and Brenna were across the table. Pads of paper had been distributed along with pens, cups of coffee, milk for Kelly, and plates of the treats from the kitchen.

Her mother pulled off her glasses. "If we're talking about early October, we have the rain issue."

Katie shrugged. "I'm willing to take my chances. I really want to be married here by the house. We can have tents in reserve. I know a terrific place that rents them. They'll give me a good deal."

Brenna leaned toward Kelly. "My sister runs a company called Organization Central. She plans parties and puts people's lives in order. Speaking as someone who can barely find matching socks some mornings, I find that very frightening."

Kelly grinned.

Katie turned to her sister. "Are you complaining already?"

"Yes. What if harvest isn't over? Have you considered that, Oh Sister-bride?"

Katie bit her lower lip. "I *hadn't* thought of that. I guess if it isn't over, you'll have to shower fast, come to the house for the wedding, then head back out to the fields to be with your precious grapes."

"Maybe I'll even stay for the reception before going back to work," Brenna said with a grin.

Everyone laughed.

Katie reached into her briefcase and pulled out a folder neatly labeled with the words *wedding gown.*

"About the dress," she said.

Francesca laid her head on the table and groaned. Her mother patted her arm.

"I know sewing isn't really your thing, dear, but it's a family tradition."

Francesca opened one eye and glanced at Kelly. "We make the wedding dress. No store-bought confections for our family. It's so much work, and I'm not very good at it. I bleed on the satin. You'd think that would be enough to get me out of helping, but it isn't. Grammy M and Katie always manage to get the stain out. How sick is that?"

Kelly giggled.

"So here are my choices," Katie said, passing around several pictures of wedding dresses.

Francesca straightened and glanced over her mother's shoulder. Her heart sank. The first dress was a sheath style literally covered with beaded lace. The second dress would be even more work. Beading swirled through the long sleeves and full skirt, then wove an intricate pattern on the train.

Francesca passed the picture to Brenna, who actually blanched. Even Grammy M looked a little concerned.

"I'm thinkin' they're lovely gowns, Katie darlin', but we're only givin' ourselves a few months to get everything ready. Even if we beaded day and night, I'm not sure we could finish this one in time. Will you be wantin' to change the weddin' date?"

Katie gazed at them all with a wide-eyed, innocent

expression. Brenna groaned, then tossed a cookie at her sister.

"I'm thinking the *B* word, Katie, and it's not *bead,*" Brenna said as she took back the picture of the heavily beaded dress and ripped it in half.

Katie laughed. "You should have seen the looks on your faces."

Relief tasted sweet. Francesca wrinkled her nose. "Aren't you the humorous one. Where's the real dress?"

Katie pulled out a picture of a sleeveless wedding gown with a scooped neck. The dress was fitted to the waist before flaring out into a full skirt. Seed pearls were scattered across the bodice and skirt. There wasn't a speck of lace in sight.

"We could practically do this in a weekend," Francesca said in surprise.

"I know." Katie looked pleased. "I love the dress and you guys are going to owe me for picking something simple. A win-win."

Kelly took the picture and studied the gown. The Grands got up from their seats and crowded around her.

"What do you think?" Katie asked, coming over and pointing at the picture.

The twelve-year-old sighed. "The dress is beautiful." She glanced up. "Do you think I could help with the beading?"

"Sure. There's plenty of work for everyone." Katie lowered her voice. "Maybe you could help Francesca. She's really awful at sewing."

"I heard that," Francesca said sternly.

Kelly giggled.

Katie touched her chest. "What? I didn't say anything."

"Uh-huh."

The Grands disappeared into the kitchen only to reappear with big bowls of salad.

"Because all the sweets weren't enough," Brenna muttered. "I've got to get out of here before I end up looking like a sumo wrestler."

Francesca followed her out of the dining room. At the backdoor Brenna pulled on a baseball cap.

"The kid seems okay. What happened to Teen-zilla?"

"I don't know. She was her usual surly self on the drive over. I guess the Grands are working their magic. If this keeps up, Sam is going to be thrilled."

"And how exactly will he show his appreciation?"

Francesca grinned. "I'm not going to tell you."

"That's okay. I can imagine, which is really depressing. Just don't go falling for this guy. Remember—Katie's relationship with Zach aside—marriage sucks."

"I know. I'm not about to go there a second time. I don't love Sam, I'm just using him for sex."

Brenna laughed. "You make me so proud."

"Their house is huge. It's really pretty and there are vineyards all around. Brenna is the sister who knows the most about wine. Katie runs some company that organizes parties, and Mia—I didn't meet her—she's in Washington, D.C., studying languages and stuff. The Grands were great. There was so much food. It was like a buffet or something, but it was just their house. And then we talked about Katie's wedding, and the whole family makes the dress. Well, just the women. But Katie said I could help."

Kelly paused and sucked in a breath. "With the sewing and stuff. And I'm going to. Not because it's like fun or anything, but to be polite."

Sam actually rubbed his eyes. He checked the clock over the stove and saw the second hand moving in the normal direction.

So if he hadn't fallen into an alternative universe, what the hell was going on?

He didn't recognize the girl sitting across from him at the dinner table. She looked like his daughter, but she didn't sound like her. Plus, this kid was smiling. Until this second he hadn't known Kelly had teeth.

"I'm glad you had a good time," he said cautiously.

Francesca gave him an "I told you so" smile. "The Grands loved Kelly. I'm afraid she might have a bruise from all the cheek-pinching, though."

Kelly rubbed her cheek. "Grandma Tessa pinches really hard, but she's still nice."

"I agree," Sam said as he cut into the lasagna. "They provided us with dinner."

"They would have given you enough for a week if I'd let them," Francesca told him. "When I mentioned you didn't have anyone to do your cooking, I thought maybe Grandma Tessa was going to move in."

"Grammy M made these scones," Kelly said. "They were really good. And there were cookies. We brought a pie back for dessert."

Sam shook his head. Francesca could crow all she wanted, and he wouldn't complain. She'd been a hundred percent right. Kelly had been transformed by grandmotherly affection and a big family.

He smiled at his daughter. "Several boxes were delivered to the office today," he said. "I'm guessing it's your things. I already put them in your room."

Kelly's eyes widened. She bounced to her feet, then actually hesitated. "May I be excused?"

Sam almost fell out of his chair. "Ah, sure," he said.

She ran out of the room.

He turned to Francesca. "Was she just polite?"

Francesca grinned. "I know. It's incredible. As it turns out, she's been hiding good manners from us. You should have heard her with the Grands. She even said *ma'am.*"

"I'm stunned."

"I'm thrilled. I think this is a big breakthrough, Sam. Kelly had a good time, but more important, she relaxed. Once she feels safe and secure, you're going to see a whole new child."

"That would be terrific. So how did it go with your family?"

She patted her mouth with her napkin. "As expected. They've picked out china for us, but not the flatware."

"You okay with that? You didn't have to take her. Not that I'm not grateful for the transformation."

She sighed. "I tell myself it's for a good cause. And it is. But there were lots of questions and speculations."

"I'm sorry about that."

"It's not your fault." She smiled. "I only have my gene pool to blame."

"But I do owe you. Kelly is a different kid, and I'll pay a lot to keep her that way." He chuckled. "Name your price."

He expected her to tease him or be suggestive. Instead her expression turned apologetic. "It's nothing so simple as money. My family has a big Fourth of July party every summer. My mom invited you and Kelly to attend. Kelly has already accepted on your behalf."

Sam didn't mind. "A party sounds fun, as long as I can bring my grandfather along. With Elena out of town, he'd be all alone."

"No problem. It's just two hundred of our closest

friends." She swallowed. "The thing is my family now thinks you and I are more than friends, and there's going to be fairly serious matchmaking. You need to be prepared."

He smiled. "Are they going to talk about how wonderful you are?"

"No, more likely they'll want to see your last two tax returns, check out your teeth, and get you to commit to a wedding date."

"The hard sell, huh?"

"They will redefine the term."

"I can handle it."

She shook her head. "You say that now, but you haven't faced them yet."

"I can handle anything."

A sudden explosion of sound made the house shake. Sam winced and glanced up at the ceiling. The steady beat of a drum vibrated through his chest.

"I guess she has a CD collection," Francesca said helpfully.

"And a powerful set of speakers."

10

Brenna sat on the edge of her desk while her grandfather paced the length of her small office.

"They're high quality grapes," she said, trying to sound calm when all she wanted to do was scream. "Those four acres have a reputation for producing some of the best Pinot Noir in the state. The buyer called to tell me he's pulling out of the deal and wanted to let me know so I could buy them. No one knows about this yet. I could make a fabulous wine with those grapes."

Grandpa Lorenzo paused in front of a map of the Marcelli property. He traced the line between their land and that of the Giovannis'.

"No."

Just like that. No.

Anger burned inside of her. The request wasn't unreasonable. What she really wanted was to buy the four acres, but she didn't have the money, and her grandfather wouldn't be interested. Not when he was talking about selling.

"Why?" she asked before she could stop herself. Arguing never changed his mind.

He stared at her, his dark eyes narrowed. "We don't buy grapes from strangers. Marcelli Wines are grown on Marcelli land. Our name means something."

"It's not going to mean shit when you sell it."

The words were out before she could stop herself, then she told herself she didn't care. She was tired of him not listening.

Her grandfather stiffened, then muttered something in Italian. She didn't understand what he was saying, which was probably for the best.

"We could start a new label," she said. "The big companies do it all the time."

"Too much work. No point."

He dismissed her with a wave, then walked out of her office. Brenna picked up her Day Runner and threw it across the room. The binder snapped opened and pages went flying everywhere.

It wasn't fair, she thought. Not that fair ever meant anything. She'd sealed her fate the day she'd decided to marry Jeff. Her other option—eloping with the enemy—would have made her entire family go ballistic, but at least then she would have been following her heart instead of her head. As it was, she had only herself to blame. Well, herself and a very stubborn grandfather.

Her phone rang.

"What?" she demanded.

"Hey, don't snap at me," Francesca said. "Whatever's going on there isn't my fault."

Brenna sagged into her chair. "Sorry. I just had a run-in with the old man."

"I'm guessing you weren't victorious."

"Am I ever?"

"Not with him." Her sister sighed. "Want to talk about it?"

"No."

"Okay, then I'm calling to invite you to join Katie and me for lunch. As she's the one with the wildly successful business, she's buying. Are you in?"

"Absolutely. I need to get away from this place."

"You look mad enough to spit," Francesca said when she walked into the café and saw Brenna already sitting at an outdoor table.

Her twin rose and hugged her, then collapsed back into her chair. "I had another go-round with our esteemed grandfather. He makes me insane."

Francesca sat and put her purse on the stone floor. "About the Pinot grapes?"

Brenna sighed. "I know better. I'm not stupid. But I went ahead and asked, and of course he said no. What's the point, right? I mean if he's really selling."

Francesca touched her arm. "You don't know that."

Brenna's dark brown eyes clouded with sadness. "I doubt I'm going to like the outcome of any plan he has. I can't believe I've finally figured out where I belong, only to learn it's not going to exist anymore."

"Okay, who died?" Katie asked as she walked over to the table.

"No one," Brenna said as she rose. "Just any chance I had at happiness."

Katie hugged her. "Okay, so we're going to need wine *and* dessert at this lunch."

Francesca smiled as she stood. "I'm thinking real dressing on our salads, too. None of that low-fat stuff."

She kissed Katie's cheek, then held her sister at arm's length. Katie wore her long reddish-brown hair up. An elegant summer dress with a short-sleeved jacket made her look like the successful businesswoman she was. Katie had always been pretty, but since falling for Zach, she had positively bloomed.

"You look great," Francesca told her as they sat.

"Thanks. It's the whole 'in love' thing. All that happiness aerates my skin or something."

"It's the sex," Brenna said. "Hot monkey sex on a regular basis is way better than any night cream."

"Is this your professional opinion?" Katie asked.

"Sure. I'm writing up an article. You'll be able to read it in the medical journals next month."

Katie laughed. "Then I'll be young forever."

"You're going to tire Zach out."

"I think he's man enough to keep up with me." Katie's humor faded. "So what's the crisis?"

Francesca and Brenna looked at each other.

"No crisis," Brenna said, then sighed. "Not yet. Grandpa Lorenzo might be selling the winery."

Katie's eyes widened. "That's not possible. He's obsessive about family."

"He doesn't have any male heirs."

"What does that matter?" she demanded. "You love the winery. You know more than he does. Whenever he doesn't listen to you, he's eventually forced to admit he made a mistake. Brenna, this is crazy."

"This is our family," Brenna said. "He's accusing me of not being loyal and not sticking around. By marrying Jeff and moving to L.A., I've proven I can't be trusted."

Katie shook her head. "We should all talk to him or something."

"You know he'd never listen. Instead he'd get mad and throw us out of the family."

"Something he likes to do on a regular basis," Katie grumbled. "I'm sorry," she told Brenna.

The waitress arrived. As this was a favorite place, the sisters all knew what they wanted. They ordered salads, extra bread, and diet soda.

When she'd left, Katie picked up the conversation. "I wish there was something we could do about this, Brenna. Have you talked to the folks?"

Brenna shrugged. "I've thought about it. I know Grandpa makes Dad crazy, too, but the thing is they work together. They live in the same house. I don't want to make them choose. Plus, going to them would make me feel like I couldn't handle things on my own."

Francesca understood her sister's reluctance to get her parents in the middle of a big fight. Brenna would consider this a fight she had to manage by herself, much as Francesca insisted on paying her own way through college and grad school.

"Are you sure you can't buy the Pinot grapes yourself?" Francesca asked. "With the money you're going to be getting from the settlement on your divorce, couldn't you rent equipment?"

The waitress arrived with the wine. All three sisters clinked their glasses together.

"I've done the math," Brenna said. "I wouldn't have enough. Plus, it would be such a small production. However, it did get me thinking. . . ." Her voice trailed off.

"About?" Katie prompted.

"Starting my own label." She held up her hand before either sister could respond. "I don't know. I'm in the 'maybe' stage. It's a little scary to consider."

Francesca couldn't imagine the work involved. Or the

money. She sucked in a breath. "Do I want to know what you're looking at in start-up capital?"

Brenna grinned. "Somewhere in the neighborhood of a million dollars."

Francesca nearly fell out of her chair. Katie gasped.

"Don't look so shocked," Brenna told them. "I would have to start big. Wine making is no longer a business for the gentleman farmer. Small wineries are failing left and right, or being bought by larger concerns. I would need to be big enough to survive."

"A million dollars?" Francesca said, hardly able to comprehend that much money. "What would the loan payment be?"

"You don't want to know." Brenna took a piece of bread and tore it in half. "Actually I don't want to know, either. Like I said, I haven't decided what I'm doing. Right now it's just a fantasy."

Katie patted her arm. "If you decide to go for it, I'm good for a few thousand. Although when compared with a million, that doesn't seem like much."

"Keep your money," Brenna told her. "You're going to need it when you start popping out babies."

Katie laughed. "We're not even married yet."

"I've heard women can get pregnant *before* marriage these days," Francesca said. "Isn't science wonderful?"

Katie threw a roll at her. "Very funny. Zach and I want to wait about a year before getting started on the whole family thing. We want to enjoy each other."

Brenna looked at Francesca. "Sex. She's talking about sex."

"I know." Francesca grinned. "Where are you going on your honeymoon?"

"Zach's mentioned Tahiti."

"One of those all-nude resorts?" Brenna asked.

"What is with you?" Katie shook her head. "I don't want to spend my honeymoon naked." She frowned. "Well, that came out wrong. Let me rephrase it. I don't want to spend my honeymoon naked with anyone other than Zach." She turned to Francesca. "And speaking of naked, what on earth is going on in your life?"

Francesca nearly choked on the bit of bread she'd just swallowed. She had a bad feeling she was blushing.

"I'm not naked."

"Maybe not, but you brought a twelve-year-old girl to the house. From what the Grands told me, you're dating the girl's father. Is this true? Do I have to hear about that kind of gossip from my grandmothers rather than my sister herself?"

"You've been busy," Francesca pointed out. "It's not like you've been calling me every fifteen minutes."

"You get crabby when I do that," Katie said. "So start talking."

The waitress arrived with their salads. Fajita chicken for Katie and Francesca, a Cobb for Brenna.

"Oh, please. Let me," Brenna said with a grin. "I want to tell her."

Francesca shrugged. "Feel free."

Brenna leaned toward Katie and lowered her voice. "Remember a couple of months ago, when we all got drunk and admitted to wanting to sleep with Nic Giovanni?"

Katie held up a hand. "Excuse me, but we all agreed we wanted to sleep with him *back in high school*. Not today. There's a difference."

"Whatever," Brenna said. "Anyway, we were both bugging Francesca about finding some guy and getting involved."

"Right. We made her promise to sleep with the next

normal, single man that she—" Katie's mouth dropped open. "You didn't actually do that, did you?"

Francesca popped a piece of chicken in her mouth and chewed.

Katie turned to Brenna. "She did?"

"Apparently. She met this guy while on one of her experiments."

Katie winced. "Not the tattooed biker chick."

"No. It's worse. She was pregnant. They talked, she came clean about her disguise, and then they had sex."

Francesca swallowed. "We went out to dinner, and I did not sleep with him on the first date."

Both her sisters looked at her. She sighed. "It was the second date, okay?"

Kate and Brenna laughed.

"Well, then," Brenna said. "It's perfectly fine. The *second* date."

Francesca refused to be embarrassed or apologize. "It just happened. I didn't mean it to, but I can't regret it. Sam is really great."

Katie looked surprised. "Miss 'I never want to be married again' isn't changing her mind, is she?"

"Absolutely not. Sam is in complete agreement with me on that, too. We're both looking for a monogamous relationship with no risk of too much emotional involvement. He doesn't want to get married again any more than I do."

"They're basically talking about cheap, easy sex and idle chitchat," Brenna said. "Honest to God, it sounds perfect."

"I don't think so," Katie said. "Where's the romance in that?"

Francesca looked at her twin. "Ever the soft-hearted one."

"Not soft-hearted," Katie protested. "Practical. Do you

really think you can have a physically intimate relationship with a man without falling for him?"

"Absolutely," Francesca said. "I've been married. Todd wasn't the devil, at least not on purpose, but there was very little I liked about being married. And look what Brenna gave up for Jeff." She touched Brenna's arm. "No offense."

"None taken," Brenna said. "You're right. I've been beating myself up about it ever since he walked out on me. Katie, you were the smart one. You waited to get married until you found the right guy. You fell for Zach and I think it's great. But neither Francesca nor I is interested in a walk down the aisle again."

Katie didn't look convinced. "I'm not sure it's possible to avoid emotional bonding. What happens if you fall for him? It could get complicated. Especially with him having a daughter. You've always wanted kids. And you love to rescue people."

"Sam is not in need of rescuing," Francesca said firmly. "And I'll admit that the kid thing could be a problem, but I will just make sure I don't bond with either of them. Sam and I want to keep this completely uncomplicated."

"Life doesn't always let you choose," Katie reminded her. "Be careful."

Francesca laughed. "We're using condoms. How much safer could we be?"

Teen-zilla had returned, Sam thought on Monday morning. There had been nearly ten days during which he'd thought having a kid around wasn't such a bad thing. But he'd been wrong.

"She smells," Kelly hissed. "And she's weird-looking."

Sam stood in front of the bathroom mirror and tucked his tie under his shirt collar.

"She doesn't smell," he told his daughter, although he'd noticed some sort of decaying plant smell whenever he was around Doreen. As for her not looking normal, Sam thought she was fine. Okay, her glasses were a little thick, and there was something strange about her mouth, but he wasn't interested in her appearance, just her skills.

"She's been working with children for twenty years," he told Kelly as he looped around the narrow end of his tie. "She has a clean driving record, no tickets in three years, she's bonded and highly recommended. If you want to get to ballet class, she's your ride."

"I put up with her for all of last week. I gave her a chance. She's horrible. She doesn't talk at all. She has no sense of humor, and she never takes me anywhere but class and home. I asked about going to the movies or the mall, and she just said no."

Sam didn't like the sound of that. "You're allowed to go places after class," he said. "I never meant to keep you locked up." Not really. "I'll talk to her when I go downstairs. I'm sure once she understands that it's all right, you can start doing more fun things in the afternoon."

"I'd rather be alone than with her."

Kelly glared at him in the mirror. She was already dressed for her dance class, in a black leotard, tights, and a short skirt. Her feet were turned out in the classic "ballerina" position—heels together, toes pointing away from the body. It made his back hurt just to look at them.

"And I'm too old for a baby-sitter," she said, her voice low but filled with fury. "Just get me a driver and a car and I'll be fine. Any car. A Town Car, even. I don't need a limo."

He adjusted the tie one last time and reached for his

jacket. "Good to know that you're so flexible, but I'm not getting you a car."

"You don't have to buy it, you could just rent it or something."

"No."

"I don't want Doreen around here. She's creepy."

"Then you're not going to ballet class, and you're going to spend the day in my office because I'm not leaving you home by yourself."

Kelly's green eyes practically spit fire. "I knew you were going to say that," she told him. "You're so difficult. You never think about what's right for me."

If only, he thought grimly. "I think about that all the time. Unfortunately our definitions are different. If Doreen is abusive in any way, then I'll not only fire her butt, I'll have her arrested. Until then, you're stuck, kid."

"Why can't Francesca take care of me? She's totally cool."

He thought so, too. Unfortunately between Kelly, his workload, and Francesca's need to finish the outline for her dissertation, he'd only been able to see her a couple of times in the past week, and both of those had been at a dinner chaperoned by his daughter. Not exactly the romantic, sexy, sensual relationship he'd envisioned.

"Francesca has her own life. She's given you more than enough of her time. I'm not going to ask her to cart you around."

Kelly folded her arms over her chest. "This isn't making me like you."

He figured the fact that she hadn't called him a bastard and run out of the room meant they were making progress.

"You're not supposed to like me," he said. "I'm your parent, not your friend."

Her gaze narrowed. "You've been reading stuff, haven't you. You didn't come up with that sentence on your own."

He was saved from answering by the sound of the doorbell. Doreen was downstairs and would probably answer it, but even so he walked through his bedroom into the hallway. He didn't usually have visitors at nine in the morning.

Kelly pushed past him and raced down the stairs. She ran to the foyer and spoke to Doreen, who retreated to the kitchen. Francesca entered the house.

Sam's initial reaction of pleasure turned to curiosity when he saw Kelly hug Francesca.

"You came," his daughter said as he approached. "You have to save me." She lowered her voice. "Doreen is awful!"

Curiosity turned to annoyance when he figured out his daughter had called in her version of the cavalry.

Francesca pulled one of Kelly's red curls. "You barely know the woman."

"She smells funny," Kelly whispered.

The corner of Francesca's mouth twitched. She glanced at Sam. "Ah, the executive look. The power suit is very flattering."

"Unfortunately I don't have much power in my own home." He narrowed his gaze. "Kelly, did you call Francesca and ask her to take you to class?"

Teen-zilla rolled her eyes. "Well, duh. I can't face a whole summer with her—" She pointed toward the kitchen. "I had to do something. I just knew you weren't going to get me my own car."

Francesca looked surprised. "You're giving away cars? Can I put in my order? I've always wanted something flashy. In red or silver."

"A convertible?" he asked.

"Oh, that would be nice."

Kelly stamped her foot. "Would you two please pay attention to me. This is important."

Sam ignored her and took Francesca's arm. "Have you had coffee?"

"Yes, but I can always use more. I'm not really a morning person."

"What are you doing?" Kelly asked in a shriek.

"Ignoring you until you can act like a civilized person," Sam said.

"I'm civilized!" Kelly yelled. "I'm polite and well mannered and you're just a stupid butthead."

Sam turned back to Kelly. She stood with her hand over her mouth. At least she looked shocked.

"I guess you're not going to have class today, huh?" he said quietly.

She dropped her hand, opened her mouth, closed it, then burst into tears. Seconds later she was running up the stairs, sobbing as if her heart would break.

Sam sighed. "I know you said to be patient, but nothing about this is easy."

Francesca squeezed his arm. "I'm sorry. Things were going so well last week."

"Probably because Kelly was getting her way. She's one determined kid."

They walked into the kitchen. Doreen sat at the table, reading the paper. She looked up at them and smiled.

"Good morning, Mr. Reese."

"Doreen. This is my friend, Francesca."

The nanny nodded pleasantly. "Is Kelly about ready to leave? I know she doesn't like to be late for her class."

"She won't be going today. She needs to learn to control her temper."

Doreen nodded. "She's at that age, Mr. Reese. They get human again in a few years."

Sam wondered if he would survive. He poured two mugs of coffee.

"I would like Kelly to stay around the house today so she can think about what went wrong this morning. Tomorrow she'll be heading back to class. As those are only in the morning, feel free to take her shopping or to the movies in the afternoon."

Doreen nodded. "Certainly."

She spoke pleasantly enough, but Sam had the idea that hanging out with a twelve-year-old at the mall wasn't Doreen's idea of a good time.

He and Francesca took their coffee onto the deck. Sam was careful to shut the French doors behind them.

"I don't think Doreen likes children that much," he said.

"She's probably more into babies," Francesca said. "Plus, Kelly can be a handful."

"She swears she's being pleasant to Doreen, and when I've asked, there haven't been any complaints. I don't know." He sipped his coffee.

Francesca leaned close. "I know you're going to hate me for siding with your daughter, but, Sam, the woman smells."

He groaned. "Great. So I have to find someone else."

"That's your call." She leaned back in the wooden chair. "It's just too bad Kelly can't get into some summer programs and meet kids her own age. Has she made any friends at her dance class?"

"A couple. She went home with one Friday afternoon. I guess it went well. The mother wasn't screaming when I picked Kelly up."

"That's something."

"My daughter can be pleasant when she chooses to be, but the rest of the time, she's a complete . . ."

Francesca looked at him. "Are you editing?"

"Yes. You'd be shocked if you knew what I was thinking."

Francesca grinned. "I doubt that. For what it's worth, I think you're doing a terrific job."

"Thanks. It means a lot."

He smiled at her, taking in her long thick hair, and the tank top and shorts. She was sexy, pretty, intelligent, and caring. Talk about a tempting package. He'd met a lot of lying, cheating, using women in his life, and she was nothing like them.

"I have my grandfather to thank for you," he said. "All those years he pounded good manners into me. They finally paid off."

She raised her eyebrows. "What are you talking about?"

"If I hadn't stopped to help you that day you were in the building, we never would have met."

"You could try telling Kelly that story," she said. "Maybe it would convince her manners have merit."

"I doubt it." He brushed his fingers against her bare arm. "I've missed you."

"Me, too."

"Want to have a sleepover?"

"More than you know, but what about Kelly?"

"Are you interested in sneaking around?"

One corner of her mouth twitched. "I've never done it before. Is it fun?"

"I've heard it's exciting and erotic."

She laughed. "You wouldn't happen to know this from personal experience, would you?"

"Me?" He pretended shock. "I don't do that sort of

thing. I'm an upfront guy." He leaned toward her and brushed her mouth with his. "Kelly's usually in bed by ten."

"I'll be at your front door at eleven," Francesca said.

His blood surged at the thought. "I can't wait."

"You can't," Sam said sometime close to two in the morning.

Francesca stretched out next to him, her bare leg brushing against his. "Of course I can. I want to. There's no way you're going to get anyone new for a couple of weeks. Tell Kelly she only has to deal with Doreen full time this week. The Fourth is Friday and that's a holiday. Next week I'll take her Tuesday and Thursday. I'm sure Doreen will appreciate the break, as will your daughter."

He rose on one elbow and stared into Francesca's green eyes. "What do you get out of it?"

"I like Kelly. She's fun." She pressed her lips together. "When she's not being a pain."

"What about your dissertation?"

She ran her hand along his back. "You are looking at the author of a completed outline. So there!"

He was torn between offering her money and telling her she didn't owe him anything.

"I want to," she told him. "Just be gracious and say yes. Or better yet, show your gratitude in a more carnal way. Be inventive. Startle me with—"

She shrieked as he suddenly flipped her onto her stomach. "What are you doing?" she asked, her voice muffled by the pillow.

He nipped at her backside. "Being inventive."

• • •

Francesca hummed through her morning. She'd been up most of the night, her insides felt mushy and sore, and she couldn't be happier. Sam Reese was a man who knew his way around a woman's body. *Contentment* didn't begin to describe the feeling of well-being that swept through her.

She pulled her date book out of her purse and flipped through the pages. If she was going to take Kelly for a couple of days for the next week or so, she needed to schedule writing time on her dissertation. An outline was one thing, but actually getting all the information together and processing it was something else.

She penciled in several blocks of time, then flipped back to check the dates of her experiments. The one in Sam's building had been just over three weeks ago, and the one before had been five weeks ago and—

Francesca frowned as she stared at the small three-dimensional box she'd drawn by the date two days after the experiment at the old mission. She'd been in a wheelchair that time, tormenting tourists. And two days later she'd gotten her period.

She flipped back a month. There was the little box indicating her start date, then she flipped forward. No box. Not even the hint of a box. She slammed the date book shut.

No way, she thought, trying to avoid panic. Not possible. They'd used a condom. Every single time. She knew. She'd been there.

Three hours later she stared at the plus sign on the slender stick. Her mind was blank. She couldn't think, couldn't breathe, couldn't believe.

This wasn't happening, she told herself. It couldn't be. She absolutely could *not* be pregnant.

11

"I *don't see the point,"* Gabriel grumbled as he poked his cane into the floor mat of the passenger seat. "Not that anyone asked me. I guess when a man reaches a certain age, his family sees him as little more than a piece of furniture to be moved around and kept out of the way."

Sam held in a grin. "You said you wanted to come."

His grandfather glared at him. "When did I say that? I never said that."

From the backseat Kelly leaned forward as far as her seat belt would allow. "Sure you did. When you came to dinner. I remember. You complain a lot."

Gabriel grumbled something under his breath. "I'm allowed to complain. It's a privilege of age."

"But you just said you get moved around like a piece of furniture because you're old. So is it good or bad?"

Gabriel turned around and eyed his great-granddaughter. "It beats being dead."

Sam quickly glanced in the rearview mirror. Kelly blinked, then grinned.

"I guess so," she said.

Gabriel chuckled and Sam relaxed his grip on the steering wheel.

After their disastrous first meeting, he'd been hesitant to have Gabriel over to the house for dinner. But he knew Kelly and Gabriel needed to develop a relationship. Also, he didn't like to leave his grandfather on his own, especially with Elena out of town. Fortunately the meal had occurred right after Sam had agreed to find a replacement for the fragrant Doreen and Kelly had been in a good mood.

"Grandpa Gabriel, I've been to the hacienda before, and it's this big, beautiful house," Kelly said cheerfully. "Sort of Spanish style with a tile roof and everything. Plus you can see the grapevines. Brenna—that's Francesca's sister—said I could come down and watch them bottling. Only not today because it's a holiday."

"Slackers," Gabriel muttered.

Sam shot him a warning glance.

"Francesca said her whole family would be at the party," Kelly continued. "Along with a lot of friends. She has three sisters, but only two of them are going to be there. Her youngest sister, Mia, is in Washington, D.C., studying Japanese. She's supposed to be this really amazing language expert. And Francesca's older sister, Katie, is getting married. She's the one I told you about, Sam. I'm going to help with her dress. It's so beautiful. Isn't it like totally cool that they all work on it so when she walks down the aisle she can know that all her sisters and her mom and her grandmothers helped?"

"Too many damn people if you ask me," Gabriel grumbled.

Kelly ignored his ill temper. "Up there," she said, pointing. "See the sign?"

He did. An arch proclaimed MARCELLI WINES. The turnoff from the highway was a long, narrow road. After about a quarter mile a sign pointed toward the tasting room and public areas of the winery. Sam turned in the opposite direction.

Kelly continued to bounce. "Do you see the house? Do you?"

"Not yet."

Then he did. The large structure in the distance surprised him. While he'd known that Francesca was a part of Marcelli Wines, he never actually thought about where she'd grown up.

The stucco house stood on a slight rise. Several other smaller buildings were clustered all around. But what really caught his attention were the grapevines stretching out in neat rows, for as far as the eye could see.

Sam enjoyed wine and knew what he liked, but the process of turning grapes on the vine to Cabernet Sauvignon in the bottle was a mystery to him.

"Look at all the cars," Kelly said. "It's gonna be a great party."

Gabriel grumbled again. Sam ignored him and parked. The car had barely come to a stop when Kelly flung open her door and stepped out into the warm afternoon.

"Francesca! We're here!"

Sam climbed out of the car and saw Francesca coming down the rear steps. He moved around the car to help Gabriel, but the old man waved him off.

"I'm not so bent that I can't stand on my own," he muttered, leaning heavily on his cane as he straightened.

Which meant Sam could focus his attention on the woman greeting his daughter. Francesca wore a loose-fitting white dress that shouldn't have looked the least bit sexy, yet sent his blood pressure rocketing up to the boiling level. She wore her hair back in a braid. Gold hoop earrings glinted at her ears and minimal makeup emphasized her features.

"What are you gawking at?" Gabriel asked, then raised his head. One corner of his mouth turned up as his gaze settled on Francesca as she gave Kelly a quick hug, then pointed toward the backdoor.

"Well, hell. If she's the woman you've been keeping company with, you're not as half-dead as I'd figured."

Sam glanced at his grandfather, but before he could say anything, Francesca moved close enough to hear.

"Hello," she said with a smile. "You must be Mr. Reese, Sam's grandfather. It's a pleasure to meet you, sir."

Gabriel cleared his throat. He nodded. "If he told you who I am, he probably told you I was as surly as a bear and as old as the hills."

Francesca laughed. "Actually he said you were tremendously charming and that I was forbidden to run off with you."

Gabriel gave a rusty-sounding chuckle. "I like being flattered, young lady. You keep it up. And don't call me Mr. Reese. That makes me sound like an old man." He winked. "I'm Gabriel."

Kelly came tearing out of the house. "Look!" She skittered to a stop in front of them and held out her hand. A flag-shaped cookie rested on her palm. The shaky flag design already told Sam the name of the artist even before she said, "I decorated it myself. Want a taste?" she asked Sam.

The question caught him off guard. "Of course. But only half. You need to eat some, too."

"Okay."

Kelly carefully broke the cookie in two and gave him half.

He took a bite. "It's great."

Kelly beamed. "Grandma Tessa said she wants to teach me to cook. That it will make me be a good wife. I told her I didn't really care about that, but I would like to be able to cook stuff so I could throw parties." She glanced at him. "Maybe when I make friends at school I could have them over and stuff."

More twelve-year-old girls filling his house? He swallowed hard. "Sure. That would be great."

Gabriel pointed toward several chairs in the shade. "I'm going to go plant these old bones. Why don't you help me, Kelly?"

The girl hesitated for a second, then nodded. "Okay. Want the rest of my cookie?"

The old man eyed the half-eaten snack, then shrugged. "Why not?"

They walked off together. After a couple of steps Gabriel reached for her hand and settled it in the crook of his arm. Kelly didn't pull away.

"I think my grandfather likes her," Sam said, surprised and pleased in equal measures.

"Kelly's not half bad," Francesca told him.

He chuckled. "Heady praise."

She smiled at him.

He was about to say something else, when her smile faltered. He looked more closely and saw shadows in her eyes.

"Are you all right?"

"Sure." She leaned close. "I've been working on my dissertation. It's not easy trying to get all the data into charts and graphs without putting myself to sleep. I would much rather just talk about what I learned. But that's not how higher education works."

"Smart *and* pretty. Do I have to worry about Gabriel stealing you away?"

"Maybe. He's charming."

"That's where I get it from," Sam told her.

She laughed. "Thanks for sharing. I'd wondered." She glanced at the house, then took his arm and led him toward his car. "You're going to meet my family today," she said and sighed.

He raised his hand to rub away the frown line between her eyebrows, then lowered his arm to his side.

"I figured I would," he said, "what with the party being at their house."

She smiled. "Good point. I just want to go over this one more time so we're all clear. When I brought Kelly over to meet everyone, I tried to tell them we weren't dating, not really, but no one would listen. For them, it's a very short journey from an introduction to happily married. Once they see you in the flesh, they'll start hearing wedding bells. These people are not subtle."

She looked worried, which he thought was charming. "I'm okay with that. Your family can't scare me."

"You say that because you haven't met them yet." She studied him. "I just want you to know I'm not implying anything behind your back."

He touched her cheek. "Francesca, I trust you. You're not a deceptive person."

She opened her mouth, but before she could speak, the backdoor opened and several people spilled out into the yard. Older, younger, and ages in between. As they approached, he thought he saw some physical resemblances. If he hadn't been sure, Francesca's groan would have told him this was her family.

"It won't be so bad," he murmured.

She gave him a pitying look, then turned to face the group. Ten minutes later Sam knew he'd misjudged the situation. Badly.

Introductions passed in a blur. Even with Kelly having explained who everyone was, he had trouble keeping the names straight. One of the grandmother's got his cheek in a wrestling lock that nearly brought tears to his eyes and both of Francesca's sisters eyed him with expressions that warned him there would be questions asked later.

"Come," the cheek pincher said, taking hold of his arm and drawing him toward the house. "You can help me. While we work, we talk, eh?"

He glanced at Francesca, who shrugged as if to say none of this was her fault. Her mother asked something and she turned away. Sam was on his own.

"You're Mrs. Marcelli?" he asked as they stepped into the house. The rear utility room gave way to a massive kitchen with a multiburner stove that would cause trouble in his house if Elena ever saw it. She'd been petitioning for a bigger stove since the first day she started work.

"You call me Grandma Tessa," the woman said as she directed him to the sink. "Wash. Use soap."

"Yes, ma'am."

He did as she directed, dried his hands, then walked over to the huge center island. Hundreds of flag cookies waited to be frosted.

She handed him a bag of red frosting, picked up one for herself, then showed him how to squeeze out the right amount of icing.

"In rows," she said. "Keep the lines straight."

Six cookies later he got the hang of it and was able to apply fairly straight red stripes on the cookies. Grandma

Tessa worked at about five times his speed, applying tiny blue dots to take the place of the stars.

"So, how did you meet our Francesca?" Grandma Tessa asked.

"She was conducting one of her experiments. I offered to help. She was in disguise and I couldn't tell. That impressed me."

The older woman looked at him. "She's an impressive girl."

"I know."

"So you have a daughter. Where's your wife?"

"On her way to Europe to marry someone else."

"And you didn't know anything about the child before?"

"Not a clue." Sam was surprised to feel a burst of anger. "She had no right to keep Kelly from me." For the first time since his daughter had shown up, he realized he'd missed a hell of a lot. Her birth, her first word, her first step. He'd missed things that could never be recovered.

Grandma Tessa smiled. "You look fierce. Good. You take care of your own."

His own? He supposed that described Kelly. "She can be a handful."

"She's getting independent. They grow up and then they don't listen. What can we do?"

He doubted Kelly had ever been much for listening.

"You have a good business? You have money?"

He couldn't help smiling. "You're not subtle, are you?"

Grandma Tessa chuckled. "I'm an old woman. I've lived long enough to say what I think. Francesca is a lovely girl. Her husband died a long time ago. She has mourned him like a good wife, but time moves on. Things change."

Sam made a mental note never to complain about

Gabriel's gruff inquires about his love life. Compared to Francesca's grandmother, Gabriel was a lightweight.

"Francesca needs to be married," Grandma Tessa said. "She comes from good stock. Her hips are a little narrow, but we can't all be built like Brenna. She's Francesca's twin."

A woman walked into the kitchen. She was about Francesca's age, but a little shorter, with short dark hair and brown eyes. She winced as she caught her grandmother's words.

"Hi, I'm Brenna of the childbearing hips," she said ruefully. "You're in luck. I'm here to rescue you."

Grandma Tessa frowned. "Sam doesn't need rescuing."

"Want to ask him?" Brenna took the icing bag from him and set it on the counter. "Come on. I know a secret way out of here."

"Nice to meet you," Sam said as he hurried after Brenna.

She took him out the front door.

"I see I didn't have to ask you twice," she said.

"I enjoyed meeting your grandmother," he said.

"Uh-huh. And the matchmaking?"

"That was a little intense."

Brenna smiled. "Marcellis tend not to do things by halves. Just remember that you owe me."

They circled around the house, coming out in the back, where the tables were set up for the party. Large trees provided shade. To one side young children ran around playing a game. He could smell the charcoal from the barbecues and something fruity he thought might be the grapes.

"There she is," Brenna said, pointing.

He followed the direction and saw Francesca talking

with her mother and her other sister. The light breeze played with the hem of her dress and a few loose strands of hair. When she leaned her head back and laughed, something caught in his gut, making him feel as if he'd been kicked.

Francesca looked up and saw them. She said something to her mother and sister and walked toward them.

"I rescued him from Grandma Tessa," Brenna said when she was within earshot. "I don't know how bad it got, but when I walked in they were talking about your skinny hips, so they'd already moved to childbearing."

Francesca stumbled and blushed. "Sorry, Sam. I didn't know it would go that far."

He chuckled. "No permanent harm done."

Brenna excused herself. He waited until she was gone to continue. "Now I know why you didn't mention dating to your family."

"It's definitely a place I don't want to go," she admitted. "For a lot of reasons." She pointed to a path. "That heads through the gardens. Up for a walk?"

"Sure. Your grandmother thinks you've been in mourning for your late husband?" he asked.

"Yes. I tried to explain that my feelings about marriage have nothing to do with being in mourning, but the Grands didn't understand. I'm not the traditional woman they want me to be. I keep my guilt in check with my craft classes."

"Have you been involved with anyone since Todd?" he asked.

"After a couple of years I dated some. But I was busy with college, and my heart wasn't in it. Honestly, it was never worth the trouble before."

He paused in front of a low fence surrounding a vegetable garden. "Why now? Why with me?"

She shook her head. "You're fishing for compliments, and I'm not going to bite."

He grinned. "Sure you are. You like to bite."

He drew her close and wrapped his arms around her. Just before he kissed her, he thought she stiffened. He straightened.

"Is this too public?" he asked. While they couldn't see any of the party-goers, they could hear them.

Francesca shrugged. "I'm just a little on edge."

He brought her hand to his mouth and kissed her fingers. "Then I can control myself until we're alone. Fair enough?"

Francesca nodded and did her best to smile. After pointing at the neat rows of vegetables in the garden, she started talking about how Grandma Tessa and Grammy M went on a planting frenzy every spring because the mundane topic kept her from blurting out what was really on her mind.

She was pregnant with Sam's baby. In the past two days she'd probably reminded herself of that truth a thousand times, but she still couldn't believe it.

Life was nothing if not unfair, she thought as they headed back for the house. Condoms were supposed to be effective ninety-six percent of the time. She and Sam had made love four times that first night. What were the odds of her getting pregnant in just four times?

Sam took her hand in his and squeezed her fingers. The gentleness in his expression made her want to cry. Or throw herself on the ground and confess all.

She was going to tell him. She had to—it was the right thing to do. But not today. Not with her family around. And probably not tomorrow, because he still hadn't adjusted to having a daughter who was twelve. What would he say about a newborn?

A baby. She sucked in a breath. This was going to change everything in her life and his. What about her studies, her goals? Could she do all that and be a single mother? There were months she had trouble balancing her checkbook.

As for Sam—she glanced at him out of the corner of her eye. He wasn't going to be happy. She mentally cringed as she remembered his shock at Kelly's arrival. At least his daughter was able to dress and feed herself. She was only six years from being an adult.

Sam was like her—he'd made it clear he wasn't interested in long-term commitments or happily ever after. He'd already had to adjust his thinking to accommodate Kelly. What would happen when he found out there was about to be another child in his life?

Brenna drove one of the small trucks to the north end of the property and stopped by the fence line. Once she'd stilled the engine, she climbed out and checked on the Chardonnay grapes.

She glanced from the tight clusters to the sky. This was the part of the season her grandfather claimed made believers of them all. They prayed for the right temperatures, for the right balance of sun, cloud, and fog. For rain to fall on certain weeks, but not on others.

Brenna straightened and brushed off the skirt of her dress. She shouldn't have left the party, but for reasons she didn't understand, the crowd had started to get to her. She'd felt out of place and awkward.

She started walking the fence line. Dammit, she thought. She refused to be missing Jeff. The ass had dumped her for a younger woman, leaving her lost, confused, and a twenty-seven year-old cliché. She didn't want him back. She didn't want anything to do with him. But this was the first time she'd had to go out in a large gathering and be a single woman again. She'd been married in a double ceremony with Francesca when they'd both been eighteen. In the past nine years she'd forgotten what it felt like to be alone.

A flash of movement caught her attention. Brenna froze in place, knowing what she would see before she turned. She only had a heartbeat to be grateful she looked better than the last time she'd seen him a couple of months ago.

She remembered everything about their encounter, from how she'd found him too sexy for words and how they'd instantly jumped from social niceties to sniping at each other. This afternoon she was determined to take the moral high ground and be only pleasant.

"Hello, Nic," she said as she turned toward the fence.

Nicholas Giovanni, sole heir to the Giovanni lands and Wild Sea Vineyards, strolled toward her. He moved with a laconic grace that made her remember being sixteen and wildly in love with the neighborhood bad boy.

Time must be a woman, because it had graced him with a few wrinkles by his eyes that only added to his dark good looks and sexual appeal.

"Brenna." He paused by the fence. "I can hear the party from here."

She turned in the direction of the Marcelli hacienda, but she couldn't see anything but grapevines. The faint sound of music and laughter did indeed carry on the light breeze.

"My invitation must have gotten lost in the mail."

"My grandfather's too old to change his ways," she said. "He'll never forgive you for being a Giovanni."

"I don't need forgiving."

Men like him never did, she thought. They sinned with impunity.

She looked at his jeans and T-shirt, the latter with cut-off sleeves. "I take it you're not celebrating at home."

"I'll be heading out later."

He stared at her. His dark eyes seemed to see past her fragile defenses to the insecurity beneath. Self-consciously she put her hand up to her short hair.

"I like it," he said, his gaze following her actions. "You look good."

Simple words. Meaningless words. She swore silently as pleasure blossomed inside of her and heat flared, as it always had when Nic was around.

"You, too," she said before she could stop herself. Mortification followed instantly. She cleared her throat and changed the subject.

"Looks to be a good harvest."

He nodded. "You heard about the Schulers going out of business? I've put in an offer."

Which was just like him. "Dammit, Nic, don't tell me you're buying them, too. Do you have to own every damn acre in the valley?"

He grinned. "That's the Brenna I know. I got worried when you were so polite. I thought maybe the family had put you on medication."

She glared at him. "Very funny. You're on the verge of overproducing."

She thought of the map in her grandfather's office, the one that showed the Marcelli's lands, along with those belonging to Wild Sea Vineyards. Over the past twenty years their rivals to the north had nearly doubled in size. "There's no way you can keep control of that much acreage. Or is that the point? Will you be hiring people to manage it for you so you don't have to get your hands dirty anymore?"

"We'll be the biggest, and the best."

"Not possible. Besides, you've already decided volume is more important than quality. I'm disappointed, but not surprised."

He leaned against a fence post. "I heard Lorenzo has put you back in charge."

"For now," she told him, thinking of her grandfather's threat to sell. "I'm going to try a new Cuvée with the whites. It's going to be a winner. You won't want to go up against me in competition."

"We don't make a Cuvée. But it's not a bad idea."

"Sure. If you can't be original, then copy."

He grinned. "I'll make it cheaper and sell about ten times as much."

He would, too, damn him.

"I'll still be the best," she told him.

"You'll be broke."

Or out on the streets if her grandfather sold. But she didn't want to think about that.

A loud burst of music made her turn toward the direction of the hacienda. "I'd better head back," she said.

He nodded. "Good to see you again."

"Oh, right. Because you really enjoy arguing with me."

He surprised her by grinning. "Actually, I do. See you, Brenna."

His statement stunned her into silence.

When he'd disappeared into the vineyard, she headed back to her truck. As she slid onto the worn seat, she remembered when it had all been different. Years ago Nic had been her universe. She had thought she couldn't possibly live without him, but she'd been wrong. In a world where Marcellis and Giovannis were sworn enemies, Nic had asked her to chose. She had . . . but she hadn't chosen him.

Francesca set a pile of flatware on the table and began to sort through the pieces. The afternoon had warmed up enough to make her grateful for the shade of the nearby trees. The party-goers clustered in large groups all around the property, while music from the band her parents had hired added to the festive mood.

Every few minutes she found herself glancing around and trying to find Sam. When she caught a glimpse of him, guilt, fear, and terror made her stomach clench and her throat close up. Neither were pleasant.

"Did you see?" Kelly asked as she raced up to the table. The preteen practically vibrated with excitement. Her face was flushed and her eyes widened.

"Look!"

Kelly pointed and Francesca turned in that direction. She frowned, unable to see what was so interesting. Two people sat together in shade. They were talking, their heads bent close together.

"It's my great-grandpa and your Grammy M," Kelly breathed. "I saw them laughing a little bit ago. I can't decide if it's really great or totally gross."

Francesca grinned. She knew what her vote would be. "It's fun," she said.

Kelly wrinkled her nose. "They're so old."

"That fact should give you hope for the future. With a little luck you'll still have a love life at that age."

Kelly groaned. "*That* is totally gross."

"You won't think so then."

"What are you two up to?"

Francesca turned and saw Sam walking up.

Kelly grinned. "Gabriel has a girlfriend."

Sam saw what was going on with Gabriel and Grammy M.

"I don't know what to say," he admitted.

"Francesca thinks it's cute," Kelly told him. "I'm not so sure."

"Love happens at every age," Francesca said.

Kelly's expression hardened. "I hate it when people fall in love. They act stupid and forget what's important. They forget about a lot of things."

She turned and ran toward the house. Sam stared after her.

"My ex-wife has a lot to answer for," he said coldly. "For what she did to both of us. She put Kelly through hell and kept me from being there to make my daughter's life bearable. I can forgive her for a lot of things, but I'll never forgive her for the lies."

12

The last of the plates were cleared away just as the sun slipped below the horizon. In the distance the fireworks were set up on a patch of graded land that had yet to be cultivated.

Francesca and Brenna strolled in the twilight, heading away from the tables and toward the house.

"I'm going to explode," Francesca said, touching her stomach. The troubles in her life had done nothing to reduce her appetite. "Why do I always eat too much?"

"Because the Grands are the best cooks in the world," Brenna said. "I've got to get out of here and get my own place. If I stay much longer, I'll weigh four hundred pounds by the end of summer."

Francesca laughed. "You look great. Quit complaining."

"I look okay," her sister said. "You look amazing. There's this strange glow about you." Brenna's gaze narrowed. "It's Sam, isn't it?"

Francesca swore silently. Glowing? She couldn't be glowing. She was maybe three weeks pregnant. The baby wasn't even a rice grain yet. "It's this new moisturizer I've been using. Really. It's fabulous."

Brenna laughed. "You are such a liar."

Francesca knew she was teasing, but the 'L' word made her wince.

"Admit you like him," Brenna said. "Commitment or no commitment, you think he's great."

At least this was something she could talk about. "Okay, yes. He's pretty amazing."

"And you like the kid."

"Kelly is a good kid."

They circled around to the rear of the house. Brenna came to a stop. "Then watch yourself, Sis, because I'm seeing sparks between you two."

"You don't have to worry. There's nothing . . ." She hesitated. Nothing serious between them? Didn't a baby count as that? "We're still not picking out rings. I promise."

"Just watch yourself. I don't want you to get hurt."

"I don't want that, either. Sam and I—"

The sound of harsh, angry voices caught her attention. Francesca looked toward the house and saw her father arguing with her grandfather.

"What on earth is that about?" she asked, heading toward them.

"Dad looks mad," Brenna said as she hurried after her.

"She knows," her father was saying as the two of them hurried up. "Brenna has always known about the grapes. What would it hurt you to listen?"

Grandpa Lorenzo waved a hand in dismissal. "This is not the time."

"You're wrong. Buying the Pinot Noir grapes was a good idea. We need to expand."

"It is not for you to say!" the old man roared. "This land is mine to do with as I will!"

"Are they drunk?" Francesca asked quietly as she and Brenna hovered a few feet from the two men.

"I have no idea."

Grandma Tessa hurried up, as did Grammy M, who was with Gabriel. Francesca's mother appeared from around the side of the house.

"Marco?" she said. "What's wrong?"

"My father," he said, obviously furious. "He's being as stubborn as ever. I just found out Brenna tried to buy some grapes, but the great family patriarch wouldn't let her."

"*I* am in charge," Grandpa Lorenzo declared. "My name is on the label of these wines."

"We all have the same name," his son blasted back. "We all care about the winery."

"I care more. I wait and wait, but there is no heir. Now what? Everything is to be lost."

His son rounded on him. "Don't you dare throw that up in my face again, old man. If anyone is to blame, it's you. Not me, not Colleen. You and Mama decided. You chose this path."

Francesca had no idea what they were talking about, but she was stunned by the guilty expression on Grandpa Lorenzo's face. She turned to Grandma Tessa and saw tears in her eyes. Even Grammy M look worried.

Francesca glanced at Brenna, who looked as confused as she felt. Their mother began to cry.

"I can't, Marco," she said softly. "I can't pretend it didn't happen. Not anymore."

"I know." Her husband put his arm around her. "It's been thirty years and it still hurts every day." He glared at his father. "Damn you for your arrogance and your pride. Damn you for making us give up our son."

• • •

Like many other party-goers, Sam had been drawn by the sound of loud voices. Now there was only silence as Marco Marcelli's words echoed in the twilight.

"What's happening?" Kelly asked quietly as she hovered by his side.

"I don't know."

Whatever it was, the family didn't need an audience.

"We should go," he said.

"But we haven't seen the fireworks."

Sam figured they had, only not the kind she meant. "We'll watch the ones over the pier back home," he said and headed over to where Gabriel stood with Grammy M.

His grandfather looked up as he approached, said something to Grammy M, then began his slow walk toward Sam.

"This is family business," Gabriel said unnecessarily. "They don't need us around."

"I agree. Let me tell Francesca we're leaving. I'll meet you by the car."

The Marcelli family clustered together. Francesca was next to Colleen, her arm around her mother. They both looked shocked.

"We're going to head out," he told Francesca.

She glanced at him and nodded, but he wasn't sure she saw him. He wanted to offer the same kind of comfort to her that she offered to her mother. Right now Francesca seemed to need a shoulder to lean on.

She managed a shaky smile. "We usually do a better job at our parties."

"We had a great time. Don't worry about it."

She nodded.

Light from the house spilled out and illuminated the side of her face. He visually outlined the curve of her jaw and the strand of dark hair curving against her neck.

"Call me if you need anything," he said. "Kelly and I will be around all weekend."

"I appreciate that."

He waved and turned toward the car.

Ten minutes later they'd left the Marcelli house behind and were approaching the highway.

"What happened back there?" Kelly asked.

"I'm not sure." Sam figured Francesca would explain things when he finally saw her. Until then there was no point in speculating.

"Mary-Margaret was damned upset," Gabriel muttered.

Sam glanced at his grandfather. "I noticed you spent a lot of time with her."

Gabriel gave a wolfish grin. "She's a fine woman."

"That is totally gross," Kelly complained.

Gabriel chuckled, then winked at Sam. "I told you I still had some life left in me, boy."

"That you did."

Francesca and Brenna stood across from Katie. All three of them were in the kitchen, while their parents and grandparents talked in low voices in the living room.

"This is completely crazy," Brenna said, her voice harsh, her eyes glazed with shock and disbelief.

Francesca knew she probably looked just as stunned, but unlike Brenna, she didn't have as much to lose if the bombshell was true. Sure, their grandfather had hinted about selling the winery, but Francesca hadn't believed that was likely. Eventually Grandpa Lorenzo would relent and Brenna would inherit. Unless there was a male heir.

"A brother," Katie repeated. "It's not possible."

"It's more than possible," Brenna said bitterly.

Francesca shook her head. "Why wouldn't they have said something? This is a thirty-year-old secret."

"Maybe Dad isn't the father," Katie said, sounding as stunned as Francesca felt.

"He said *our* son," Brenna reminded her.

"What about all the times Grammy M said the family was being punished by God?" Francesca asked. "We never figured out what that meant. What if it was about this?"

Zach, Katie's fiancé, walked into the kitchen, then paused. "You want me to go wait somewhere else?"

Katie glanced at Francesca, who shook her head.

"I think it's a little too late for secrets," Francesca said, trying to lighten the tone.

"Now what?" Brenna demanded. "I can't believe it. This is complete bull."

Francesca touched her twin's arm. Brenna's pain was as real to her as the ache in her own heart.

"Now we go find out the truth."

Katie's mouth twisted. "Grandpa Lorenzo already sent us away. You know if we go in there, he's going to threaten to throw us out of the family. Speaking as the last person that happened to, it's not fun."

"We don't have a choice," Francesca told her. "I'm sorry about what happened before. We should have stood together. That's what we'll do this time."

"You think he bothers you," Brenna said bitterly. "Try working for him." She took her sisters' hands. "Come on, we're joining them." Zach put his arm around Katie.

The four of them walked into the living room. Her parents sat together on the sofa. Her mother was in tears. She pressed a tissue to her face with one hand and held on to her husband with the other. Grammy M huddled next to her daughter. For the first time Francesca realized her grandmother was an old woman. Pain emphasized the lines in her face and pulled at her mouth.

Grandma Tessa sat alone on a chair by the fireplace and Grandpa Lorenzo stood next to her.

They all looked up when Francesca, her sisters, and Zach entered. Grandpa Lorenzo frowned.

"This is not your business."

Francesca ignored him and crossed to the sofa. She squeezed in next to Grammy M and took her frail hand in hers. "Are you all right?"

Her grandmother offered a trembling smile. " 'Tis something I knew would have to come out one day. None of us meant to hurt you girls. You have to believe that."

"Mary-Margaret!" Grandpa Lorenzo roared. "You will be silent!"

Grammy M flinched.

Francesca rose and faced her grandfather. "There has been too much silence for too many years. We are all a part of this family. You can threaten us, Grandpa, but you can't scare us away. We want to know what's going on."

Her parents exchanged a look of silent communication. Grandma Tessa looked at her husband. Grammy M nodded slowly.

" 'Tis time," she said softly.

"I agree." Her father stood. "It's long past time."

13

It took a few minutes for everyone to get settled. Francesca found herself on the sofa between Brenna and Grandma Tessa. Her mother sat next to Grammy M on one loveseat, while Katie and Zach shared another. Only Lorenzo and his son stood alone.

They glared at each other from across the living room. Tension filled the air, nearly crackling with intensity. Francesca wondered how long they had been avoiding this particular topic—how many years had they needed to clear the air. She and her sisters had always known there were secrets, but they had assumed they were silly, inconsequential bits of information that might be interesting, but would never impact their lives. They'd been wrong.

Still glaring at his father, Marco spoke first. "You girls know that your mother and I dated in high school."

All three of them nodded. Francesca watched her father turn his gaze from Grandpa Lorenzo to his daughters. He smiled at each of them. She saw the love in his eyes, and the unspoken promise that they would survive whatever he had to say. Some of her tension eased slightly.

"We were young and very much in love." He shifted his

attention to his wife, who gave him a warm and tender smile, despite the tears in her eyes.

"What you don't know is that our families were opposed to our relationship."

Francesca straightened. She glanced at Brenna, then at Katie. Her sisters seemed as shocked as she felt. She turned to Grammy M for confirmation.

"You didn't approve of Dad?" she asked.

Grammy M twisted her hands together. "It was a long time ago, darlin'. Things were different."

Grandma Tessa shrugged. "We wanted a good Italian girl for our Marco."

"But that was in the 1970s. Did people really care about those things back then?" Brenna asked.

Her mother gave her a sad smile. "More than you can believe. Your father and I had a lot of family pressure to stop seeing each other. We were both fighting with our parents. In the end, we agreed to keep the peace, but continued to see each other in secret."

Grandpa Lorenzo opened his mouth to say something, but his son cut him off.

"I'm telling this story," Marco said curtly.

Grandpa Lorenzo hesitated, then nodded.

Brenna shifted closer and took Francesca's hand in her own. Francesca tried to give her sister a reassuring smile, but had a feeling it didn't come out very well.

"Your mother was only sixteen when we found out she was pregnant."

"He proposed right away," her mother said, picking up the story. "We'd planned to get married anyway, but this moved up our timetable. Unfortunately the news didn't please either of our parents."

Francesca couldn't begin to imagine what that must

have been like. Two teenagers surrounded by disapproval. They must have been terrified.

"We sent her away," Grammy M said softly, tears filling her blue eyes. "Lord forgive us."

Grandma Tessa nodded, withdrew her ever-present rosary from her pocket, and kissed it lightly.

Colleen sighed. "I was sent to a school for unwed mothers before I could run away with your father. No one knew where I was. They thought—" She cleared her throat. "We all thought . . ."

Grammy M stared at her daughter. "You'll not be takin' the blame for what others made you do." She turned to her granddaughters. "My Connor, God rest his soul, Tessa, Lorenzo, and myself decided it would be best if they were givin' up the wee one for adoption. Colleen and Marco were just babies themselves. But they were stubborn and they fought us. In the end we won, though."

She didn't sound especially happy about that.

Francesca looked at her mother. "You had a boy?" she asked.

"Yes. I never saw him. They said it would be easier if I didn't." Her mother swallowed as tears returned to her eyes. "I'm not sure anything could have been harder. They took him away and I came home." She turned her attention to her husband. "Marco was waiting for me. Our parents insisted we stop seeing each other, but we didn't listen. When I turned eighteen, we married."

Marco crossed to his wife and took her hand. "That's all," he said quietly. "Now you girls know what happened."

Francesca wondered who was going to tell Mia, but decided that could be determined later. Next to her, Brenna caught her breath.

"So he's out there somewhere, with no idea who is he or what's waiting for him here?"

Francesca swung to face her sister. Brenna's expression was stark and empty. Her twin's pain slammed into her as if it were her own. Francesca wanted to point out that a male heir couldn't possibly matter at this late date, that Grandpa Lorenzo would never give the winery to a virtual stranger, regardless of his connection by blood, but she knew she was wrong. It was more than possible.

"God punished us," Grandma Tessa said. "We shouldn't have insisted she give up the baby."

"Don't be ridiculous," Grandpa Lorenzo snapped. "We're not being punished." But he didn't sound as sure as he could be.

Francesca couldn't absorb all she'd been told. How could events from thirty years before have such an impact on their lives? And yet in a matter of minutes—with only a few words of information—everything was different.

"Has anyone contacted him?" she asked.

"We never thought there was a need," Grandpa Lorenzo said.

Francesca stared at him. "This isn't about need, it's about family. You have a grandson out there. We have a brother. My parents have a son. Does that matter to you?"

"We weren't sure," Colleen said quietly. "We didn't want to interfere with his life. We didn't know if he would be interested in hearing from us."

We didn't know if he would forgive us.

Her mother didn't speak the words, but then she didn't have to. Everyone heard them.

Katie clutched Zach's hand. "Why didn't you tell us before?" she asked.

Their father shrugged. "There was never a good time."

Katie started to protest, then stopped. Francesca wondered if she was thinking about the secrets each of them kept from the family. Katie had had secrets about her broken engagement all those years ago. Francesca had never confessed the truth about the state of her marriage to Todd, and Brenna . . . Francesca studied her twin. What secrets did Brenna keep?

"We need some time to absorb all this," Francesca said. "I think we should let the subject drop for a couple of days and talk about it again at Sunday brunch."

Katie nodded. "I agree. This is no longer just your issue. We all have a stake in what happens now."

Grandpa Lorenzo glared at her. "Be quiet," he ordered. "You are not the head of this family."

"You're right, Grandpa," Brenna said. "*You're* the head of the family, and in this matter you've done a real lousy job."

Grandpa Lorenzo sputtered, but before he could say anything, Brenna stood. Francesca rose as well, followed by Katie. The three sisters moved to stand next to each other.

"We decide together," Francesca said, facing her parents. "Agreed?"

"Yes," her father said. "We'll talk on Sunday. We'll decide as a family."

Katie led them out of the living room. By silent agreement they didn't talk until they were upstairs in the old bedroom Francesca and Brenna had shared. The room Brenna had returned to when her marriage had ended. They sat on the two beds and stared at one another.

"Happy Fourth of July," Brenna said grimly.

Francesca touched her arm. "Are you okay?"

"Not even close. You?"

"In shock."

"Me, too," Katie said. She flopped back on the bed. "Why on earth didn't they say something ages ago?"

"That's what I want to know," Brenna said.

"You're upset," Francesca said, eyeing her twin.

Brenna shook her head. "What I am is screwed. It was bad enough to find out that Grandpa Lorenzo was thinking of selling the winery. I figured I might still have a shot because he wouldn't want strangers on the land. But if there's an heir floating around out there somewhere, I don't have a prayer."

Francesca wanted to offer some words of comfort, but she didn't know what to say. Everything had changed, and she had a bad feeling their lives would never return to normal again.

It was a perfect summer's day, but Francesca couldn't summon the enthusiasm even to open the drapes. Instead she curled up on the sofa, her legs pulled to her chest, her forehead resting on her knees.

How had everything changed so completely in such a short period of time? One minute she'd been well on her way to achieving her goals while dating a terrific guy who not only made her see stars in bed, but who wasn't interested in marriage or forever. The next she was pregnant, unsure how to tell Sam, and suddenly had a long-lost brother who could inherit the winery and break her sister's heart.

There were also all the subtleties that went along with the new circumstances. Things like the logistics of being pregnant and having a child, how to tell her family, how to tell Sam. What to tell Sam. That her parents had lied to her and her sisters for years, that Mia had to be told, and that while she didn't want anything like a commitment or a permanent relationship with Sam, she couldn't help wishing he were with her right now. She could use a good hug.

She sighed softly and shook her head. No point in wishing for the moon, she told herself. It was a perfectly good Saturday afternoon. He was probably taking Kelly sailing or to the beach or for a drive along the coast. Or pulling his hair out because Kelly was driving him crazy. Whatever the circumstances, he wouldn't be thinking about his sometime bed partner, except in the context of being grateful that he hadn't committed to her or her insane family.

This line of thought wasn't making her feel any better. "So think about something else," she told herself.

Like what? That she hadn't had any symptoms of her pregnancy, but that didn't make it any less real? That she had to get to a doctor and start taking vitamins or something? And didn't she need to be drinking lots of milk to get her calcium?

A knock on the door interrupted her musings. She straightened and rose. It was Brenna, she told herself as she walked to the door. No doubt her sister wanted to talk about what had happened with—

It was Sam.

Francesca stared at him. He smiled.

"I thought you might need a friend," he said.

He looked good. Too good. Shorts, a T-shirt, and slightly mussed hair. Staring at him made her throat get all sore and her eyes burn. She had a bad feeling she was thirty seconds from bursting into tears.

She stepped back to let him in.

"You okay?" he asked.

She nodded and swallowed. "Thanks for coming by. That was really nice."

"I couldn't stop thinking about what happened last night at the party. I wanted to make sure you'd survived the bombshell."

She motioned to the sofa, then crossed to the window, where she opened the blinds and let the morning sun spill into the small room.

"I'm still processing information," she admitted as she sat next to Sam and angled toward him. "I can't believe I have a brother, that he's been alive for all these years and my parents never mentioned it."

His mouth twisted. "I know all about parental secrets," he muttered.

She wanted to protest that her parents hadn't acted at all like his mother, but she supposed there were some similarities.

She told him what her parents had shared with her. "I guess that once they gave him up for adoption, they tried to move on." She shrugged. "But honestly, I can't decide if not telling us about him was for our good or theirs."

"I hate the lies," Sam said.

Francesca shivered. She was currently sitting on a really big secret of her own. She would tell Sam—she not only had to, she wanted to. It was a matter of timing. She wanted things to be more stable with Kelly, and honestly, she wanted a little more time with Sam. She knew that as soon as she came clean, nothing was ever going to be the same.

Was it so wrong to want a few more days of him liking her?

Before she could answer, he slid toward her and pulled

her close. She snuggled against his warm body and let herself relax.

"I didn't mean to run out on you last night," he said. "I figured you needed family time, not guests."

"It was fine. We sort of all abandoned the party to have it out with our parents. Thank goodness my mom always has a staff in charge of events like that. We know our guests got fed and that someone started the fireworks." She glanced at him. "The ones in the sky, not the verbal ones."

"Kelly and I went down to the pier to watch the fireworks," he said. "She stayed pretty normal the whole time, which was nice. I think hearing your family argue shocked her."

"If she brings it up, you might want to tell her that we're just like everyone else. We get mad and we get over it. My grandfather likes to throw people out of the family for weeks at a time. Eventually all is forgiven and life returns to normal. At least as normal as we get."

Sam kissed the top of her head. "I wish there was something I could do."

"I appreciate that. But to quote someone we both know, you didn't sign up for this kind of trouble."

He looked at her. "Francesca, you've been the only life raft I've had to cling to these days. If you hadn't been around when Kelly showed up, I don't know what would have happened."

His words made her smile. "Thanks."

"That's my point. So now it's my turn. I want to help. I might not know much about raising kids or extended families, but I'm in security. I have access to some interesting databases. I'm sure I could find your brother."

She drew back so she could stare at him. "You know how to do that?"

He grinned. "I'm the best."

"And modest." She considered the offer. "Let me check with my parents, before I tell you for sure, but I can't imagine they wouldn't want to get in touch with him. Now that he's not a secret, he should be a part of the family." She touched his cheek. "I don't know how to thank you."

He shrugged. "You don't have to." His tawny gaze locked with hers. "You know what? I think we've changed the rules."

She swallowed. He couldn't have guessed about her pregnancy, could he? "In what way?"

"Our uncomplicated, monogamous, sex-only relationship has evolved into a friendship."

Oh. "I know."

"You okay with that?"

"Yes." Right up until he went ballistic when he found out about the baby.

"Me, too." He leaned forward and brushed his mouth against hers. "More than okay."

She felt the exact moment the tender kiss became passionate. Heat flared and his hug tightened slightly. Low in her belly, muscles tensed.

Despite the trauma, the questions, the knowledge that she was going to have to come clean, she couldn't help responding to Sam's closeness, his touch. There was a whisper of guilt, but she pushed it away with the promise that she would tell the truth in a few days. Just a few days of him still liking her, wanting her, and everything being the same between them.

"Francesca," he breathed as he slid his hand down her back to her hip, then up to her breast. "Am I pushing you with this?"

His question filled her with warmth. Not the heat of

passion but the comforting protection of tender concern.

Instead of answering directly, she covered his hand with hers and squeezed. His fingers closed around her breast.

"My bed is smaller than yours," she murmured. "That means we're going to have to be a lot closer. I hope you don't mind."

He sighed heavily, then pressed his mouth to her neck. "The sacrifices I make to satisfy you."

"Every one of them is appreciated."

He licked and kissed his way down to her collarbone. She arched her head back, giving him room, encouraging his attentions. At the same time he cupped her breasts and rubbed his thumbs against her sensitive, tight nipples.

The contact was exquisite. Fire roared through her, melting her from the inside out. Her panties were already damp, her body swollen. She wanted and needed with a fierceness that matched the first time they'd been together. Somehow she would have thought that intensity would fade some with time, but it hadn't.

When he tugged at the hem of her T-shirt, she helped him. She was the one who unfastened her bra and pulled it off. Sam dipped his head and drew her sensitive nipples into his mouth.

The sensual tugging made her catch her breath. She clutched at his head.

"Don't stop," she gasped as her body clenched in pleasure.

Even as he continued to caress her breasts, he dropped his hands to her hips and urged her to straddle him. She moved over him, then settled her dampness against his thick erection.

Even through the layers of his clothing, she felt the

pulsing need of his arousal. He wanted her as much as she wanted him. His rapid breathing told her, as did the urgency in his hands as he squeezed her and drew her closer. Suddenly he pulled away.

"Condom," he gasped.

Her first thought was that they didn't need to bother. Her second was there were other reasons to be protected. Her third was that she didn't want to have that conversation right now.

Fortunately their decision to become lovers had propelled her to the drugstore, where she'd bought a box of protection. Just in case Sam ever visited.

"Get naked," she said as she stood and hurried into her bedroom. She found the box in her nightstand and tore it open. Clutching a condom in her hand, she returned to the living room, where she found a very undressed Sam sprawled on her sofa.

She slowed as she took in the broad chest, flat belly, and impressive erection. Pausing only to slip out of her shorts and briefs, she tossed him the package, then waited until he had sheathed himself before straddling him again.

They resumed their positions, his mouth on her breast, her hands on his shoulders, his hands on her hips. But this time when she lowered herself, he slipped inside of her.

Her body shivered in pleasure, as the familiar stretching, tensing, filling brought her to the edge. That, combined with the gentle tugging of his mouth on her nipples, made her want to scream. It was too much and she never wanted any of it to stop.

"Oh, Sam," she breathed as she raised and lowered herself. She wrapped her arms around his neck and tried to hang on to control. It would just be too embarrassing to come this quickly.

But she couldn't stop herself. Everything felt too good.

The hands on her hips urged her to go faster and faster still. Friction increased, as did tension. And then she would have done anything, said anything, because when her body convulsed into perfect release she could only ride him, crying out his name until he stiffened and lost himself in his own orgasm.

The waves of pleasure slowed, receded, then faded. She leaned back, just as he looked at her. Neither of them smiled, neither of them spoke. The connection between them lingered, growing in the silence until she wanted to crawl inside of Sam and be as much a part of him as his heart or his blood.

She didn't know what the feelings meant, and they scared the crap out of her. Still, when he rubbed his thumb against her mouth and asked if she would like to spend the day with him and Kelly, she could only nod mutely and hold him close.

Kelly sat in the front seat of the truck and glanced at Francesca from under her lashes. Francesca had been quiet all morning. While she always claimed *not* to be a morning person, she'd never been this out of it before.

"Are you, um, okay?" she asked at last.

Francesca glanced at her and offered a sad smile. "Sorry. I have a lot on my mind."

Kelly thought about the angry conversation she'd overheard at the Fourth of July party nearly a week before.

"Is your family fighting?" She shifted uncomfortably. "I wasn't trying to spy or anything, I just—" She sighed. "You know. We sort of heard."

Francesca nodded. "I'm guessing everyone heard.

Things got a little loud." Her grip on the steering wheel tightened. "We're okay now, but things were a little shaky for a couple of days."

Kelly wanted to ask more, but knew it wasn't polite. Normally being polite wasn't a high priority, but she liked Francesca and was really trying.

"My folks started dating while they were still in high school," Francesca said. "Neither set of parents approved."

"Why?" Kelly asked. "Everybody in your family loves each other."

"That's what I thought. Apparently things were different before. Back then they faced a lot of disapproval. They refused to break up and started dating secretly. Then my mom got pregnant."

Kelly caught her breath. "Wow. Her mom and dad must have been really mad."

Francesca smiled. "I doubt they were happy. They ended up sending my mom away to a special place for pregnant girls. After she had her baby, he was given up for adoption. That was thirty years ago. We've been talking about the situation, and we've decided we're going to try to find him and bring him back into the family. Your dad offered to help with that. Apparently security experts can also find people."

Kelly was less impressed by her father's abilities than what Francesca's parents had done. "They gave their baby away?" She knew people did that sort of thing. Of course they did. But she'd never known anyone who was adopted or anyone who'd let their baby be taken away. The thought of it made her feel cold inside.

"From what my mom said, they didn't have a choice. It's sad for everyone."

Kelly didn't like to think about being abandoned. She

wasn't sure she'd ever spent one whole day feeling safe and wanted. Not with her mom and not now with her dad.

They pulled up in front of the ballet school. When Francesca turned into the parking lot, Kelly touched her arm. "You don't have to stay. I'm going home with Cindy. Dad said it was okay."

Francesca hesitated, then shrugged. "Okay. Have fun."

"I will."

Francesca watched Kelly as she headed for the side entrance. Despite being only twelve, the girl moved with a grace that made Francesca envious. When Kelly waved and disappeared into the building, Francesca backed out of the parking lot, then headed home.

Once there she flipped through her dissertation. Her mind raced with thoughts of her long-lost brother, the paper she should be working on, and her pregnancy. Nearly another week had passed. At some point she was going to have to come clean with Sam. And she would. Very soon. Just as soon as she figured out what to say.

She finally settled down to work about eleven. At three-thirty the phone rang.

"Hello?"

"Is Kelly with you?" Sam asked abruptly.

"No, she's—"

He cut her off with a strangled growl. "If she's not with you and she's not home, where the hell is she?"

Francesca arrived at Sam's place less than twenty minutes later. She walked into the house and found him pacing the length of the entryway.

"I haven't heard from her," he said, obviously furious

and worried in equal measures. "Who is this Cindy person and why didn't you get a phone number?"

Francesca wasn't willing to take the fall on this one. "She said you had told her it was fine. I assumed you had."

Sam had pulled off his suit jacket and tie and rolled up his sleeves. Even without all the trappings of success, he still looked powerful and angry.

"She told you I said it was okay and you believed her?" he asked, sounding incredulous. "We're talking about a kid who thinks nothing of lying to get her own way."

Francesca refused to be intimidated by his size or his temper. "When has she lied? To the best of my knowledge, Kelly is completely upfront about her wants and desires. Are you saying this morning she didn't ask you about going to Cindy's and you didn't say it was all right?"

He opened his mouth, then closed it. Rage faded from his eyes.

She put her hands on her hips. Now it was her turn to glare. "What?"

He turned away and walked into the kitchen. "I was reading the paper this morning," he mumbled.

She followed him. "So?" Then the pieces clicked into place. "Oh. You were reading and not listening. In fact, you can't remember one thing your daughter may or may not have said. So for all you know she *did* tell you about going to Cindy's. You might have even agreed."

"Couldn't you at least have gotten a phone number?" he asked, turning to face her.

"Couldn't you have at least listened for thirty seconds?"

"I listened."

"Obviously not. Kelly is your child and your responsibility."

"You think I don't know that?" he yelled. "I can't take

a breath without thinking about it. I didn't ask for this responsibility, but I'm doing the best I can. Everything about my life is different, with no warning, no explanation."

Francesca tried not to panic. Sam hadn't actually come out and said he didn't want his child, but he'd skated close to it. Close enough to make her press a protective hand over her stomach. This was not good.

Just then the front door opened. "I'm home," Kelly called. "Francesca, you're here. Did Sam call and ask you to—"

Kelly walked into the kitchen and looked from Sam to Francesca and back. "What?" she asked, suddenly looking wary.

"Did you ask permission to go to Cindy's this morning?" Sam demanded.

Francesca winced at his harsh, accusing tone.

Kelly took a step back. "Of course I did and you said it was fine. I even wrote down her telephone number."

Sam blinked. "You did what?"

Kelly stalked over to the pad by the phone and pulled off the top sheet. She carried it back to her father and slapped it down on the counter next to him.

"Well, hell," Sam muttered. "I guess I overreacted."

Kelly's gaze narrowed. "Why are you all mad? I didn't do anything wrong."

"I know," Sam said. "I came home early and when you weren't here, I got worried. When I called Francesca, she said you were at a friend's, and I didn't remember us talking about it."

Kelly took a step back. "You weren't listening to me?" she asked, sounding both insulted and hurt. "Was I too *boring?*"

"Of course not. I was—"

She cut him off with a shake of her head. "You were reading your damn paper."

"Don't you swear, young lady."

"Why not? You don't listen. I thought you were different!" she yelled. "I thought you weren't like her. But you are. You're a lousy parent. You're horrible. I hate you!"

Sam stepped toward her. "Kelly, I'm sorry I hurt your feelings. I never meant to."

"You didn't hurt my feelings. I don't care anything about you. No, that's not true. I'm sorry you're my father. I wish you weren't. I wish I'd never come here."

She ran out of the room. Francesca hesitated, not sure if she should go after her.

Sam leaned against the counter and rubbed his eyes. "That would be my parental screwup for the day. Why can't I get control of this situation? I can manage everything else in my life. Why not Kelly?"

"If you talked to her—" she began.

"I don't want to talk to her." Sam walked to the refrigerator and took out a can of soda. "I don't want to have to deal with any of this. I want things like they were before she ever showed up."

He offered her the can. Francesca could barely breathe, but she managed to shake her head. Her throat was tight, her heart heavy. She'd known Sam was still adjusting to having Kelly around, but she'd thought he was coming to care about his daughter.

"Unless you need me to stick around," she murmured, "I should be going."

"I'm sorry I called in a panic," he said.

"You were worried. That's okay."

He walked her to the door. Francesca said a quick goodbye and hurried to her truck. She had to get away before she gave into the need to burst into tears. She'd been a fool, because in her heart of hearts, she'd actually hoped Sam might be happy about the baby. Now she knew he would consider the child nothing but an inconvenience and her little more than a liar who had tricked him into a situation he didn't want.

Sam waited an hour before heading up to Kelly's room. She didn't answer when he knocked, but the door wasn't locked. He considered that a good sign.

When he stepped inside, she was stretched out on the bed, her back to the door. He crossed the room and sat on the edge of the mattress.

"I'm sorry," he said. "I should have listened."

"It doesn't matter."

"Sure it does." He studied her red curls and the curve of her back. When she was going toe-to-toe with him, she seemed so grown-up, but here, curled up on her bed, she was small and defenseless. A child. His child.

He wanted to be in control, but Kelly was her own person. Maybe the best he could hope for was an alliance between them.

He smiled as he remembered plenty of fights with Gabriel. No doubt he'd been just as stubborn and difficult when he'd been growing up.

"What was it you called me before?" he asked. "A pinhead?"

She turned to face him. Her eyes were swollen and red, her face damp from her tears. The sight of her pain stabbed him right in the gut.

"A butthead," she whispered.

"Hmm. I'm not sure I'm comfortable with that. How

about if you call me a pinhead, I promise to listen, and we're even?"

Kelly stared at him without speaking.

He leaned toward her and lightly touched the back of her hand. "I'm really sorry. You followed the rules. You asked for permission, you left a phone number, you even told Francesca. I was wrong."

"You want to buy me a DVD player to make up for what you did?" she asked with a sniff.

"No. But I know a great rib restaurant that has a pretty cool video game room in back. I'll front you five bucks' worth of quarters."

"It's not a DVD player."

"I'm aware of that."

She sat up. "Thanks for apologizing."

"You're welcome."

"Are these Chicago-style ribs?"

He groaned. "They're ribs. Meat, bone, barbecue sauce. Just ribs."

Kelly sighed. "You don't have to have a hissy fit just because you don't know what kind they are."

He growled. She giggled, then smiled. Without thinking, he held open his arms. Kelly stared at him as if he'd turned into a rat. But just as he was about to lower his arms, she moved close.

He hugged her, and for the first time since she'd shown up on his doorstep, he felt how small she was. Thin and frail. But full of life. His daughter, he thought with pride. His child.

14

The late morning sun was warm as Francesca adjusted her straw hat and wove her way through the row of grapevines.

"What are these?" she asked her sister.

Brenna stopped walking and pressed her lips together in an expression of disgust. "I can't believe you don't know the different kinds of grapes."

"They're red," Francesca said helpfully.

"Wow. You can do your colors. What's next? Shapes?"

"Hey, don't mock my intelligence," Francesca told her. "I was the slow learner, remember? I'm very sensitive about my abilities."

Brenna shook her head. "That was nearly twenty years ago. Since then you've gone to college, graduated summa cum laude with a bachelor's degree, and you're in a Ph.D. program. That 'I'm not the smart one' card doesn't play anymore."

Francesca started to protest, then stopped herself. She still remembered her frustration at being unable to read while everyone else in her class caught on so quickly. She'd been nine before she'd suddenly figured out what the jumble of letters meant and saw they could form words and sentences and entire thoughts. No one knew what had caused her learning disability. A few doctors had speculated there was a part of her brain that had simply taken longer to mature. Regardless, she's spent a lot of years feeling stupid and slow.

Had that really been almost twenty years ago? When she thought of it in those terms, she was forced to admit she'd come a long way.

"So now I'm smarter than you," she said, teasing her sister.

Brenna bent over and checked the trellis holding the grapevine in place. "Not about growing grapes or making wine."

"Good point."

Brenna straightened. "And we're both idiots when it comes to men. Unless you've improved through practicing on Sam?"

Francesca didn't want to think about him. "Not really."

"We won't even get into the family problems."

"I think we should. We have to talk about it, Brenna."

Her twin shrugged. "Is that why you came by?"

"It's part of the reason. I've been worried about you."

About them both. There was so much going on right now. Francesca didn't think she could handle one more thing.

"They want Sam to find him," Brenna said. "Mom already called him and he agreed."

Francesca wasn't surprised. She'd passed along Sam's offer. Her parents had still been in shock, but when that faded, she knew they would want to get in touch with their firstborn.

"Did he tell you they'd accepted?" Brenna asked.

Francesca glanced at the rows of grapevines. "No, but we haven't actually seen that much of each other in the past week or so."

Not since Kelly had gone to spend the afternoon with a friend and Sam had gone ballistic.

"Do I want to know why?"

"Different reasons."

"That sounds ominous."

Francesca brushed aside her concern. "That's not important. I've been worried about you. About how you're handling all this. Grandpa Lorenzo talking about selling was one thing. It could have been a lot of bluster on his part. But finding out about another child . . ."

Brenna plucked at a leaf. "Not just a child. A grandson. Our sexist grandfather is so happy he positively beams. I'm guessing he has visions of bringing the long-lost man into the folds of family and teaching him all he needs to know to run Marcelli Wines."

Francesca wanted to say that wasn't possible, except she knew it was. It might even be likely. "Maybe he won't be interested."

Brenna's expression tightened. "Marcelli Wines is worth about forty million dollars. Would you walk away from that?"

Francesca swallowed. "Forty million?" She'd known the land and the vines had value, but that much? "Tell me again why I'm scrimping and saving to put myself through college."

Brenna smiled. "Because you have integrity, kid."

"Oh, right. Think I could get a cash advance on my inheritance?"

"You're probably going to have to talk to your brother about that."

A brother. She still couldn't believe it. "They should have told us a long time ago. We would have understood."

"It wouldn't have hurt so badly," Brenna murmured.

Francesca agreed. Keeping secrets created trouble, which was something she'd been telling herself.

"Are you going to tell me what's wrong?" Brenna asked.

"Nothing. Why?"

"You've been acting weird since the Fourth. And don't tell me it's about our long-lost brother, because you were weird before that."

Francesca tried to smile. "Gee, thanks for the endorsement."

"You know what I mean. I can tell there's something off. So what is it? Did you go and fall for Sam? Are you starting to think that marriage might not be such a bad thing?"

Her sister's guess was so far from the truth that Francesca laughed. "Not even close. I'm—"

Brenna waited.

Francesca sighed. Maybe it was time to come clean, if not to Sam then to her twin sister. "I'm pregnant."

Her twin's eyes widened and her mouth dropped open. "Holy shit! Are you kidding?"

"No. I took a pregnancy test about ten days ago, and it was positive. I haven't gotten my period since, so there's no reason to think anything has changed."

Brenna leaned over the row of grapes and hugged her. "Wow. This is so amazing. You're going to have a baby!" She straightened. "Okay, so this isn't exactly how you had your life plan set up. I know you don't want a husband, but kids are different. Aren't you thrilled?"

"I don't know."

Brenna smiled. "You should be. A baby! Remember how

we used to talk about how many kids we'd have and how they'd all grow up playing with each other, like you, me, and Katie did? How we'd take them to that grove of trees and let them play dress-up? You're having a baby!"

Francesca touched her still-flat stomach. "Honestly, Brenna, I don't know what I feel. I'm scared, I'm excited, I'm worried. And if we're going to have our kids all playing together, then you'd better get a bun in the oven of your own."

Brenna grimaced. "That would require me having sex, and right now that's not likely to happen. But with Katie getting married, there will be cousins for your little one."

Brenna stopped talking and sucked in a breath. "You haven't told Sam yet, have you?"

She shook her head. "I don't know what to say."

Brenna stared at her. "How about something along the lines of 'Hey, big guy. One of your little tadpoles got a bit too frisky.' "

Despite her emotional angst, she couldn't help smiling. "You really want me to call him 'big guy' and refer to his sperm as tadpoles?"

"Maybe not." Brenna turned toward the winery. "This is sure going to change your life."

"Tell me about it."

"So why haven't you told him?" Brenna asked.

"A lot of reasons. For one thing, I've been in shock. We used a condom. I know they're not a hundred percent effective, but having me get pregnant the first night seems really unfair."

Brenna looked at her. "That's a pretty lousy argument."

"Agreed. I'm . . . scared. At first I didn't want to say anything because he was dealing with Kelly showing up in his life and—"

Brenna swore. "Kelly! I'd forgotten all about her. Oh, kid, you are in big trouble. Practically the same week Sam finds out he's the father of a teenager, you turn up pregnant. Talk about lousy timing."

"You're not making me feel better," Francesca told her. "But you're also right. That's why I waited. I didn't want to dump this on him, and I was still getting used to the idea myself. Then I found out we had a brother and it's been crazy."

"And?"

Francesca sighed. "And Sam is having a tough time adjusting to Kelly. She's a great kid, but a handful. Last week he got really angry and said some things about her disrupting his life and how he didn't ask for the responsibility."

"If he doesn't want Kelly, he's not going to want your baby?"

Francesca wasn't surprised Brenna understood. "Yeah. Plus, things have been really good with Sam and telling him is going to change all of that."

"You think?"

"I'm so screwed," Francesca muttered.

"You're also not 'fessing up to the most important part."

"What?"

Brenna stopped walking and faced her. "You don't want to tell Sam because you don't want to hear what he has to say. Not because he's going to reject your child, but because you have this fantasy in mind. One in which he sweeps you off your feet and confesses undying love."

Francesca rolled her eyes. "That's so much bull."

"Is it? You're nearly as romantic as Katie. You're like the middle child, seeing everyone's point of view, rescuing the world. Sam is a great guy. After years of not wanting a man in your life, you finally hook up with him and he's terrific. Sexy, smart, successful. It's okay if you fall for him."

"I didn't fall for him. I don't love him. I don't want anything from him but sex. Now we're having a child and that complicates everything."

"No way," Brenna told her. "The baby is just logistics. If you weren't worried about getting hurt, you would have told him. You have to work out details like custody. If your heart weren't engaged, stuff like that wouldn't matter."

Francesca didn't like anything her sister was saying. "You're wrong."

"You don't want to admit I'm right because it scares the crap out of you and because you don't like me figuring out something about you that you couldn't figure out yourself. It violates your view of yourself as psychologically superior."

The verbal slam caught Francesca like a blow. "That is so unfair."

Brenna shrugged. "It's true. You planned this whole affair with Sam as if you were shopping for a wardrobe. Oh, you need a little black dress, so go to the stores until you find the right one. But this isn't a dress. It's sex. And you're not shallow enough to give your body without your heart being engaged."

"It's not about being shallow. It's about being sensible. I don't want a man in my life right now."

"According to you, you don't want one ever. You're afraid, Francesca. Like I said, it's been twenty years since you were the dumb kid in class, but you can't let that go. I remember you crying yourself to sleep because you felt stupid. And when you confessed your fears to our wonderful, caring Grandfather, he told you not to worry yourself. That you were so pretty some nice man would always be around to take care of you. Which Todd did and you hated."

Francesca wanted to run away. Why was Brenna turning on her? What was going on?

"This is all old information, and it doesn't have anything to do with Sam."

"It has everything to do with Sam. You got scared, Francesca, and I don't blame you. For so long you were afraid you couldn't measure up. Todd acted as if you had the mental acuity of a stamp. He wanted you to shut up and look pretty, which you did. But you weren't allowed to be a person. You've spent the last six years becoming your own person. Of course you're afraid of being with a man again. All your life you've been told that only the men matter. That we have to take care of them. If you get involved with Sam, you risk losing yourself."

"I'm not involved, and I haven't lost myself."

"You're not *going* to lose yourself," Brenna told her, obviously annoyed. "That's my damn point. You're not that insecure teenager anymore. You're a successful woman. You're confident and capable, and it's okay to admit you care about Sam."

"I don't care!" Francesca yelled. "I'm not involved! I'm just pregnant!"

A sharp intake of air made them both turn. Francesca nearly fainted when she saw her grandfather standing not five feet away from them. She and Brenna had been so busy arguing, they hadn't heard him approach.

Panic flared, and with it a sense of her life spinning out of control. Just when she'd decided it couldn't get any worse, she was fighting with her sister and had just spilled her secret to the person least likely to keep it quiet.

"Don't say a word," she told her grandfather. "You didn't hear that."

The old man wasn't the least bit impressed with her instructions.

"Is it Sam? That young man who was over at the party?"

She couldn't lie and she didn't want to tell the truth. "Grandpa, this is my problem and I'll deal with it."

His gaze narrowed. "Men who get women pregnant have a responsibility."

"No. You're not talking to Sam. I mean it. You're not to say anything. I'll handle this."

"He should marry you."

"No, he shouldn't. And he doesn't know about the baby yet, so don't you even think about telling him. Grandpa, you can't!"

It was like bargaining with the weather. No matter how much energy she put into the process, she had absolutely no control over the outcome.

He didn't say anything. Instead he looked from her to Brenna, then turned and started for the winery.

Francesca folded her arms over her midsection. "This is bad. This is really, really bad."

"It's worse," Brenna said. "Sam and Kelly have been invited to dinner tomorrow night."

"I thought we'd head out to the mission," Gabriel said as he settled on a kitchen chair.

Kelly put down her spoon and pushed her cereal bowl away. "You don't have to worry about me," she said. "I'll be fine on my own."

"Nonsense. You and I can take the day to get to know each other better."

Kelly wasn't sure about that. She thought her great-grandfather might like her more if they *didn't* get to know each other. "The new nanny starts the day after tomorrow. With my dance class canceled for the day, I can just hang out. You don't have to bother."

"It's no bother." Gabriel leaned his cane against the table. "I've made reservations for a boat cruise this afternoon. It goes over to the Channel Islands. They're just south of here."

She eyed the tall, white-haired man sitting across from her. She could kind of see bits of her dad in him. Gabriel wasn't exactly friendly, but he wasn't too scary. The odd-smelling Doreen's last day had been the previous Friday. Sam had stayed home yesterday, and Gabriel was with her today, while Francesca was taking the Wednesday shift. Kelly had lobbied for Francesca to take care of her the whole week, but Sam had said they'd bothered her enough already.

Kelly didn't like the sound of that. She'd thought Sam was interested in Francesca and that they might want to get married or something. Kelly wouldn't mind having Francesca around more. Sometimes her dad was okay, but sometimes he made her crazy.

Now she had a grandfather to deal with.

"Are you going to be all right on a boat?" she asked. "Is it safe?"

Gabriel drew his bushy, white eyebrows together. "Are you saying I'm too *old* to go on a boat?"

"I don't know. Are you?"

"I'll have you know, young lady, I've forgotten more about boats than you'll ever learn."

"If you've forgotten it, then you're not going to be much help, are you?"

The words were out before Kelly could stop them. She flinched slightly, waiting for Gabriel to get mad. Sam would never believe it, but she'd really been working hard to think before she spoke. With Tanya nothing had ever mattered because her mother was too busy with her own life to care. But here things seemed to be different. Fortunately Gabriel only chuckled.

"Good point," he said with a grin. "Good news that I'm not the captain, eh?"

She nodded.

"You been on a boat before?" he asked.

"One of the maids took me on that tour around Manhattan once. It was pretty cool to see the whole city that way."

"Where was your mother while this was going on?"

"I don't know. Out, I guess."

He frowned. "You miss her?"

Kelly considered the question. "It's weird to be here instead of there, you know? But miss her?" She shrugged.

Not really. She'd never spent any time with Tanya. The staff were always taking her places, not her mother.

Here it was different. Sam was in her face all the time, but he wasn't so bad. Maybe he didn't spoil her, and she really hated not having a DVD player, but they had some good times. They'd started going out to dinner a few nights a week. Different places with different kinds of food. And they'd gone to the movies. He'd refused to take her shopping, but he'd promised the next nanny would. And honestly, thinking of Sam in the teen department of a mall store was kind of funny.

"Your father's a good man," Gabriel said.

"You're his grandfather. You have to like him."

"You're his daughter."

"I guess." She turned her spoon over in the bowl. "I don't really know him."

"You'll get there. And he'll get to know you."

His words were meant to reassure, but they made Kelly feel all cold inside. Staring at a few floating bits of cereal, she cleared her throat. "What about after?" she asked, her voice quiet. "When he sends me away. Do you think it will be to a boarding school or something?"

It was the thought of the "something" that terrified her the most.

"What the hell are you talking about? Sam's not sending you anywhere."

Kelly looked at her great-grandfather. "My mom said he'd probably keep me around for a couple of years and then he'd send me away when I got to be too much trouble. Maybe one of those boarding school places or even to a dance school. I guess that would be okay."

The last bit was more to convince herself than because she believed it. She didn't want to go anywhere. She wanted to be a part of a family. She wanted to feel safe.

"Do you want to go away?" Gabriel asked.

Kelly opened her mouth, then stunned both of them by bursting into tears.

"Silly girl," he muttered as he shifted his chair close to hers and drew her against him. "This is where you live now. I know it's hard to adjust, especially with your mother dumping you like this. But we're your family now. You're stuck with us."

Kelly wanted to believe him. Really. "Sam gets mad at me."

"Of course he does. I used to get so angry with him that

I wanted to lock him in his room forever. But I got over it. Then he screwed up again. It's what kids do. Think of it as your job."

He smelled of peppermint and sports cream. His arms were thinner than Sam's, but being in them made her feel just as safe. She raised her head and looked at him. "Yeah?"

"Absolutely." He brushed her hair off her forehead. "My late wife was one of the most beautiful women I ever had the pleasure of knowing. Whenever we'd walk down the street, the other men would watch her and wonder how somebody like me got so lucky. Want to know a secret?"

Kelly swiped away her tears. "What?"

"You look just like her. She had red curls and green eyes, too."

Wonder filled her. Wonder and something light and warm that made it feel as if her heart was floating. "Even freckles?"

"Especially freckles. Freckles just like yours."

Francesca parked in front of the hacienda. Kelly raced toward the backdoor and burst inside, but Francesca was slower to follow. If she hadn't had Kelly for the day, she might not have had the courage to show up at all. Except with Sam due for dinner, she hadn't had a choice. There was no way she could let him face her family without her first knowing what they knew and what they planned to say.

Oh, but she didn't want to go inside. Not now. If Grandpa Lorenzo had told anyone . . . She leaned her forehead against the steering wheel. *If?* Was there any alternative universe in which he *wouldn't* spread the news? She wouldn't be surprised to find her father standing just inside the door, a shotgun in one hand and a list of available priests in the other.

The only bright spot was that she knew no one would say anything to Kelly. Her family would never hurt or upset the girl. If only they felt that way about their adult daughters, she thought wryly.

Unable to avoid the inevitable, she climbed out of the truck and made her way to the house.

The kitchen was the usual chaos. Even though it was only early afternoon, the Grands were in the midst of preparing dinner. Pots bubbled, vegetables lay on the countertops, and something delicious baked in the oven. Her mother stood with Kelly, next to Katie, who was sitting at the table and working on a list. As she entered, they all turned to look at her. There was a second of silence, and in that second she knew that they knew. Francesca braced herself against the need to bolt.

"Hi," Francesca said weakly.

Her grandmothers rushed forward to embrace her. When she'd been squeezed, hugged, and cheek-pinched, Grammy M offered tea and Grandma Tessa told her to sit "and take a load off your feet."

As the baby wasn't even as big as a pencil eraser, worrying about her carrying around extra weight seemed excessive, but Francesca knew they all meant well. She tried to look on the bright side, but all she could think about was what was going to happen when Sam arrived.

Katie gave her a sympathetic look, then rose. "Kelly, I'm going to start beading the train. Want to help?"

Kelly grinned. "Sure. You mean you'd really let me sew on your dress?"

"Absolutely. There's a special pattern for around the hem. I thought you'd like to work on that."

"Wow. Okay. Great!"

Katie led the girl from the kitchen. Francesca watched her go with a sense of impending doom. Her mother crossed the kitchen, stopped in front of her, and reached for her hands.

"How far along are you?"

She'd been a fool ever to hope Grandpa Lorenzo had kept her secret for a second. "Did he run right back to the house to tell you or did he announce it at dinner?" she asked.

Grandma Tessa frowned. "Lorenzo is very worried about you. We all are."

"Francesca, darlin'," Grammy M murmured. "Are you feelin' all right? Are you happy about the wee one?"

"I'm dealing with it." She couldn't commit to *happy*. Not when she was still floundering in *confused*.

"Does Sam know?" her mother asked.

"No. And I don't want any of you to tell him."

Her mother looked disapproving. "Francesca, if he's the father—"

"Of course he's the father. I don't go around sleeping with more than one guy at a time. And for the record, there haven't been any other guys in a long time, okay?"

Grandma Tessa pulled out her rosary and started murmuring. Francesca crossed to the table and sank into a chair. This was not going well.

"I know I have to tell Sam and I will. I just need a little more time to sort some things through."

"Don't be takin' too long," Grammy M said. "The weddin'—"

Francesca stared at her. "There isn't going to be a wedding. Let's make that clear. No marriage. No Mr. and Mrs. I'll be having the child on my own."

The three women looked as if they'd just witnessed a murder. They were stunned, shocked, and more than a little disapproving.

"If you're concerned about Sam, your father will be happy to have a talk with him," her mother said.

"No!" Francesca rose. "No talking. No anything. This is my life and you're not to interfere. Do you understand?"

"Francesca—" her mother began.

"No. I'm going to make my own decision. I don't want you to get involved. I mean it."

The three women looked at one another, then back at her and nodded. Francesca knew it was the best she could hope for. They had agreed not to interfere, but that didn't mean she believed them.

Sam exited the freeway for the two-lane highway that would take him to the hacienda. The late July afternoon was warm and clear—perfect California weather. While he should be back in his office, dealing with any number of crises that were bound to crop up in his absence, here he was playing hooky instead. The thing was, there wasn't anything he would rather be doing.

He was even willing to admit the reason for his good mood—he couldn't wait to see Francesca. Since the party on the Fourth, nearly three weeks ago, they'd barely spent any time together. Between his work, getting to know Kelly, Francesca's need to work on her dissertation, and a five-day crisis involving the kidnapped son of a French banker, they hadn't had much time alone.

Funny how in the past couple of weeks he'd found himself missing her. He missed talking to her, listening to her. He missed the sound of her laughter and looking at her across the dinner table. He missed her in his bed.

At first he'd been able to ignore the ache inside, but it hadn't gone away. If anything it had gotten worse. Deeper, darker, more uncomfortable. He wanted to see her smile. He wanted to touch her face, kiss her, tease her, see her blush, watch her taking care of his daughter.

Basically, he had it bad.

Telling himself all the reasons he shouldn't get involved didn't seem to be helping. He didn't want to believe he was thinking with the wrong head, but there didn't seem to be another explanation.

So here he was, driving to the hacienda, grateful her family had insisted. They'd wanted to thank him for looking for their son. He glanced at the file folder on the passenger seat. To make the visit more official, he'd brought along what he'd been able to find out about the Marcelli's firstborn.

He turned from the highway onto the long private road that led to the house. The grapes had grown since his last visit. Heavy clusters swelled in the afternoon light. He rolled down the window and inhaled the scent of earth and fruit. There was a heady sweetness in the air. The promise of harvest only a few weeks away. At least, that's what it smelled like to him, he thought with a grin. Like he knew anything about making wine.

He was still chuckling as he parked the car in the driveway behind the hacienda. He cut the engine and stepped out in the shade. The afternoon was still and quiet. Santa Barbara wasn't a huge city, but it was a major metropolis when compared with the solitary splendor of the hacienda.

"Sam?"

He turned and saw Brenna walking toward him. She

wore shorts and a T-shirt, with a large hat covering her head. The wide brim protected her face.

He studied her as she approached, looking for similarities between her and her twin. Their eyes were the same shape, but different colors. Francesca's features were more of a blend of the two families, while Brenna had inherited Italian features from the Marcelli side. She was full-breasted and full-hipped to Francesca's slender lines. Her beauty was less obvious than her sister's but just as powerful.

"I know you're not here to help with Katie's dress," she said when she stopped in front of him.

"Is that what they're doing? Working on the dress?"

Brenna grinned. "It's a real estrogen fest in there. Want to take a walk until they're ready to break? I suspect if you go in too soon, they'll put you to work."

He shuddered. "I'm not into beads."

"As your daughter would say, well, duh. Come on. I'll let you admire my grapes."

He followed her back the way he'd come. She headed into the rows of vines closest to the house, pausing every now and then to bend down and study the growing clusters.

"We're having a good year," she said. "So far."

"Could that change?"

"Sure. In a heartbeat. Too much sun, not enough sun, rain at the wrong time, no rain, too much rain. If it gets too cold, too hot, too foggy."

"Sounds like you're lucky to get any harvest at all."

"Some years we are." She stepped back and pointed to the grapes. "Chardonnay."

"How do you know when they're ready?"

"Experience. This is my first harvest in a long time, so I'm a little nervous."

Sam frowned. "I thought you were the sister who was completely into the vineyard. Francesca told me you love it here."

Brenna shrugged. "That's true, but what she apparently forgot to mention is that I'm also an idiot."

She started walking and he followed along. Several questions came to mind, but he didn't want to go anywhere dangerous. Just when he was about to change the subject, she started talking again.

"Per family expectations I got married when I was eighteen. Jeff was just entering medical school, and someone had to pay the bills. He was at UCLA, so I couldn't be married to him and still work here. So over the course of a few years I became less and less involved with the winery. Life went on, I missed it, but I knew my place was with my husband."

She glanced at him. "That would be the idiot part."

"Because the marriage didn't work out?"

She nodded. "I became a twenty-seven-year-old cliché. Dr. Jeff left the wife who had supported him all those years and took up with a younger woman. They're getting married in a couple of months."

"I'm sorry."

"I'm just plain relieved to have it behind me." She shoved her hands into her shorts pockets. "I was too young to marry anyone. Even being with the right guy would have been a challenge. But family expectations can be a real pain in the ass."

There was something in her tone of voice that caught his attention. "What are you trying to tell me?"

Brenna shrugged. "My parents are pretty anchored in this century, but not the Grands and Grandpa Lorenzo. They don't take to newfangled ideas. They're traditional."

"Are they concerned because I divorced Kelly's mother?"

"What? No. It's just—" Brenna pressed her lips together. "I love my sister. She's annoying at times, but I love her. They love her, too. You're a single guy with a daughter. Francesca's single. There's been talk."

The lightbulb went on. He grinned. "You're warning me that they're not going to be subtle in their matchmaking."

She hesitated. "Something like that."

Before he could figure out an answer, Kelly ran out from the backdoor of the house, calling his name. She waved when she saw him and ran up to greet him.

"You're here!" she said, sounding delighted. "I've been working on the dress all afternoon. It's the most beautiful dress I've ever seen. We've been using shiny beads and little glass balls to make tiny flowers and a vine pattern. I haven't even pricked my finger once today, but Francesca did." She paused to suck in a breath. "She bled and everything, but Grammy M says she can get the stain out and Katie said she was sticking herself to get out of having to bead the dress because she's not very good at sewing, but she's good at lots of other stuff, so that's okay."

She stopped to breathe again. This time he laughed. "So you're bored and want to go home, right?"

"Not even close. I may never leave. I love it here. Francesca and her family are so cool."

A noise made him look up. He saw Francesca standing in the doorway of the house. She wore shorts and a shirt. Her hair was loose and a little messy. There was a Band-Aid on one finger and a smudge on her cheek. She shouldn't have looked beautiful. She shouldn't have looked anything.

In that second, as he stared at her and she stared back and their eyes locked together, fire flared. It burned bright and hot. In that heartbeat, all his determination to avoid messy relationships, to listen to his brain and not his hormones, faded away. He wanted her—in bed, out of bed, whatever was available he would take, and the hell with the consequences.

15

"S*am, would you help me for a second?"* Colleen asked.

"Sure." He followed her into the kitchen, where she put him to work washing tomatoes for the salad.

"I don't know what we're going to do with all the vegetables we have in the garden this year," she said as she peeled zucchini. "I hope you don't mind if we send you and Kelly home with a few pounds of our bounty. We're being overrun."

Sam held up the tomato he was washing. "Only if you send them with instructions for preparing them. Otherwise this is about all I can handle."

Colleen Marcelli, stylishly dressed in light-colored pants and a coordinating short-sleeved shirt, raised her eyebrows. "I thought Francesca could take care of that for you."

He thought of his recent warning from Brenna and held in a grin. "She's not at my house all that often, but when she is, I rarely put her to work in the kitchen. After all she's done to help me out with Kelly, I think it would show a lack of gratitude."

"I know Francesca enjoys spending time with your

daughter very much. She's always liked children. Then I suppose most women do."

He thought of his ex-wife. But then Tanya wasn't like most women.

Colleen finished with the zucchini and went to work on several red and yellow peppers. "You never remarried."

"No, ma'am."

Francesca's mother smiled at him. "I'm prying, I know. It's just . . ." She sighed. "I worry about my children. Francesca is very special. She deserves a world of happiness. Sometimes life gives us situations that at first don't seem ideal, but over time we come to see that it all worked out for the best."

Sam stared at her. When had he lost track of the conversation? "Mrs. Marcelli—"

"Colleen," she said with a smile. "Please."

"All right. Colleen. I think Francesca's great and I want her to be happy, as well."

"There's also Kelly. Being an only child can be so—"

"Mom!"

Sam looked up and saw Francesca standing in the doorway to the kitchen. Her eyes were flashing with temper.

"What are you doing?" she demanded.

Colleen ducked her head. "Sam and I were just talking."

"Then it's time for the conversation to be over." Francesca turned to him. "Come on. Let's take Kelly for a walk."

Sam wiped his hands on a paper towel and followed her out of the room. He didn't know what was going on, but there were enough undercurrents to float a ship in this place. He hadn't noticed them at the party. Was that because there'd been such a large crowd around, or had something happened in the past few weeks? Something other than the mystery brother. Something he didn't know about?

• • •

Nightmare didn't begin to describe dinner, Francesca thought when the meal was finally finished and the family moved into the living room. The family matchmaking had abandoned anything remotely subtle and risen right to hard sell. While Sam had laughed off most of the more obvious comments, she'd sensed his confusion as to the intensity of the attack. Her family was keeping her secret, but only just. If she didn't want the Grands to break out the yarn and start knitting receiving blankets in front of Sam, she was going to have to come clean and soon.

All decisions for another time, she thought, forcing her attention to the situation at hand. At dinner Sam had said he had news about the long-lost Marcelli son. Everyone gathered to hear what Sam had to say. They all watched as he opened the folder he'd set on the wood coffee table.

"I've found him," he said, addressing his words to her parents.

Her mother gasped and clutched her husband's hands. "So soon?"

"His name is Joe Larson. He was taken in by Cynthia and Joseph Larson when he was four days old. They lived in San Diego."

Francesca listened as Sam sketched out her brother's life. Where he went to elementary school, that he had no other siblings.

"His adoptive parents were killed when Joe was twelve."

Francesca froze. Her parents gasped, her mother began to cry, as did the Grands.

"He was alone?" Grandma Tessa asked.

Sam consulted his notes. "No other family members stepped forward. He went into foster care."

Her mother covered her face with her hands. "No. That's

not right. It can't be right. Why wouldn't they tell me?"

Sam didn't answer, but Francesca already knew the truth. When the baby had been given away, all rights and responsibilities had been lost. The state would have placed him with strangers rather than returning him to the mother who had decided she wasn't interested in raising her child.

Grandma Tessa pulled her rosary from her pocket and began to finger the beads. Grandpa Lorenzo paled. Sam continued to read from his report.

"Joe went into the Navy after high school. They tapped him for OCS right away. Officer Candidate School. A year after graduating, he entered Navy Seal training. That's what he does now. He's a Seal."

"Is there a picture?" her mother asked.

Sam reached forward and pulled it out, then passed it to her. She studied the photo for nearly a minute, before closing her eyes.

Francesca took the picture. A man in his late twenties stared back at her. She saw the likeness immediately, the blending of Irish and Italian features. He favored his father's side more than his mother's. He was good-looking. A stranger who was her brother.

Brenna stared over her shoulder. "He's really one of us," she said quietly.

"Was there any doubt?" Francesca asked.

"I was hoping for some," her sister admitted.

"You'll want to confirm the relationship with a DNA test," Sam said, "but it wasn't a difficult trail to follow. He's the missing Marcelli."

"We'll need to get in touch with him right away," Grandpa Lorenzo said as he took the picture. "Tell him who he is. He has a history here. A heritage."

"An inheritance," Brenna muttered.

The old man nodded.

"I don't know," her mother murmured. "It's been so long. He must hate us."

"He won't," her husband told her.

"Whatever he's feeling, this is going to be a shock," Francesca said, unable to imagine finding out she had an entire family somewhere. "Joe Larson has lived his life for thirty years without knowing about us. He'll need time to absorb everything. You can't just spring it on him. This needs to be planned out."

"There's no time," Grandpa Lorenzo said. "He's family. That's what matters."

Brenna stood and left without saying anything. Francesca watched her go. For Brenna, the arrival of a long-lost son was the death of a dream.

"Francesca is right," her mother said. "When I was sixteen I listened to all of you and did what you said. What I should have done was listened to my heart. This time Marco and I decide."

"He's not just your son," Grandpa Lorenzo said. "He's my grandson. He could be my heir."

"No."

Colleen and Marco rose to their feet.

"You'll stay out of it," Colleen said firmly. "We'll decide what we want to do."

She brushed away her tears and turned to Sam. "Thank you for finding him."

"I was happy to help. I'll leave the contact information here," he said as he dropped a card into the folder and handed it to her.

Kelly shifted next to her father. Francesca turned her attention to the girl and gave her a smile. "You okay?" she asked as her parents left the room.

Grandpa Lorenzo was still muttering. The Grands alternately hugged each other and wiped away tears.

"It's really weird," Kelly said. "I feel bad for everybody."

"Families are complicated," Francesca agreed.

"Do you think he's going to like finding out he has a family?"

"I don't know. I hope so."

"Are you happy about all this?"

"I think this information is going to change a lot of lives," Francesca said.

Kelly nodded. "Like when Tanya sent me to live with my dad." She glanced at Sam, who had risen and was talking with Lorenzo. "It was weird at first, but it's better now."

"I'm glad," Francesca said and meant it more than the girl could know. If Sam could adjust to life with Kelly, maybe he wouldn't freak out at the thought of having a second child. Or was that just wishful thinking?

Sam touched Kelly's shoulder. "Ready to head home?"

Kelly nodded and rose. "I want to say good-bye to the Grands and Katie."

As Kelly crossed to be with the rest of the family, Sam moved close to Francesca.

"How're you doing?" he asked.

"Fine. We're all in shock." She looked at him. "I'm sorry about tonight. I know my entire family went crazy with the matchmaking thing."

"I survived." He lowered his voice. "At the risk of facing a shotgun wedding, what are your plans for this weekend? I thought we could spend some quality time together." He leaned close. "Kelly and I are going to the beach Saturday afternoon, then she's staying at a friend's house for the night. I thought we could have a sleepover, too."

Francesca studied his face, the crinkles by his tawny

eyes, his easy smile. She was still trying to recover from his "shotgun wedding" remark. He had no idea how close he had skated to the truth.

A few more days, she thought. She would be with him a few more days. Next week she was watching Kelly, and that Friday, just over a week from now, she would tell Sam about the baby. It was past time.

"I'd like to spend the night," she told him with a smile, even as she knew it might be their last time together. "But only if I get to sleep on top."

The night was warm and they'd left the balcony doors open. Night creatures serenaded them with soft music, while their rapid breathing provided counterpoint and rhythm.

She stood with Sam in his bedroom. They'd made it that far without ravishing each other, but she had a feeling they couldn't hold out much longer.

The hand cupping her cheek moved slightly as long fingers stroked her skin. She wrapped her arms around his waist. His hard back muscles rippled at her touch. She moved her hands up and down, feeling his strength, the hard planes of his body.

She returned her attention to the still-chaste kiss. He'd kept the contact light, so it was up to her to entice him. She licked his lower lip. Instantly he groaned. She licked his lip again. He groaned. When he opened for her, she swept inside, eager to explore, to play, to excite. Anticipation swelled. Heat ignited in her belly before spiraling out and settling between her legs. When her tongue touched his, sparks flared. His taste, his warmth, the way he moved with her, the way they moved together. The opening moves of their sensual dance left her trembling and hungry.

He raised his other hand to her face and cupped her jaw. Suddenly he was back in charge. He deepened the kiss before closing his lips around her tongue and sucking gently. Pressure started between her legs, and her breasts began to ache.

She arched against him, wanting to be closer. She could feel the dampness of her swelling, the heat of her rising passion. Sam broke their kiss only to nibble his way along her jaw toward her ear. He licked the outside curve before sucking on the sensitive skin just below her lobe. His hands moved to her breasts.

"We're both way too dressed," he breathed.

"I agree. We should do something about that."

He kissed her collarbone just as his thumbs brushed over her tight nipples. She gasped. He cupped her breasts, squeezing gently. Her head fell back.

"In a second," he whispered. "I don't want to stop kissing you just yet."

His fingers circled her curves, then his thumbs flicked against her nipples again, and fire shot through her.

"Hell," he muttered.

With one swift, fluid move, he pulled his polo shirt free of his jeans and tugged it over his head. "Touch me," he said, taking her hands in his and placing them on his skin.

He was warm. The light dusting of hair tickled her palms and made her fingers tingle. While she explored hard, male contours, he went to work on the buttons down the front of her dress. Just as she had discovered the pleasure of stroking him from shoulder to waist, he pulled her dress over her arms. She straightened and the garment fell to the floor.

She stood there in bra and panties, along with her sandals, which she quickly kicked away. Sam skimmed his hands down to her breasts and cupped them. She sought out his erection. He was hard, long, and he flexed into her touch. She explored the length of him, then rubbed her thumb over the tip. He groaned, then kissed her deeply.

"Bed," Sam mumbled against her mouth.

He started urging her to step backward. As she complied, he moved his hands around to her back and expertly unfastened her bra. The garment fell away.

He broke their kiss and lowered his head to take her nipple in his mouth. Warm, damp heat surrounded her. Rational thought fled. She came to a stop and cupped his head to hold him in place.

Tension flooded her. Heat made the balls of her feet burn and her toes curl. As he licked and sucked on one breast, he used his hands on the other. Dual pleasure swept through her. She whispered his name, then spoke it louder. He shifted mouth and fingers so her other breast now received his kisses. The ache between her legs intensified to actual pain. Heat spiraled. Need grew. Tension flared higher and higher. His fingers moved back and forth in a rhythm that made her head spin.

Sam straightened and kicked off his shoes. Before she knew what was happening, he'd pulled off her panties and shed his jeans. His briefs went with them. They were naked in a heartbeat.

She barely had a second to anticipate how great it was going to be, when she found herself being lowered into a sitting position on the bed. Somehow her legs were apart and his hand was easing between them. He kissed her and slipped inside of her at the same moment.

Tongue and finger in perfect synchronization. He withdrew once, twice, then a contraction began deep inside of her. As always with him, her orgasm exploded with little warning and incredible intensity. She couldn't control it or herself. She clung to him. He shifted slightly and brushed his thumb deep into her wetness until he found that one swollen point of need. He circled it once and she was lost.

Her entire body shook as her release overwhelmed her. Her legs opened wider, her breath stopped, her head fell back. Every muscle in her body tightened, then relaxed in rhythmic surrender. Hot pleasure rolled through her until her mind went blank and she could do nothing but accept and feel.

She opened her eyes to find Sam watching her. He smiled.

"God, you're so amazing," he said before kissing her mouth, her cheeks, her nose, her eyelids. "I'm shaking. I want you so damn much and I want it to be good, but how the hell am I supposed to hold back after watching that?"

"No one said you had to."

"I have a reputation to uphold," he reminded her as he reached for his jeans and pulled out a condom. "I wouldn't want to disappoint you."

She shifted back on the bed and held open her arms. "Sam, that's not physically possible. You just have to show up and I'm ready. Flash that at me"—she stroked his erection—"and I'm three quarters of the way there."

"You're pretty easy," he said, slipping on the condom. "It's one of your best qualities."

She was still chuckling as he knelt between her thighs and slipped inside her.

Her body stretched to accommodate the familiar length and breadth of him. He stroked her breasts, then gently squeezed her nipples with his thumbs and forefingers.

"I want you to come for me again," he said, his voice low and husky.

She opened her eyes and found him watching her. "If you insist."

"I do."

He dropped one hand to her stomach, them moved lower. Once again he moved his thumb deeper, slipped it between their bodies.

"Don't close your eyes," he whispered. "Watch what we're doing for as long as you can."

Watch?

She lowered her head slightly. They were both naked, he was inside of her *and* touching her, and she could see it all. He found the one place designed for pleasure and began to slowly circle it. At the same time, he withdrew, then entered her again.

She could see and feel all at the same time. In and out. Slowly, except for his thumb which moved faster and faster. Her breathing increased. The combined sensations were irresistible. Her muscles began to tense.

"Yes," he breathed. "Come for me, Francesca."

She raised her gaze to his face and saw he was watching as well—what they were doing and her. He leaned forward and kissed her. At the same moment his thumb brushed over her most sensitive place and he plunged inside of her.

It was too much. No, it wasn't enough and then it was and then the contractions began again. She clung to him all through the whirlwind of sensation. At some point his hands settled on her hips as he drove himself into her again and again. She felt him stiffen and knew he was close. The realization was just erotic enough to make her climax one last time, surrounding him with a pulsing massage that sent him over the edge.

They held on to each other until they were both still and their breathing had slowed.

"I screamed," she said when she finally gathered the strength to open her eyes.

Sam smiled. "I know."

They slept, they awoke sometime in the night, made love, and slept again. Francesca got up sometime before dawn.

She pulled on her clothes and crossed to the balcony doors that still stood open. From there she could see to the ocean, and to the horizon. It was still dark, although there were hints of gray at the edges of the sky.

Behind her Sam lay sprawled across the bed. She'd had to slide out from under the arm he'd rested across her belly. He'd been warm and relaxed. The powerful man relaxed in sleep.

Awake he was many things. Strong, gentle, caring, seductive. When he smiled at her . . .

Brenna's words came back to haunt her. That the reason she hadn't told Sam about the baby was that she was afraid of what he would say. And the reason she was afraid was because he mattered.

While she'd been busy enjoying her first ever adult sex-only affair, and helping him with his daughter and enjoying his company, had she really allowed herself to fall for him? Was love a possibility?

No, she thought firmly. There was no way she would ever allow the rules to change like that. She hadn't wanted the complication. She'd wanted something easy. Fun. A diversion, nothing more.

Only this was a lot more, and now there was a baby to think about.

She turned and watched Sam sleep. She'd promised herself she would tell Sam and she would. Friday. Six more days. Just six. And then . . . then she didn't know what was going to happen.

"You wanted to see me, boss?" Jason asked as he entered Sam's office.

Sam nodded at the leather club chair in front of his desk. "Have a seat. I've been on the phone with a couple of clients finalizing holiday party plans."

Jason sighed. "It's July. Even the department stores don't have their Christmas decorations up yet."

"You know we book up early."

Jason nodded. "What seems to be popular this year?"

"The usual. Aspen, London, Paris."

Sam's company provided protection to some of the world's wealthiest families. When those families decided to entertain, the workload increased as the firm was expected to protect guests, as well.

"We also have three corporations requesting increased security for their senior executives and one former Mafia informant looking to live into his senior years."

Jason drew his eyebrows together. "Aren't we having a planning meeting on Friday?"

"Sure."

"So why are you telling me this now?"

Sam kept his expression neutral. "The Johnsons just phoned about their holiday plans. They plan to travel."

Jason groaned. "Sam, no. Not another trip to the wilderness. I don't even have all my shots yet for that African safari. We're going inside the blue zone. Do you know what that means?"

Trying not to laugh, Sam shook his head.

"The blue zone is African airspace where there isn't much in the way of traffic control. No one is in charge, so planes have a real good chance of running into each other."

"Sounds dangerous."

"It's hell," Jason muttered. "Pure hell."

"The Johnsons don't want to go to Africa."

"Where do they want to go?"

"They asked for you specifically. Apparently their youngest adores you."

"Sam," Jason growled. "Where are they going?"

"Did you know that winter for us is summer in the southern hemisphere?"

Jason's dark eyes widened. "Holy shit. Not Antarctica."

"You can get there by boat."

"Sam."

He allowed himself a slight smile. "Monaco, Jason. They're spending Christmas in Monaco."

Jason slapped his large hands on Sam's desk and grinned. "No shit."

"I know."

Just then they heard a familiar uneven step in the hallway.

Jason rose to his feet as Gabriel walked into the room. "Morning, sir," he said, holding out the chair he'd just vacated.

"Jason." Gabriel nodded. He glowered at Sam, then sank into the chair Jason offered.

"Hallway's getting longer," the old man grumbled. "It used to take me only a few steps to get to your office."

"Morning, Gabriel," Sam said, ignoring his grandfather's complaints. He'd made the mistake of offering the use of a wheelchair once before and had nearly had his head chewed off.

"You're out and about early," he said instead.

"I'm looking for some information." His grandfather stared at Jason. "Sit down. You'll give me a crick in my neck if you just stand there."

Jason winked at Gabriel. "Yes, sir."

"My grandson works you too hard."

"I think so."

Gabriel muttered something under his breath and turned his attention back to Sam. "There's a restaurant by the Four Seasons Hotel. Supposed to be a nice place. What do you know about it?"

Sam stared at his grandfather. "You're eating out? You hate restaurants. Do you want to come stay with Kelly and me for a few days?"

As soon as he issued the invitation, he wanted to call it back. His need to be alone with Francesca grew exponentially every day. Having one more person in the house would only complicate an already difficult situation.

"I'm fine on my own," Gabriel growled. "Why can't a man go out to dinner once in a while?"

Jason made a choking sound. When Sam glanced at him, he seemed to be having some kind of spasm.

"You have a problem?" Gabriel snapped.

"No, sir." Jason cleared his throat and straightened in his chair. "I'm familiar with that restaurant. It's excellent. What kind of food does the lady like?"

Lady? Sam nearly fell out of his chair. "You have a date?" he asked his grandfather.

"I'm taking Mary-Margaret out for dinner, yes. Not that it's any business of yours."

Mary-Margaret? The pieces fell into place. "Grammy M?"

Gabriel glared at him. Sam would have sworn that the old man was blushing.

"She's a fine figure of a woman," Gabriel told him. "Been widowed for some time. She makes me laugh. No law against that."

"None at all," Sam agreed, more than a little impressed.

"I'm sure you'll both be pleased by the restaurant," Jason said.

"Good to know." Gabriel pushed himself to his feet and leaned heavily on his cane. He headed for the door.

"You two get back to work," he called over his shoulder.

Sam waited until his grandfather was out of earshot, then leaned back in his chair. "Who would have thought?"

Jason chuckled. "You should see the look on your face."

"I don't know what to think about my grandfather dating after all these years. On the other hand, I'm pleased to know the Reese family sports equipment works well into the golden years."

16

Early Monday morning Francesca walked out of her apartment only to find Brenna leaning against her truck. She slowed her step as she studied her twin. For once Brenna actually had a dress on, and makeup.

"This is a surprise," Francesca said when she reached her twin.

Brenna shrugged. "I thought you might want company."

Considering how quickly news traveled through the family, Francesca found it amazing that no one had said a word about a long-lost brother for nearly thirty years.

"Mom and Dad called last night," Francesca said. "When did you find out they'd asked me to get in touch with Joe?"

"About fifteen minutes after they hung up. I didn't think you'd want to go on your own."

Francesca hadn't, but after the fight they'd had in the vineyard, she'd been uncomfortable calling Brenna.

"You might have been right," she said by way of apology.

Brenna raised her eyebrows. "About what specifically?"

Francesca pushed her toward the front of the truck. "Get in and I'll grovel all the way to San Diego."

Fifteen minutes later they were on the freeway, heading south.

"Didn't you have Kelly this week?" Brenna asked.

Francesca nodded. "I had to call Sam last night and explain I couldn't pick her up from ballet today. He's taking her to work with him when she's finished with class, which is a good thing. They can hang out together and bond. I'll have her the rest of the week."

Brenna glanced at her. "I'm guessing you haven't spilled the beans about the little one yet."

"Friday. I wanted to get through this week first."

"Scared?"

"Terrified." She smiled. "Because you were right. I do care about him. And don't ask me to define what *care* means. He matters. That's all I know."

"The details aren't important." Brenna leaned back in her seat and sighed. "I love being right. It's a good way to start the day."

Francesca laughed. "Fine. If you're so smart, have you figured out what we're going to say to our big brother?"

"I haven't a clue. Although I've considered the fact that we don't want to piss him off. Joe Larson is a Navy Seal. Doesn't the military train those guys to be killing machines? He can probably take us out with a cocktail napkin."

"Tell me about it."

Two and a half hours later they entered San Diego County. Brenna shifted uneasily in her seat. "Maybe this was a bad idea. Me coming along, I mean. I don't know if I want to meet this guy, although I'm sure he's going to be thrilled at the possibility of inheriting millions."

"You really think Grandpa Lorenzo will offer Joe the winery and he'll say yes?"

"Wouldn't you? Even if he's not interested in it, he can sell it and pocket the cash."

"Grandpa Lorenzo wouldn't let that happen."

"I'm not so sure. I think he'll be blinded by the thrill of finally having a male heir. It's been his dream since we were kids. Regardless of how or where he was raised, Joe is family. You know what that means in our house."

Francesca couldn't argue. Family was everything. She still wasn't used to the idea of having a brother. What would he be like? Would he be angry about being given up for adoption?

They entered the city. Thirty minutes later they pulled up into the hotel parking lot. Her parents had used a lawyer to arrange the meeting in the lobby-level coffee shop.

"Here goes nothing," Brenna said as they climbed out of the car. "If I start to go for his throat, hold me back."

"If he has all the training you claim and you go for his throat, he'll be able to take care of himself."

"Good point."

They walked into the open hotel lobby. A small sign pointed the way to the café. The lush plant life and sound of a nearby fountain should have been soothing, but Francesca found herself fighting nerves. She placed a hand against her stomach.

Brenna squeezed her arm. "Me, too," she admitted. "I've been trying to think of a funny opening line, but I can't seem to get beyond 'Hi.' "

"How about 'Hi, I'm your sister.' "

Brenna rolled her eyes. "You're the professional psychologist here. Wouldn't you want me to be more subtle?"

"Maybe. But sometimes getting everything on the table is a better idea."

They approached the café. The waiting area was empty. Brenna glanced at the chairs. "Want to sit down?"

"I can't."

"Me, either."

They tried to make small talk. Francesca scanned the people in the lobby, looking for a dark-haired man with Marcelli features.

"Do you think we'll recognize him from the picture? After all he could—"

Just then a man turned onto the path and approached the café. He was tall, dark-haired, and nearly the spitting image of their father. Francesca's mouth went dry. Beside her Brenna sucked in a breath.

"I'd been hoping there was a mistake, but obviously there isn't," she murmured.

The man, well-built and handsome, wore jeans and a T-shirt. When he caught sight of them, he raised one eyebrow. His mouth curved up in a grin.

"Very nice," he said when he was within earshot. "When that lawyer guy called and asked me to meet you here, I nearly blew him off. Glad I didn't. Looks like my lucky day."

Francesca blinked. She couldn't think of a single thing to say.

"You're kidding, right?" Brenna told the man.

He grinned. "I've never done a threesome. But hey, I'm open to it."

Francesca blanched.

Brenna simply smiled. "Joe Larson, in about two minutes you're going to think that's the most disgusting thing you've ever said."

He didn't look the least bit worried. "You two vice cops?"

"Worse. We're your sisters."

"But this is just an office," Kelly said as she looked around the large open space of her father's business. "I thought it would be . . ." She shrugged. "Different."

Sam grinned. "Like the workshop in the James Bond movies?"

Kelly considered the question, then nodded. "Yeah. What about really cool machines and stuff? Things to help you take down the bad guys?"

"Sorry. These are just offices."

"But you have to have, you know, like weapons and ray guns."

His eyebrows rose. "Ray guns?"

"Didn't you ever watch TV? There are a lot of secret weapons on the black market."

"We try to keep our operations mostly legal."

"Mostly, huh?" She smiled. "Want to tell me about the other parts?"

He pulled one of her curls. "Not even on a bet."

At first Kelly had been kind of upset when Francesca had called to say she was going to San Diego to meet her brother. Sam had already let Doreen go and the new nanny wasn't starting until next week. She'd been surprised when he'd told her he would bring her to work with him after her ballet lessons. Although she would never admit it, not even if she was tortured or threatened with a ray gun, she sort of liked hanging out with her dad. When he wasn't being too domineering or stubborn. He could be nice.

But she wasn't going to like it too much, she told herself. Because Sam could still get tired of her and send her away.

They rounded a corner just as a huge man stepped out of his office. He was tall, with massive shoulders and dark skin. His head was shaved. He was like old and everything, maybe even over thirty, but he was gorgeous.

"Hey, boss."

"Jason." Sam put his hand on Kelly's shoulder. "This is my daughter. Kelly, Jason Carlton. He runs several special security operations for our most demanding clients."

Jason grimaced. "What your dad means is he puts me in charge of the crabby rich people."

Kelly giggled.

Jason winked. "So you're giving her the grand tour, Sam? You show her the gadgets?"

Sam shook his head. "Kelly is already dangerous enough without her learning how to use a gun."

Kelly was about to say she wasn't sure she *wanted* to learn how to use a gun when Jason sighed.

"Not that kind of stuff. The other things. Infrared, night-vision goggles."

Sam glanced at her. "Would you like to see that?"

Kelly wasn't sure exactly what it was, but it sounded fun. She nodded eagerly.

Sam glanced at his watch. "I have a call coming in from Germany in a few minutes, but maybe after that—"

"Don't sweat it, boss," Jason said cheerfully. "I've got the Johnsons' African safari all planned. I'll take Kelly through the playground."

Sam hesitated. "All right, but keep her away from anything dangerous. I don't want her taking me out in my sleep."

Kelly watched him walk away. She was pretty sure her dad had been kidding, but not a hundred percent. Didn't Sam trust her? She sighed. Tanya never had.

Before she could think about that too much or get sad, Jason lead the way to the rear of the office. They stepped through a set of double doors and into a mock street with buildings on both sides. There was a huge locked cabinet against the wall by the door. Jason pressed his thumb against a small glass square, and the doors swung open. He dug around and came up with an assortment of goggles, head gear, weapon-looking devices, and small discs he tucked into his pocket.

"Just so you don't get any ideas about breaking in on your own, kid," he said as he closed the doors and motioned her forward. "Give it a try."

She glanced at him, then at the small glass square. "Will it hurt?" she asked.

He grinned. "Not even a little. Suck it up, little girl."

Hesitantly she pressed her thumb to the glass. A female computer voice announced, "You are not authorized to open this unit. If you attempt to gain access, an alarm will sound. Please return to the front office immediately for processing."

"Cool," Kelly breathed.

"Isn't it? So don't be thinking you can bring your friends over and impress them."

"I won't."

"Good." He set a pair of goggles on her head. "We're going to night vision first, then we'll do infrared."

He handed her a long rifle-looking gun thing. It was big and really lightweight.

"These only work on targets," he told her as he pulled on his own goggles. "We program them, depending on the training session." He showed her a small pad in the butt of the weapon. "They fire a burst of light that's picked up by the sensors on the target." He grinned. "Ever play paint ball?"

She shook her head.

"After this game, you'll be an expert."

Francesca, Brenna, and their brother sat at a table, ignoring the food they'd ordered. Joe pushed around the French fries on his plate.

"My adopted parents died when I was twelve," he said. "It was a car accident. I'd been spending the night with a friend, or I would have been with them. They didn't have any relatives, so I got shoved into the foster-care system."

His dark eyes no longer sparkled with humor. Francesca leaned toward him. "But if you knew you were adopted, why didn't you tell someone? Wouldn't they have tried to get in touch with your family?"

"I'd already been given up once. Why would I think anyone had changed their mind?"

"Is that why you didn't try to find your birth parents?" Brenna asked.

He shrugged. "I've been meaning to go to one of those registries. I figured I could leave the information there. If someone was looking, they would find me."

The simple statements told Francesca a lot. Joe was willing to give them a second chance. He'd listened while they'd told him the circumstances of his birth and how desperately their parents wanted to meet him. That had to count for something.

"We've found you," Brenna said, swiping a French fry from his plate. "Now what?"

"You tell me."

Brenna shrugged. "You should come get to know your family."

"The Navy is my family now."

"Actually there are three generations of Marcellis dying to get to know you," Brenna told him.

"Uh-huh."

Joe didn't look real impressed. Francesca turned her attention to her twin. Brenna had the most to lose if the long-lost Marcelli heir made an appearance, yet she was the one who had clicked with Joe.

"Scared?" Brenna challenged.

Joe didn't bother answering. He leveled his steady gaze on her and didn't blink.

Brenna only smiled. "Going to threaten me with a really big knife?"

"I don't need props."

"You don't intimidate me, Joe. But I think we terrify you. I think you're finally looking at the one thing you've wanted all your life. So why would you walk away from it? Your parents, *our* parents, want to get to know you. Is that so terrible?" Brenna shrugged. "Then there's the matter of the inheritance."

Francesca stared at her. "What are you doing?"

"He's going to find out about it eventually."

Francesca recognized the pain in her sister's eyes and suddenly understood Brenna's plan. Her twin wanted to know if Joe was going to be interested. She would rather know now than wait and wonder. Brenna had always been the gutsiest of the Marcelli sisters.

Joe leaned back in his seat. "What inheritance?"

"Ever hear of Marcelli Wines?" Brenna asked.

"Maybe." He frowned. "Same Marcellis?"

"You got it. Just pictures acres and acres of vineyards, one traditional grandfather who owns it all, and four sisters. Not a male heir in sight. Until now."

Joe's expression didn't change. "You're shitting me."

"Nope. You just won the jackpot."

His mouth curved into a slow grin. "How much is it all worth?"

Brenna swallowed. Francesca felt her pain and it tore at her.

"About forty million. Think you might make your way north for a visit now?"

"Sure. Hell, I'd visit for two million."

"As long as we know you can be bought."

Joe's grin never faded. "Every man has a price. Every woman, too."

"Mine's only a million," Brenna said.

"What about her?" He pointed at Francesca.

Brenna shook her head. "She has principles."

Joe's gaze settled on Francesca's face. "Money's a whole lot more dependable. Speaking of which . . ." He slapped a twenty on the table. "I have to get back to work."

"Out to kill and maim?" Brenna asked.

He smiled. "Yeah. That's just how I spend my day."

They all rose. Francesca scribbled the house number on a piece of paper. "Please call."

He took the number and stared at it. "Sure." He studied them both. "Nice meeting you."

"You, too, Joe," Francesca said.

He turned and walked away.

Francesca watched him go. "He's not what I expected."

"Me, either. The hell of it is, I sort of like him. Except for him wanting the money, which I don't like but I understand."

"Me, too. Think he'll call?"

Brenna picked up her purse. "In a heartbeat. Wouldn't you?"

Francesca touched her arm. "I know you're not okay. Is there anything I can do to help?"

Brenna blinked several times. A single tear rolled down her cheek. "I'll get over it. Just give me a few days. I need to come up with a plan or something."

Getting over the possibility of losing everything she'd ever wanted? Francesca knew it was going to take a whole lot longer than a few days.

"It was so cool, Gabriel," Kelly breathed as she sat on her great-grandfather's desk and clutched a can of soda. "There were these terrorists and they had hostages and we caught them and everything. I had a sixty percent kill rate."

Gabriel glanced at Jason. "Are you sure Sam is going to approve of this?"

The large man shrugged. "She had fun. She's good, too. Must be in the genes." He winked at her. "You're turning into a Daddy's girl, huh?"

Kelly had never had a father before, so she wasn't sure what was involved with being a Daddy's girl, but she liked the sound of it.

"I'm glad you had a good time," Gabriel said.

His phone rang. As he picked up the receiver, Kelly slid off the desk. She started to leave the office, but before she could go, he waved her back. When she stepped close, he put his arm around her, pulled her close, and kissed her forehead.

Kelly walked out into the hallway. Wow. Gabriel had

just acted like he really liked her. That had to be good, right?

"What do you have planned for the rest of the afternoon?" Jason asked.

"I don't know. I'm staying here until my dad's ready to go home."

"Then why don't you come with me. I have to run an errand, and I could use some help."

"Sure."

She followed him into Sam's office. Her dad was on the phone, too. She thought security was about being a bodyguard, but a bunch of it was just talking on the phone.

Jason made an unlocking motion. Sam reached into the top of his desk and drew out a key attached to a bright blue key ring. A plastic disk hanging down was printed with the words SECURE FILE.

Jason led the way into the supply room. He unlocked the file cabinet with the key. Inside were various forms along with a small metal box.

Jason motioned to the paperwork. "Top secret," he said in a low voice, then opened the box. Inside were a stack of bills. He took several twenties and closed the box.

"You keep cash around here?" she asked.

"Sure. There's always an emergency stash in case someone has to leave the country and the bank's not open. Plus there's petty cash for things like birthday parties."

He paused expectantly.

She stared at him. "Who's having a birthday?"

Jason locked the cabinet, then put his hand on her shoulder. "Your dad, Kelly. His birthday's in a week. I'd like you to help me pick out a cake. We have to choose the lunch menu, too. We're having food brought in. Sam hates the fuss, which is one of the reasons I like to do it."

Jason was grinning and Kelly tried to smile back at him, but inside she felt kind of weird. It was her dad's birthday and she hadn't known. What if she'd missed it? He would get really mad.

She would have to get him a really cool present, she thought as she followed Jason out of the building. But what? And how? He'd canceled her credit card, and she didn't have any money. She would have to think of something and soon.

Sam turned out of the parking lot. He felt pleased about the afternoon. Kelly had seemed to enjoy herself in the office. Jason had taken care of her for much of the time, and he'd only had good things to say about her behavior. Maybe Teen-zilla was gone for good.

As he waited at a signal, he glanced at Kelly. While he could see Tanya in her, he also saw his grandmother. Yet much of Kelly was uniquely herself.

"How about Italian for dinner?" he asked. "We could go back to that place by the beach."

Kelly shrugged.

"What's wrong?" he asked.

She faced him. "Nothing. It's just—you need to give me an allowance, okay? I mean, I'm twelve. I've more than proved I know how to handle money. I've had my own credit card for years. But you took that away from me. I need to have some cash to buy stuff."

Her voice was an odd combination of pleading and defiant. He turned his attention back to the road. When the signal turned green, he stepped on the gas.

"What do you need money for?" he asked.

"Does that matter? Do I need to give you a list?"

"Maybe." An allowance. While he didn't agree that her having her own credit card meant that she was capable of handling money, he knew she would need to learn. An allowance might accomplish that. But how much? And how often? Should he tie it to chores or just give it to her?

Too many questions, he thought as his head began to pound. "Let me think about it."

She rounded on him. "You are so mean. How can you not say yes? You don't give me anything I want. Not ever. How many things have I asked for lately?"

She continued to rant. When they pulled into the driveway, all he could think about was that he'd been too hasty when he'd assumed she'd morphed into a normal child. Apparently raging Teen-zilla still lurked just under the surface.

"Kelly come out of your room right now!" Sam yelled through the closed and locked door.

"No. I'm fine. Go to work and leave me alone."

Leave her alone? Not likely. He glanced at his watch and groaned. He had a nine o'clock meeting with clients who had flown in from Brazil. Kelly had been in a temper all the previous evening, still upset about the allowance discussion, but he'd expected her to be over it by morning. Obviously, he'd been wrong.

Their relationship could definitely be defined as two steps forward, two and a half steps back. He wished he could find a way to get through to her so they could communicate like rational people. Between her being a teenager and him being a clueless father, that wasn't likely.

"Kelly, I know you're angry, but sulking isn't going to change my mind. If you don't get out here right now, you're not going to ballet class for the rest of the week."

He heard something that sounded like a sob. "F-fine," she told him, her voice thick with tears. "Just leave me here. Okay? Just go away."

While her temper got on his nerves, her tears made him nervous. "Kelly, dammit, tell me what's going on. Are you sick?"

"I don't—" She sniffed. "No. It's not like that. I can't tell you. Just stop asking me, okay?"

It wasn't okay. He rattled the door handle. He knew with a screwdriver and thirty seconds, he could have the door open, but something inside told him that wasn't the best way to handle the situation.

"If you won't talk to me, will you talk to someone else?" he asked. "Gabriel or Francesca?"

He heard Kelly crying. Then there was silence and finally she said, "I'll talk to Francesca."

"Okay. I'll get her on the phone, then you pick up."

He practically ran to his bedroom, where he dialed the number from memory.

"Hello?"

"Hey, it's Sam. I'm sorry to bother you so early. I know you wanted to work until you have to pick up Kelly after class."

"It's fine. What's up?"

"Hell if I know. Kelly won't come out of her room, and she won't tell me why. But she agreed to talk to you."

Francesca sighed. "Oh, Sam, I thought things were getting better with you two."

"So did I. Obviously they're not. Can you talk to her?"

"Sure."

He hurried back to Kelly's room and knocked on the door. "Francesca's on the line. You can pick up."

He heard a click, then Kelly's voice. "Sam, hang up now. I mean it."

He hesitated, then did as she requested.

As he paced the hall, he heard murmured conversation. Three minutes later the phone rang. He grabbed it.

"What?" he demanded.

Francesca laughed. "Don't sound frantic. She's fine. I promised not to tell you what's wrong. Don't freak out about that. I'm coming over now and she and I are going to talk, and then I'll call you at work and tell you all about it."

"What's going on?"

"Sam, you're going to have to trust me on this. Just go to work and I'll be in touch."

Trust her. He relaxed. That was one thing he could do. "Please call before noon."

"I promise."

"Great." He smiled. "Thanks, Francesca. I owe you."

"No, you don't. Bye."

He hung up the phone. "I'm going to work," he called through the door. "Francesca will be here shortly."

"I know. Everything is fine now, Sam. Don't worry."

He heard the relief in Kelly's voice. The tears seemed to have disappeared. Somehow Francesca had worked a miracle in just a few minutes. Damn, she was good. Better than good.

He'd long ago learned that women lied to get what they wanted, that they couldn't be trusted under any circumstances. But Francesca wasn't like that. She was honest, straightforward, and she would never manipulate him. He could trust her. And he did.

17

"*This is just too gross,*" Kelly said as she came out of her bathroom and flopped on the bed.

Francesca thought about pointing out she would get used to the process over the next thirty or forty years, then decided that was too depressing to consider. Better to focus on the positive.

"At least you know you're growing up."

Kelly glanced at her and smiled. "I kind of already knew that was happening." She winced slightly and pressed a hand to her stomach. "How long does it take for the pain to go away?"

"Give it a half hour or so." She pointed to the hot pad she'd brought along. "Try that. It really helps."

Kelly pulled the flannel-covered square over her midsection, then picked up the control and hit the On button.

"I thought I was gaining weight or something," she said. "I've been kind of puffy for the last couple of days."

"Good old bloat. It happens."

"Along with cramps and that disgusting bleeding. Who thought that up?"

"It's all part of the flow of life, if you'll excuse the pun."

Kelly wrinkled her nose. "Not funny."

Francesca lay down next to her. "Are you feeling better?"

Kelly nodded. Her lower lip trembled slightly. "I knew all about it and stuff. My mom had said a few things, and we'd talked about it in school, but hearing about it and seeing blood are *not* the same thing. For a second I thought I was dying. Then I remembered, but I couldn't tell my dad and I didn't know what to do."

Francesca stroked her bright red curls. "I'm glad I could help."

"Me, too."

"We'll take it easy today. Just relax and hang out. Tomorrow, if you feel up to it, you can go to class. In the afternoon I'll need to stop by my adviser's office for about a half hour. Otherwise, I have no plans for the week."

Kelly smiled. "I like the idea of hanging out today. Maybe we can use the DVD player in the family room, seeing as I don't have one up here."

"That's right. How sad. Imagine having to go through life without your very own DVD player. Maybe you could write UNICEF and ask for one. Oh, wait. They're busy feeding starving children in poor countries."

Kelly swatted away her hand. "I get it. I'm a spoiled brat who doesn't appreciate all she has."

"Something like that."

Kelly grinned. "Okay. I'll stop complaining about the DVD player."

"I would if I were you." Francesca sat up. "I have to call your dad."

"No way! I don't want him knowing."

"It won't be a surprise to him. Sam's been around women before, and he completely understands the process."

"But he's my *dad*. Telling him is completely sick."

"Getting your period is a natural part of life. Kelly, he has to know what had you upset this morning."

The preteen sighed heavily. "All right, but I don't want to talk to him about it. *Ever*. I mean that."

"Fair enough. Why don't you sort through your movie collection, and I'll talk to him."

Francesca had to wait on hold for a couple of minutes, then she heard Sam's chocolate-on-velvet voice.

"So what was the crisis?"

"Kelly got her period. It was her first one and it freaked her out, which is completely understandable. Plus, she wasn't prepared with supplies, and she was too embarrassed to tell you."

"That was it?" Sam asked. "Her period?"

Francesca frowned. "It's a big deal. Girls have a lot of ambivalence about the whole concept of growing up. This is physical proof things are never going to be the same again. Plus, it's not like a guy's first wet dream. There's no pleasure and usually a lot of pain."

"Whatever. She can't hide out every time she has a problem. Look, I'm in a meeting and I have to get back to it. Thanks for letting me know what's up. I'll deal with it when I get home tonight. Bye."

He hung up. Francesca stared at the phone. "Whatever?" she repeated, more than a little outraged. "That's your entire response to this incredibly significant event in your daughter's life? And now you're going to deal with it? I don't think so."

Kelly walked into the kitchen. "Everything okay?"

Francesca set down the phone and smiled. "Absolutely," she lied cheerfully. There was no point in upsetting Kelly. Not when the poor kid wasn't feeling well. Francesca would make sure to corner Sam before he could talk to Kelly. Somehow she would make him see that he had to give his daughter a break and show a little more sensitivity.

Sam could feel another headache coming on. They were a regular occurrence ever since Kelly had appeared in his life. He ignored the wine rack on the counter and went right to the hard stuff. After collecting a glass, he headed for the wet bar and opened a bottle of single malt scotch.

"I'm not kidding, Sam," Francesca said as she followed him. "You are *completely* in the wrong. This is a female thing and you can't possibly understand. You're going to have to believe me."

He drank half the contents of his glass in two swallows. The liquid burned its way to his belly.

"She could have told me."

"No, she couldn't. She was embarrassed and scared. You try waking up to blood everywhere and we'll see how you react."

He wasn't comfortable with the visual image, so he ignored it. "She locked me out of her room, she wouldn't come out, and she wouldn't tell me what was wrong."

"With a good reason."

"I'm her father."

"You're a stranger. It's been what—a month? That's not enough time to get to know each other." She leaned against the bar. "You haven't even decided if you like having her around."

"Sometimes I don't," Sam admitted. He crossed to the sofa and sat down. "Sometimes . . ." He shrugged.

Francesca perched on the edge of the club chair and leaned toward him. "Give her a break on this."

"She was wrong to lock me out of her room. This weekend I'm taking the lock out."

"Fine, but don't be in a snit when you do it."

He looked at her. "Why are you taking her side? I thought you were on my team."

"I'm a neutral third party."

He didn't like the sound of that. "Francesca, I've had a hell of a day. I have clients in from out of town, I was worried about Kelly all morning only to find out she'd fussed about nothing."

"It's not nothing to her."

He wasn't convinced. "I just want to spend a quiet evening. No fighting, no misunderstandings, no lectures. Is that too much to ask? We could order in, you could stay for dinner, then for breakfast." He smiled.

She didn't smile back. "You're missing the entire point. Kelly had a hard day, too. She needs to be cuddled and pampered. She needs to feel special. She needs you to understand. Right now she has to be the most important thing in your life."

He swallowed the rest of his drink. "Why the hell not? She's ruining it anyway."

Francesca rose and glared at him. "I can't believe you said that."

His guilt was faster than her accusation. "I know. I didn't mean it." He hadn't. It was just he didn't understand Kelly. Every time he thought he had her figured out, he found out he couldn't be more wrong. He cared about her; he just wished she wasn't so frustrating.

"Get to know her, Sam. Make some effort to spend some time with her."

"I do."

"Not enough. You don't understand her, and that's why

this isn't going smoothly. You're the adult in the relationship. Maybe you should act like it."

With that, she turned and walked out of the room. Seconds later the front door slammed.

Sam leaned back on the sofa and closed his eyes. Looked like he wouldn't be getting any tonight. His morning had started badly, and his evening wasn't showing signs of improvement.

He heard a noise from upstairs. Kelly.

Get to know her, Francesca had said. He *was*. Sort of. He'd taken her to work the previous day. Okay, she'd spent most of her time with Jason, but still . . .

"Hell," he muttered and set down his glass. Francesca was right. Again.

He walked upstairs and knocked on Kelly's door.

"Come in," she called.

He opened the door and found her curled up on her bed, reading.

"How're you feeling?" he asked.

She eyed him warily. "Fine. I know Francesca told you and everything, but I don't want to talk about it."

Thank God. "What do you want to do?"

She shrugged.

Great. That was helpful. He thought about what he used to do with his grandfather when he'd been Kelly's age and it had been a cold, rainy day. He smiled.

"Ever play chess?"

She rolled her eyes. "Could you be more boring?"

"Probably not, but that doesn't answer the question."

She sighed. "No, and I don't want to learn."

"Too bad. Because if you were to win a game, I'd get you a DVD player."

Her eyes widened. "No way."

"Way, kid."

She dropped the book. "Just one game."

"That's all it would take."

She scrambled off the bed. "Show me the way."

"You have to tell him, Francesca."

Francesca curled up on her small sofa and watched her mother pace the length of her living room.

"I will."

"When?" Her mother stopped and faced her. "Your grandfather has already started threatening to contact Sam himself. You don't want that to happen."

Francesca had to agree. Having Sam told about the baby and threatened in the same sentence would probably send him into heart failure.

"Lorenzo is expecting an engagement out of all this."

Francesca straightened and set her feet on the ground. "It's not his decision to make."

Her mother walked to the sofa and sat next to her. "Don't you love Sam?"

Admitting to her mother that she'd slept with a man she didn't love wasn't her idea of a good time. "It's not that." Not exactly. She hadn't loved him at first. But now . . . now she was pregnant, confused, and a liar.

"Then what?"

"Sam isn't the marrying kind."

"When they fall in love, they all are."

But that was the thing. Sam *didn't* love her, and she . . . well, she didn't know what she felt about him. Was wanting to be with him all the time love? Was adoring him and his daughter and imaging a future together enough?

"We both agreed the relationship would be casual," she said at last and held her breath.

Her mother only looked mildly disapproving. "I see."

"It's just, I don't want to be married," Francesca blurted out, then groaned. "At least I didn't use to."

"Because of Todd?"

"Partly. Because I was never sure of myself." She thought of the conversation she'd had with Brenna last week. About it being time to let go of the past. "I've never felt capable before. Confident. Growing up, I was the stupid Marcelli sister. With Todd, I was arm candy. I don't want that."

"Do you think if you love a man you're going to lose yourself?"

"I used to."

"And now?"

Now everything in her life was a mess. Sam, Kelly, the pregnancy. "I don't know anymore."

Her mother cupped her chin and looked into her eyes. "Francesca, whatever you and Sam decide about your future, he must know about the baby."

"I'm going to tell him."

"When?"

"Friday. No matter what. The new nanny starts Monday. Friday is the last day I have Kelly."

Her mother shook her head. "Don't wait any longer. You weren't raised to be a deceptive person."

Francesca winced. The statement was perilously close to the "I raised you better than this" complaint that always made her feel about six years old.

Her mother dropped her hand to her lap. "One more thing. Whatever you do about Sam, do it because it's what you want, not because of what other people say. Not even me."

Francesca knew she was thinking about her decision to give up Joe for adoption. "I will."

"Promise, Francesca. Promise to follow your heart. Even if you're afraid. There is no greater regret in life than not having tried. Believe me. I've lived with that one for thirty years."

Francesca hugged her mother close. "I'm sorry."

"You don't have to be. You've done nothing wrong. Not yet. I'll hold off your grandfather until Friday, but no longer."

"Fair enough."

Although she had no idea what she was going to say. Telling Sam about the baby was one thing, but telling him about her heart . . . she wasn't sure what she wanted. Somehow life without him didn't seem as appealing as it once had. She liked being with him, talking to him. She liked Kelly. But Sam was a man who didn't forgive lies. Would he understand why she'd waited to tell him about the baby, or would he see her as little more than yet another woman who had set out to deceive him?

Francesca's second unexpected visitor arrived shortly after nine the following morning. She opened the door to find Sam standing there.

He wore one of his power suits and looked good enough to appear in a calendar. Her heart gave a little flutter, her chest tightened, and her thighs went up in flames. If she didn't know better, she would think she had malaria. Or that she'd fallen in love.

She stepped back to let him into her apartment, then closed the door behind him.

"You were really mad at me last night," he said by way of greeting.

"That's true."

He shoved his hands into his pockets and rocked back on his heels. "So I was wondering if you were still going to pick Kelly up from her dance class."

"Of course. Why wouldn't I?" Then she got it. "Just because you and I were fighting doesn't mean I'm going to duck out of my responsibilities."

"I know." He looked at her. "I'm sorry. You were right."

She stared at him. "About?"

"Kelly, her getting her period. That I didn't get it. I see now that it's a big deal for girls."

Francesca felt more amused than vindicated. "You've been reading your teenage parenting books."

He grinned sheepishly. "Maybe." He straightened. "Kelly and I had a long talk last night. About her life here, and how things are different. About getting to know each other better. We're each going to write down a list of our expectations and how we'd like the family to run. Then we're going to talk about them and negotiate. We've set up a meeting for Saturday morning. Kelly suggested you be there to mediate and I agree."

"I don't know what to say," Francesca told him honestly. She was thrilled that Sam was willing to meet his daughter halfway *and* get to know her. She was touched that they both wanted her to be a part of the family meeting. She was terrified to think how things could be between them, come Saturday.

"As Kelly pointed out last night, you're as much a part of the family as either of us. Maybe not by blood, but certainly by time and effort."

She desperately wanted to agree, but didn't feel she had the right.

He pulled his hands out of his pockets and moved

closer. "I know this isn't what we agreed to," he murmured as he brushed her mouth with his. "It's a lot more messy and complicated, but is that such a bad thing?"

"I d-don't know."

It was impossible for her to be rational while he was kissing her. Her mind went fuzzy, her body surrendered, and all she wanted was to take Sam to bed.

He nipped her lower lip. "Well, think about it," he said as he released her and moved toward the door. "I'll see you tonight."

And then he was gone. Francesca leaned against the wall and closed her eyes. She didn't mind *messy* or *complicated.* Not if things turned out well in the end. But would they? Time was ticking. Come Friday, where would she and Sam be?

"How are you feeling?" Francesca asked that afternoon as she and Kelly drove away from the ballet school.

"Better. No cramps, but the bleeding is still too incredibly gross for words. Oh, and I'm not bloated anymore, so that's something." Kelly pulled out the pins holding her hair back and fluffed her curls. "You said you had to see your adviser this afternoon, right?"

"Yeah. If it's okay with you, I thought we'd stop and see her first, then head out to a café I know by the beach afterward."

"Sounds good."

They chatted about movies and fall fashions until Francesca drove onto the university grounds.

"It's really big," Kelly said, looking around.

"Have you been on campus before?"

"No. I didn't know it would be so pretty."

Francesca pointed out several buildings, then parked close to the psychology labs. "My adviser has an office in here."

"We aren't going to see anything icky, are we?" Kelly asked as she climbed out of the car. "No cats with wires in their heads or anything?"

"Not even close," Francesca said as she stepped onto the pavement. "We torture people here. Not animals."

Kelly grinned. "Good."

They walked along the pathway toward the double doors.

"So what do you do here?" Kelly asked. "You're like still in college, but how is grad school different?"

"I already have a bachelor's degree," Francesca explained. "Do you know what that is?"

"Uh-huh. It takes like four years, right?"

"Yup. After that people can come back for more education. I'm in program where I'll get both a master's degree and a Ph.D. In fact, I'm supposed to be writing the paper for my master's right now."

"You just turn it in and get a grade?"

"I wish," Francesca said, leading the way down the long corridor. "But there's a little more to it than that."

She briefly explained about research projects, committee approval, distilling data, and coming up with a topic.

Kelly's eyes widened. "You could be going to school forever."

"I hope not. I plan to have a life of my own eventually."

"But you have to be willing to make a big commitment."

"I agree. Some people have trouble with that, but getting my Ph.D. is really important to me. When you want to be good at something, you have to be willing to work hard."

"Like my dance," Kelly said as they climbed the stairs to the second floor.

"Exactly."

They walked to the end of the hallway, then entered the main lab. A reception area fronted several observation rooms. The offices were on the left.

An older woman sat behind the front desk. She smiled when she saw Francesca.

"You've been avoiding us," Marg Overton said with a grin. "I want to think you've been home typing your fingers to the bone, but somehow I doubt that."

"Not even close," Francesca agreed. "Marge, this is Kelly. Kelly, Marg. While there's a department head in charge, Marg actually runs this place. We'd be lost without her."

"Of course you would," Marg agreed.

Kelly smiled shyly and said, "Hello."

"What's going on today? Any interesting work?"

"Dan is working on his association game with some four-year-olds."

"Good." She turned to Kelly. "You'll enjoy watching that. I'll get you settled before I head to my meeting."

"Okay."

Five minutes later Kelly sat next to a red-haired grad student in the observation room. Dan pulled out his computer-generated graphs and began explaining them to Kelly.

"She's twelve, Dan. Don't get into the calculus," Francesca said as she walked to the door. "Kelly, if he starts to bore you to death, I'll be in the first office on the left."

"I'll be fine," Kelly said.

Francesca chuckled. Dan would probably be talking in techno-jargon in about thirty seconds, but he was a good guy with a real dedication to children.

She crossed to the first office on the left and tapped on the open door.

"Francesca," her adviser said. "You finally remembered where to find me."

"Yeah, yeah, I know." Francesca walked in and settled in front of Emily's desk. "I've finished my outline."

"You're kidding." Her adviser, an attractive woman in her forties, picked up the papers Francesca held out. "I've been telling you that you can't spend all your time tormenting innocent bystanders, but I wasn't sure you were listening."

"I always listen to what you say."

Emily smiled. "If only that were true." She drew on her glasses and pushed her dark hair off her forehead. "All right. What have we got here?"

One of the four-year-olds picked up a kid-sized chair and threw it at the boy across from him. Kelly's mouth dropped open.

"Are they supposed to do that?" she asked, pointing at the second boy, who promptly hit the first. They both burst into tears.

Dan muttered something under his breath and raced out of the observation room. Kelly wasn't exactly sorry to see him go. Some of his theories were interesting and stuff, but he'd gotten way too technical. At first she'd been insulted that Francesca had said she was only twelve, but after ten minutes of listening to Dan, she understood why.

She stood and strolled out of the room, back into the hallway. Francesca had said she would be about a half hour and that time was nearly up. She spied a chair by the office Francesca had told her she would be in and plopped down to wait.

She and her dad were supposed to play chess again that night. Last night Kelly had barely figured out how the different pieces moved. She knew now that she'd been tricked. It would be years before she was good enough to beat her dad and win that DVD player, but that didn't bother her at all. He'd known what he was getting into when he made the offer. Maybe he was planning on keeping her around for a while. While he was kind of a stick in the mud about some things and annoying, he wasn't really so bad. He was—

Kelly jumped as she realized she could hear what was being said in the office. She leaned back against the frosted glass window so the words would be more clear, then stiffened when she heard her own name.

"Kelly is the daughter of a friend of mine," Francesca was saying. "She's a wonderful dancer and takes classes all the time. We're hanging out together this week. It's been lots of fun."

"Sounds like a great mini-vacation."

"It is. Kelly is really easy to be with. Basically a great kid."

While Kelly didn't appreciate the "kid" remark, Francesca's words made her feel good.

"I saw you two walk in," the other woman said. "She has beautiful hair."

"I know. She hates the curls, but I think they're amazing."

The other woman laughed. "I tried to get a perm that would do what her hair does naturally. Eighty dollars and three hours later, I looked like a badly cut poodle. It was very disheartening."

Kelly bit back a smile.

"She also has the most adorable freckles," Francesca said. "I think they're charming. Ah, to be that young and pretty. When I watch her dancing, I feel like an old crone by comparison."

"Honey, by comparison, you *are* an old crone."

Francesca laughed. "Gee, thanks."

Kelly stood up and quickly walked to the far end of the hall. Her face burned and her stomach was all jumpy. Every time she'd overheard her mother talking about her—which wasn't very often because only a few friends even knew she existed—Tanya said mean stuff. Nothing like this.

Francesca thought she was pretty. Francesca liked her. If Francesca and Sam got together, then Kelly might never have to worry about being sent away.

She thought about how her mother had always hidden her and ignored her. Francesca would never do that. She would never leave her child. She would never forget birthdays, or say things that hurt Kelly's feelings. She knew a lot of her friends had stepparents, and while some of them were okay, others were really awful. What if her dad started seeing someone else?

That couldn't happen, she told herself. Francesca was exactly who she and her dad needed in their lives. Somehow she would find a way to bring them together.

18

Wednesday morning Sam adjusted his tie, then stepped back into his closet to collect his cell phone, wallet, and jacket. He had another meeting with the Brazilian clients, then a working lunch with his office manager. A local business association wanted to sponsor a mini film festival the following summer and had asked Sam to meet with them to discuss security.

He glanced at his watch. Francesca was going to be taking Kelly to dance class that morning, so he could get into the office early and get a head start on his day. Without her, he couldn't possibly get everything done. She was—

He reached for his wallet, but instead of grabbing it, he accidentally knocked it onto the floor, where it fell open. As he bent to pick it up, he noticed a strip of silver. Anger exploded.

"Damn her hide," he muttered.

Straightening, he examined the platinum credit card. It was right where it was supposed to be. Right where it hadn't been the afternoon before when he'd stopped and gotten gas.

"Kelly!" he roared as he walked out into the hallway.

His daughter poked her head out of her bedroom. She was already dressed for her dance class. Her hair was a mass of curls, and she held a white ribbon in one hand.

"Stop yelling," she told him. "I'm right here. What's up?"

She was so casual about it all, he thought, fighting the need to put his fist through the wall.

"You took my credit card," he said, his teeth clenched.

"What are you talking about?"

She sounded concerned and baffled, as if she had no idea what he meant. But he'd known her long enough to recognize the slight tension in her thin shoulders and the stubborn set of her chin.

"Yesterday I noticed my Visa card was missing from my wallet. This morning it's back where it belongs."

She rolled her eyes. "Right. So you want to blame me. Maybe you misplaced it or didn't see it when you looked before."

"It wasn't there. So I called and canceled it last night. Funny how there had only been one charge on it. To a clothing store on the Internet." He narrowed his gaze. "I canceled the order, too."

"You did what?" she demanded. "That is just so typical. You want to ruin everything."

He'd caught her stealing, and he expected her to go on the attack, but he was still stunned by her blaming him for stopping the order.

"You stole from me!" he yelled.

"You stole from me, too," she said as she stepped into the hall and glared at him. "You had no right to take away my old credit card. I wasn't doing anything bad with it. And I wasn't doing anything bad this time, either."

"You were stealing. Maybe that's okay in New York, but it's damn wrong here."

"I asked for an allowance, and you said you'd think about it. You haven't said anything since, and I couldn't wait any longer. I didn't have a choice."

"So this is *my* fault? What is wrong with you? If you're grown-up enough to steal, why aren't you grown-up enough to take responsibility for what you've done?"

"I'm only twelve. What do you want from me?"

"Better behavior than this. You're grounded."

"There's news." She folded her arms over her chest. "So you really like being a bully, don't you. When you were little, did you beat up on the smaller kids?"

He hadn't thought it was possible to get more angry, but he'd been wrong. "Do not make this about me, young lady. You are the one who stole from me. I can see I'm going to have to start locking up my money and credit cards, which is a pretty sorry state of affairs around here."

"Why don't you just lock me up, too?" she taunted. "It's what you want to do."

"It could just be me, but from where I'm standing, it sounds like both of you need to take a deep breath and calm down," Francesca said.

Sam turned and saw her leaning against the railing by the stairs. Relief flooded him. At least she would know what to do.

"When did you get here?" he asked.

"Somewhere between the opening shot and the last salvo," she said. "Want to talk about it?"

Kelly glared at her. "He's a hundred percent wrong. Don't you dare take his side."

"Don't speak to her in that tone of voice," Sam ordered.

Kelly huffed. Sam glared. Francesca had the feeling she should have slept in and avoided the whole fight. But now she was here, stuck in the middle of what could be a sticky situation. Because as much as Sam had the right to be furious with his daughter, there was one piece of the puzzle missing. Why had Kelly taken the credit card?

In the past few weeks her stuff had arrived from New York, she'd been to the mall to flesh out her wardrobe, and from what Francesca had been able to tell, she was adjusting well and pretty happy. So why would she risk her father's wrath and steal his credit card?

She turned to Sam. "Tell me what happened."

He recounted going to get gas the previous afternoon, finding his credit card missing, and then calling to cancel it.

"There had only been one charge that day," he said. "To an Internet clothing company." He glared at his daughter. "We all know how Kelly likes to shop with a keyboard."

Francesca ignored the sarcasm. "Okay, Kelly, let's hear it. Did you take the credit card?"

Sam started to say of course she had, but Francesca held up a restraining hand. "Please let her answer."

The preteen sighed heavily. She ducked her head so her curls fell in her face. "It's not what you think."

"See?" Sam said.

Francesca ignored him. "Kelly, are you going to answer the question?"

Kelly raised her head and thrust out her chin. "Okay, I took it, but it's not what *he* thinks."

Francesca studied the girl's green eyes, seeing the shadows of pain and fear. This hadn't been an act of defiance, she realized. It was something else entirely.

"What I think is that you took it and used it without permission," Sam said, still sounding furious. "And you're going to be punished."

Francesca agreed that no reason was good enough to

avoid all consequences, but she still wanted to know one more thing.

"Why?" she asked softly.

"What?" Sam turned to her. "What does it matter why? She wanted more clothes. More whatever she doesn't think she has enough of."

"You're so stupid!" Kelly yelled. "You think you know everything, but you don't. You don't know *anything*!"

Francesca sighed. "Kelly, you know better than to speak like that. Calling an adult stupid is never a good idea. You're making your father more angry, and you're using up your good-will with me."

Kelly's mouth trembled. "It doesn't matter. Just punish me. I don't care."

She cared so much, it hurt Francesca just to look at her. "Tell us why, please."

Kelly sucked in a breath and faced her father. "It was a leather jacket for you," she said, her voice high and shrill. "For your damn birthday, okay? I asked for an allowance and you blew me off. You didn't even want to talk about it. Your birthday is next week, so what was I supposed to do?"

Sam's expression tightened. "Don't you swear at me, young lady. You're already in enough trouble."

Francesca nearly fell over. All he'd gotten from Kelly's confession was that she'd used a bad word? What about the fact that she wanted to get him something for his birthday? The means might suck big time, but the motive was pure.

Kelly's mouth trembled. Francesca knew exactly what she was thinking. That she'd tried to show she cared, that her father mattered to her, and he'd thrown it back in her face.

Without saying a word, she turned and raced into

her bedroom. The door slammed and the lock clicked.

Sam groaned. "Great. I was waiting until the weekend before taking out her lock. I can see I should have done it last night."

He headed for his bedroom. Francesca hesitated, not sure who to go after first, then she remembered Sam would be leaving for work in a matter of minutes while Kelly would be around all day.

"Sam, wait," she called as she hurried after him. "You can't leave yet."

She found him in the closet, slipping into his jacket.

"I have out-of-town clients," he said. "This will have to wait. I don't want Kelly to go to dance class today. I don't want her going anywhere. She should stay in her room and think about what she's done wrong. We'll talk about it tonight."

"You and she may talk about it tonight, but you and I are going to talk about it right now."

He sighed. "Francesca, I don't have time for this."

"Then you'd better make time." She faced him. "Sam, you're wrong about this. I don't approve of what Kelly did. There's no excuse for her taking your credit card."

"Good. We're in agreement." He picked up his briefcase and stepped around her.

"No." She grabbed his arm. "She bought you a birthday present. She found out it was your birthday and wanted to get you something really nice. Doesn't that matter to you?"

He shook his head. "She could have made me a card or something."

"She's twelve, not five. She asked for an allowance first, so she was willing to use legitimate means to get you something."

"A leather jacket?" he asked, sounding incredulous. "We're talking a lot of money. I don't know the going rate for an allowance for someone her age, but it better not be enough for her to buy a leather jacket in a week."

"I agree. But can't you see she's trying to show you she cares? That you matter? That she wants you to be a family together?"

"I see that, but you're missing the fact that she lied and stole." He drew his eyebrows together. "I can forgive a lot of things, Francesca, but not deception."

Francesca swallowed. "I'm not defending her actions."

"How strange. Because that's exactly what it sounds like to me."

He turned and left.

Francesca walked to the top of the stairs and sat down. She felt queasy, but didn't think this was the onset of morning sickness. Instead it was a combination of fear and guilt. If Sam got this angry when Kelly acted out, what would happen when he found out the truth about her little secret?

She told herself she had two days left before the big confession. If things could just stay calm between now and then, maybe he would relax enough to understand. Of course, it could start raining silver coins in the morning, too.

She wasn't sure how long she sat there, trying to find the right combination of words to explain it all to Sam. At some point she heard a door open, then quiet footsteps on the carpeted landing. Kelly settled next to her on the top stair.

The twelve-year-old pulled her knees to her chest and wrapped her arms around her legs. "I really blew it," she whispered.

Francesca nodded slowly. "That's as good a definition as any."

"I guess I didn't think it through. I found out it was his birthday, and when he wouldn't give me an allowance, I panicked."

"You could have come to me for a loan."

Kelly looked at her. Tears filled her green eyes. "You don't have any money. I was afraid you'd say yes when you couldn't afford it, and then you'd have to go without food or something."

Francesca didn't know if she should laugh or cry. Instead she put her arm around the girl and hugged her. "I might be a struggling grad student, but I have enough for the basic necessities. Besides, the Grands always send me home with enough food to take care of the entire population of Baltimore." She leaned her head against Kelly's. "But it was sweet of you to worry."

Kelly turned toward her and held on tight. "He said he canceled the order. That means I don't have a present for him."

"Honestly, kid, I think that's the least of your problems."

"But I wanted to get him something nice. It's the first time I'm going to be here for his birthday."

Francesca heard the intensity in her voice and remembered feeling every emotion, every nuance when she'd been the same age. Life was so much more raw.

"I understand, but do you know why your dad got so mad?"

Kelly ducked her head and nodded. "I took his credit card and that was wrong. And maybe stupid."

"Maybe?"

Kelly gave a strangled laugh-sob and looked up. "Okay. It *was* stupid."

"Good. We're making progress. Now do you want to tell me what you could have done instead of just going for the plastic?"

Kelly sniffed. "I don't know."

"Sure you do. You're a smart girl. What other alternatives did you have?"

She thought for a second, then straightened and rubbed her fingers across her damp cheeks. "I could have talked to you. Or Gabriel. I sort of forgot about him. He might have loaned me the money and maybe even taken me shopping."

"What else?"

Kelly looked at her. "You want me to say I could have told my dad why I wanted the money, but that would have spoiled the surprise."

"Yes, but it would have been honest."

"Being honest is more important?"

Francesca felt as if there were a scarlet *H* on her chest. Talk about being a hypocrite. "I think so, and I suspect your dad thinks so. He has this thing about people lying to him."

Kelly flinched. "He was so mad."

"You're going to have to apologize to him when he gets home."

"No way. He was wrong, too."

Francesca sighed. "I can't make you, but I'm going to tell you a secret. Things will never be right with your dad until you say you're sorry, and the longer you wait, the harder it's going to be."

Kelly looked doubtful. "I'll think about it."

"I think you should."

She sighed. "I guess we're not going to dance class this morning, huh?"

"Nope."

"At this rate I'll never be a professional dancer."

"Let's concentrate on getting you all the way to age thirteen first. Then we'll sweat your career of choice."

Kelly smiled, then threw herself at Francesca. "Thank you for understanding. You're the best."

Francesca hugged her close. Kelly and Sam both had a lot of tough times ahead of them, but she knew they would be okay in the end. Wouldn't it be wonderful to be a part of this family? To watch the evolution of the relationship between father and daughter? She found herself wanting that chance more and more.

Sam walked into the house shortly after six. He found Francesca putting cooked chicken and a sauce onto dinner plates.

"Chicken Marsala," she said. "My mom stopped by to see me last night and brought along enough to feed ten or twelve. I thought I'd share the bounty."

He set his briefcase on the counter. "How was your day?"

"Fine."

She wasn't looking at him as she spoke. He had a feeling she was still annoyed.

"If I tell you that I think I should have listened to you, will it make things better?" he asked.

"Do you mean it?"

"Yeah. I need to take a deep breath before I react. Maybe listen more."

She stopped working and glanced at him. "Want to share the details of that thought process that got you there?"

"I was mad this morning. Too mad to think clearly. What Kelly did is inexcusable, but you're right. Her motives put a different light on the situation." He held up a hand. "Not that I'm saying she shouldn't be punished."

"That sounds more reasonable than what you were saying this morning."

Francesca set down the pan of chicken. He took that as a sign of forgiveness and moved toward her. She melted into his embrace.

"You have no idea how much I need you," he said as he stared into her eyes.

"So we're talking gratitude?" she asked lightly.

"Some, but it's more than that." He kissed her. "You're very important to me."

More than important, Sam thought. Vital.

He was about to tell her just how vital when she stepped free of his embrace. "You should probably head upstairs and put your daughter out of her misery. She's convinced her punishment is going to include being banished to a small cot outside and surviving on little more than leaves and tree bark."

"I was thinking along the lines of no TV for a week."

"I'm sure that will be a relief." She gave him a little push toward the door. "Go on. I'll get dinner ready, then I need to head home."

He'd been about to ask her to spend the night, but if she didn't want to . . .

Sam headed out of the kitchen. He wanted to clear things up with Kelly, but as he climbed the stairs, he couldn't help thinking there was something going on with Francesca. It was almost as if she'd known he wanted to talk about their relationship, and she hadn't wanted to have the conversation. Which made him wonder why. Was all this too much for her?

He didn't want to think about that. Losing her would be a disaster. Not just because of Kelly, but because of how much he'd grown to care about her. He needed her. He trusted her.

He came to a stop at the top of the landing. Need. Trust. Desire. Longing. Well, hell. Somehow, when he hadn't been paying attention, he'd gone and fallen in love.

Still stunned by the revelation, he crossed to Kelly's room. When he opened the door, she looked at him. He could see the fear and regret in her eyes.

Neither of them spoke. He wasn't sure what her reasons were. His were about not wanting to get it wrong. Finally he held out his arms. She raced toward him and flung herself into his embrace.

He held her close. "One of these days we'll get it right," he murmured.

She nodded. "Think it will happen soon?"

He chuckled. "I sure hope so." He exhaled. "You know you're still in trouble."

She snuggled close. "I know. It's okay."

Funny how suddenly it was.

19

Kelly watched herself in the floor-to-ceiling mirror. She raised her left leg a little higher, trying for the perfect line.

"That's right," Miss Angelina said approvingly. "Stretch. Like Kelly, girls. See how hard she tries."

Kelly felt a sharp pain in her leg and her hips, but she ignored it. Perfection came at a price. How many times had she been told that? Dance class was the only place she never screwed up, so she was determined to be the best here.

Against her will, her gaze slid from her own reflection to the window high in the opposite wall. She could just catch a glimpse of blue sky and part of a palm tree. If she closed her eyes, she could imagine the sound of the surf. She knew if she asked, Francesca would take her to the beach later. That they would talk and have fun. That Francesca would never say anything more about Kelly apologizing to her father, even though Kelly knew she wanted her to.

Kelly knew it was the right thing to do, too, but it was hard to say the words. Hard and scary. Because what if he was still mad? What if saying she was sorry wasn't enough? What if she didn't matter?

"And turn," Miss Angelina called.

The instruction caught Kelly off-guard. She began to rotate, then something happened and she was falling. Her ankle twisted painfully as she slammed into the ground.

"Kelly!"

She glanced up and saw Francesca rushing forward. Her notes for her paper lay scattered on the floor. Miss Angelina crouched by Kelly.

"Where does it hurt?" the instructor asked, reaching for her ankle. "Not broken, I think. Just a slight strain."

Pain shot through her, but that wasn't why Kelly started to cry. Instead the tears formed because she was tired and because she desperately needed her dad to be proud of her and to maybe even love her, but what if he didn't?

It was too much. All of it. What she wanted was to go home. So when Miss Angelina made her stand and put her weight on her sore ankle, it was so much easier to simply fall into the pain, let her eyes roll back, and faint.

Sam hurried into the house. "Is she all right?" he asked when he saw Francesca coming down the stairs.

"She's fine. The doctor says it's a strain, not even a sprain, and she'll be dancing her heart out by Monday."

"I don't think I can take any more," he muttered as he set his briefcase on the floor and loosened his tie. "This has been the week from hell."

"Tell me about it," Francesca murmured.

"At least tomorrow's Friday."

"Oh, goodie."

He glanced at her. "You don't sound happy the week is almost over."

She shrugged. "Like you say, it's been one thing after another."

He pulled off his tie, then shrugged out of his jacket. "We'll make sure we have a quiet weekend together. Just the three of us. How does that sound?"

"Good."

Francesca smiled, but he could see there was something bothering her. Before he could ask what, she stepped back and pointed upstairs. "Why don't you go check on our patient."

"Sure." He gave her a light kiss, then started up the stairs.

Kelly lay on top of her bed, her right foot propped on two pillows. Sam crossed the room and sat on the edge of the mattress.

"A sports injury, huh? Are you scarred for life?"

Kelly rolled her eyes. "I'm fine. It was just a silly twist. I don't know why I wasn't paying attention more."

"Francesca said you fainted, too. It must have hurt pretty bad."

She shrugged.

"Tough, huh?"

"Maybe."

He brushed her curls off her forehead. "Are you supposed to ice your ankle?"

"For the first twenty-four hours. We're taking a break." She stared at him. "Are you mad?"

He frowned. "Why would I be?"

"You had to leave work early and stuff. I thought . . ."

Kelly didn't want to say what she was thinking. That she hadn't wanted Francesca to call Sam because if he didn't come home, it would mean he didn't care. And she wanted him to care. But she didn't want to know if he didn't.

Still, he was here, and he looked worried, which was good.

"I wanted to know you were all right," he said gently, and smiled. "You're my daughter. I care about what happens to you."

Her chest tightened. "Really?"

"Absolutely."

She stared into his eyes and tried to see if he meant it or not. She wanted to believe him so badly she could barely breathe. Maybe if she apologized for taking his credit card, he would say something else really nice.

She opened her mouth. "I know I was—"

Francesca walked into the room. "So maybe it's time to come up with a different hobby," she said with a grin. "Something safer, like painting."

Irritation ripped through Kelly. As much as she liked Francesca, she hated that she'd just waltzed in here when things were going so good with her dad. If Francesca hadn't interrupted, she, Kelly, could have apologized.

"Unlike you, I actually have my life together," Kelly snapped without thinking. "I don't intend to be a poor struggling student when I'm almost thirty. I intend to be successful."

As soon as the words were out, she knew she'd made a really big mistake. She felt small and mean and sick to her stomach. But that wasn't the worst of it. The really bad part was the look in her father's eyes when he turned back to stare at her, and the pain and betrayal on Francesca's face.

Francesca made a small, choking sound and quickly left the room. Sam stood.

"Dammit, Kelly," he muttered. "What is wrong with you?"

Tears filled her eyes. "I don't know. I'm sorry."

"You're telling the wrong person."

Horror filled her. She'd hurt Francesca, which she'd never meant to do. "I didn't mean it."

"But you said it." He shook his head. "You might have your life planned out, but at the rate you're going, you'll be living it alone because no one is going to want to be with you."

She was crying too hard to see very much, but the silence that followed told her she'd been left all alone.

Francesca made it down stairs, but she couldn't find her purse. She was still fumbling through the kitchen when she felt Sam come up behind her. He turned her, pulled her into his arms, and held her close.

"I'm sorry," he murmured.

She shook her head, trying to say it was okay, that she understood, only it wasn't and she didn't. Kelly's words had pierced her like poisoned arrows. They'd struck deep and true, wounding her to the soul. In a couple of short sentences she'd reduced Francesca to that scared, stupid kid she'd always been. The one who was afraid of never being smart enough to make it in the world. The girl whose grandfather had told her over and over that she wasn't to worry her pretty head about it—some nice man would take care of her. But Francesca had never wanted to be taken care of. She'd wanted to be strong enough to stand on her own. And she was. Only it didn't feel like it.

"Oh, honey, I know it hurts," Sam whispered into her

ear as he stroked her back. "You've been on Kelly's side since the second she walked into this house. You've put yourself out for her, and this is your reward. I wish I could change things."

He drew back and cupped her face. "For what it's worth, I think you're amazing. These past few weeks have shown me that you're a very special woman, and I've been lucky to have you in my life."

Light poured from his eyes. A warm, gentle light that bathed her in a glow that should have made her happy enough to float.

Instead, it terrified her.

"Sam, don't," she said, pushing away from him. "Don't say anything nice about me."

He stiffened. "Because I'm changing the rules? Because I want more than something casual?"

It was as if someone had ripped her heart from her chest. If she hadn't been pregnant, if she hadn't spent the past month lying to him, she couldn't have been happier to hear those words and know that he cared about her. Maybe even loved her. Because over the past few days she'd come to see that he mattered more than anyone ever had.

She could imagine a life with him, a future. She could see them growing old, being happy. Sam didn't see her as a pretty face, or an ornament. He saw her as a confident, capable woman. He depended on her, believed in her. He thought she was strong. He thought of her as his equal. A partner. With him, she'd finally found everything she'd ever wanted.

But could she keep it?

"Please sit down," she said, moving to the kitchen table and pulling out a chair. "We have to talk."

He grimaced. "Four words every man hates to hear." He

took a seat. "Let me guess. You're not interested in anything more than an affair."

Tears burned in her eyes, but she blinked them away. "You couldn't be more wrong."

He brightened. "Great. Then what's the problem?"

There was no easy way to break the news, so she went for blunt and simple. "I'm pregnant."

He stared at her, then laughed. "Right. So tell me. What's going on?"

She sighed. "I'm not kidding. I'm pregnant."

He didn't speak, didn't react. Instead he just sat there, looking at her. She tried to read his expression, but she couldn't.

"When?" he said at last.

She wasn't sure if he was asking when she'd gotten pregnant or when she'd found out. Neither was going to please him.

"I'm about seven weeks along. It must have happened the first night we were together."

He stood up and very deliberately pushed in the chair. Tension tightened his body and his face. His mouth got pinched, his eyes narrowed.

"Pregnant?" he asked, his voice low and disbelieving. "You're having a baby?"

She nodded. "I know this is a shock to you—"

"A shock?" He paced to the far counter, then leaned against it, his arm folded across his chest. "A shock? How the fuck did this happen?"

The attack shouldn't have surprised her, but it did. She gripped the table. "The usual way."

"We used a condom."

"I know. I was there." Something occurred to her. "Are you doubting that this child is yours?"

"Of course not. I don't think you've been sleeping around, if that's what you're getting at, but holy hell, did you have to go and get pregnant? Isn't having Kelly drop into my life enough for one month?"

She'd known he wouldn't be happy, even though that had been her fantasy. She shouldn't be surprised he was upset. Neither of them had wanted this. Except after she'd recovered from the shock, she'd found that she liked the idea of a baby—especially Sam's baby.

"I didn't do it on purpose," she said. "I would say we have equal responsibility here."

He shook his head. "I know. I'm sorry. I don't mean to blame you. But a baby. Now. I didn't want . . ."

His voice trailed off, leaving her to fill in the rest of the sentence. He hadn't wanted Kelly and he certainly didn't want a baby? Was that it? Or was it even worse? He didn't want to tell her he refused to have anything to do with their child?

"I'll be fine," she said as she rose. "You don't have to be involved."

He frowned. "I'm not going to abandon my responsibilities here."

His responsibilities. Because of course he didn't *want* the baby.

"How long have you known?" he asked.

She was so caught up in feeling rejected that she spoke without thinking. "About five weeks."

The quality of the stillness in the room changed to something dark and dangerous. Francesca instinctively took a step back.

Sam didn't move, but that didn't mean he was still the same caring man she'd grown to love. He seemed to get bigger, angier. Whatever last hope she might have clung to died when his expression of frustration and confusion turned to loathing and contempt.

"It's not what you think," she said quickly. "Dammit, Sam, don't give me that look. I'm not the enemy here. I didn't tell you because Kelly had been in your life all of two or three weeks. You were still in shock and you didn't need one more thing to worry about."

"The words sound right," he said, his voice low and almost silky. "Tidy, reasonable. You were thinking about my feelings. I really appreciate that."

"Stop it," she demanded. "You don't need to be sarcastic."

"Then tell me what I need to be. You lied to me. You betrayed me."

She knew the danger in him thinking that. "I didn't lie."

"You withheld the truth. In my book, there's not much difference." He glared at her. "You've been lying for weeks. I let you in my house, in my life, in my bed. I made love with you. I thought you were different. I thought you weren't anything like Tanya, but damn if I wasn't wrong. Looks like I picked another winner."

The unfairness of the accusation froze her to the bone. "No! That's not true. I've been here for you. I've been good to you and to Kelly. I don't deserve this."

"What made you finally want to tell me? Do you need money?"

She felt as if he'd slapped her. "How dare you say that to me?"

"I can say anything I damn well please. When I think about all the times I've listened to your advice. Like you knew what the hell you were talking about. Like you weren't in it for yourself."

He moved toward her, which made her walked backward until she bumped into the stove. He stopped less than a foot from her and loomed over her.

"You're nothing but a liar, and if you think for one second you can use this against me, you're wrong. I don't care what it takes, but you'll never get a piece of me or my daughter again."

Horrified didn't begin to describe what she was feeling. What about their baby? What about her feelings and his? He cared about her—she'd been sure of it. How could that have died so quickly?

"You're wrong," she said. "About me, about all of it."

"Get out."

He turned and walked out of the kitchen. Francesca stared after him. She didn't know what to do, and then it didn't matter because she couldn't be in this house one second longer. She ran to the foyer, where she found her purse by the front door. After picking it up, she raced outside and vowed never to return.

Kelly carefully held on to the stair railing. Her ankle throbbed, but that wasn't the reason she couldn't seem to move. Nothing was right. Maybe nothing would ever be right again.

She'd started to come downstairs to apologize to Sam and Francesca. She'd wanted to make everything right. But instead she'd heard them fighting. It had been bad. Way worse than anything that had happened with Tanya and her boyfriends.

Francesca was pregnant. Kelly had figured out that much, and if Francesca was going to have a baby, then she didn't need Kelly to be a part of her family. Not when she was going to have a child of her own. And Sam had thrown Francesca out. Which meant they weren't going to get married. And if Sam found someone else, she might be as horrible as Raoul. He might decide that his new fiancée wouldn't want a twelve-year-old hanging around, and then he would send her away.

He would send her away, and she didn't have anywhere else to go.

20

Sam didn't sleep. He spent the hours until midnight pacing downstairs, then around one in the morning he started walking the grounds. By the time the sun came up, he was exhausted, sore, and not completely convinced he'd handled the situation with Francesca as well as he could have.

She'd lied. He was still having trouble reconciling what she'd done with the woman he'd grown to love. If she had been anyone else, he would have dismissed her from his life and never thought of her again. That's what he'd done with Tanya, with the other women he'd met. Even with his mother, after she'd died. He turned his back on bitter memories and had vowed never to make that mistake again.

Until now he'd succeeded. He'd kept his relationships superficial. No one had gotten under his skin, no one had mattered, and no one had betrayed him.

He'd wanted more of the same with Francesca, but that hadn't happened. Kelly had shown up, throwing his life the kind of curve designed to show the measure of his character. He figured he'd succeeded as much as he'd failed with her. And any part of his success was due to Francesca.

Damn her hide, but she'd made him look at things he hadn't wanted to see. He and Kelly might have a long way to go before they had something close to a normal father-daughter relationship, but if not for Francesca, they would still be spending all their time screaming at each other.

Francesca had taught him to listen, to be calm, to look at Kelly's side of things. Francesca had given him hope that he could learn how to be a good father. She'd made him believe in himself, in her, in them.

He'd fallen in love with her. Only to find out she was just like all the rest of them.

But he couldn't get his mind around that last thing. That she was like Tanya. Because Tanya had never cared about anyone but herself. And his mother had only been interested in manipulating those around her, using whatever means she could to manage the outcome. He'd known women who were in it for the money, the house, the family business, or the name. So what was Francesca in it for? A baby?

He shook his head. No. He would bet his soul that she hadn't gotten pregnant on purpose. They'd used protection and it had failed. So he wasn't angry because of the baby, but because—

He stopped in the middle of the garden, cold, damp with dew, and barely able to see straight. The first fingers of pink light had barely crept over the house. They were going to have a baby.

He'd heard the words when she'd said them, but he hadn't internalized them. Not until that second. A baby. An infant.

His brain filled with pictures of diapers and blankets, of

rocking chairs and car seats. Of a baby smile, a toddler, of a first step, a first word. All the things he'd missed with Kelly. No, not missed. All the things that had been stolen from him.

He clenched his hands into fists and raised his face to the sky. If there was one woman in the world he would have been willing to have a child with, Francesca was the one. He loved her. *Had* loved her. And she'd betrayed him.

Why had she kept it a secret? Five weeks. Not a couple of days or even one week. Five. She'd made love with him, knowing she carried his child. She'd laughed with him, smiled at him, held him close, all the while living a lie.

How could he reconcile what he wanted with what he knew?

There weren't any answers. At least not here in the garden. Tired beyond words, he headed for the house and walked into the kitchen. Maybe a couple hours of sleep would make things more clear. Maybe he would wake up and find out this was all just a bad dream and that it was still okay to trust and give his heart.

Didn't anybody on the planet carry cash anymore? Kelly wondered angrily as she tried yet another key in the door of Security International. The third one worked, the lock giving way with a loud *click*.

It was nearly six-thirty on Friday morning. She figured she had a couple of hours before office staff started showing up, but she wasn't taking any chances. Not when there was so much on the line.

Sam had been up all night. She knew because she kept checking his room. Finally, just after dawn, she'd heard him go into his room. He'd been snoring when she left fifteen minutes later.

She really hated that she'd had to come to the office first, but when she'd gone through his wallet around midnight, she'd found all of twenty dollars. Not nearly enough to allow her to run away and not ever be found. Which meant she needed more cash, and she knew only one place to get it.

After carefully closing and locking the front door behind her, she made her way to Sam's office. There she went through the key ritual again until she found the one that unlocked his desk. She pulled out the key that would open the cabinet holding the petty cash box and crept down the hall.

She didn't want to steal. Not really. But what choice did she have? It wasn't like she had her own credit card anymore. And not having a credit card had meant having to look up the bus routes and then take the right one to get her to the office. She'd lost a lot of time. But she had a plan. Once she had the money, she would take a bus to San Francisco. She figured a bus was really safe because Sam would assume she was taking a plane. While he was busy checking first-class reservations, she would disappear into the city.

She walked into the storeroom and opened the cabinet. She was in the process of counting out the bills when a hand dropped onto her shoulder. She screamed and the money went flying. When she turned, she found her great-grandfather standing right behind her.

"You're up early," he said.

She opened her mouth, closed it, then burst into tears.

Sam woke at eight-thirty. A shower and two cups of coffee later he still felt like roadkill. By nine-fifteen he decided he'd better check on Kelly. She'd been hurting last night, and he felt badly for not talking to her at the time. Francesca's announcement had thrown him.

As he climbed the stairs, he wondered how he was going to tell Kelly about the baby. Maybe he should wait on that until he knew what was going to happen. They could discuss it—

She was gone.

Sam stood inside her room and stared at the neatly made bed. There weren't that many things missing, but he knew in his gut that she'd left. Run away.

Panic didn't begin to describe what he was feeling. His daughter, he thought frantically. Where would she go?

Just in case his gut was wrong, he carefully searched the house, then checked his wallet. His credit cards were all there, but the last of his cash was missing.

He grabbed the phone on his nightstand and punched in Francesca's number. A thick, tear-filled voice answered.

"Hello?"

"Is she with you?"

Francesca cleared her throat. "What? Sam?"

"Is Kelly with you?"

"No. Of course not. What happened?"

"She's missing. She ran away. I was up all night, so it must have been sometime this morning."

"No. Oh, Sam, she can't be out on her own. What are you going to do?"

"Find her."

"Do you want me to help?"

Frustration, fear, and the need to get moving steeled his resolve. "I don't want anything from you," he said before hanging up.

• • •

"You're all fired," Sam announced at noon the following day. "Every single one of you is fired. We're the most successful security company on the West Coast, and you're telling me we can't find one twelve-year-old girl?"

The portion of his security staff in town gathered in the main conference room. Sam paced in front of the dry erase boards. Gabriel sat in a chair by the door.

Jason ignored the news of his job loss. "We've checked all points of departure, boss. Airports, train stairs, bus depots. We've talked to cab companies, limo companies. Hell, even car-rental companies in case she had fake ID."

Sam glared at him, not bothering to point out the obvious—that Kelly was twelve and unlikely to know how to drive a car.

"No one's seen her. There aren't any clues." The man shifted uneasily in his seat. "It's like she vanished."

Sam turned his back on his staff. "Get out," he said wearily. "All of you, get the hell out."

There was movement behind him, then silence. He turned back to find Jason and Gabriel still in the room. He crossed to the table and sank down next to Jason.

"Now what?" he asked quietly.

Jason looked as tired and worried as Sam felt. "It's time to talk to our liaison at the police department."

Sam didn't even want to admit defeat—to go to the police when he knew his people could work faster by avoiding all that messy legal protocol. But never had he felt the sharp blade of failure more acutely than today.

He stared at his friend. "We have to find her, Jason. Dear God, she's out there by herself. Anything could happen."

Gabriel excused himself and walked wearily from the room. His limp had gotten more pronounced over the past twenty-four hours. He was showing his age.

Sam and Jason made up a new list of plans. When they were finished, Sam covered his face with his hands.

"This is all my fault," he said. "The last thing I said to Kelly . . ." Just thinking about it made him sick to his stomach. "She can't be gone. She just can't. I missed so much with her. All those early years. I can never get them back, but I want the future we were supposed to have. I want to watch her grow up and teach her to play chess. I want to be there on her first date." He dropped his hands. "And scare the shit out the guy."

Jason gave him a weary smile. "You'll do a good job at that."

Sam nodded. "I want to help her pick out a college." His throat got tight. "Dammit, Jason, I just want to hold her in my arms."

"Daddy?"

The soft voice, the single word, made his heart stop in mid-beat. He turned toward the door and saw Kelly standing just inside the conference room.

A thousand thoughts flooded his brain, but he couldn't focus on a single one. Instead he could only stand and move around the table. Then Kelly was running toward him.

She threw herself against him just as he grabbed her and pulled her close. She was warm, alive, breathing, and crying.

"You're okay," he said, unable to process the information. "You're here."

"I've been here the whole time."

Sam stroked her hair, her back, then touched her chin so she looked up at him. Her green eyes were wet with tears, but still precious to him.

"You're all right?"

She sniffed, then nodded. "I was running away. I came here to get cash and Gabriel found me."

Sam couldn't feel anything but happiness. He glanced over her to where Jason sat grinning like a fool. "You know about this?"

"No way. The old man pulled one over on both of us."

Sam remembered his grandfather showing up within minutes of being called. He'd insisted on searching the house while Sam had been on the phone calling staff members. No doubt the wily old bastard had used the time to slip the keys back into place. Sam had never noticed they were gone.

He sighed. "No one bothered to check the office, right?"

Jason shook his head. "Sorry, boss."

He rose and left, just as Gabriel stepped into the room. The old man looked very pleased with himself. Sam noticed the limp didn't seem so bad now.

"You fooled us all," Sam said, too relieved to be angry.

"I only wanted to fool you."

Sam sat down and pulled Kelly onto his lap. "I'm sorry about what I said the other night. About no one wanting to be with you. Not only was that mean of me, it was wrong. I'm so sorry."

"It's okay." She wrapped her thin arms around his neck.

"Kelly, you mean the world to me. I know things haven't been easy, but I think we're making progress. Good progress. I can't—" He couldn't imagine life without her. He cleared his throat. "I love you."

She straightened. "Really?"

"With my whole heart. I'd be destroyed if you left."

Her eyes widened. "So you don't want to send me away?"

"No. Not ever." He took one of her hands in his. "I can honestly tell you that never crossed my mind. Not even once." He gave her a slight smile. "You're stuck with me, kid."

"That's okay." She looked at him, ducked her head, then blushed. "I called you Daddy before."

"I know. I liked it."

She sighed, then smiled. "Me, too."

She flung herself against him and he held her close. As he rubbed her back, he glared at his grandfather.

"You and I are going to have words later, old man."

Gabriel shrugged. "It was for a good cause."

"You nearly gave me a heart attack. I know you needed to let Kelly know how much she mattered to me, and I'm glad she got the message, but you shouldn't have carried things on for so long. When I thought Kelly was out there by herself . . ." He shook his head, not wanting to think about it.

Gabriel chuckled. "Sam, you're such a horse's ass."

Sam stiffened, Kelly gasped and sat up, but Gabriel didn't stop talking.

"You think I did this for Kelly, when the truth is, I did it for you. You're the one who needed to figure out how much she mattered."

Sam glared at him. "Why you meddling, old—" He stopped and leaned back in the chair. Well, hell. Gabriel had taught him a lesson and a half. The last twenty-seven hours had been a living nightmare he would never forget. If that's what it had taken to make him realize how much he loved his daughter, then maybe it had been worth it.

"I don't approve of your methodology," Sam muttered as he touched Kelly's cheek. She smiled at him.

Gabriel settled into a chair. "That's fine with me. I've

always been a cowboy at heart, doing my own thing." He nodded at Kelly. "She told me a real interesting story about you and Francesca. So you've got another one on the way, huh?"

Gabriel sounded more proud than surprised, which was fine, because Sam was shocked enough for both of them.

"You knew?" he asked Kelly.

She nodded. "I was coming downstairs to apologize to Francesca for what I said and to you for taking your credit card."

Gabriel chuckled. "You've got to admit, the kid is damned resourceful."

Sam ignored him. "And you heard about the baby?"

"Uh-huh." She wiped her cheeks. "That's why I ran away. Francesca was always the one making things right with you and me. I'd been hoping the two of you would get together or something. But when I heard about the baby, I knew she wouldn't want me anymore. Not when she was going to have one of her own." New tears spilled down her cheeks. "Then when you told her to get out, I figured you weren't going to get married and that I wasn't going to be allowed to stay."

"Oh, honey."

Gabriel making a tisking sound. "You're going to have some groveling to do, boy."

Before Sam could respond, there was a loud commotion outside.

Gabriel glanced at his watch. "Right on time."

"Who is that?" Kelly asked.

"The Marcelli family. I called them when you went missing." The old man chuckled. "They've been worried and wanted to know what to do. I suggested they show up here this morning." He winked at Sam. "I figured you'd be at your breaking point about now, and Kelly and I would take pity on you."

Kelly jumped off Sam's lap and hurried toward the door. "They were really worried about me?" she asked, sounding delighted. "Wow. That's so cool."

When she'd stepped out of the room, Gabriel looked at Sam. "It seems they all know about Francesca's bun in the oven. Lorenzo's not taking it well. He was expecting an engagement announcement, followed by a quickie wedding."

Sam rose. "They knew? Did everyone know but me?"

Gabriel shrugged. "Looks that way."

Sam headed into the hallway. Sure enough, the Grands, Grandpa Lorenzo, and Colleen and Marcus stood around talking with various staff members. He supposed he should be pleased that Katie and Brenna hadn't tagged along.

His daughter was being hugged, squeezed, and cheek-pinched by the Grands. The pleasure on her pretty face eased some of the tightness in his chest. It had been a hell of a morning, and it didn't seem to be getting any less stressful.

"Thanks for stopping by," he said above the din. "As you can see, Kelly is fine."

Conversation ceased. Five adults looked at him. Five pairs of eyes turned reproachful. Sam suddenly felt as if he were eight and had just hit a baseball through the church window.

He tried to smile and somehow couldn't make his mouth move. Grandpa Lorenzo stepped toward him.

"You dishonor my granddaughter. We have a word for men like you."

Sam didn't want to know what it was. Nor did he know how to defend himself against the much older man. While he knew enough moves to take out Lorenzo twenty times over, it seemed in bad form to use them against a soon-to-be great-grandfather.

Lorenzo started muttering in Italian. The Grands didn't look any more friendly. He didn't want to know what Francesca's parents were thinking.

"You're going to marry her," the old man said. "It's the right thing to do."

"No, he's not."

Everyone turned and saw Francesca walking down the hallway. She walked over to Lorenzo and got between him and Sam.

"Leave him alone."

Her grandfather roared. "You're pregnant. He's the father. He should do the right thing."

Sam turned and saw Gabriel leaning against a wall. "Did you call her, too?"

"Sure. She needed to be here."

"Any more surprises?"

"That's up to you."

Great.

Francesca glared right back at Lorenzo. "Sam and I will do what is right for us. Not what you want, not what my parents want, not what anyone else wants."

"But the baby—"

"Will be fine. I've already married one man I didn't love. I'm not doing it again."

She didn't love him? The words burned deep. "You don't love me?" he asked without thinking.

She whirled on him. "Do you really want to have this conversation right here?"

He glanced around at her family, at Gabriel and Kelly and most of his staff hovering in the background.

"I thought I'd fired all of them," he muttered, then motioned to the conference room. "How about in there?"

"Fine."

She swept past him.

He followed and closed the door, all the while trying not to think about everyone out there pressing close and listening.

Francesca paced the length of the room. When she reached the far end, she turned back to him but didn't speak.

Sam studied her—the long brown hair that swayed with each movement. The shape of her greenish-hazel eyes. The set of her mouth. He remembered the first time they'd met. She'd been seriously pregnant. Maybe it had been a sign.

She was having his baby. He recalled being furious with her just a couple of days ago. He'd said a lot of things he now regretted. After the last couple of days, he understood why she'd kept the truth from him. He'd been reeling from dealing with Kelly. She'd wanted to give him time. She hadn't acted anything like his ex-wife. He—

"You have a lot to answer for," she said, her voice thick with tension. "You were a real bastard, Sam. And you don't fight fair."

Her sharp words were so at odds with the warm and friendly thoughts he'd been having that it took him a second to switch gears. "Me?"

She planted her hands on her hips. "You. If we're going to fight, we're going to fight fair. No name-calling and no walking out. We stay here until it's settled. No matter how long it takes."

She was right, he thought. "Fine. I'm sorry I called you a liar. I was stunned and wounded and I lashed out, but it's not an excuse. It won't happen again."

She didn't looked convinced, but she nodded. "I'm sorry I walked out. I should have stayed and fought with you, no matter how upset I was. And just to make things clear, I didn't keep the information from you just to entertain myself. I found out about the baby right before the Fourth of July. I didn't want to tell you then because I didn't believe it myself. Then I learned about my brother and there was all that. Then there were problems with Kelly. I wanted to give you time."

"You shouldn't have made that decision for me. It wasn't yours to make."

"I know that. I was wrong and I apologize." She sucked in a breath. "But that's not the only reason I didn't tell you. I knew you'd get upset, and I didn't want things between us to change."

What? "We're having a baby. Of course they're going to change." He couldn't believe that he loved her and wanted to yell at her in equal measures. "How could things not change?"

"I knew they would be different," she said, her voice rising. "That's the point. I liked being with you. I liked what we had. I was starting to care about you, which not only broke the rules, but scared the crap out of me. So I hid the truth. And I felt really guilty."

He matched her volume with volume. "You should have trusted me."

"Don't yell at me."

"You started it."

She stomped her foot. "Dammit, Sam, I am a calm, rational person. Not a screamer."

"You seem to be a screamer with me."

Her gaze narrowed. "Don't you dare bring up sex right now."

"I meant when we fight. You yell."

"I do not."

"You're yelling right now."

"I'm—" She pressed her lips together, then dropped her voice. "You bring out the worst in me."

Color stained her cheeks. She was breathing hard and standing her ground. In that second, he knew she would always go toe-to-toe with him. If she thought he was wrong, she would tell him. Whether it was about Kelly, their baby, or any other part of their lives.

He circled around the large table and walked toward her. "I love you, Francesca Marcelli."

In the silence that followed, he heard not only her gasp, but a sigh from outside.

She shook her head. "You can't. I lied. I knew how much you hated deception, and I did it anyway."

He walked closer and took her hands. "Tell me why."

"Because." She blinked back tears. "I didn't want to lose you and I thought I might. I . . . I love you, Sam."

His heart did a double beat. "Yeah?"

She nodded. "Even when you make me crazy. You don't treat me like I'm stupid. With you I'm an equal. You listen to me, you trust me. At least you did."

He leaned forward and kissed her. "I still do. How could I not? You do the right thing, even when it hurts. No matter what happens, you keep showing up."

She sniffed. "You do, too. Having Kelly appear without warning really messed with your world. But even when you were angry and frustrated and backed into a corner, you kept trying."

He glanced at the door behind them, then lowered his voice. "I said some things I regret. About being sorry she was around."

Francesca nodded. "But you said them to me. In private. It's okay to have doubts. We're judged by what we do with those doubts. You kept on trying. Working the program. Falling for her."

He smiled. "I love her." He pulled her close. "I love you, too. I want us to be a family, Francesca. I'm still in shock about the baby, but I'm excited, too. I want you to marry me. Not because it's the right thing to do or because of pressures outside this room, but because you want to. Because you can't imagine life without me."

Francesca kissed him. If she'd had any doubts about her feelings for Sam, the last twenty-four hours had destroyed them. She'd been more than miserable: she'd been lost.

"I need you," she whispered.

He chuckled. "Not half so much as I need you. Say you'll marry me. Promise to love me forever, which is almost as long as I'm going to love you."

She held him and sighed. "I do love you, Sam. With my whole heart. And yes, I'll marry you."

There was a loud cheer from the hallway.

"So we don't have to make a formal announcement," he murmured.

"My family doesn't exactly stand on ceremony."

"Neither do I," he said and kissed her.

POCKET STAR BOOKS
PROUDLY PRESENTS

THE SEDUCTIVE ONE

SUSAN MALLERY

Available in paperback
from Pocket Star Books

Turn the page for a preview of
The Seductive One . . .

Borrowing a million dollars from the devil was one thing; picking a fight with him while doing it was something else.

Brenna Marcelli considered herself to be above average in intelligence. With her future on the line, there was absolutely *no* way she would be anything but perfectly pleasant during her conversation with Nicholas Giovanni. She would be confident, persuasive, even charming. She would not get crabby, beg, or think about sex. Especially not sex. No matter how good it had been.

But it *had* been great, she thought as she paced the length of the waiting area in the executive offices of Wild Sea Vineyards. Better than good. One time they'd done it on the beach, and that night on the news there'd been a report of an unexpectedly high tide. Brenna had always wondered if she and Nic were somehow to blame.

"History," she murmured as she clutched her portfolio more tightly to her chest. "Ancient history. This is a new decade—a new century even. I am empowered. I am impervious. I am really annoyed that he's keeping me waiting."

She turned and glared at the closed door leading to

Nic's private office. When his assistant had asked her to wait and promised the man in charge would be with her shortly, Brenna had believed her. Now, nearly ten minutes later, the assistant had disappeared and there was still no sign of Nic.

"Just a power play," she told herself, then took a calming breath. "I'm not going to buy into it. He can keep me waiting as long as he wants."

Except her stomach was in knots, she had serious regrets about that fifth cup of coffee, and she had a bad feeling that if she stopped moving for too long, she would find that her knees were shaking. Not exactly the picture of professional confidence she wanted to portray. She really needed to—

The office door opened and the devil himself walked into the room.

Okay, maybe calling Nic the devil was a bit strong, but he was dark, dangerous, and at this point she would sell him her soul to get what she wanted. A rose by any other name and all that.

"Brenna." Nic spoke her name with a smile. As if they met on a regular basis. "Good to see you."

If only, she thought. She hadn't set foot on Giovanni land in ten years. And with good reason.

"Hi, Nic."

He motioned toward his office and she stepped into the inner sanctum. The room hadn't changed a whole lot since she'd last seen it. Still massive, still dominated by a desk built in the eighteen century. The computer was new, as was the owner. Ten years ago Nic's grandfather had occupied the space. From here he'd run all of Wild Sea Vineyards. Now the old man was gone and Nic was in charge.

In charge and going places, she thought as she crossed

to the map on the wall opposite the opulent desk. She studied the shaded area that detailed the Giovanni holdings, noting how much expansion there'd been in the past seven years. Nic had always wanted to be the biggest and best. He'd achieved that in spades.

Of course, focusing on the map allowed her not to think about that damn desk. Unfortunately, she was going to have to turn around and stare at it sometime. It wouldn't be so bad if she and Nic hadn't, well, done it on that desk.

It had been about three A.M. on a Saturday morning. The night had been still, cool, and incredibly romantic. Of course, when she'd been seventeen and in love, watching paint dry had been romantic.

"You're welcome to sit down," he said, a trace of amusement in his voice.

Sure, she thought as she squared her shoulders and turned to face her past. Nic worked here every day. He'd probably forgotten what had happened on that carved slab of wood. But not her.

She made her way to an oversize chair and sank onto the smooth leather surface. Nic walked around his desk and sat facing her.

"I was surprised to hear you'd made an appointment to see me," he said easily. "I hope everything is all right with your family."

"They're fine. Great, really. Francesca's engaged." More than engaged, but that conversation was for another time.

"That must make your grandfather happy."

She nodded and found her gaze settling on his face. Strong features, she thought, remembering the boy as she stared at the man. He'd always had strong features. Compelling eyes, a straight nose, a determined, maybe even stubborn chin, and a mouth that had once been able to kiss her into another time zone.

Despite the warm August temperatures, he wore a long-sleeve black shirt, dark slacks. Not exactly the jeans and T-shirts she was used to seeing.

"You're dressed for success," she said.

"In honor of our meeting."

He smiled, a slow, sexy smile that made her remember other smiles. Like the one he'd used to convince her it was really okay to make love late at night in the vineyard. It had been their first time and she'd lost her virginity to the sound of crickets and—

Let's stop this right now, she told herself. Trips down memory lane were only going to get her into trouble. She was here on a mission that had nothing to do with sexy smiles or the heat flaring to life low in her belly.

She forced herself to relax in the leather chair. She carefully crossed one leg over the other and tried for a faintly amused, possibly bored expression. Who knew if it really worked.

"All that trouble for me? I don't think so."

He chuckled. "All right. I have a meeting with several foreign distributors later this afternoon. I figured jeans would put them off."

Not if they were women, Brenna thought before she could stop herself.

"So you're expanding again," she said instead.

"Always. Be the biggest and the best."

"You're certainly going to win on volume."

"Don't they say size matters?"

"Only those who don't know how to use what they have." She remembered her vow not to argue with him about eighteen seconds too late.

"Sorry," she murmured.

He raised his eyebrows. "For disagreeing with me? There's a first. Now I'm even more intrigued." He grinned and leaned forward. "All right, Brenna. You're here, you're wearing a suit, and you're carrying what looks like a thick stack of papers. Why don't you tell me what's going on?"

So they were going to get right to it. She cleared her throat and set her portfolio on his desk. At that moment her brain hiccupped and every single intelligent, logical, financially sound sentence she'd practiced flew out of her head.

"I'm one of the best in the business," she began, then hesitated, wondering if that sounded too arrogant.

At least he didn't break into hysterical laughter. "I'll admit that I wouldn't want to go head to head with you in competition," he said.

The compliment boosted her confidence and made her want to wiggle in her seat. She satisfied herself with a slight smile. "As my grandfather says, aside from him, I'm the only one in the family with a passion for wine. I've lived it most of my life."

He started to say something, but she rushed on. There was no way she was going to let him remind her of the ten years she'd spent away from Marcelli Wines. Ten years she'd spent being an idiot.

"My grandfather has put me in charge of the winery. I know what's needed to take our success to the next level."

"So you're not here for a job."

"No." She flipped open the portfolio. "I'm here for a loan."

Nic straightened. "Why? You don't have a cash-flow problem."

"Marcelli Wines doesn't. Business has never been better. But I'm not them. I work for my grandfather. The company still belongs to him."

"You'll inherit."

If only. The truth shouldn't still hurt, but it did. It hurt a lot. "My sisters and I inheriting has become less of a sure thing." She paused, knowing that there was no point in holding back. He was going to hear about it eventually.

"It seems my parents had a child out of wedlock, as they say. A son. They were both still in high school. Due to family pressure, they gave up the baby for adoption."

Nic was cool as always. Instead of letting any emotion show on his face, he leaned back in his chair. "That would change things," he admitted. "When did you find out?"

"At our big Fourth of July party. It was our version of fireworks, to say the least. The point is, the long-lost baby is now a thirty-year-old man."

The Marcelli and Giovanni families might not have spoken in nearly three generations, but they had both grown up with the same traditional Italian values. Feminism had yet to arrive at the shores of their respective vineyards. Nic got it right away.

"Your grandfather is old-fashioned enough to be more comfortable leaving the family business to a male heir. I'm guessing the long-lost brother is interested?"

"It's a ton of money. Wouldn't you be?" she asked with a lightness she didn't feel. "All of which leaves me on the short end of the inheritance stick." Now came the tough part. "I've learned that the wine business is in my blood. I don't want to do anything else with my life."

"If you're right and your brother inherits, why wouldn't he keep you on to run things?"

"He might, but I'm not willing to wait around and see. Besides, I have my own ideas and plans. I want to start my own label."

He pointed at the portfolio in front of her. "Your proposal?"

She nodded. "I've detailed everything. What grapes I want to buy, the price of the inventory, barrels, storage. There's also some land I'm interested in."

"Starting a label doesn't come cheap."

"I know."

His dark gaze never left her face. "Where else did you go for financing?"

"Everywhere short of a loan shark."

He nodded. "Let me guess. They want to know why you can't get the money from your grandfather."

"That's some of it. They were also concerned that I don't have any collateral. I've explained that the wine is collateral, but that doesn't seem to impress them." She shrugged. "You're a man who likes to take risks, but only when they pay off. I'm the closest to a sure thing you're going to find."

He raised his eyebrows. "Really?"

Brenna could have cheerfully thrown herself in front of a moving delivery truck. She could feel the heat on her face, but with her olive coloring, the blush wouldn't show. It was a small consolation, but one she clung to like a life preserver.

"You know I can do this," she said, as if she hadn't caught the embarrassing word play.

"Maybe," he said. "But why would I want to add to my competition?"

For the first time since driving onto the property, Brenna relaxed. "Oh, please. If I'm lucky I'll be able to match ten percent of your production in five years. I don't think you're going to sweat me putting you out of business."

"Fair enough. Why did you come to me?"

"You're the only person I know with extra cash."

"Your parents would have helped you out."

"Possibly. But I didn't want to make them choose

between me and my grandfather. You're a neutral party."

"I'm a Giovanni. Doesn't that make me second cousin to the devil?"

Gee, just what she'd been thinking earlier, only in her eyes, the relationship had been a little closer.

Coming to Nic was her last hope, but also a calculated risk. The Marcelli and Giovanni families had been feuding for years. Her grandfather might find out about the loan if she'd secured it through traditional sources such as a bank, but he would never know if Nic funded her. Grandpa Lorenzo would cheerfully rip out his tongue rather than *speak* to a Giovanni.

Brenna and her sisters had never been all that interested in the feud. Nic hadn't been, either, which he'd proved the first time she'd met him. But to her grandparents—hostilities were alive and well.

"There's a certain irony to this conversation," she admitted. "I would think that appealed to you."

"Rumor has it I'm a ruthless bastard," he said casually.

"I've heard. Should I be scared?"

"You tell me."

She could remember everything about being with Nic—the way he touched her, the way he kissed, the scent of his skin. She knew the boy he had been, but not the man. What was the same and what had changed? Or did it matter?

Ruthless bastard or not, she wanted the money.

"I don't scare easily these days." She pushed the proposal toward him. "Look it over and tell me what you think."

He rested his hand on the leather cover but didn't open it. "How much?"

The butterflies appeared in her stomach and began to fly in formation. She thought they might be practicing touch-and-go landings. Her mouth got dry, her palms got wet, and the room lurched once for good measure.

"A million dollars."

Nic didn't react in any way—at least not on the outside. He didn't blink, didn't shift in his seat, he didn't even smile. But on the inside, his mild amusement and intrigue turned to impressed amazement. Brenna had gone and got herself some balls.

She watched him, her big eyes betraying her nervousness. She was at the end of the line and they both knew it. If he turned her down, she wouldn't get her loan. Any dreams of starting her own label would be squashed. Oh, sure, she could buy a few tons of grapes on the open market, borrow equipment, and set up few dozen cheap barrels in a garage somewhere. She might get a loyal following, a little notice, maybe a write-up in *Wine Spectator.* But without an infusion of cash, she would never have the chance to make it big.

Not that he gave a damn about that. What mattered to him were his goals. How did her request fit into the big picture?

He rose and circled the desk until he stood in front of her, then he leaned against the surface, his arms folded over his chest. It was a position designed to intimidate. To challenge.

Brenna reacted by uncrossing, then recrossing her legs. In the silence of the office the sound of her silk stockings brushing and shifting grated against his ears. He found himself watching the movement, staring at the hem of her skirt, picturing her thighs underneath. And above her thighs?

Paradise. At least that's what her body had been ten years ago. Dark, slick, secret—the road to redemption. Instead she'd steered him right to hell. Because of her, he'd been sent away from his home. He'd been exiled, abandoned, and written off for dead.

Unfortunately, the reminder didn't do a damn thing for the unexpected tension crawling through him. He tore his gaze away before he distracted himself with the wrong kind of memories.

"I'm not saying no," he told her.

"You're kidding!"

She sprang to her feet, which put her less than a foot in front of him. Close enough for him to see the various shades of gold and brown that made up her irises, and the tiny scar by the corner of her mouth. Close enough for her perfume to invade his personal space. The scent was different; his reaction to it was not. Long forgotten heat awoke, stretched, and went searching for sustenance.

He ignored the temperature and the hunger. This was not the right time nor the place, and she was sure as hell not the right woman.

The thing was, he had a plan. Over the years he'd learned that a well thought-out plan ensured that he always won. When the goal was revenge, it paid to be patient.

His instincts told him that Brenna's loan request was as unexpected as a home run off the first pitch. All he had to do was toss down his bat and circle the bases. But he wanted to be sure.

"It's a lot of money," he said.

She nodded as her mouth curved in a smile. "I know. I've detailed every penny. It's all going into the wine. I'm not taking a salary. Oh, Nic, the land I want to buy is just perfect for Pinot Noir. There's a sweet valley at the base of a hill that gets just the right amount of midday sun. That, combined with the fog and the salt from the ocean creates perfect grapes. You'll see."

Her enthusiasm was as tangible as the hand she put on his arm. He acknowledged the contact—and his reaction to it—by sliding away and picking up her portfolio.

"I'll look this over in the next couple of days and get back to you." He raised his eyebrows. "How exactly do I do that?"

Brenna chuckled. "I suppose a phone call to the hacienda would cause problems for both of us. My cell number is on the proposal. If you don't get me, you can leave a message and I'll call you back."

"Fair enough."

She clutched her hands together. "Nic, I know it's a lot of money and that this is a risk for you, but I can do this. If you take a chance, you won't be sorry."

"I won't do it if there's a chance I will be."

Her excitement didn't flicker. "You're going to be impressed. I promise."

He had a feeling she was right. Besides, one of his rules in life was to take advantage of every unexpected opportunity. If he agreed, he would insist on keeping close tabs on what she was doing, which was the same as keeping close tabs on Brenna herself. Being close to her had only ever led to one thing.

So money wasn't the only risk. Was that good or bad?

He didn't have an answer, but he knew time spent with Brenna wouldn't be boring. Once again, they could be entering dangerous territory. The difference was this time he would be the one calling the shots.

Brenna drove back to the Marcelli winery, taking the long way round so she drove past the ocean. She rolled down the windows of her ancient Camry and let the warm salty air brush over her skin. Her suit jacket and high heels lay where she'd tossed them on the passenger seat. She had the radio cranked up and sang along with an old Beach Boys tune, delighting in the fact that although they'd been current years and years before her time, she knew all the words.

At this moment in time she felt free and wild and happy and so excited, she probably could have taken flight, if not for the seat belt anchoring her. She leaned her head back and laughed out loud at the sheer pleasure pumping through her.

She'd done it. *She'd done it!*

Oh, sure, Nic hadn't said yes, not yet. But somehow down in her gut she just knew he was going to. He'd been willing to listen, something no one else had done, and listening was all she needed. Her carefully thought-out proposal was going to blow his socks off. Maybe even his pants.

"I hope I'm around when that happens," she murmured, then grinned at the thought of a bottomless Nicholas Giovanni.

Until this past spring she hadn't seen him in nearly ten years. He could have gotten wrinkled and paunchy, but instead he still had the power to make her entire body go up in flames. And maybe, just maybe, she'd seen a flicker of appreciation in his beautiful sex-god eyes.

After several years of a crappy marriage, abandonment by a creep of a husband, and nine months and seventeen days since her last sexual encounter, male admiration—especially that coming from Nic—was a balm to her battered and horny soul.

Not that anything would happen, she reminded herself. If Nic agreed, make that *when* Nic agreed, they were going to be business partners. There was no way she was going to be foolish enough to mix business and pleasure. Not with a million dollars and her future on the line. No one was *that* good in bed.

She turned into the entrance to the Marcelli Winery and sighed. Okay, from what she recalled, making love with Nic had been spectacular. Incredible. Life-altering. But not worth a million dollars.

She shifted uncomfortably. All this reminiscing about sex was getting to her. If she'd been a cat, she would have been rubbing herself against the nearest door frame. Not only was she going to have to avoid any sexual contact with Nic, she was going to have stop thinking about him as anything but her loan officer. Nothing personal. Not again.

Fortunately her resolution coincided with her arrival at the family hacienda. Judging from the number of cars crowding around the rear entrance, the entire family was home.

The three-story Spanish-style home had been built in the late 1920s. Her great-grandfather had found plans for a house designed in the late eighteen hundreds by a Spanish nobleman with ten children, which made for lots of bedrooms. Good thing, she thought as she came to a stop in the shade of an old oak tree and turned off the engine. Currently the permanent residents of the hacienda included her paternal grandparents, her maternal grandmother, her parents, and herself.

"Humiliating but true," Brenna said as she slipped on her pumps and grabbed her suit jacket. "Twenty-seven years old and living at home."

Actually she'd moved back the previous spring when her jerk of a husband—a newly licensed cardiologist without a speck of gratitude or decency—had left her for a younger woman who happened to be a former cheerleader. He was poised to marry the bimbo the instant the computer print was dry on the divorce decree.

Brenna had no desire to have her soon-to-be ex back in her life, but she wouldn't mind a little justice. Her current favorite fantasy was some kind of genital infection that left him unable to enjoy the wedding night. Ever.

All revenge aside, one of these days she was going to take the time to find a place of her own. For now, it was nice to be where a houseful of people loved her.

She made her way up the rear steps and into the kitchen. As usual, the entire female contingent of the family collected there. Her two grandmothers held court over the food, with Grammy M stirring something on the stove and Grandma Tessa chopping vegetables. Her mother sat at the kitchen table, a box of wedding-invitation samples open in front of her. Katie, Brenna's older sister, and Francesca, Brenna's fraternal twin, stood in front of their mother.

Their defiant posture made them look like five-year-olds who had just been caught spray-painting the dog.

"What?" Brenna asked as she draped her suit jacket over her arm. "I was gone two hours. What happened?"

"Nothin' terrible," Grammy M—aka Mary-Margaret O'Shea—said from her place at the stove. "Francesca has the most wonderful news."

Brenna's mother didn't look all that excited. "But we'd already picked a date and were about to order the invitations."

Wedding talk.

First baby sister Mia had come within weeks of marching down the aisle, only to call the whole thing off. Then Katie had gone and gotten herself engaged to Mia's exfiancé's father. Twisted, but so California. Francesca had fallen for the handsome CEO of a security company who found out within days of their meeting that he had a twelve-year-old daughter he'd never known about. A few weeks after that, Francesca had turned up pregnant.

Only Brenna had managed to escape love's sticky snare and the ongoing soap opera that was the Marcelli family. Her current plan was to avoid romance and focus on work. She might be open to a little meaningless sex, but a relationship? She didn't have the time *or* the energy.

She crossed to the kitchen table, grabbing an iced cookie on her way. After six months of her grandmothers' cooking, she didn't want to think about what her cholesterol level must be.

"Tell me everything," she said, stopping next to Francesca and eyeing her very beautiful, very *thin* twin.

Nearly two months pregnant and was Francesca showing? Not even close. Brenna knew that if *she* was ever to play host to a marauding sperm, she would plump up overnight and look as if she were giving birth to a watermelon by week nine.

Francesca shrugged. "I know we all talked about waiting, what with the baby and all, but Sam and I have changed our minds. And Katie and I want to have a double wedding."

"We're willing to put the wedding date back to give us all time to get everything done," Katie said.

"You could have the weddings at Thanksgiving," Brenna said as she nibbled on her cookie. "We all know everyone in this family will be doing the happy dance to see two sisters married. For years everyone has despaired ever getting us all hitched. Now we're halfway there. That gives us so much more to be thankful for."

Grandma Tessa muttered something Brenna couldn't hear. She half expected to see the older woman whip out her rosary for a quick trip around the beads. Fortunately

Grandma Tessa contented herself with a couple of dark looks.

"Turkey-day weekend works for me," Katie said. "We could have the wedding that Saturday."

Francesca shrugged. "Sam doesn't care about the date. As for a dress, I'll pick something simple and flowing."

"Don't bother," Brenna told her. "You'll be nine months pregnant and still not showing."

Their mother raised her head. "I don't know. As it is, we'll be sewing day and night."

Family tradition dictated that any Marcelli bride have a wedding gown handmade by the women in the family. A great idea in theory, but beading lace took forever. Brenna wasn't worried about the additional sewing duties. She had a winery to run and therefore was excused from most of the needlework.

Their mother pulled out a pad of paper. "If we're going to have a double wedding, we need to start making lists."

The three sisters looked at one another and shook their heads. When Mom started making lists, an entire afternoon could fly by. Better to escape now.

"I'll get the drinks," Brenna said, heading for a rack on the far wall.

"I'll get chocolate," Francesca said.

Katie walked to the cupboard. "Cheese and crackers or cookies?"

"Cookies," Francesca and Brenna said together.

Their mother shook her head. "You girls aren't going anywhere. We have two weddings to plan."

Katie snaked a plate of cookies from the counter, kissed both Grammy M and Grandma Tessa, and hurried out of the room.

"Love you, Mom," she called over her shoulder.